Providence

This extraordinary story classically captures the mindset of the 1940s. Addie and her friend Kate reflect the voices women hear as they face confusing dilemmas 75 years later—my first read kept me up into the wee hours. I will refer my readers to *In Times Like These*!

Patricia Evans, author of
The Verbally Abusive Relationship,
Controlling People,
and other books listed at www.VerbalAbuse.com

Wartime brings out the best and the worst in people. I loved the way Addie and Kate, each in her own way, dug down inside to become more than either had ever dreamed. *With Each New Dawn* will inspire you toward resilience and personal growth even as it keeps you riveted with each page turn.

Sonia C. Solomonson, freelance writer and life coach
Way2Grow Coaching

Gail Kittleson introduces us to a small town community, under the strains of World War II. The everyday lives of the town folks unfolding their thoughts and concern for the husbands and brothers fighting for their country. The family and friends dynamics in this story keeps the reader wanting to turn page after page. The author knows how to keep the reader engaged. Looking forward to Ms. Kittleson's next book.

K Currie

The pages almost turned themselves. Great period piece exploring family dynamics and interpersonal relationships as well as the growth of self-esteem and the importance of friendship.

Lisa Lickel

Kittleson's writing style fosters instant empathy as her quiet heroine, Addie, struggles through daily living in Iowa during WW2. Readers are introduced to Addie through patriotism, friendship, and self-realization. "I've spent my whole life in fear instead of living each day," highlights Addie's growth in overcoming an emotionally abusive husband. Highest recommendation.

Carolyn Cobb

Kittleson deftly writes strong female characters facing heartbreaking tragedies. *Until Then* features two: Marian, caught in the Blitz, and Dorothy, a surgical nurse whose work with the 11th Evacuation Hospital has taken her to North Africa, through Sicily and into France. Their stories intertwine in a narrative that touches then heals the soul. Highly, highly recommended!

Literary Soirée

In Times Like These clearly portrays the difficulties for women during WW2. First, there are the challenges of raising food, preserving it, making money stretch, wisely using ration cards and just plain living in fear of the war. But then the overlay of Addie's controlling husband made me instantly empathize with the main character. His verbally abusive and cold treatment of Addie unfortunately is not just a problem from another era. God's provision for her was intriguing. The value of faith, friendship and compassion are evident in this book. I personally enjoyed the food tips and recipes, as well as vivid descriptions of farm life. This may be my favorite book by Gail Kittleson. It is the first in the series, *Women of the Heartland*. Be sure to read the books in order.

Cleo Lampos, co-author of
The Food that Held the World Together
A World War 2 Holiday Scrapbook

Women of the Heartland Series
With Each New Dawn
A Purpose True
All for the Cause
Until Then
&
Kiss Me Once Again
a Women of the Heartland story

and

In This Together
Catching Up With Daylight
Land That I Love
The Winds of Change
Love at the Lanvender Farm

Providence

a novel of the West

GAIL KITTLESON

WordCrafts Press

Providence
Copyright © 2024
Gail Kittleson

ISBN: 978-1-962218-67-2

Cover concept and design by Mike Parker.
Original art ©Lewis_Royal; ©Shooting Star Std/Adobe Stock

Published by WordCrafts Press
Cody, Wyoming 82414
www.wordcrafts.net

To Cora, whose adventurous spirit inspires me.

*Thank you to Lynn Dean,
Texas researcher extraordinaire,
for your help with this story's logistics.*

War makes for chaos. It's unwise and virtually impossible to compare wars, but the American Civil War stands right at the top for messiness. And the state of Texas provides us with a template for the untidy nature of this particular bloody war.

Most other seceding Southern states heartily signed on with the Confederacy. True, some border states fell into utter disarray, leading to Bleeding Kansas and other tumultuous situations. We will never know for sure how many lost their lives in this type of mayhem.

Though Kansas fought on the Union side, many Kansans remained pro-slavery, leading to the Lawrence Massacre in 1863. Neighboring state, Missouri, exhibited even more havoc, with over 1,200 battles being fought within its borders from 1861–1864. Having the Mississippi River as its Eastern border made this state all-important to both Union and Confederacy.

110,000 Missourians fought for the Union, and at least 40,000 for the Confederate Army. Many others fought with Confederate bands of bushwackers, and Missouri's Confederate government-in-exile fled to Marshall, Texas, which also became the Confederate capitol west of the Mississippi after the fall of Vicksburg.

In these border states we might say nothing was orderly about the war. But in Texas—a unique circumstance. The vote to secede from the Union and enter the Confederacy brought about the resignation of Governor Sam Houston, hero of the Texas Revolution and twice-elected President of the Republic of Texas. Sam Houston refused to sign articles of allegiance to the new government.

We have to wonder how his choice affected the average Texan, if such a person existed. For in general, Texans, a strong-minded lot, had endured an incredible amount of change. Before even becoming a state, they'd thrown off the rule of a Mexican dictator to become a Republic.

With such great land mass and a history more politically complicated than most other sections of the United States, Texas brought a frenzied past to the verge of the Civil War. Along with this came great internal conflict.

The state government held a referendum to settle the legality of secession on February 23, 1861. The results for the state as a whole were 46,153 for secession and 14,747 against. Roughly one-third.

And Sam Houston stood staunchly in that one-third. Imagine the talk on main streets, in local government offices, and around hearths as individuals considered this result. Knowing that their honorable leader elected to relinquish his position must have heartened some and brought dismay to others.

This circumstance could only have strengthened the backbone of those who opposed the Confederacy. Some, like hearty German pioneers near Comfort, Texas, fled South, but were hunted down like prey by Confederates from the neighboring town of Kerrville in the Nueces Massacre.

Men who stood by their personal convictions and vowed loyalty to the Union faced grave danger. At the same time, staunch proponents of States' Rights felt the North must be opposed. Along with their political ideologies, Texas citizens experienced tests in other areas.

Until the Union blocked off all Mississippi River trade in mid-summer, 1863, ranchers supplied beef and horses for the Confederate Army. But the blockade caused an economic conundrum. What were ranchers to do with their herds?

Unfortunately, solutions were hard-won, and as men left for the fighting, many herds went feral for lack of care. Into this scenario, let us insert the maverick nature of certain Texans. Thinking on their feet (or on their horses) they devised ways around parameters forced upon them.

The word *maverick* originally referred to an unbranded calf with unknown origins and ownership. The meaning expanded to refer to the maverick spirit of individuals with an independent way of thinking. In today's terms, we might label this the ability to think outside the box.

Somehow, these folks made-do with what history handed them—sometimes within the law; sometimes not. In this story, we meet some men mavericking their way north despite the war.

In the meantime, tens of thousands of Eastern and Midwestern Americans still made their way by wagon train across this great nation. Led by a fierce devotion to Westward Ho, they left all—family, property, and in many cases, a good life. Their sacrifices, like some of the Texas mavericks, chronicle the meaning of steadfastness and determination.

What an era to be alive! How vast the choices for those willing to forfeit control. For the journey, in essence, required this—trust in a wagon master who had traveled this long route before and pledged to guide them safely through mighty river crossings, unexpected blizzards, drought, deprivation, and the precarious dangers lying in wait in Injun Territory.

In his 1820 address celebrating the two-hundredth anniversary of the Mayflower Landing at Plymouth Rock, Daniel Webster observed, "New England farms, houses, villages, and churches spread over and adorn the immense extent from the Ohio to Lake Erie and stretch along from the Alleghanies onwards beyond the Miamis and towards the falls of St. Anthony. Two thousand miles westward from the Rock where their fathers landed may now be seen the sons of pilgrims cultivating smiling fields, rearing towns and villages, and cherishing, we trust, the patrimonial blessings of wise institutions, of liberty and religion…. Ere long the sons of the pilgrims will be upon the shores of the Pacific."

Thus it was nearly forty-five years later. Settlers of immigrant heritage entertain Western dreams and forged their way to the high plains of Wyoming Country—as yet not even a Territory—or even to the Pacific Northwest.

In spite of the war raging in their nation, these settlers set their hopes on distant destinations. But they would discover their own personal battles along the way.

The Oregon Trail

To enjoy such a trip… a man must be able to endure heat like a Salamander, mud, and water like a muskrat, dust like a toad, and labor like a jackass. He must learn to eat with his unwashed fingers, drink out of the same vessel as his mules, sleep on the ground when it rains, share his blanket with vermin, and have patience with mosquitos. He must cease to think, except of where he may find grass and water and a good camping place. It is hardship without glory.

~anonymous settler
writing in the St. Joseph, Missouri Gazette

Starting out ahead of the team and my men folks, when I thought I had gone beyond hearing distance, I would throw myself down on the unfriendly desert and give way like a child to sobs and tears, wishing myself back home with my friends.
~ young woman on the westward trail
1860

February, 1863

"Oh, read them all!" Lissa begged

Meta could scarce say no to her baby sister, with the family all gathered for her wedding.

Garrit, whom just an hour ago she had pledged to have and to hold, to love, cherish and obey, had gone out to the wagon with her brothers. An apt time for the womenfolk to gather.

In this cozy parlor, with Mama, Meta's sisters Margita and Lissa, and Margita's two little girls, reality struck. After tonight, at nearly eighteen, she would no longer be a girl but a woman. And in just a few weeks, she and Garrit would take their leave to meet a wagon train bound for the Oregon Trail.

For ten years, Garrit had worked and scrimped to follow his dream. When he spoke of the horse ranch he planned to establish, his eyes brightened and the years between them faded. He might be one of the fellows at school she had known for many years.

But apart from their talk about the journey and the recent loss of his father, the last of his family here in Mitchell County, they barely knew each other. Still, she had yearned for a dream like his ever since her eldest sisters, Alma and Greta, left for the wilds of Nebraska.

Such vivid recollections of that day—true, she'd been young, but the desire had taken hold in her heart. As years passed, the government's encouragement to settlers—free land if homesteaded for five years—had rooted the longing even deeper.

"I…" Something caught in her throat. "Margita, could you please do me the honor? I don't believe I…"

"Surely. It's only natural for you to be overcome…such an auspicious moment in your life."

Lissa added, "This will be one of the last times we shall all be together." She meant no harm, but her words brought a gush from Meta.

Mama hurried to her side with a hankie. "There, there now. All will be well with a good night's rest. For days now, you have been working so hard…"

"Yes, even sewing, though you hate it!" Lissa's proclamation turned Meta's tears to laughter.

"So right…how will I ever make a fit housewife?"

"Ah, that will all come naturally, sister. Each of us learns day-by-day." Margita opened one of the missals from friends and well-wishers. "Here, let me read what Miss Brunner wrote:

> *Dear Meta,*
>
> *Always, I have seen in you unique strength. …a spirit still, and bright, with something of angelic light. To tide you over during the long drive, please accept this small volume of poetry. Hold onto your angelic light, my dear, through the long journey ahead and as you begin your new home out West. If anyone can succeed, I believe you will.*
>
> *Please write me—I shall always be interested in what you are doing and especially the flora and fauna of your new home. I will write back to you with hundreds of questions.*
> *Sincerely,*
> *Miss Brunner*

"Angelic light? What is she talking about? Do angels climb trees with their brother Martin, rip their skirts, and come home all muddy?" Margita's grin defied her fierce words.

"They do indeed," Mama spoke up right away.

"That Martin—he watched out for you so carefully, and you two had such times together," Mama continued. "Oh, I do wish he could be here tonight to celebrate your wedding." She shook her head, "The youngest of our sons…"

"Off to war." Lissa sat back and began humming, "May God Save the Union," and Margita reached for the second envelope.

> *Dear Meta,*
> *My friend, I should love to be there as you say your vows, but Mama took ill this week. I remember our school days, when you helped me with my numbers and reminded me of my lines in the Christmas play—you always looked out for others.*
> *We send our heartiest wishes for you and Garrit. I hope you will find good use for this towel and think of me when you use it.*
> *Elmira Perkins*

"That's our Meta." Mama clasped her hands to her throat. "This whole community will miss you, dear, but I have no doubt you will reach out to those around you on the wagon train and in your new environs."

Meta started to reply, but Margita's daughter Sarah giggled, "Won't that be mostly animals, Aunt Meta?"

"I will not be surprised if that proves true, but hopefully other settlers will soon come."

As Margita continued with several more notes, good memories flooded in. So many heartfelt sentiments from dear friends, so much pleasantness from childhood to remember through the years.

"There would be one more of us here, too, if…"

Mama looked as though she might shush Lissa. But then she admitted, "Yes, we must never forget our sweet Bergita." But she could not bring herself to mention Papa, so no one else did, either.

Within minutes, Meta's oldest brother, Friedrich, entered through the back porch, along with Henry, the next-in-line. Their skin, leathered from all the weeks they spent planting and haying and harvesting, shone in the lamplight, and so did Garrit's. They must have been discussing how best to pack the wagon.

"Any supper in here for us working men?" Friedrich's tone held humor, but also honest hunger.

"Why, of course." Mama jumped right up. "For a time, we lost ourselves in all of the worthy remembrances Meta's friends have sent." Glancing at Garrit, she gestured with her hand. "Do join us. I shall don my *kepi,* and supper will be ready in a minute."

Puzzled lines filled Garrit's forehead—of course, Mama spoke in English, and he may never have heard of the Union caps worn by soldiers like Martin. Meta reached out her hand, and he made a step toward her, but only one, so she rose and took his arm.

As Lissa went to help Mama in the kitchen, Margita's youngest boy entered the back porch and called, "There's baby puppies out in the barn, everybody!"

Margita's girls both ran for their coats, and one of them tugged at Garrit's hand. "Come with us, won't you?"

Something in Garrit relaxed—the tension left his shoulders. "Yah! Yah!" When he ducked down to their height and scrambled off with them, Meta followed.

Watching him in a back stall of the barn, kneeling in dingy shadows with the children and tenderly holding one pup after another, her cares faded. Again, he spoke in German, which Mama discouraged in their family, but the children understood both.

Surrounded by familiar scents—animal hide, dusty straw, a milky aura from the evening's chores, and plain, rich Iowa soil, he seemed at home once more. This man, strong as the oxen who would pull their wagon on the trail and as determined as the Union Army—this man she had wed.

Chapter One

March 22, 1863

Savoring the lavender essence of Mama's quilt, Meta Tolzmann Rausch eyed the starry sphere above. Beside her, Garrit's steady breathing relayed a message—safe in the hands of Providence. Oh, to embrace that truth!

A chilly wind seeped into the wagon, though two long oak trunks hedged some nasty March weather. Spring would surely arrive soon, but for now, woolen scarves remained a mainstay.

After long miles on the trail, Garrit's warmth soothed her aching muscles, but nothing could assuage her hankering. Each day took them further away from home, with no return. Already seven days to the western border of Iowa and then three more to meet the wagon train at Council Bluffs. And their trek had only begun.

As she floated between wakefulness and sleep, Garrit draped his arm around her.

"Ve vill haf many children, *mein schatz*." His breath, a mix of strong coffee, bacon, and sourdough, brought home to mind.

Home and Mama. Those two would always intertwine, no matter how far she traveled or where Garrit found a claim.

"Garrit, a solid name—you have found a strong husband, daughter." Mama's blessing, spoken after their wedding vows and as clear as the stars above, allowed Meta to release her cares at last.

Spring sunshine grazed the sparkling Missouri, sprouting grass and prairie sage on either shore. Meadowlarks signaled their mates and a flash of tawny red stirred the tall grass as Meta fetched water from a creek.

A morning breeze off the Missouri dried the dishes she scrubbed and made quick work of the wash water she tossed behind the wagon. After arranging the dishes for today's trek, she found her pen, a jar of ink, and the black leather journal her sister Margita gave her when they parted.

A hangnail caught on the leather, so she sought the tin medicine box where Mama had stocked liniments and ointments, a brown bottle of sweet oil, and a glass vial of her special sage salve for skin ailments. Way in the back, Mama tucked medicinal recipes—*receipts*, she called them.

As a child, helping chop and boil beeswax, stirring in herbal oils, and pressing medicines into vials had provided a basic understanding of healing. Soon, Meta would be the one to care for any mishaps on their claim, and having these recipes written out loosened the tension in her shoulders.

No Conestoga wagons here—overlanders who had gone before learned that their size and weight became an obstacle on the trail. Those huge heavy conveyances depleted even the sturdiest oxen before the journey was two-thirds complete. And two-thirds might be just about in Wyoming Country, where Garrit longed to settle.

As Meta sailed to earth, a sudden morning wind whipped through camp, so she re-pinned her dark hair. Sunshine found her forehead as she chose a stump beside their campfire.

"Forgot my bonnet—Mama would say my freckles will blossom." But the ink bottle on a small folding table received Meta's pen. "I'm not taking the time to climb back into the wagon. Surely this short period in the sun will make no great difference."

She dipped her pen and thought of Miss Brunner as she began to write.

March 29, 1863

Missouri Crossing somewhere near Omaha. Seventeen wagons speckle this endless prairie like so many small shanties. We expect thirty-five more. The wagon master, a bearded mother hen, scuttles about like brother Friedrich, all business.

Yesterday, Betsy Bishop and her brother Ben welcomed us. They are traveling all the way to Oregon where Betsy's husband is building a cabin. They left Ohio some weeks ago with five children and an infant. Such a resolute example she provides—I shall not complain.

Dear Martin—I think of him often and wonder where his unit was when they heard the news of Mr. Lincoln emancipating the slaves. What a hopeful beginning to this new year, after the Union's terrible struggle in the Vicksburg campaign. I do so wish for this war to end.

"The Worm Moon of March holds Spring in the air… thawing brings both mud and worms, but soon the Pink Moon will rise and showers will wash away Winter's waste." A settler in our train told Garrit this last night—'twas too dark to see who was speaking, but always, someone seeks him out.

Spring in the air—I can scarcely wait. As it is, nightly gales chisel right through our wagon's sides.

Smells of rich boiled coffee, frying bacon, and rising biscuit dough wafted over the camp. Down a hill glittered the tireless Missouri, as if to say, "I await your crossing."

"Our time to cross will come soon enough." A calm thread undergirded Betsy's voice yesterday as she and Meta climbed a bluff to view the great river and glimpse the other side. "We are near where Lewis and Clark first held a council with the Indians so long ago, Ben says."

With a clutch of young'uns and four-month-old Michael in her arms, she still managed to converse.

"Ferrymen know their task, but things can go awry. In our

Ohio crossing, one family lost all of their goods. Can you imagine, after working so hard to purchase and load everything?"

"No. That would drive poor Garrit to distraction."

"They were Welsh, and their daughter taught me a word to ponder—*hiraeth*. It means a homesickness for a place to which you can never return, perhaps a place that never even was."

"Had they come from Wales?"

"Yes. Already they had left so much behind back in the Old Country. Then to suffer the loss of their provisions—they had to remain behind to replace everything and start over."

"Do you think they will?"

"Oh yes. And I won't be surprised to meet them again in Oregon one day."

Other accounts circulated of wagons tottering into sinkholes during crossings like this. Three years ago, Garrit's cousin crossed here after waiting weeks for amenable conditions, and now Garrit hankered to reach the other side. Tension emanated from his chest. He took each delay as a slight, but Meta agreed with Betsy.

"The race is not always to the swift. It will do the oxen good to rest before we start out again in earnest."

"I think this crossing is better." Garrit kept his head low as he and two other settlers studied the wrinkled paper he held. Meta had seen it before amongst his things, but they were about to cross in the morning. Why bring up this alternative?

TO CALIFORNIA AND OREGON EMIGRANTS
Good Crossing near St. Joseph
Whitehead's Ferry, 4 ½ miles above St. Joseph, on the
Missouri River, is on the nearest and best route from St. Joseph,
Fort Kearney, and all other places on the northern route to
California and Oregon, beyond these points.
The undersigned has two good boats in good order and

*can cross from 5 to 700 head of Cattle per day. He also has good
and sufficient lots on each side of the River for the accommo-
dation of the Emigrants with large herds of stock, which will
be provided gratis to those favoring him with their patronage.*

*In conclusion I will say that you may rely upon being
crossed at my Ferry with safety and dispatch. Mistake not the place.*

James R. Whitehead

*My Ferry is within one-half mile of the Prairie on the
other side of the River and no brush intervening. Opportunity
of losing cattle very poor.'*

Surely Garrit would not want to travel more hours south
to St. Joseph…the crossings would begin so soon now. With the
men still debating, Meta climbed into the wagon—best to try
sleeping early tonight. She did not hear Garrit come inside, and
by morning, he seemed calm and ready for the crossing.

Thomas, Betsy's eldest, burst into the campsite after the
morning meal. His wide hazel eyes sparkled like his Mama's.

"First wagon's 'bout t' cross the river. Mama says, will you
climb the hill to watch with us?"

Garrit glared at him, then at the fire. Meta waited, but he
remained silent, distant—such a sudden change. If only he would
speak his mind! Betsy's young emissary kicked at a stone. "Didja
know the feller who started this ferry founded the city of Omaha?"

"No, I hadn't heard."

"And pioneers been stoppin' over here for a long time. Bet
my Papa mighta been one of 'em."

"My older sisters and their families, too. I wish I had paid
more attention to their letters from along the trail."

Thomas fidgeted. "Ma'am, what shall I tell Mama?"

"When I have straightened things here, I shall come along."

Ramrod straight and wordless, Garrit tramped away. A niggling sensation wedged in Meta's chest—how might one possibly
know a man's thoughts?

Like a prairie chicken, Thomas ran off. Mama always chuckled, *With their stubby wings, those birds fly about as well as pigs!*

Mustn't leave the featherbed hanging like a limp skirt—heaven forbid it should get damp. Plumping its folds in an inside corner and arranging the cooking pot, Meta hung her apron on a stake and sought about for any neglected responsibilities.

Her morning conversation with Garrit lingered. "Our wagon master shows too much caution—such a long passage ahead, why wait to cross the river?" Attempts to smooth the permanent furrows in his forehead had taught her to stay quiet. "Bide your time, sister," Margita would advise. "Day-by-day, one learns how to respond."

The woman from the next campsite over shooed her brood up the hill, along with nearly every other mother in the train. Everyone wanted to watch the crossing—what harm could lie in that?

Meta tied her bonnet strings. Twice before starting out, she called for Garrit in vain. Two minutes later, Betsy's gaggle overtook her. Full of giggles and games, they swarmed like butterflies. Carrie, the youngest, latched onto Meta's forefinger.

Such appealing midnight eyes and rosy cheeks—like Margita's last child. Hoisting Carrie, Meta slowed her pace. "What a big girl you are and as strong as your brothers!"

"Like frisky lambs, aren't they?" Betsy laughed as some barefoot youngsters tackled Thomas, and they all rolled into a six-legged ball. "Oh, won't my John be surprised to see how they have grown?"

Within sight of the crossing, she and Meta claimed a large rock as the little ones scampered about. Other women found spots nearby as the first wagon neared the river.

Friendly chatter carried on this clear day full of longing and hope. Near the river the men clustered like grapes around the first wagon.

Betsy shaded her eyes. "Did you hear about the meteor showers back in '60?"

"I don't think so."

"In July, they lighted the skies of New York State in a singular way—Mama's sister lives out there and wrote about them. Then, in November, more came—I think they were called comets—after the Federals sentenced John Brown but before his execution. Now, scholars are calling the showers in the skies portents of this nightmarish war."

"Miss Brunner, my teacher, must not have heard this, or she surely would have told us."

"No matter what we believe about portents, so many of our boys have already perished." Betsy took Meta's hand. "And we are about to cross a great river and enter a vast wilderness. Where two or three gather.... Pray with me?"

"Of course."

"We beseech thee, Heavenly Father, guard this crossing and the trail ahead. Especially send your angels to protect our precious little ones."

The first and second wagon made the crossing—a third and more, accompanied by unanimous sighs. Most women brought breakfast leftovers, and small groups formed under an arching sun. As the seventh wagon entered Nebraska Territory, the youngest ones napped on flower patch blankets

An hour later, Betsy gathered her family. "Come, children. Our turn will come soon—our wagon sits second in line now, and Uncle Ben will be watching for us."

Grabbing two pudgy hands, Meta plunged off with them. "I could keep the little ones while you cross."

"Thank you, but I could never bear one to be missing. See you on the other side." Near the Bishop's wagon, Betsy's brother hailed them and helped everyone into the wagon.

With Garrit nowhere to be found, Meta climbed the hill again. Soon, the Bishops crossed with Michael and Carrie in Betsy's arms, her other young'uns huddled behind her, octopus arms protruding around her waist.

"Another one across." Matilda Hanson, a sturdy woman with her own cache of babes, released a long breath.

After descending, they bade each other good fortune on the morrow. Time to prepare the evening meal. Near their wagon, hands tight behind his back, Garrit paced. "Where haf you been?" His harsh tone scalded Meta's ears, and her reply in English deepened his pout.

"We all watched from the hill. Everything went well, don't you think?"

Silent, he strode off to busy himself with the harness. Somewhere, a mourning dove issued its first woeful evening refrain. The solid iron skillet Mama had bequeathed them weighed on Meta's arms.

Even as she filled it with beans, the afternoon loveliness dwindled. Such a momentous day tomorrow—she had planned to join Garrit on the seat as they crossed the river, but now her teeth grated at the thought. Mama came to her rescue sometime before dawn. Such a steady, trustworthy voice: *According to Alma and Greta, who also married their husbands not long before they went West, the journey itself multiplied the trials of their first months as wives. But they managed, and so will you.*

Still, the actual crossing left a let-down sensation. Garrit guided the oxen onto the wide wooden planks of the ferry, and another wagon accompanied them. Its driver, Hildegard Mueller, kept her brood hushed and inside with her husband.

How pleasant it might have been to share this momentous occasion, but Hildegard made no attempt at friendship and looked away when Meta glanced her way. This woman drove her family's wagon as skillfully as any man and did not seek a comrade.

Instead Meta set her attention on how the ferry functioned—a strong rope system, stout work horses straining all day long, and a fellow who knew how to take charge. All of this would make for an interesting letter to send Miss Brunner, who would surely use these facts in her classroom.

No doubt she already explained the complications of Nebraska Territory becoming a state. Mama might even have shared Alma and Greta's letters bemoaning the long process, with Congress complicating the will of the citizens.

But here they were, having crossed the wide Missouri! On the west side, Betsy, Ben, Thomas, and the rest of the Bishops shouted a hearty welcome. Even Garrit felt obliged to raise a responsive hand at their exuberance.

Perhaps one day, he might feel more at ease with them, even though they spoke no German at all. This single gesture, the simple rise and fall of his hand, signaled hope.

Chapter Two

April 21, 1863, Eastern Nebraska.

Frost gives way to warm afternoons now, and another train has joined ours. Nearly seventy wagons gather to parade the prairie. One month past the vernal equinox, each day seems a bit longer than the previous.

The other day Betsy mentioned hearing "peepers" at night. She said in Ohio, these tiny frogs waken from hibernation in the mud every spring and make a sort of chirp, also like a song. I must listen closer.

Later, we smelled something clean, earthy and fresh, like geranium. Not sweet, and stronger than a faint carrot scent. Matilda solved the mystery—"Sage, or salvia, from the mint family. My auntie called it the no-nonsense herb—square-stemmed and down-to-earth—and swore by sage tea for swelling and pain. I drink some each month during my time."

We vowed to gather some later in the season. Who knows what will grow in the Wyoming Country? One thing is for certain: our medicine boxes cannot contain too many remedies.

"Have you ever seen such tall grass?" In early evening light, one settler addressed Garrit. He toted an eight-inch green sprout and spoke English with a Norwegian accent.

"Taller than oats back home." Little-by-little, Garrit's English was improving. "They say it grows a foot high." The two ambled off, Garrit's shoulders half again as wide as his visitor's. Did men seek him out because of his size? No, he looked them in the eye and spoke the truth—even though his German often garbled his meaning. A good man, as Mama declared. Why then, could he not look into her eyes and say what he meant? This seemed to occur most often when Betsy was involved, although Meta could not comprehend why. Garrit went about his business in the mornings and after long days driving, made friends throughout the camp. Why would it upset him so for her to have a companion, too?

"You can love someone without liking everything about them." Thus went Margita's advice just before she and Garrit left. "Of course you will have disagreements. Keep in mind, you have been married only a few weeks."

When the sun lent its final rays, Garrit's familiar gait sounded. As Meta skipped toward him, he scooped her up in his muscled arms.

"Where go you, young miss?"

"Wherever you go, *mein mann*." Such a glow of gold and vermillion over the landscape as twilight settled. Surely no other sunset had ever offered such beauty. What a gift—this moment to treasure.

And herein lay the solution to all of her pondering. What she did not understand, Nature taught her to attend. Yes, simply attend, without casting judgment. Miss Brunner, who loved American poetry as much as English, rehearsed a line from Ralph Waldo Emerson as Meta savored Garrit's closeness.

Adopt the pace of nature: Her secret is patience.

Chimney Rock rose like a red pillar, or an enormous finger, or forty-five other objects the children imagined as Betsy played a word game with them. Someone said it seemed to beckon the train onward from a distance after so many weeks of travel. A good omen.

Along the way from Courthouse Rock, twelve miles behind, wagon ruts gouged the prairie like cruel, scraping fingers. After a violent bump slid Meta across the seat and nearly overboard, she raised her hand to signal Garrit to stop. He hated to slow the wagon, but she ignored his incensed expression and climbed down to some women herding children.

A whip sailed the air as Hildegard Mueller snapped her reins. At Mr. Fortune's meetings, this heartily-built woman always spoke for her husband—shy, thin Rudolph. Hildegard's beak-like nose curved to match the downward turn of her lips. Not just any woman could handle a team the way she did—her meaty arms bespoke a lifetime of hard labor.

Nothing to do but simply accept her ways and leave her to her business, yet Hildegard's unpleasantness grew by the day. She seemed to dislike being part of the camp. Her outbursts drifted to every ear.

One evening, Garrit and Meta fetched water together, three pails between them. A flighty breeze made for a peaceful evening until they passed near Hildegard's wagon, and she yelled, *"Dummkopf!"*

A streak of crude names followed. Garrit showed no sign he heard, so Meta quickened her step. A few moments later, the Mueller's youngest, a four-year old, careened from the wagon and rolled to a stop at their feet. Seeing him sprawled there, Meta set down her pail, and Hildegard's insults rained down as she brushed dirt from the child's face and hands. "Oh my. Are you hurt?" She traced his tears with her finger.

Tugging on the middle handle, Garrit drew back and issued a command harsh as tree bark. "Leave him alone! If he cries, his mother will beat him more."

"Der, mein kinder," Meta whispered. *"Der, Der."*

"Komme sie hier!"

Under a ragged shirt, the boy's slight shoulders trembled. A gash along his forearm called for attention.

"Beill dich!" Hurry up! But how could he, bruised and bleeding?

The terrified boy got to his feet and took a step. Garrit

clamped his hand around Meta's arm, but she waited until the little fellow reached his wagon where Hildegard dumped him inside like a bag of turnips. Hands on her hips, she still glared their way.

Near the river, Garrit hissed. "The Good Book says we must not take on others' problems."

"But we are to care for the helpless."

"We must not make an enemy."

"Garrit, the child fell at our feet." Stiffness radiated from him, but Meta could not hold back. "He might have been killed. Surely you don't think—"

His stony face flushed dark red. "Meddling in other people's business leads to a bad end."

Heat stung her eyelids.

Turn away from a child in danger? No, *never*—Mama would have intervened. At their campsite, she prepared supper while Garrit tended the oxen. With the potatoes ready, she summoned him.

Such a lovely eventide, with families settling in for the night, but Garrit ate and left without a word. Tonight, even a robin's cheerful evening tune failed to lighten Meta's heart. Early crickets made their peculiar music. Above a cacophony of moos, dishes and clattering pans, Hildegard's harsh commands still carried over the camp in the haze dividing dusk from daylight.

What a nasty woman—and Garrit had been so sharp-tongued tonight. Meta visualized rebelling somehow, like the colonists when they threw shiploads of British tea into Boston Harbor. But what could she do?

A fog of dark thoughts slipped around her, invaded her being. How could any mother treat her child like Hildegard? True, she had so much work to do, yet she could choose how to speak, how to behave.

And so can you. In the onset of evening, all alone and so at odds with Garrit, Mama might have stood right here beside her. Nothing quieted her like Mama's sentiments, and this was no exception. Yes, she had a choice.

Later, Garrit returned in silence, but accepted a cup of coffee and sank beside the fire. Darkness gradually enveloped them as voices lowered around other fires. At last, Hildegard's barbs decreased.

As Meta stared into the flames, full night fell—often she had pondered how this occurred…from daylight to utter darkness. The transition occurred imperceptibly, without a sound.

Things cannot always be black and white. Mama again. A sleepy wand loosened Meta's shoulders. Today, the women had discussed the first wagon train to Oregon Territory—someone's aunt had arrived there a widow who lost two of her sons in Indian attacks.

"So much they suffered to pave the way for us. Papa told us about those days, with Henry Clay in Washington and Andrew Jackson the President."

Another woman broke in. "Yes, back before Texas became a state. Those were wild days—the government encouraged people to settle in Oregon because England and Russia had eyes on the Territory, too. A miracle anyone survived that first overland journey, but in time, Oregon became our thirty-third state."

"Thomas, are you listening?" Betsy glanced over at her eldest. "Take this as your history lesson for this week—so much change so quickly in our nation. And now, this insufferable war."

An older woman named Elsbeth chimed in. "But so far, our train has been safe."

Recalling the afternoon's conversation, gratitude slipped into place once again. Ah, yes, Mama always pointed to gratefulness as the key.

Then, as if it were last February, the final injunction of Meta's wedding sermon came to mind.

Never end a day in anger.

At Fort Kearney, several Swedish families observed the Sabbath with a gathering. Two men brought violins and another gave a brief talk.

In a soothing draught from the west, Garrit surprised Meta by agreeing to come. They rested against a wagon wheel as thirty or forty voices fanned the prairie. On the other side of the fire, Ben and Betsy corralled their sleepy charges. Ben, tender but strong, had a way with his nieces and nephews, always teaching them about Nebraska or engaging their minds with riddles.

As music spired around them, Hildegard's outbursts punctuated the meeting. Betsy caught Meta's eye. Earlier, she had declared, "I would take her children if I could!" They made a pact to pray whenever they heard her irritating voice—which meant quite often. Near Betsy sat Elsbeth. Her rich brown eyes, like Mama's, revealed a mix of light and pain. Perhaps one day she would share her story.

Chapter Three

May 10, 1863

Nothing to see but Indian and Buffalo trails leading to water. Very quiet here, only sounds of birds chattering and the wings of the locust or the wave made by the wind on the tall grass. Very depressing... We saw many Indians riding along on ponies with lowered heads... encountered thunder storms with lightning. The streams raised during the hard storms and often ran through our tents... high wind storms flattened our tents like mushrooms. Many of the immigrants were frightened out of their wits by the Indians. No plow had ever turned a furrow on the black loam. Our wagons were packed with boxes, bundles, bedding, tin cans and, in short, all the equipment of a camper who, as it were, took his life in his hands and had gone into an unknown land for a length of time where he will be cut off from communications without any base of supplies.

~Mary Jane Smith Watkins, b. 1835
Emigrated with her parents from Indiana to Oregon.
En route she married, but her new husband died before
reaching Oregon, as did both her parents.

"Oh, for the wide easy track we followed earlier." Meta clenched the rough box as the wagon lurched through a ravine.

"You dream, *shatz*."

Northward, Meta's sisters Alma and Greta had homesteaded. How she yearned to turn off and surprise them. She dared to break the silence with a vibrant memory.

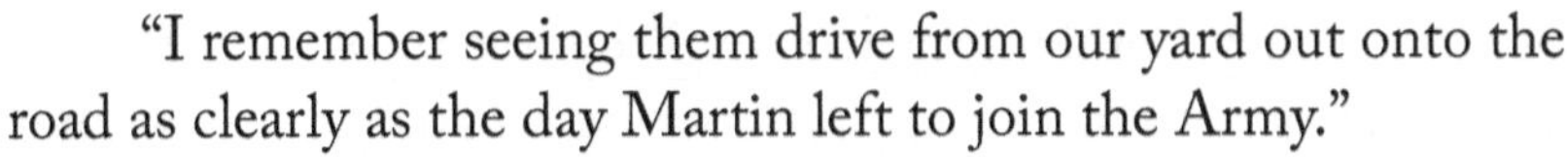

"I remember seeing them drive from our yard out onto the road as clearly as the day Martin left to join the Army."

Garrit squinted into the distance.

"Greta's firstborn, Heinrich, turned ten last December, so I must have been seven. Friedrich and Henry, Martin and Lissa still lived at home."

Muscles taut, Garrit wiped his forehead.

"Do you recall your older brothers and Henrietta leaving home?"

At last, a slim reply slipped out

"*Nein.*"

Thirteen years separated him and his oldest brother, Helmar. Henrietta and Peter, the twins, had married by the time Garrit came along. Now, like her brother Martin, his younger brother Fritz had joined the Army.

Garrit's replies, single words at most, failed to satisfy. The thought of her sisters living so close grated like fingernails on a chalkboard. To be so close to family, yet oceans away…The lump in Meta's throat became insurmountable.

After a while, she walked with Betsy, dreaming aloud. "My sisters live nearby—oh, how I wish we could see them."

"How long has it been?"

"About ten years. I think perhaps the wanderlust struck me when they left for Nebraska Territory—the adventure seemed so exciting."

"You have always wanted to come West?"

"Yes. So when Garrit said he was making plans, I—"

"You welcomed his dream. I did the same with John—dreams have a way of taking us in with the slightest encouragement, don't they?" Betsy's sigh joined the trail dust. "Did you write to your sisters? They might have come to see you."

"Mama sent letters to Greta and Alma, and they wrote back. But in the flurry of getting ready, I never thought…"

Could a meeting have been arranged? Ah no—Garrit would never have consented if it meant the least inconvenience.

Distant thunder growled from the northwest. Nothing to do but persist. Later, Thomas and his friends happened upon some male prairie chickens in their mating dance. They called. "Come see this!"

Issuing tympany-like moans from globular bright gold organs on either side of their necks, the males put forth their best efforts to win female hearts. Betsy's young'uns gasped when a black and white male leaped into the air in quite the show, and the women chuckled over the sight.

Someone asked, "Does this remind you of your suitors?"

"Yes—one of them went on like this for about a month!"

"Indeed—my father worked so hard at keeping the boys away, but he failed to realize that John, our hired man's son, had eyes for me." Betsy's giggle carried afar. "And John won my heart. Now, he is leading me so far away, Father will never find us."

Others joined in with tales of their own as Meta pondered. Other suitors? Not really, although Martin said his friend Hans expressed some interest in her. But at the next barn dance, Hans had been too shy to approach her.

Mitchell County offered plenty of sturdy young women who knew how to work, but for some reason, Garrit had never married. And then that old *Westward Ho* had wooed her, and in the end, she had been the one to seek him, hidden away on his father's farm.

More than ten years older than she, he might have continued a bachelor, but his steady labor and determination lured her. Looking back, even meeting him outside of church services, seemed unlikely. But then one day after his father's death, Mama sent her to the Rausches with a *kuchen*.

She had handed Garrit a basket filled with the sweet, cinnamon-laced bread. He said thank-you, and his eyes revealed his recent loss. Something about his manner stirred her heart, and she lingered longer. He would leave for the Wyoming Country in late March, he said, only ten weeks away.

Now, nearly six months had gone by, and these other women's

courtships seemed enticing. Hers had involved a simple, *Yes*, when Garrit gained the courage to ask for her hand, and centered around preparing for this journey. Apart from working together to provision the wagon, they barely knew each other when they said their vows back in February. But Mama had not known Papa well when they wed, either.

Now, as these paternal wild chickens pounded the prairie, leaped into the air, and drummed out their inmost desires in wild dance, Meta joined in the women's laughter. Impossible to imagine Garrit dancing under any circumstances.

Word came of even rockier country ahead. Already, Garrit had fixed one of their wheels, and the smithy could barely keep up with breakdowns.

That night, the wagon master visited each campsite. "Mr. Rausch, Ma'am. We'll be holdin' over here a day and a night."

"Why? May has already come and gone." Garrit's inquiry issued none too friendly.

"Folks need time to make repairs."

"Can we afford to waste time?"

"Better than having our wagons break down in Injun country." Meta held her breath. She had never spoken with Mr. Fortune, but since Garrit *huffed* and headed toward the oxen…

"Sir, how far is the German settlement north of Fort Kearney?"

"Eleven, mebbe twelve miles."

A half-day's ride. Her sisters lived that close.

"Thank you."

"Ma'am."

Garrit led the oxen to the Platte. With wooden arms, Meta took out corn flour. The coffee bean lid popped off, and as she knelt to rescue the precious beans, tears burned the backs of her eyes. "Betsy is right. We might have seen them."

With two pails, she headed for the water, staying as far as

possible from Garrit's route. She stumbled over a short branch, kicked with all her might, and sent it spinning.

Only one chance in life to see Alma and Greta. Oh, why had she not thought ahead? A pool invited her to refresh her weary feet. Nearby, a low, cooing hum sounded—perhaps a grouse making ready her nest.

Tepid water received Meta's sore toes, and little-by-little, small ripples quieted the roaring in her ears. Then a history lesson from school surfaced. The state of Iowa had begun with conflict, Miss Brunner said, when citizens rejected the proposed constitution in 1845. Since Congress had reduced the state's land area by almost a third, they rebelled.

After another year of negotiations, Congress bowed to the stalwart settlers and returned the boundaries to what former Governor Lucas, the chairman of the Committee of Boundaries, had originally proposed. And in 1946, the vote for statehood became law.

As Margita would say, "A pleasant marriage takes hard work, time, and many compromises. We must not try to hurry what is meant to last a lifetime."

Ah, such a dear older sister—so much like Mama. Always, Margita offered practical wisdom. If only the two of them could visit for even a few minutes. A gush of yearning swept Meta. Sobs welled in her throat—that Welsh traveler Betsy met had been right—this longing would accompany her for all time.

May 23, 1863
Today Mr. Fortune announced that General Grant has begun a siege of Vicksburg. Oh that the Rebels give up easily— then the Confederacy will be split in two and Martin can return home from the dreadful fighting. I hope Erma Hirsch waits for him.

The sights and sounds here intrigue me—so many new plants, but the sagey scent reigns over all the others. And new creatures, too. I could have watched the prairie dog colony forever. Each one so alert, so committed to each other and their common life. I can imagine Miss Brunner reading part of my letter aloud to her students, although I may not be able to mail it soon.

The prairie dogs' example is not exactly true of our train, for Betsy has mentioned two men near their wagon who cannot get along and even resorted to fisticuffs. To be expected, Mr. Fortune would say, as he has made this trip so many times. He issued a warning. One of them will soon bring up the rear, should their spats continue.

West of Chimney Rock, the wagons' wild sway set many women walking. Matilda Hanson's resonant laugh heartened them all—though heavy with child, she always found a bright spot.

Michael stirred in Meta's arms, so she held him close and sang a ditty. For a few minutes, he fell back to sleep, but soon wriggled again.

"All right, then, we shall find your Mama." Not far off, Betsy anchored a rope of young'uns searching for the color of the day but hurried over, delivering three sets of sweaty hands into Meta's keeping. "All right, then. What new colors have you found today?" One of them held up a fistful of tiny purple flowers and spurted, "Betsy says it's hellotro."

"Ah—heliotrope. Indeed. Now, shall we play follow-the-leader?"

They liked her idea, and May heat and dust whipped Meta's skirts as one of the older boys pulled everyone into a heap. She fell, too, her yellow calico bonnet collapsed around her neck. Such a messy pile of appendages, skirts, and giggles. As always, Betsy came back as content as Michael.

"I needed that rest. Do you think Nebraska Territory will ever truly end?"

"At least we can take the Rockies' pass instead of the north way. Thank Providence for the explorers who passed before us."

"Holes ahead!" One woman shouted the warning as she helped another who turned her ankle.

"Well, we can always hope Nebraska does not last forever."

"Garrit calls my hopes fantasies. He clicks his tongue as if I were—"

"My older brother did that too. He fumed, '*Achh mein. Sie arger.*'"

"He called you *trouble?*"

"Yes, but Ben always protected me. Now he has taught us a song about the cliffs ahead; Crown Rock, Dome Rock, Eagle Rock..."

"Sentinel and Saddle."

"You've heard it too, of course. Ben will climb up and carve 'Bishop' there. John passed this way late last summer—maybe we can find where he carved his name. Wouldn't that be something?"

As Meta transferred fresh cornbread to their plates, Garrit reached for her hand.

"*Komm, Herr Jesu; sei du unser Gast; und segne, was du uns bescheret hast.*"

Come Lord Jesus, be our guest. And let these gifts to us be blessed. Mama would proclaim, "We are Americans—we must speak English!"

But like many folks who settled around Emmanuel Church, Garrit's family rarely did. After all, Pastor Schulz conducted services in German, and Miss Brunner taught school in German as well.

But each night, Mama read to her children in English. When the boys complained, she bristled.

"People will come from many other countries, and they will all learn English—we will do business in English. Then you will be glad for your studies at home."

Garrit cleaned his plate and handed it over. "*Schmeckt gut.*"

"You have provided well for us."

"Your Mama helped." He almost smiled, and Meta decided to take a risk.

"I heard that folks climb Chimney Rock to scratch their names."

"*Ach!*"

"Wouldn't it be good to leave our names for others who come after us, to see that we passed through here?"

No reply, but his baleful look answered for him.

The sun disappeared. The fire cast longer shadows, like burnt orange phantoms. Suddenly, in the slim light of evening, Garrit looked so very old.

"In two days, we will see Scott's Bluff. Mitchell Pass edges the badlands and parts west. The Cavalry and the overland stage have smoothed the way somewhat, but prepare your wagons—you men-folk, batten down everything that moves."

Something about Mr. Fortune's manner grabbed Meta's attention—folks said he'd been a mountain man and scouted for the Cavalry for years. If anyone knew the tribes out here, it would be him. Besides, he never seemed to raise his voice, but folks trusted him. Well, most of them.

For days, rain slanted down. In long, hot weeks, how they had looked for the smallest cloud. But now, women and children huddled inside their wagons as oxen broke through muddy seas.

Hardly a glimpse of Scott's Bluff or the majestic cliff formations of the Pass. Meta closed her eyes and dreamed of Martin at Vicksburg, but then a high-pitched call alerted her. When it came again, she crawled toward the front to listen.

Another scream. A cold finger traced her spine. Then she recognized Betsy's voice.

"Stop!" She clambered forward, pounding on Garrit's shoulder. "Stop! Stop!" Two rods to the right, Betsy wallowed to her knees in brown slime, buffalo grass binding her ankles.

Garrit kept up the pace, so Meta gathered her skirts. When

she took to the air, he lunged for her but fell short. Against the onslaught, Betsy enfolded Michael in her arms, so Meta supported her toward the Bishop's wagon. Any other time, they remarked with delight at the thick buffalo grass, but today, these wiry strands transformed into a painful threat. Finally, they reached the wagon and Ben leaned out to pull them in. Aldrich reached for his Mama, and Carrie tumbled to Meta, her eyes full of concern.

"Mayda, Mayda… baby all dirty."

Chapter Four

Nebraska is a miserable, unpleasant place indeed, and can never be inhabited except by Red men.
~Journal of emigrant Harriett Sherrill Ward, 1853

Like a stuffed doll, baby Michael drooped in Betsy's arms.

Ben tore him from Betsy, but even as he breathed into his tiny mouth, an odd grey-blue infused the baby's skin.

Time stopped. Ben tried again... again.

Finally, he pressed his forehead against Betsy's, with Michael between them. "I'm afraid he has left us, sis." Betsy's wail broke Meta's heart, and little Carrie hid in Meta's skirts.

"Mama cry, Mayda."

An impossible truth swirled as Meta lifted Carrie. Time seemed to halt. Then Mr. Fortune summoned Ben to the back opening. Embracing Betsy and the children, icy shivers coursed Meta's back.

"No! No! Not my sweet Michael—"

Garrit stood outside, rain slashing his shoulders. A cold wave ransacked Meta, and she turned away. Only yesterday, Elsbeth described losing two of their children, taken by a raging fever on the trail from out East to Wisconsin. Now, Betsy fell into the older woman's arms.

Uncle Ben entranced the children with a story as the metallic scent of blood on wet wool convulsed in Meta's throat. Insensible wind moaned. Some time later, a low voice beckoned her in broken English.

"You vill come?"

She staggered towards the back, into the everyday smells of wagon grease, wood smoke, and lye soap. Loose locks slapped her neck as Garrit carried her to their wagon and wrapped her in a woolen blanket. He climbed back outside and returned with water.

"*Washen sie sich.*"

Wash myself. Yes.

This copper taste—these red stains on her dress—how could all of this be true? But something far more alarming burned in Garrit's eyes.

Fumbling, he unbuttoned her top two buttons. She took over, and he left as she washed her face and arms. Sodden undergarments heaped on the floor, intermingled with muddy grass, fine golden baby hairs stuck to her dress. When she found her breath again, Mama's quilt waited, and she buried herself in its folds.

Finally, the rain beat into a drizzle, and outdoors, Garrit struck his flint. When the fire crackled, he fetched her a cup of hot coffee. One strong sip and he turned on her. "You could have been hurt or killed." His stolid stare challenged her to respond. But why should she?

His squint sent a chill through her bones. Then his boots grated against loose stones as she stifled a sob.

Later, Betsy's face lingered so very near, and silence from the campsite told her Garrit had left. She could take some tea to the Bishops. The steeping minutes calmed her, as did the short walk.

White as new potatoes, Betsy rocked her baby. Elsbeth murmured as sawing and pounding echoed. "Ben and Adolph, building..." Her meaning throbbed in Meta's temples—they were fashioning sweet Michael's coffin.

Later, the men shuffled into the firelight with a small wooden box. Like pendulums, Ben's hands dangled at his sides. Then he reached toward Betsy.

"No. You cannot have him." Betsy clung to Michael. Someone

pushed a warm blanket from the darkness, and Elsbeth draped its folds in Betsy's lap.

"Let me hold him, sis. We'll stay right here with him."

"Yah, ve sit vit you." A child cried from inside the wagon, and a sleepy voice murmured, "There, there."

An hour passed watching the flames, perhaps two. Then rough fingers moved along Meta's shoulder. Garrit's voice came, softer than ever before. "Vill you come again?" She turned and reached for him.

Within twenty-four hours, rain, hail, snow, and sleet deluged the train. Winter's early June surprise. Those prairie chickens—where was their bravado now?

Drivers could not avoid the small grave beside the trail. Earlier, Ben had lowered Michael's rough-hewn box into a hollow next to two Indiana children sharing a cross. Another stormy day dawned and passed. Betsy's words still echoed. "John never even got to see his son."

During the long night, visions of Bergita, the sister Meta could scarcely recall, played in her mind. No wonder Papa never recovered from her death. As the mud trail wound on day after day, she rode in the wagon back or sat like a stone beside Garrit. But one morning, she reached out.

"Now I understand more about Papa."

Garrit said nothing.

"You know he backed the wagon over Bergita?"

"Yah."

Of course. Everyone in their small community knew. Another silence. Oh for even a few moments with Martin, for he alone had always been willing to talk about Papa and Bergita.

Later, the camp quieted. She tried again when Garrit put his arm around her in the wagon bed

"Michael had a smile every time I took him. And now—"

She curled into a ball as his steady breathing became a snore. Long afterward, she lay awake, more alone than she ever dreamed possible.

Before the Missouri Crossing, Betsy had prayed for protection. How could she possibly bear this? How had Mama borne Bergita's passing, or Elsbeth her children?

Heavy clouds scuttled a slim moon. Finally words came, but no relief. *Man is born unto trouble as the sparks fly upward.* The following days blurred. Then one evening, cattle mooed near the camp.

"A Texas herd has joined us." Mr. Fortune almost grinned. "Extra guns bode well in Injun country."

The lowing carried Meta back home where placid Herefords ambled the pasture. She and Martin rode old Tobias through grass mown by their grazing.

Here, the pungent odor of sage reached her—a mixture of camphor and turpentine. Mama praised this plant as an unguent. The creaky wagon lumbered forward, ever forward, and her very bones ached for Betsy, but this cleansing aroma bespoke healing.

June 7, 1863

Nebraska Territory still languishes. I can think of nothing but Michael and dear Betsy.

But today another cloud, enormous and black, approached our train. Like a sudden mist, but rapid and snorting, a buffalo herd ran our way—what might we expect?

Tails like small dark kerchiefs, noses to the earth, the huge mass plunged toward us with a thunderous roar. I grabbed Garrit's arm as the earth trembled.

The stampede handily destroyed one wagon near the front of the train and overturned another, leaving injured folks behind. But the men shot several of the massive beasts and baked their tender humps and tongues over campfires.

In addition to this fine feast, someone passed about a

helping of the marrow from a large bone baked in the coals.
Such rich fare—nothing has ever tasted quite so mouthwatering.

Crossing into Wyoming Country, another loss loomed at Fort Laramie, the end of the Oregon Trail for some wagons. But the Bishops continued westward—so did Hildegard and Rudolph, with their shy, skitterish children. The morning after they reached the fort, Meta left Garrit beside the wagon. These last days, nothing she did pleased him. His words stung while hers suffocated in her throat. Swallowing them seemed her only option, for if she spoke her mind, he drew away even more.

Healing, cleansing, starting over again—the promise of the sage—could this still be possible? Had Margita or Mama ever felt so distressed? But at this moment, losing Betsy weighed her down even more. In such a short time they had become so close.

"Write me, do you hear? I would never have survived these last weeks without you." Betsy clung to her, and they fought back sobs. "Hurry, Mama!" Hannah and Florence danced about, excited to continue the journey.

Another embrace. "I will never forget you."

"Nor I you."

Betsy had borne up for her other children, but a numinous shade clouded her eyes, and Meta vowed to write her when they staked their claim. No, sooner. From Garrit's cousin Herman's place in Cheyenne—maybe her letter would reach Oregon before Betsy did. Like time departing forever, the Bishop wagon shifted into line. With each turn of its wheels, devastation crushed Meta. But there could be no turning back.

Meanwhile, Garrit visited the blacksmith for his sore tooth. Before the Bishops left, Mr. Fortune had stopped by with some news. "The Fort raises prices ten to twenty times higher than in St. Louis."

So Meta tended camp, washed clothes, and cooked a thin soup. Nothing any mercantile offered could repair the emptiness shrouding her. Cattle bawls reminded her—they always sounded distressed, solitary in this world.

With their wagon, the drovers and three other families would follow the Laramie River for a time. One by one, they would turn off for their destinations—time was a'wasting. She must get to know these women better.

But they all had families of their own. Besides, an insatiable desire for sleep stymied her. But on the morning of the last leg, a thrill laced Garrit's tone.

"Our land lies near." In spite of his swollen face, he managed a crooked grin that pleaded with her to put everything behind them. Somewhere she had heard of ships stuck at the mouth of the Amazon River, mightier than the Missouri and Mississippi combined. Believing themselves becalmed in salt water, sailors sometimes died aboard ship, not realizing the Amazon's powerful currents spurted two hundred feet into the ocean, so fresh water lay just over the side.

Like those sailors, she needed help. As the wagons fell into their jagged rhythm, this singular word preoccupied her.

Help.

An old Indian path led them forward. On either side, stark oxen and cattle skeletons baked under the noonday sun.

"How could anything grow in this country?" By now, she expected no response, but after a while, Garrit answered.

"Remember Ezekiel and the dry bones living again?" Little solace. Even Mama's raspberry preserves tasted sour this morning.

"One day, we will sell many horses to the Cavalry."

At the Chugwater Creek ford, Tom and Matilda Hanson wheeled aside. Close to giving birth, Matilda ambled over to say good-bye. "Do visit us if you head to the Fort. We may not live so far apart." Her cheerful eyes ignited possibilities.

"You really think so?"

"At least hours instead of days."

After she left, Meta trailed the shallow creek water with

her fingertips while Garrit helped another fellow. Birds caroled afternoon songs as sunlight filtered through a dense pine stand.

The land's humble beauty beckoned. Simple—no mountains or cliffs, yet lovely. Somewhere, a single thrush warbled.

"Help me, please. I need to forgive Garrit..." As dried out as the bones along the trail, she shrank against a sapling.

Be still and know that I am God.

A divine message in Mama's quiet voice. The heaviness in Meta's chest receded a bit. She ought to be getting back, but her bodice ballooned as one low branch caught her toe and plopped her into the shallow pool. How to explain to Garrit—shoes and stockings drenched, hair streaming like a veil onto her soaked dress... But oh, the coolness! Who would know if she took time to bathe?

With four-wing saltbush leaves, she lathered her petticoat and hung it on a limb before scrubbing all over. Stains on her stockings and skirt needed work, and her petticoat, too. Finished, she climbed out and onto another massive rock face. Its warm surface invited her to stretch out, and in a gentle waft of sage, she fell asleep.

When she startled awake, her dress stuck to her. She hurried into her stockings and shoes, slinging her petticoat over her arm. Perhaps Garrit had started talking with someone and hadn't noticed her absence.

Suddenly, boots crunched, sending alarm up her spine. She turned to see a tall slender fellow bend and retrieve something white, though clay-speckled.

One of those Texas cowhands—heat rushed her cheeks as she drew back. How often had Garrit repeated Mr. Fortune's warning?

This man's slim build made his muscular shoulders even more obvious. As if balancing a dead mouse between his fingers, he took a step back. Then he held out an undergarment.

"Ma'am—you might have dropped something?" For a sheer

second, his eyes showed, long enough to reveal a unique violet-blue. With another long backward step, he lowered his gaze as she snagged the petticoat.

"I... thank you, sir."

He tipped his hat and vanished among the boulders.

Chapter Five

"The beauty and charm of the wilderness are his for the asking, for the edges of the wilderness lie close beside the beaten roads of the present travel."

~Theodore Roosevelt

Raising a vast dust cloud, the drovers swerved south. Ten minutes down the trail, urgent *moos* still echoed. What must it be like to ride in that dust? Even now, that cowhand's eyes stayed with her—only one patch in Mama's quilt came close to their distinctive hue.

When the waterway branched out, the oxen followed the south fork beside a high-banked creek boasting willows, tall cottonwoods, and plenteous juniper pine. The arch above the water drew Meta's eyes upward as she fixed a simple supper. By firelight, she and Garrit lazed under wild plum blossoms as sunset melded sleepy bird chatter with a rusty orange sky.

How foolish she had been, laughing with Betsy at the thought of Garrit lunging about like a prairie chicken. Now, they faced life together, and his vigor would see them through.

"This land is *gut*." Here, in *their country*, something in him eased.

The next day, he calculated their location about four miles north of the Lodgepole River. Following what must be an old Indian trail, they made steady progress, until a small cabin topped a rise above a cut bank.

Garrit slowed the oxen. "I take a closer look." He climbed

the bank while Meta washed away trail dust in the cool water and whispered to the oxen. "We might come back here. This could be our new home."

Then a shout sounded.

"*Aufkommen!*"

Someone stood dwarfed by Garrit's height. He appeared almost gnome-like, bowed legs and a thick buckskin-covered chest. Coarse rock ground into pebbles led Meta to abundant growth as far as the eye could see. The trapper held out a gnarled hand and gave hers a good shake.

"Got beans and bacon cookin'." His mustache straggled into his beard like grey-white weeds.

"Ve vant to make Cheyenne by nightfall."

"Thet's a long haul. But ya gotta eat."

They followed him to his campfire, where he motioned them to sit.

"A'ready et, m'self."

He poured steaming water over a spoon and plate and shook them dry before ladling beans and meat. His eyes flashed sapphire beneath heavy white eyebrows.

"Lookin' t' settle here?"

Garrit swallowed his portion and handed the spoon to Meta.

"Maybe. My cousin in Cheyenne vill help us."

"Plenty o' land fer th' takin' out here. Right glad t'meet ya folks."

"*Danke.*"

"Hope ya come back thisaway." The fellow's comment followed them down to the water, where they turned and waved.

Garrit's English might be lacking but using it on their journey had helped. Scrabbling back down to the creek, the gleam in his eyes matched the water's sparkle, and she quipped, "We have met our first native."

"Yah. You tink he is Indian?"

"No. But likely he knows some of them."

The wagon rolled on, and after a while she crawled inside. "I forgot to ask that trapper's name. Oh, my, I must start to *think* again!"

The sweet scent of Mama's quilt received her whisper. Reliable hoofbeats lulled her to sleep.

Voices outside the wagon. Meta shook herself. Muscled like a blacksmith, Garrit's cousin Herman helped her down as Anna rushed forward.

"*Wir haben auf dich gewartet!*" A warm embrace and an apron like Mama's spilling kitchen aromas. Eyes brown as Martin's pet woodchuck and a smile wider than the Missouri, Anna's presence hummed, *home.*

Over fresh bread, sauerkraut, and tender beef, Herman described this land. Anna filled their plates and herded four lively children. "The best land lies north of here."

"Beyond the Lodgepole?"

"Yah. Less sand and plenty of water."

In the morning, Herman and Garrit wasted no time visiting the solicitor, who housed the land office. While Anna worked in the restaurant, Meta washed their clothes and played with Helga and Gustav. Soon, Garrit burst across the yard and twirled her by the waist.

"We have our claim! One day, horses will graze from the creek to those cottonwoods on the hilltop, *shatz.*"

Herman slapped Garrit's shoulder. "Finally, another Rausch in Wyoming Country! Tonight, we make merry."

Time to write Betsy, as Garrit reinforced the wagon wheels. Still a long month of travel for the Bishops to reach the Willamette. Later, Anna made a batch of sweet dough while Meta peeled potatoes. Soon, the aroma of rising warm *kuchen* satiated the kitchen.

"If only you would settle closer. You must travel so far."

"Garrit has his heart set on selling horses to Fort Laramie." Meta dropped a potato into salted water. "But you must visit us."

"Will you come back for Christmas?" Anna slapped her dough a final time and dug into a second hefty mound. "The children need an Auntie."

Little Helga's dress created a banner as she raced by, followed by Gus. Helga squealed when he tackled her.

"Garrit bartered for a horse and cow and promised your neighbor our oxen in return. We will have to bring them back here."

Helga's squeals turned to yelps as Anna finished another *kuchen*. She held up greasy palms.

"Now she will cry. But I always have the next meal to prepare."

Soon her prediction came true.

Squatting beside a squalling Helga, Meta drew Gus close. "Get some water for Helga and sit under this table. Such a big boy you are—help your sister count the stones in the floor. I am certain you can do it."

Gus fetched the water and started counting and pointing for Helga.

"We must be sure the men must think this is their idea."

As Meta washed dishes near an open window, Anna headed outdoors. Every syllable from the men carried as Anna joined in.

"Fritz at the livery is selling eight prime pullets. Surely you must have laying hens on your claim, Garrit?"

Garrit squinted toward the house, searching for Meta. But she stayed in the shadows as Herman added his opinion. "Yah. You need chickens."

Garrit's eyebrows rose—he agreed with Anna? Then Herman winked. "I know—this will be your vedding gift."

Eying the kitchen again, Garrit stiffened. But to no avail— Anna had already accomplished her mission.

The milk cow slowed their progress to the claim. Most of the day, Meta led the animals, and having a milk cow lightened her step. And chickens stirring in their cages—King Midas never felt so rich. When they stopped for water, she soaked her feet while the animals drank. Back at the wagon, she found Garrit filing a rim.

"I think we should name our cow Della. And what shall we call the mare? She'll be the first of our herd."

"Yah." He rubbed the stubble on his chin.

"What about Hope?"

"Sounds *gut*." A grin picked at Garrit's lips. "Vill you name the chickens too?"

For two weeks, Garrit felled trees. His clothing swam with fine clinging dust and wood chips, so rancid, Meta washed his shirt in the creek and hung it on the wagon brakes to dry overnight.

All day long, she cared for the animals and prepared meals. One morning she rigged an oven using Mama's big iron skillet and the plowshare.

At midday Garrit wolfed down three slices of bread before noticing the plowshare. "*Vas is das*? My plowshare in the fire?"

Certain the flames would cause no harm, she had prepared for this. Her answer waited at the ready, but he sealed his lips.

Anna had sent more than cheese and sauerkraut with them. She also offered lessons on how to deal with a husband.

"See how well it works?"

"*Schmeckt gut*. Back to work, *mein shatz*."

Chapter Six

Courage is resistance to fear, the mastery of fear—not the absence of fear.

~Mark Twain

The last floorboard slid into place. Meta mudded the inner walls while Garrit labored over the roof and floor—their cabin, almost finished!

Finally they made countless trips from the wagon with their belongings. The feather bed, in one corner on the heavy trunks, displayed Mama's quilt.

"I saw a doe up on the hill." Garrit's eyes lighted. "She will taste fine this winter when she fattens." He wiped his brow in the intense July heat. "How big do you want the table?"

"It has to serve as my cutting board and bread board. How about half the size of the cabin?"

"Someday, I will build you a house like Herman's; two stories. And a place just for your sewing."

"Ach!"

Knowing how she disliked needlework, he chased her outside. Down the cut bank, she tore off her shoes and splashed in. Water caressed her parched skin in a pond large enough to paddle across, and Garrit followed her onto a wide jutting boulder to bask in late afternoon sunlight.

Was that a flicker protesting from a high branch like the flashy red-feathered cardinals that claimed Mama's yard as their personal territory?

Especially against snow, like bright red zinnias, they chirped, *All is well. All is well…cheerio!*

Ah, a lovely memory. But this new home offered other species to watch.

"Our life here has just begun, *mein Schatz*."

The prelude to sunset displayed an array of shades—had sunset been so beautiful back home, or had she simply not noticed?

"No fox vill ever get in." Garrit's declaration impressed the hens, whose dark eyes glimmered from their cages. Doubled and re-doubled, not even the hungriest wolf could chew its way through this wire.

"I can make the latches." And Meta did, her fingers so sore at eventide that she applied Mama's ointment. But these tedious measures would prove worthwhile—one morning an egg would rest in a nest.

Next, Garrit set about building an enclosure for Hope and Della. Late wildflowers scented the breeze, and in the evenings, autumn tinged the air. Their second turning of the seasons together—winter brought no fear, with Garrit to stock the fire and care for the animals.

So far, he had not mentioned returning the oxen, but perhaps some settler would pass and be willing to take them. Visitors— wouldn't that be something? But that trapper might happen by, at least. Oh, that she had asked his name.

Busy cutting wood for the barn walls, Garrit had found his place. *A good man,* as Mama said, *so strong.* A few days later when he set the foundations on the south side of the cabin, he took a minute to survey his work. "Almost ready for winter. Next, I will fill our wood pile." Satisfaction eased the deep lines between his brows. "Let the snows come—they will find us ready."

A wild north wind blustered as Meta gave the beans another stir. This storm brought those terrible Nebraska gales to mind—unforgettable. Grey eyes downcast, Garrit clumped into the cabin.

"What is it?"

He shunted off his dripping coat and slumped onto a chair. His wide face took on a strange cast, causing Meta's heart to thump.

"Garrit?"

"Della has wandered off. *Einfaltspinsel!*"

He opened the door and stared out into the torrent as if Della, the simpleton, might suddenly appear. "Vat if she tries to cross the creek?"

"Perhaps after we eat, the storm will die down so we can look for her?"

He returned to the table. She filled his plate with two slabs of bread and ladled the beans.

"After their normal prayer, he added, "*Und* Della."

When had he ever done such a thing? They spoke scarcely at all, and afterward, he drummed his thick fingers on the table.

She cleared the dishes, filled the dishpan, poured coffee. *Clump, clump, clump* back and forth—what would he do?

"As bad a storm as—" Garrit hushed—he meant Mitchell Pass. But mentioning those difficult days had become *verboten*. No matter the urgency, he took time to think things through. While she waited, Meta's rash judgments paraded before her. Those first weeks on that endless trail had brought out the worst in her. His differences seemed to be signs of weakness, but perhaps he only moved slower…more purposefully. As time passed she saw that he cared as much as she did.

"Would you like more coffee?"

He gulped down a swig and spread his palms. How tall he stood in this small space now, nearly grazing the rafters! Finally, he met her eyes.

"We must find her. I may have to wade the creek."

He put on his coat. The late day growth on his chin left a

tingle when their lips brushed, and she held onto him a moment. Warm earthiness engulfed her before he swung over the threshold and vanished into the twilight.

Leaving the heavy door ajar, she held the canvas he had hung over the stoop. Great swaths of rain obscured even the creek bank, but the sound transported Meta to spring tornadoes back home.

Though they built the cabin far from the cut bank, erratic lightning flashes revealed their claim saturated. Miniature gullies became rivulets giving way to wide trenches rushing toward the creek.

As though mesmerized by the sound, she startled at a coyote's howl. How long had she been gazing into the night? But still no sign of Garrit. At last she shut the door. He must be struggling with Della in tow, or perhaps found some hapless shelter.

What would they ever do without milk and butter?Desperate enough to pick up her knitting needles, she attempted a pair of stockings for Garrit. Twice, she fed the fire and lighted a candle while the downpour still raged. Her feeble flame offered a fragment of hope, even as an insistent cord constricted her breath.

Where, oh where could Garrit have gone?

Grief is itself a medicine.
~William Cowper 1731–1800

The storm's endless wail continued, but as night faded into a hazy dawn, Della's complaint somehow reached Meta. Could she be dreaming? No, the insistent mooing grew even louder.

The downpour had muddied the known world, and each tenuous step threatened to suck her away along the cabin's south wall. Shivers overtook her as she forced the stool from the muck and milked Della. Only then did the shredded tether catch her attention.

"How did you get home, girl?" Della blinked as though she would like to answer. "Such a storm. Garrit must have gone to check on something else."

Gripping the milk pail, Meta retraced her route to the cabin door. Struggling for breath, she narrowed her eyes against the wind. *Snap! Crash!* The gale downed a cottonwood and kept blustering.

In similar fashion, an incessant question hounded her.

Where could Garrit have gone?

Hours passed, and the downpour subsided into a drizzle. Thick sludge dogged Meta's every step. Around the corner, her hens cackled. Della's affectionate brown eyes glimmered a welcome, and from the grain sack, Meta parceled out a few hands full to her and the oxen.

Hope whinnied, so she patted her muzzle. "Sorry, girl. Too much grain may make you flounder."

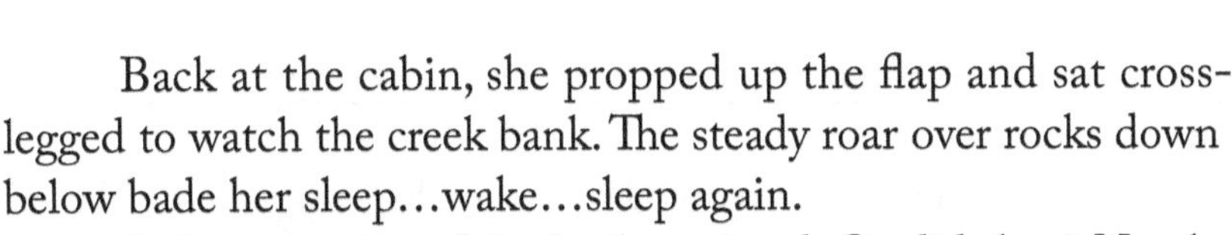

Back at the cabin, she propped up the flap and sat cross-legged to watch the creek bank. The steady roar over rocks down below bade her sleep…wake…sleep again.

At last, the tips of the bushes stirred. Or did they? Nearly impossible to separate reality from the fictions her mind devised, but a slight rustle stirred the leaves again. Trembling overwhelmed her as boggy *stomps* squished, like frogs in a pond. Closer. Closer.

Boots appeared, causing her heart to gallop. Handmade buckskins, and gradually, a hat showed. Not Garrit's. No, this wide-brim slung low on a fellow much shorter and stockier. He pushed aside the branches, and his crystalline eyes ignited a memory. The trapper they had met on the way to Cheyenne—he had shared his meal.

"M'on, Ethel!" With a mighty thrash, his mule broke through and the trapper hailed Meta. "Howdy, Ma'am. Where's yer husband?"

Below his deep forehead, his eyes glinted like candles in the night. She and Garrit had hoped to visit this fellow again, and here he was.

"He went out last night after Della and—"

The trapper's brows met in a bushy white line. "Della?"

"Yes. Our cow." At just the right moment, Della mooed.

"H'ain't come back? Lemme have a look."

Meta gathered her shawl to follow. One step into the liquid earth, and she swayed. "No day t' be out. Be right back."

But she shadowed him up the hill east of the cabin, slipping and sloshing. He found level ground, then bent over something in the brush.

"What…?"

He looked off into the distance, anywhere but at her. "Missus Rausch? Yer husband—" He face twisted. "He was here, choppin' somethin', but—"

Against her will, she followed his gaze. From a heap of mire and branches extended a human hand, the coat sleeve stuck on some nettles. Caught halfway between two branches lay an axe.

And Garrit's boot.

Why, his trouser leg had torn clear through and was covered in dark red.

The trapper swept brambles away, pulled and pulled. "Blamed if I kin see..." He wrenched around. "Thet cow got loose?"

A voice—surely not hers—replied. "Yes, last night."

"Musta got caught in this here brush. He tried t' chop 'er loose. Musta bled out."

A scream sounded, and Meta sank to the earth. Someone lifted her, and from some foreign sphere, a voice filtered like so many falling stars.

"Most terr'ble sorry, Ma'am—that I am."

The rafters... Mama's perfect quilt stitches. She had fallen... Yes, but now...

A swarthy face swam above her.

"Goin' t' bury yer husband now, Ma'am."

"Bury?" This visitor seemed so far away, and his lips moved so slowly.

"Gotta git 'im b'low ground, understand? Got somethin' t' wrap 'im in, a blanket mebbe?"

Blanket. If she did this man's bidding, perhaps he would leave, and Garrit would come home.

"An ol' blanket'd do fine."

A frayed corner stuck out between their two trunks—a piece of the wagon canvas—the remains of their prairie schooner.

Meta dragged its stiff mass across the floor.

"Might want t' come, Ma'am." He handed over her boots. "Best put these on."

She obeyed ,and dragging the canvas, he guided her up the hill. Shovel tackled rock—the scraping hurt her ears. She touched Garrit's cold forehead, ashen blue like Baby Michael's. No, surely not. If Mama were here, she would pick those pebbles out of his skin. She would wash him and prepare him, as she did Bergita long years ago, and as Betsy swaddled baby Michael. But only this trapper, no womenfolk, stood here. A cry rose from the depths, more animal than human.

"Garrit—no!"

Over and over, her doleful melody resounded, as if from someone else's mouth. Finally, the trapper set the shovel aside and unfolded the canvas. Grunting and snorting, he prodded until the bundle edged the waiting hole.

"Sech a fine pair a boots…"

On her knees, Meta nodded. With more panting, the trapper pulled at one. Another, and set them near her.

"Ma'am, this ain't a fittin'." He scratched under his hat. "Have ya said yer fare-ye-wells?"

Buzzing filled Meta's ears—*fare-thee wells?* Whatever could he mean?

"Y'know…'tain't right not to say somethin'." His bright eyes begged her to say something.

But speech forsook her. She could only stand here, silent and broken. Finally came the patter of pebbles pummeling the canvas.

The trapper turned, and his scent—leather and earth and jerky—almost made her swoon.

"Oughtn't we say somethin' b'for he's done covered?"

He cranked his jaws back and forth as if to stir up phrases. At last, he intoned, "Garrit Rausch, we commit ya t' yer Maker."

The eerie cold wind bore down as he finished his work. A heap of earth in the wilderness. A heap of earth upon a hill.

"Best git back, Ma'am. Them wolves'll soon start prowlin'. Days is gettin' shorter."

Later, he produced some jerky and coffee, but she could not eat. Still, she lingered in the doorway as he built a campfire a few yards away. His final words circled her like phantoms. "Be right here if'n ya need me in th' night."

From Texas to Wyoming Country

When a government has ceased to protect the lives, liberty, and property of the people...and...becomes an instrument in the hands of evil rulers for their oppression...it is a...sacred obligation to their posterity to abolish such government, and create another in its stead.

~Governor Sam Houston

Richmond, Virginia, 1862

The Confederate Congress passed a conscription law ordering all men from 18 to 45 years of age to be placed into military service. Exceptions: ministers, state, city, county officers, and certain slave owners holding twenty slaves or more.

In the Union, the Conscription Act of 1863 established the first national draft system requiring registration by every male citizen and immigrant who had applied for citizenship between the ages of 20 and 45. The New York Times called the Conscription Act "the condition of victory," but the law provided an exemption for those who could pay a $300 fee. Critics argued that the law punished the poor. Others insisted that it interfered with states' rights, since state-based militias had fought in previous wars.

Despite conscription laws, both the Union and Confederate armies relied mostly on volunteers.

Let me tell you what is coming. After the sacrifice of countless millions of treasure and hundreds of thousands of lives you may win Southern independence, but I doubt it. The North is determined to preserve this Union.

They are not a fiery, impulsive people as you are, for they live in colder climates. But when they begin to move in a given direction, they move with the steady momentum and perseverance of a mighty avalanche.

~Governor Sam Houston

Chapter Eight

Grass is the forgiveness of nature—her constant benediction.

~John James Ingalls
Senator from Kansas

"Accept the things to which fate binds you and love the people with whom fate brings you together—with all your heart."

By his elocution, this fellow surely might be an orator, but his breath came straight from a bottle.

Who could this be, out in the wilds of North Texas? And why foist his views on a cowpoke in an isolated hovel pretending to be a saloon near the border of Indian Territory? Intent on his sarsaparilla, Clay Burns hunkered down.

"Good advice, don't you agree? From the highly honored Marcus Aurelius." With a flourish, the crude philosopher tipped his tawdry hat. Clay shifted to the next stool—only one remained—but the dense fermented odor still pervaded. The bartender intervened.

"Now Edgar, keep your cogitatin' to yerself t'night."

"But this young bloke's a thinker, I can tell. A Texan, for certain. Betcha he knows all about the government's doings—how we're under Jeff Davis and the Confederates, and every last one of us, eighteen to sixty-five, is s'posed to fight."

The intoxicated man lurched toward Clay again. "But here you are, headin' North. Whadd'ya think of ol' Sam Houston giving up his governorship for the Union? He refused to take an oath to the Rebels, y'know?"

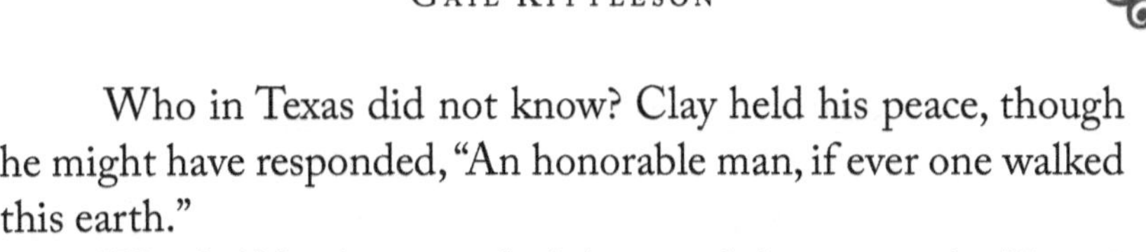

Who in Texas did not know? Clay held his peace, though he might have responded, "An honorable man, if ever one walked this earth."

"Headin' North so you don't have to fight against the Union? Rather risk your hide to the Injuns?"

Once again, Clay maintained silence—things had become so complicated with this war. Some folks reduced all of the angles to slavery versus freedom, but far more was involved.

"If I was young like you, I'd do the same thing. Yes I would, indeed. Join up with folks on their way to the Territories." The man swayed close enough to reveal deep stains on his shirt collar and grime under his fingernails.

Clay grabbed his glass, swerved and caught the bartender's eye.

"But you know, the U.S. Congress just passed the Enrollment Act, and that includes us too—I'm for the Union, you know, though Queen Victoria has proclaimed my homeland neutral. Every man, even immigrants, from twenty to forty-five's s'posed to stand for the Union."

He dragged a dirty kerchief under his nose. "So either way, we're s'posed to be in the fight." He kept veering closer, intent on who-knew-what.

But the barkeep had other plans.

"That's enough, now." He reached out for Edgar's arm, and Edgar took a wild swing. But the barkeep ducked before subduing him with a single blow to his jaw. Edgar splayed torso first over the bar, and the bartender reflected over his collapsed form.

"Come over here from England, Edgar did. Some kinda professor, they say, and he's got more brains than sense. But he lost his whole family in a runaway a couple years ago. Hain't been the same since—cain't even teach young'uns no more.

"He still brings us our news in these parts. At times, he's downright brilliant—explains the battles so's we can get the meaning."

Sarsaparilla tingled down Clay's throat as someone dragged

the hapless Edgar away, his boots slapping back and forth on the floorboards. Best to finish his drink and get back to the herd.

Strangely, Edgar's assessment had been correct. If not for Clay's incessant pondering—so many unanswered questions, and many of them unrelated to the war—sleep might come easier at night. Besides that, he had not yet heard about the Enrollment Act.

The barman still observed him.

"Was Edgar right? You a thinker?"

Swigging down the dregs, Clay set down the correct change. In smoky shadows, a table of poker players with hat brims cloaking their faces attended to their cards, paying him no mind as he sought fresh air.

This shanty boasted tarpaper sticking through crevices—one strong wind could take down the entire structure. Not even a paper window rubbed with candle stubs for waterproofing let in a bit of light.

Nothing here for him, although the other cowhands seemed to long for places like this. But then, he had never professed to be a normal cowhand. A short ride east, a few hands watched the herd while others slept. Spotting one of the younger ones, Clay tugged the reins and yelled in his best Spanish.

"Hey Antonio, I'll take your watch."

"But this might could be your last night off before we meet that wagon train."

"Take it or leave it."

"Yippee!" Antonio squashed down his hat and spurred his horse toward the unnamed outpost in this grassy wilderness.

Meanwhile, muffled evening sounds blanketed cattle weary from the long day. These doggies would arrive at their destination in a matter of weeks—a ranch in high plains country. Thanks to the continuous munching sounds around him as the animals tore at abundant grass, they would meet their owner not much worse for the wear.

"And you—what is your destination?"

The question gnawed at Clay. For now, all he knew was that they would accompany the wagon train into Indian country—Wyoming Country—where no government enrolled a man to fight.

Accept the things to which fate binds you. Did that mean he ought to veer Northeast instead to join up with a Federal Army unit? Father Bernard used to read passages like this and present them for Clay to interpret. His childlike answers always left something to be desired, but Father Bernard knew how to stretch a child's imagination.

"Take whatever happens as it comes."

Father Bernard always waited for more, so Clay thought harder. "You meet people for some reason, and you're supposed to love them."

"How, son? You must consider the entire content."

"With all your heart?"

"Indeed. But now, might you define the meaning?"

"Like your life depended on it?"

"Is that your answer?"

"Yes sir."

"You have reasoned well, son. Now let's see what mischief we can find."

Recalling how he once followed Father Bernard around the mission, Clay threw an extra log on the fire. Followed him until—the memory roused a groan.

Before Father Bernard arrived, trouble had been no stranger. More often than not, one of the Sisters administered welts to his backside with the razor strap, and his pride festered along with the bruises.

But still, he had a place to sleep and food to eat. Father Bernard taught him to be grateful. "Think, son, what would have happened to you if the rangers had not brought you to the Sisters?"

"I expect the wolves woulda got me, or a bear."

"But you were rescued. Ah, what consolation! Saint John of

the Cross said desolation comes to us all. But he also believed we must learn to recognize and embrace life's consolations."

This concept kept Clay unsure, but desolation, he knew. One night, local bandits torched a building for sport—the lean-to at the mission where he and the other orphans slept. Witnesses said Father Bernard rushed from his small quarters to save seven children, Clay one of the first. He stood back from the terrific heat and watched a main support buckle. Then the priest flung himself out a window with a young girl in his arms.

In the fire's aftermath, Father Bernard displayed fits of violent coughing, but still shared aloud his ponderings concerning desolation and consolation. Though years had passed since his death, to this day his ponderings meandered inside Clay's head. More than once, kneeling beside his bunk, Father Bernard had touched his forehead. "This little one—how can I thank Thee for saving him?"

Father Bernard often took Clay on excursions, so he could learn about the land and develop his skills. On one such adventure along the Guadalupe River, the priest became ill. Local folks told a family north of New Braunfels, the Evendsbergs, who brought a wagon to tote Father Bernard to their homestead.

With nineteen orphans to watch over, work filled every moment on their settlement, but this German couple made time for a stranger. And for Clay.

When Father Bernard succumbed to his overwrought lungs, his resting place became the closest Catholic cemetery in the Hill Country, St. Peter and St. Paul in New Braunfels. These folks knew all about desolation—they had buried hundreds of immigrants in a cholera epidemic soon after they arrived here from Germany.

Desolation enveloped Clay as he stood with the Evendsbergs at the graveside. Father Bernard lying in that grave, passed all too soon from this earth…what would he do now?

The family invited him to stay on, so he did. They included him in meals, work, games, singing, and evening prayers. As weeks passed, he realized that though quite different, Father Bernard and this German pastor had much in common.

During this time, he began to apprehend his legacy. Father Bernard had taught him to read, listen well, and think. He knew how to pay attention to what truly mattered and had studied the wise men of the ages.

But along with his ability to reason well, something else endured—a bitter seed. Father Bernard had been short-changed. He would never have murmured about this, since he took everything as it came. But truly, his earthly life had been cut short by those heartless marauders who burned the orphanage.

"To which fate binds you? Fancy words, but empty!" Clay fumed to the campfire's flames. "Who wants to be bound to wickedness? And what if destiny brings you murderers straight from hell?"

The fire consumed his questions as he gave sway to unsure memories. "The mission sat somewhere around Fort Worth. How many days did it take Father Bernard and me to reach the Guadalupe…maybe four or five?"

Despite his figuring, no answers arrived, but a warm rush prevailed as vivid scenes entered his mind. Father Bernard cooking supper over a campfire or reading nighttime meditations; Father Bernard instructing him concerning history, geography, foliage, and animal life.

And each night without fail, he tucked Clay in with a touch to his forehead and a word of peace. Those moments, still with him, ought to make his sleep easier, but such was not to be.

"Edgar was right about me being a thinker, but he has no idea where I come from. If he did, he'd have saved his fine words to spout elsewhere." All around, tall grass swayed in a late evening breeze as Clay banked the fire and greeted the next watch.

Seeking his bedroll, he muttered. "I say if you come upon hellions straight from Hades—rogues set on destruction—you seal up your heart."

In a few days they would meet the wagon train, and all

drovers received strict instructions from Red, the trail boss, to keep to their own. The announcement seemed unnecessary—who wanted to consort with settlers intent on fencing in this free range? Besides, they would travel together only a short time.

Like everything else he had tried, this situation would be temporary. As planned, Red found the wagon train—he and the boss, a Mr. Fortune, knew each other somehow.

And things went well as they followed the train, with no sign of Indians. At Fort Laramie, most of the wagons proceeded to parts west while the few that stayed found their own way soon enough.

Finding their own way—Clay had to give those incomers credit. Life on the train offered little ease. Settling a claim in what they called Wyoming Country seemed foolhardy to him, but these stalwarts—many of them hard-faced German and Norwegian immigrants—entered into this believing they could do anything they set their mind to.

"There she is—the Oak Bar Ranch, like a big ol' lizard sunnin' herself of an afternoon." Two days after they departed the wagon train's company, by then dwindled to only a wagon or two, the trail boss pointed toward broad plains extending to the horizon.

"Where are we, exactly?"

Clay's inquiry brought hee-haws from two other hands. The older one wiped his mouth with his sleeve.

"This here's no man's land. B'longed t' Oregon Territ'ry, but in '53, Congress gave it t' Wash'ton. Last year, 'fficials moved it t' Idaho. Now they's attachin' these plains t' Dakota, but they say in a few years, we'll be standin' in Wyomin' Territory."

He spat in the general direction of Clay's boot. "Name means *big plains* but nobody in Wash'ton knows what to do with this here big ol' piece of land. Jest like they didn't know what t' do at Fort Sumter or Bull Run, n' got this whole big war started. One thing

we don't need to worry 'bout here's gettin' conscripted—Wyoming Country ain't nowhere' a'tall."

On August twenty-first, the cowhands sat down in the bunkhouse to steaks dripping over their plates. The ranch owner, about as lean and tall as a man could get, shocked Clay by joining them.

He talked with them as if he had known them all of his life, and used his hands like Father Bernard. Midway through the meal, he asked for their attention.

"I'm Owen Dunbar. Welcome to the Oak Bar. Red will divvy out your pay tonight, but you're welcome to stay over." His eyes stopped on each man.

"Much obliged for the way you brought the herd here in safety. In this treacherous time to be forging a trail from the Panhandle to here, you might have suffered an Indian attack, or one from devoted soldiers on either side of the war. The Union is clamping down on trade between the North and the South, but you made it through.

"We figured since you made your passage far west of the Mississippi, the armies would have enough over there to keep them occupied. Not all of our conjectures prove true, but I'm mighty glad this one did, and you're all safe and sound."

After the meal, with his earnings in his saddlebag, Clay walked the length of the path leading to the ranch house, pondering Mr. Dunbar's words. When had a rancher ever expressed gratitude for paid labor? With Mr. Crady, the owner of the ranch where Clay learned this trade, cowhands were fortunate to even see the boss.

Some of the hands talked longer, but he stretched out on his bunk. Sleeping had never come easy, and being cooped up inside made things worse—but still, resting sounded better than conversing.

Finally he napped, and when he wakened, morning had come,

and some men had already taken their leave. One named Wilson figured he'd go fight for the Rebs and see some of the country while he was at it. Another, Gordon, headed out West.

Staring down the path from the ranch, Clay's ever-present questions rose. Which direction should he ride? Maybe beyond Fort Laramie, into Powder River Country, farther North than he'd ever imagined. But there, he might easily meet his fate at the hands of some merciless tribe on the hunt.

After breakfast, saddle soap in hand, he rubbed his boots and chaps. Sunshine sneaked over his bench as Red strode up.

"Boss wants t' talk t' you."

Putting the final sheen on his belongings brought Father Bernard's instructions to mind. *Always respect others' property and care for your own.*

Finishing his work, Clay veered toward the Oak Bar ranch house. He might have changed his mind, but as he neared, Mr. Dunbar opened the door and stepped out on the porch.

"Clay Burns?" The rancher gestured him into a cedar-lined office. "Have a seat."

Clay remained standing while Mr. Dunbar sat behind a large desk. "Red says you're one of the best cowhands he's ever seen."

Clay fidgeted with his hat.

"That true?"

"This ride taught me a lot. Red really knows his business."

Mr. Dunbar stroked his chin. "True. And I trust his judgment. Truth is, we could use an experienced hand around here, and he's been keeping his eye out for one. They say this winter will be as hard as the last, and the cold troubles my bones more each season." A shadow crossed his face. "Got a cabin up north. I would hire you to keep watch there, because cattle have a way of straying across the Lodgepole River."

Something leaped in Clay's chest—a place to go. But he tempered his reaction.

"You might not get to report in until April." The rancher

paused. "It's a job—unless some girl's waitin' for you in Texas, or you're fixin' to sign up on one side or the other."

"No, sir. Nobody's waiting for me. I'll take you up on your offer."

Mr. Dunbar's left eyebrow squiggled. "I'd like to ride the land with you. Need another day before we head up there?"

"Nope."

"Meet you outside in half an hour. Get ready for more beans and bacon."

"I was hopin' for beefsteak and gravy again tonight."

Mr. Dunbar grinned and extended his hand.

Walking away, Clay welcomed a slight breeze. Sometimes it was a good thing to have no one waiting for you; to have no commitments. He flicked a fly from his arm. He had hardly tried, but just like that, his destination had appeared.

"Missus, ya a'right?"

The substantial door fought Meta, but she forced it open—so sturdy, Garrit's careful work. The trapper stood before her, a dawn sky in the background. His mottled beard put her in mind of Pastor Schultz—had she somehow traveled back home?

"Need anythin' 'fore I go?" Blue eyes locked onto hers, but no sound came when she opened her mouth.

"Got 'nough food, Ma'am?"

He glanced at several hams hanging from the rafters.

"Bar th' door at night, ya hear? Keep watch on them animals, too."

She gripped her shoulders as if she would break apart. Behind him, the trapper's mule brayed.

"Hear me, Missus?"

His eyes flooded as he held out a gnarled hand. "Name's Ross. Franklin Ross."

The mule wheezed. Tears burned the backs of Meta's eyes, but she stood frozen. This man would leave, and she would be all alone—surely there must be something she could say.

"Let them animals graze everythin' right down to th' nubbins, hear? The grass is Wyomin Country's gift to ya. Cain't let it go t' waste." With this injunction, Mr. Ross backed off, but turned once more to meet her gaze. He gave his burly head a shake before heading toward the creek bank and vanishing into the brush.

Bar the door Garrit fashioned. Stumble to the bed Garrit built. Mama's quilt—these soft folds would sustain her, certainly

they would. The wind groaned through the trees, the creek roared beneath it all, and Meta could only listen.

Such a large pack Mr. Dunbar loaded before he swung into his saddle.

"It's almost a day to the Lodgepole, then two hours north to the ranch."

By late afternoon, the Lodgepole sparkled beyond a mild slope, a silver-blue thread running into forever. Beans and bacon it was, but huckleberry pie made the meal a feast.

"Nothing like a campfire to settle a man."

Clay grunted. Why not let the spectacular northern lights do the talking?

"Where were you headed before you signed on?"

"I'd been working at a ranch, but hadn't made any plans."

"Your family?"

"All gone." This game, Clay could play. "Where were you born?"

"In Minnesota. Pa always had the urge to move farther west and this must've looked like home to him."

"He was one of the first settlers?"

"The Cooks came thirty years before, but wolves and Indians still reigned when Pa turned up. He learned the Indian lingo and made friends wherever he could. My mother died four years later, leaving five of us for him to watch over."

Some men became storytellers near a campfire, but Clay set judgment aside. This tale rang true.

"Pa took my older brothers and me out on the range, Johnny and Pete on a pinto and me hugging Pa's saddle horn. Camped here many a night while our older sisters kept house."

The silence brought to mind those wilderness trips with Father Bernard. But why should their outings interest anyone?

"Your people hail from out East?"

"A Texas Ranger found me somewhere in the Panhandle. Told the Sisters at the Orphanage my parents might be Czech."

Owen Dunbar remained quiet—most folks did at this point. But then, "How far was that from Fort Worth, son?"

Clay gave thanks for the shadows—no one but Father Bernard called him *son*. "Maybe a couple days' ride."

"Indians killed your parents?"

"Comanches, the Sisters said. I got thrown out of their wagon and somehow the warriors missed me. Rangers found me down in a gully."

"So you have no real ties now."

Ties? The Evendsbergs? They would welcome him back, but weren't true family.

"How'd you join the drive?"

"For some years I worked further west, for a German fellow. He and his wife took in some orphans after an epidemic."

"Got my share of German blood on my Mama's side. Mind sharing his name?"

"Evendsberg."

"Hmm. He raised cattle?"

"Milk cows and enough to butcher. But one of the immigrants, John Meusebach, cross-breeded German Friesens with Longhorns."

"Is that right? Seems like my daddy mentioned a fella like that—he had some connections down that way. So you met Red…"

"The Evendsbergs were Union sympathizers and encouraged us to head out of Confederate country after the vote went for the Confederacy. Plus, I had the itch to travel—wanderlust, I guess."

"Hmm. It isn't often we snag a trustworthy cowhand. Think the isolation out here'll bother you?"

Trustworthy, yes. Isolation? "No, sir."

"I answer to *Owen*." Mr. Dunbar banked the fire and pulled up a blanket. "Night."

Clay had already covered his face with his hat, but long

after Owen slept, memories held sway. They troubled him less than ones that ravaged his sleep with painted faces and vivid war cries.

Other times, a blaze broke out. He could never wake soon enough to save himself. Under cover of darkness, the flames took on a life of their own. Gunshots and flames—two things he hoped to avoid. Two good reason to flee from war.

Sometimes a woman's pasty face cinched in heavy black linen drew near and sent his heart wild with the crack of her razor strap. When he wakened, her stale breath still lingered.

Mentioning Father Bernard tonight re-wakened some recollections, but mostly good ones. This might still bode well for sleep, for he believed that miracles still occurred on this earth. Comanches or no, Clay maintained that God's angels had watched over him from the beginning. Not far away, a soft nicker reminded him of one distinct miracle. Pax, his faithful horse, had come to him as a gift from the most unlikely person.

Around mid-morning, a small dark square appeared ahead. Soon the Oak Bar's carved brand etched on a wooden marker led the way to a corral.

Clay eased down. Pax whinnied and nudged his shoulder.

"Here we are. Thirty feet behind the cabin, the ground cuts down to the creek. Always good water here." Owen pushed open the door to reveal a corner bunk and small table. A larger table boasted two chairs. Behind it, orderly shelves filled the wall.

Tin plates, containers labeled salt, flour, sugar, coffee, and cans holding spoons and knives lined the shelves. A medium-sized cook stove completed the outlay. On iron hooks, a large iron skillet and some other receptacle—what was that, anyway?

"You noticed our coffee pot? Ordered it in from Frederick and William Niedringhaus at the St. Louis Stamping Company. Immigrants keep bringing such useful items, and these men just happen to be shirttail relations on my mother's side. I'll show you how it works later—uses a filter."

"Couldn't have been easy getting that stove way out here."

Dust sailed when Owen blew on the table. "Nope. We have a little cleaning to do, but I think you'll find everything you need here, son."

Clay tried to hide his wince, but clearly failed—only Father Bernard called him *Son*. Owen squeezed his eyes shut for a moment.

"Sorry. You remind me of..." The rancher leaned toward a small one-paned window.

"You'll have to scrub this glass to get some light in here. Come on, I'll show you the boundaries."

They rode northwest. Stark, some would say, except for ravines filled with sagebrush or black sagebrush. Rough and unfettered, the wildness of the landscape offered its own beauty. When they dismounted at a creek, Owen kicked some stones. "There's been one light snow here already."

How could he know? Clay yearned to grasp this art, but swallowed his question. At another rise, the sky shown azure, but intermittent haze lay low over the land. Something in the air seemed different. Moist.

"Snow?"

"Yep. Day after tomorrow, I'd say." Owen sniffed. "Long enough to get me home." On the way, they counted twenty-seven cattle lowering their heads into lush grass. At the Lodgepole's south curve, Pax perked up. Could he already know they approached their new home?

In a few minutes, Mr. Dunbar swung down. "How about I start supper while you take care of the horses?"

The small barn held brushes, shovels and other tools, clean straw, stacks of hay, and a manger. In another room, a bag of oats sat next to two buckets. From a rafter hung two more bags. Down the incline, clear water swished westward so it didn't freeze.

Concerning this observation, Father Bernard would stage

a debate: "Or is it the other way around—does the water move because it hasn't frozen?"

His constant lessons once wearied Clay—some of them seemed hopeless circles, like the chicken or the egg coming first. But oh, what he would give for just one more session! Did other people only recognize what they had after they lost it?

The dull pounding in Meta's head coursed down into her neck. From the very top of the wall, where it connected with the ceiling, came a cool draft of air. Garrit would be upset—she must climb up there today and do more mudding.

Careful as she had been, this mudding error taunted her— she had missed the mark. Before winter's storms she must make repairs. As Mama would say, "Today is the day to start."

But she stayed abed as recollections stirred of the Missouri crossing, of Nebraska's endless stretches, of Mitchell's Pass, of Betsy and Michael... The incessant wind kept her grim company, so she sought pleasant memories—their wedding day, idyllic childhood afternoons with Martin and Old Tobias, weeding with Mama in the garden, cheerful times with Margita's family.

But always, baby Michael's image returned. "Betsy will mourn him the rest of her life." These comprised her first words since... a sob caught in her throat as Garrit's helpless figure came to mind. Slouched over that bush, his leg gashed, bled out. The certainty seemed impossible, yet she could not deny that image.

Mama would say the Psalms held power to comfort, but the sting of his death rendered Meta lethargic, made any action appear fruitless. She could almost hear Martin ask, "Lethargic... do you mean sluggish or slothful?"

His bright mind hid beneath the typical farmer façade of country manners and his work overalls, but he could thrash her when they practiced vocabulary. To think of him engaged in mortal combat now increased the throbbing in her neck.

Ah, dear Martin—so kind, so gentle, gone off to such a cruel war. Fighting for the right, surely, but such an unlikely soldier.

One low scraggly pine branch scratched the cabin like a nervous horse. Amidst the scraping, Betsy's parting words floated. "Write to me, hear? I would never have survived these last weeks without you." Had the letter mailed in Cheyenne reached the Willamette yet? The last time Meta looked into Betsy's eyes near Fort Laramie, both Mama and Elsbeth stared out at her—women forever grieving lost children. As she pondered, a simple truth surfaced…perhaps their losses had prepared her for her own. For this.

Perhaps. But still, her longing remained for Garrit to stride into the cabin to report fresh progress on their claim. How could this yearning exist alongside what she knew was true—never again on this earth would he enter this place.

She dozed, and later, gathered her willpower to mud that hole. Then the exquisite afternoon called to her. Time for some sunshine. Hope and Della grazed as she sat on the hill, where a pile of rocks covered Garrit's grave.

Mr. Ross had shielded the site, ensuring Garrit's peaceful sleep. But at one edge, some creature had already been at work, leaving scattered stones. The sight twisted Meta's insides.

A whistle pig, perhaps? They normally lived on higher ground, but near Fort Laramie, one of the women, perhaps Matilda Hanson, had heard some of them screaming from her wagon and spied a colony.

Time to move Hope and Della to fresh grass again and go inside. Would she ever stop expecting Garrit to lift the door flap? Instead, a lusty wind rose and began to sneer taunting accusations. Her stubborn, impulsive nature had riled him time after time. Why had she been so weak? To honor and obey him as she had vowed, could that have been so difficult? And farther back, how had she allowed her desire to move west blind her so?

Her craving had begun a fateful series of events—apart from her foolhardiness, Garrit would not have died. But it was too late to change anything. Now she could only be faithful to the dream he cherished.

Keeping these sinister thoughts at bay, each day she brushed and fed Hope, milked Della, let the oxen graze, led them to the creek, watched the hens scratch for bugs. Simple tasks.

All the while her thoughts roamed. From here to Iowa, to Martin in the fighting, to Mr. Lincoln at the Capitol, faced with so many difficult decisions, and back again. This wild country, only one small portion of a great nation—in truth, not even a Territory yet—how could she possibly carry on here all alone? Hardly a stir in the leaves, hardly a sound in the brush above the creek. Insects rubbed their wings, that she could count on—such short lives that would end with the first frost.

A hen pecking for grubs found something to cackle about and Meta whispered. "Soon, eggs will appear in your nest, just you wait and see." Another evening passed. Another long night. If she never rose, if she never opened the door in the morning, who would know? She covered her head with Mama's quilt and finally slept.

Then came a *moo*. And another. As she opened her eyes to the light, the calls became more insistent. She sat up and swung her feet to the floor.

Della would care. So would the other animals. Meager comfort, but comfort, still.

The wood would not chop itself, and a chill swept her shoulders as she stepped out. Each day grew a bit shorter—someone must chop wood before winter.

Later, she dropped a twenty-pound chunk of lumber on the block and hefted the axe. Just then, a movement on the incline caught her eye. "Probably a bird taking off."

Twigs snapped. She held her breath, and then came a tuneless whistle. Someone was coming up the bank.

Her breathing quickened—did Indians whistle?

And then, when she felt she could take no more, Mr. Ross

stepped out. Tears sprang to her eyes at the sight of his forehead shining in the sun, his eyes like the sky.

She must welcome him, but before she could assemble the words, he neared her and grabbed the axe.

"Gimme thet! Hain't no job fer a woman."

He motioned her back and sent a resounding, *Craaaack* through the air. "But—"

Late September rays reflected Mr. Ross's shiny scalp as he lanced blow after blow. Wood chips flew like insects. Nearby, his mule looked on. "Well then. I shall..."

He paused, axe in midair. Fixed his eyes on her.

"I shall stir up a cornbread and fry some ham."

"Mr. Ross, would you join me for a meal?"

The trapper looked up from working on Ethel's hoof. To his left lay a pile of logs ready to be stacked. "I made some cornbread." Meta held out a mug of fresh coffee, and Franklin accepted.

"Will you come in, then?"

"Mebbe."

Uncertain, she returned to the cabin. Not much later he hesitated at the threshold, looking every bit the frightened child.

"Ma'am?"

"Do come in." His shuffle, so unlike Garrit's sure gait, caught her attention. He sat, but fidgeted. After a few bites, he peered her way.

"Right good corn pone. Where'd ya git this fine honey?"

"We brought it from Iowa. Soon I will have eggs so the bread will be far better." His brows squeezed into one white line. "Goin' t' Cheyenne fer th' winter? Headed thar m'self."

"No. I must stay here with my husband."

Piercing eyes searched her face.

"Th' crick'll freeze solid. What'll ya do fer eatin'?"

"I will store up water. Della gives plenty of milk, and there's still a sack of corn meal and some vegetables."

He frowned up at a sagging burlap bag that once bulged with Iowa onions, potatoes, turnips, and carrots. "We—we were too late for a garden. But when the hens start laying. . ." Seeing him angle his head, Meta continued. "Garrit meant to add a barn to the cabin, and I will work on that over the cold months."

With some effort, Franklin rested his elbows on the table.

"I can hunt, too. My brother Martin taught me to shoot. I can bring in squirrels, rabbits, maybe even a deer."

The lines around his mouth eased.

"Got plenty o' powder?" At her nod, he rubbed his beard. "Kin ya sew?"

"I can."

"Kin ya knit?"

"Yes, sir."

"Need me some socks afore the cold comes, n' somethin' fer m' neck. A shirt, too. Would ya trade yer handwork fer me buildin'?"

It would never do to be beholding to this neighbor, but he proposed a fair trade. If he knew how much she hated to sew..."I will sew for you, Mr. Ross."

"Franklin. I'll jest stay on till ya got plenty o' wood, if'n ya don't mind."

No more chopping for a while—her legs and back already ached from dragging fallen logs over rough ground."I kin bring ya supplies."

"Oh, thank you."

After he returned to his work, a sudden desire emerged, such a simple everyday need. Back home, eggs had never been in short supply, for Mama kept two hundred hens.

"If only the hens would lay, I could make homemade noodles." If Garrit heard her speak this way, he would say she dreamed, but pullets did become laying hens, as she had witnessed many times. They *did*—nature had its way.

"I would have eggs for breakfast, and could bake bread pudding, maybe even a cake."

The comforting echo of Franklin increasing that pile of firewood accompanied her as she checked the chickens. Their obsidian eyes observed her from their roosts like so many pairs of fine gems.

Five-foot poultry wire surrounded the individual cages. Above this, Garrit had rolled wire every six inches to form a strong ceiling. Not one hen lost thus far, but winter made predators bolder—this shelter needed walls and enough space for Della and Hope. A cool late-September breeze rattled the cages. The wire gave under Meta's prodding, and she checked under the first pullet.

One beautiful egg—oh my! Her eyes burned as she carried this treasure into the cabin and returned with a basket. In the final set, more plunder awaited—two more lovely eggs. Inside again, she fell to her knees. "I have been so lost. I have not prayed and yet... These eggs... and Franklin... ."

Her breathing reminded her of something Mama once whispered.

You needn't look far, children. The Creator of all dwells as near as the air around us and hears our cries even when we cannot call out.

Chapter Ten

My paramount object in this struggle is to save the Union, and is not either to save or to destroy slavery. If I could save the union without freeing any slaves I would do it, and if I could save it by freeing all the slaves I would do it; and if I could save it by freeing some and leaving others alone I would also do that. I have here stated my purpose according to my view of official duty; and I intend no modification of my oft-expressed personal wish that all men everywhere could be free.
~Abraham Lincoln to Horace Greeley, Aug 22, 1862

"Best git some walls up 'round this here coop. Gotta hide this here wire—cowhands see thet n' they'll..."

"Are there any cowhands around here?" A fleeting memory appeared of the cattle drive that had joined their train.

"South o' here. Rancher's a good man, but them hands, ya never know..."

Franklin sniffed the air. "Zacly like last fall—tough winter ahead. In January, cattle south o' here froze t' death tryin' to bust through a fence in a fearful snowstorm."

The grizzly image made Meta shudder.

Again Franklin eyed the wire. "Don't want no one thinkin' ya fancy a fence." He studied the coop top to bottom. "Yer man done good, but we'll jest finish this here job."

That evening, he launched into war news. "Heer'd 'bout the Battle of Chicamauga. Them Rebs forced our troops t' a siege—lost a passel o' men fightin' hand-to-hand fer two whole days.

"Most as bloody as Gettysburg a few months back. Fella called Bragg from Tennessee s'prised Rosecrans when he crossed Chicamauga Creek. Forced the Fed'rals into a siege at Chattanooga." Franklin studied her. "Think yer brother mighta been there?"

"Maybe. The last I heard, he fought at Vicksburg. Did the Union win that siege?"

"Sure 'nuff, they did. Forty-seven days, but thet durn fool Pemberton fin'ly gave up."

"So the Union controls the Mississippi."

"Yep, Mr. Lincoln says the key's in 'is pocket now."

"But they keep on fighting. How long can this horrible war go on, Franklin?"

"Don't rightly know, gal. When menfolks gets t' fightin' fer a cause, well… Don't rightly know."

Sunset splayed outrageous colors as Clay latched the barn door and took a few minutes to survey this infinite plain. In every direction, nothing but land. No wonder this country lured settlers—gold had its attraction, but land surely charmed its share of men.

Out here, a man could make his way, fend for himself. No one lived anywhere around, and like the sudden ravines he came upon, fertile and green, this terrain offered surprises. No matter your past, this vast territory spread out its arms and took you in.

Father Bernard would like this image, full of promise and possibility. He might liken it to eternal love…the Father inviting all people.

No red sky tonight, only azure deepening into cobalt. Next, indigo alone endured until purple coaxed it into utter darkness. Not a shred of light from any quarter, but for a reluctant moon.

Red sky would come in the morning, he would stake a silver dollar on it. And Father Bernard might well agree. "Colours which appear through the Prism are to be derived from the Light of the white one." Ah, Sir Isaac Newton, one of Father Bernard's favorites.

Sir Isaac's study of light and planetary motion intrigued him, for Newton had risked his own sight during his experiments and in the end, divided all light into red and blue. Before his time, scientists agreed that color came into play only when light passed through a prism, but Newton challenged their theory.

Ah…his theories and axioms—*to every action there is an equal and opposite reaction. A body remains at rest, or in motion at a constant speed in a straight line, unless acted upon by a force. When a body is acted upon by a force, the rate of momentum change equals the force. If two bodies exert forces on each other, these forces have the same magnitude but opposite directions.*

Father Bernard never tired of reading about Sir Isaac and even tested some of his theories. Although years had passed, a random axiom might still set Clay to pondering.

Newton cited plenty of evidence for gravity—if a person pressed his finger on a rock, the same amount of pressure would be returned. But statements like this ignited more questions. How could one truly test this notion…how could one measure the pressure returned?

Indeed, memorizing axioms did not equal comprehending them. Not at all—but as Father Bernard would say, isn't this the purpose of knowledge, to spur us to seek more wisdom?

When Clay finally opened the cabin door, a strange warmth rippled through him. Mr. Dunbar, stirring spoon in hand, was making biscuits. Bacon sizzled in lantern light, and a friendly fire beckoned. A hearth, a stove, a place to sleep—what more could he want?

But when Clay took a seat at the table, heaviness descended. Such a long day with little sleep for the past two nights.

Minus his hat, Mr. Dunbar's bare scalp showed on the crown of his head. Did he have a wife? Children? Sure would be easier if a person could tell these things without having to ask.

The rancher set a steaming cup before Clay. Even before he took a sip, the coffee worked magic.

Mr. Dunbar slid into the opposite chair and broke the silence. "Worn out tonight. How 'bout you?"

"A little." Might as well ask a question before his host did. "You built this place yourself?"

"Brought up a couple of men for a day, and then we worked on it over a summer." Mr. Dunbar drank some coffee. "My son James put in the window."

The catch in his voice sounded an alarm. Time to change the subject.

"Ever get tired of ranching?"

"Every day holds a surprise—an orphan calf or a busted fence needing attention. Having the Indians sent north has helped, but... I do get weary. Never thought about aging much, but now my bones remind me a little more each morning."

The biscuits were browning—they both stood up at the same time. Mr. Dunbar transferred them while Clay served the beans.

Before he could take up his fork, the rancher bowed his head. "We thank Thee for this food and for bringing Clay here. Keep him safe through the harsh months ahead. Amen."

"Amen." Clay's part in Father Bernard's prayers seemed as natural as taking his next breath, and for some reason, sleep came as soon as he bunked down near the hearth.

"Take care of yourself. If you need anything, a trapper lives up that way a few miles."

Mr. Dunbar pointed northwest. "Name's Franklin Ross. He knows these parts better than anybody."

He mounted, and the dust from his departure dissolved in early morning darkness. Daylight would soon waken the plains—Clay's favorite time of day.

But now he returned to the cabin to explore.

His cabin—his own cabin!

Poking into every corner, lifting the lid of each tin on the shelves, he breathed deeper. Mr. Dunbar thought of everything. Above the washbasin hung a cloudy mirror, and on the bedside table lay a thin brown book. The drawer even offered extra kerchiefs, folded and ready for use.

Sinking on the bed, Clay picked up the small volume. *Pilgrim's Progress*—Father Bernard had read him this years ago. As the first rays of light struggled with darkness, he thumbed the pages, and the story came alive once more.

The next thing he knew, Pax whinnied. *What?* Mr. Dunbar had started home early this morning... Ah. He'd been reading about Pilgrim, who had suffered greatly on his trek, but found his beautiful palace at last.Frost still lined the fence rails, but the best hours of daylight had passed. Had he ever slept this late?

A nervous whinny greeted him, and Pax happily crunched a handful of grain.

"Not used to being cooped up so long, are you?" Out in the fresh air, Pax nickered his thanks.

Clay ran his hands over the sleek bay's muzzle. "How about we go for a ride?"

The big horse nudged his shoulder.

"Good boy. You're a good boy." He saddled Pax and ran for a swig of coffee and some jerky.

Once again, the air foresaw snow—and soon.Following Mr. Dunbar's instructions, they searched for cattle. "I don't expect a real close count, just keep track of the main section—about four hundred head. Settlers keep building fences—lost some cattle that way last year. You have much trouble with that in Texas?"

"Nope." Clay might have said, "Mr. Crady would have shot anyone who tried building one."

"One rancher lost a quarter of his herd. We aim to keep good relations yet need to make our boundaries clear. We expect to lose some to wolves and disease, but humans—that's a different story.

"If I see anything..."

The rancher clasped Clay's hand. "Good to have you taking

care of things, but if you get sick or have an accident you can't do your work. After a storm, wait until the wind blows the snow off a little... no use trying to hurry. The weather's like a woman, changing day to day." He clenched his jaw and paused. "See you after the first real thaw."

Now, Clay gave Pax free reign over rolling ridges. Father Bernard might label this simple beauty all around them the rhythm of the hills.

About halfway across, a strange zigzagging trail appeared, heading north. A steer, most likely diseased. An inner voice cautioned, *A crazed steer will eventually die of thirst. Let it go.* But another one urged Clay to follow the tracks. Half an hour later, the steer began running in wide circles toward a patch of low trees. Just as Clay aimed his gun, a wolf had other ideas, charging the steer from a ravine.

Beyond the scene sat a black object—perhaps that trapper's cabin or a settler's? No sign of fences here, but this place bore watching. As if by some hidden communication, a vulture circled overhead.

What would Sir Isaac surmise right now?

Asking Franklin yet another favor went against the grain, but Meta headed toward his worksite this morning. Might as well do this now.

"In Cheyenne, Garrit traded our oxen for Della and Hope, so I need to return the oxen to his cousin Herman. I cannot think of another way but to ask you."

Fighting a chilly wind from the creek, Franklin added a log to his fire. In budding light Meta sank on a nearby log.

"Want I should take 'em back fer ya?"

"I hate to ask you, but..."

Franklin pulled on his beard.

"An Injun's meetin' me down the trail. He kin help."

"An Indian?"

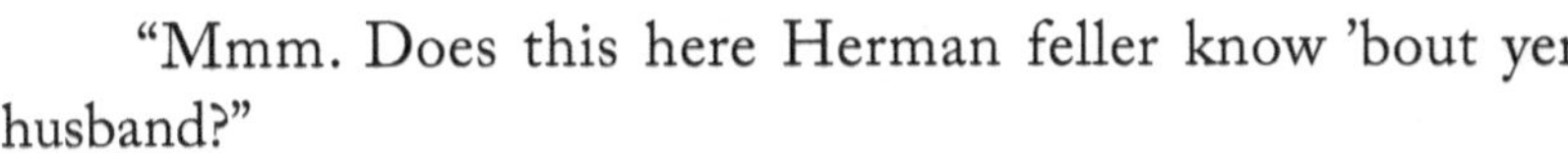

"Mmm. Does this here Herman feller know 'bout yer husband?"

"Not yet."

"Kin tell 'im, too." Franklin drew a long breath as he glanced around.

"Th' barn'll be done tomorry."

Doubts swarmed Meta as she retreated to her cabin. Would Mama praise or chide her choice to remain here? Both sides of the argument lined up like soldiers on guard.

Having Franklin here—combined with her hens producing fresh eggs—helped to still the spiteful voices in her head. No, life and death did not lie in her hands—Garrit would have gone after Della even if he had lived here alone.

But those inner adversaries seemed poised to pop up again, like the prairie dogs in Nebraska that charmed the children so. And this decision to stay on their claim ignited them. But at the same time, something way down deep—her intuition, some might call it—remained fixed. She must stay.

Two days later, Franklin set out with a promise. "Be back 'fore November." A packet of Meta's letters rode along—to Betsy, Mama, Margita, and Garrit's older brother Peter. Telling bad news took a toll, yet each sealed envelope somehow strengthened her. Her circumstances she could not help, but this claim she could preserve simply by living here.

That rule, the government had made…although Wyoming Country remained apart from its jurisdiction, still. Surely it would become a Territory some day, just as Oregon Territory had, and then a state. Carved from other Territories, perhaps Wyoming Country fit her to perfection—born an Iowan, with roots far back in Germany, she had come here, and this land belonged to her.

Nearing the cabin, she proclaimed it. "I am who I am. What if I was born for just such a challenge?"

That night, the derisive whisper that had wheedled her for weeks seemed a bit less insistent. Way back when Papa died, she had learned how to hold her head high and ignore sneers from schoolmates.

Mama had instructed all of her children, "Stay close to each other—watch out for your brothers and sisters during this time. Remember, people mock what they do not understand, and no one on earth understands what happened with your Papa."

But this was different—no schoolchildren looking down at her, only specters in the night. It was as if they realized the best time to badger her, when loneliness and weariness held her captive. But she had taken a stand.

Just before he left, Franklin tried again to change her mind.

"If ya come 'long, I kin bring ya back after th' first thaw."

"But what about my hens. What about Della?"

His *tch, tch* reminded her of Martin. Such a kind, sensitive brother, aware of her faults but also her strengths. How many times had he supported her? "Have no care, Meta, you can do this. You're such a strong girl!"

"The animals will keep me company, and now the barn helps warm the cabin. Thanks to you."

Franklin's beard quivered. "Hits one thing fer a feller t' face a winter here, but somethin' else fer..."

A woman? Yes, but a farmwoman, one who has endured the Oregon Trail. Surely that counts for something, but she held her peace.

Earlier, after they had feasted on hot porridge, biscuits, and gravy, Franklin inspected the stone fireplace. "Keep a watch on these here cracks."

"I can never thank you enough—"

The flash in his eyes proclaimed he would not bear another smidgeon of gratitude, but for the very first time, he drew her close for a moment. The *thump-thump* of his heartbeat assured her he would return.

Now, with a final shake of his head, he addressed Ethel.

"Come 'long, then." His humble parade began its long trek.

The thick log walls and ceiling surrounding her chicken coop eased Meta's mind—surely no predator could surmount the protection of this barn. And nothing could repay Franklin for all he had accomplished, though she had cooked every specialty over the past days. Now for the chinking. Hauling mud for the cabin had nearly destroyed Garrit's wool trousers, but they would still suffice. Bucket in hand, she hurried to the creek for mud, much like making mud pies with Lissa years ago.

Using her small iron soup ladle, she emptied the oozing bucket little by little. Reddish brown mud slipped into the first crack—now, to pack it in. Thus far, she had not used Garrit's knife, but the blade could push mud deep, and if no light pierced the mudding, she had succeeded. Of course, as with the error near the roof, holes might still show up later.

Time after time she traipsed up and down the hill under Hope and Della's watchful eyes. Such faithful listeners, these two!

"Thanks to Franklin, you have a secure home now, and we will be all right while he's gone. But every time he comes back, we'll be even better."

By midmorning, the animals had grazed the grass to the ground. She led them south of the cabin where grass still flourished under wild plums and scrub oaks.

Weeks ago, falling leaves pronounced Autumn's arrival—that meant winter could not be far behind. But each trip up the bank diminished the hard knot that formed in her chest when Franklin left. Talking to herself helped, too.

"He will be back in November. This work will make the time go quickly."

A vibration passed through her feet, something running hard against the earth. No time to get Della and Hope to safety. Transfixed, she stared south as a whitish blur stampeded over the hill. Then her instinct to flee took over.

By the time she reached the cabin, her hand trembled so, she fumbled with the latch. But inside, her heart finally stopped pounding.

"Please keep the animals safe." Not knowing what to expect, she waited as mud dripped onto the planks.

Time seemed to stand still until finally she peeked out. Calm and serene, Hope and Della moseyed between patches of grass. A bird twittered its lazy afternoon song.

A few steps from the barn, she paused to listen. Nothing. But she had heard something running—felt it in her feet and legs. And she had seen something white, most likely an animal. President Lincoln himself could not convince her otherwise.

As she pondered, a childhood memory returned.

Something had wakened her, and she'd padded down the hallway. At the stairs, Papa's portrait in its heavy oval frame looked down at her. That night, he seemed to lean out through the thick glass as she paused for a time. Did this really happen? How could she know, since Mama forbade any talk of him? Maintaining silence became all-important, even when someone harassed one of the boys at school.

"Shush! Our family's business—ours alone," Mama chided Martin and Henry, who had taken some older fellows to task.

Like Papa's death, Garrit's passing still seemed unreal. Just when she had begun learning how to live with him, he perished. Now, she still expected him to appear around any given corner. Heading back to the creek, her empty mud pail clattered against her leg. No matter what Papa had done and no matter what anyone else said, her brothers and sisters had always been there for her.

Then came Garrit. But now, no one shared her time and challenges.

Chapter Eleven

To live in hearts we leave behind is not to die.
Thomas Campbell, 1777–1844

Inch-by-inch, a flash of pink tongue washed a seasonal patchwork of rabbit fur. How could animals' tongues stay wet for so long? The closest water flowed a mile away—one more puzzlement fit for Father Bernard.

Mr. Dunbar had mentioned artesian springs out here, bubbling up with no visible source, but thus far, no free-flowing water had appeared as Clay traversed the plains. Steppes in basins grew giant sagebrush, along with black sagebrush or cushion plants. On the most alkaline soil, Gardner saltbush and greasewood thrived.

Closer to moisture, big sagebrush and silver sagebrush flourished, and some rugged ravines extended for hundreds of square miles. Elsewhere, treeless, low rolling hills seemed to go on forever.

But an artesian spring, defying the forces of gravity… what would that be like? Better keep his eye out for one, although listening for one might make more sense.

The rabbit turned to stone against red clay when Clay adjusted the reins. Slender ears, slightly flesh-colored, still showed, though winter masked the animal's coat in grey and white.

Fresh meat for supper and an easy shot, but… the furry tuft wiggled its nose. Rabbits, like cowhands, settled wherever they happened to land. Why not let this creature live? It would die a natural death soon enough.

Some cowhands hunted for sport, but Father Bernard taught

that all life belonged to God and merited honor. The same with women—even the ones the cowhands met along the way.

Every human being, every creature, deserves respect, resounded in Clay's head. No wonder this lonesome starlit range won out over saloons.

Mr. Dunbar had brought plenty of bacon, and several hams hung from the cabin rafters, along with sacks of onions and potatoes and enough jerky to sustain daily range rides well into spring. Tonight might call for something a bit different, perhaps porridge with ham and biscuits. The rabbit launched like buckshot when Clay nudged Pax. Its startled movement reminded him of that woman from the wagon train—the one he had met so briefly beside a creek. The same fear filled her eyes.

A similar sense of alarm once controlled him too, especially under the Sisters' sway. The slightest action intimidated him, and they used him as an example for the other children. When he moved to the Crady ranch, the owner, whose son shared his callous nature, eyed him with suspicion.

Not much older than Clay, Allan Crady often reminded him of his status: "Stinkin' orphan." But he did teach that orphan a cowhand's life, as his Pa ordered. And above all, Pax came to Clay at the ranch.

A sudden burst of wind sent Pax's mane flying. If Clay lived a hundred years, he could never give enough thanks for this fine horse, brought in by ranch hands to train over the winter. One day in March, Mr. Crady called to him from the corral fence. "Want a horse of your own?"

The ranch owner, addressing him?

Inside the corral, the geldings pawed the earth, all muscle and sinew and spirit.

"Well, do you?"

"Yes, Sir."

"Then pick one."

"Pick…?"

"Hank says you're a good worker. You need a horse." The rancher's nostrils flared. "Hurry up, boy, or I'll change my mind!"

All through the winter, one horse had impressed Clay. But to own him? Unthinkable.

"That bay over there, Sir."

Mr. Crady nodded to Hank and left.

Hank told Clay to choose a saddle and bridle. Oh, the wonder of outfitting the bay—could this truly be happening? The tremulous moment when he first gripped the saddle horn still throbbed as if it were yesterday.

Hank put a hand on his shoulder. "Fine horse. Ya picked the best one."

Years had passed, but to this day, Mr. Crady's sudden generosity perplexed Clay. The next winter, the boss nearly died of consumption, and Hank dropped a clue after a long day together searching for strays.

"Boss said he recollects bein' a orphan hisself."

Hank faded into the darkness, leaving Clay to ponder. *Mr. Crady, an orphan? And now he owned this whole spread?* It took only a week for Pax to receive his name. One day the idea came, and Clay whispered it like a litany.

"Think I'll call you Pax."

Now, Pax picked up his pace as the scent of snow strengthened, and Clay's stomach rumbled. Another day on the range, full of thinking and memories. Not enough work to make a man really hungry, yet supper could not come soon enough.

Autumn, 1863

I cannot say the date for certain, but surely November must be close. The cold seeps in through every hidden entrance, in spite of our careful mudding.

Like sorrow. Like guilt—the reasons I have neglected to write. But now, with the sure knowledge of Franklin's return and the pullets laying, and Della giving milk like always, hope has taken up steadier residence in my heart.

Who can know their weaknesses? If anything good comes of loss, I expect this sort of understanding might qualify. Frail of faith, fragile of mind, and scrawny of will—ah, how clearly I see myself now.

And yet, I continue to live. Providence knoweth all and so must see some good in me.

Another thing I know: a friend at hand means all. On the trail, Betsy became my comrade. I would never have imagined a scruffy mountain man might take her place. And yet, I await Franklin like a good omen. Unlike anyone I have ever encountered, yet solid as the frozen earth outside my door, he has become my mainstay.

Carrying a heavy log from Franklin's woodpile to the cabin, Meta forsook her coat. She continued working until a stack five feet high surrounded the structure for insulation. Later, a shiver took her, so she donned her shawl to climb the hill to Garrit's grave. Though nothing could bring him back, at least she could remember him and honor him.

The morning he left, Franklin gave her another task. After checking the remaining sacks of corn and oats, he explained, "Plenty of good grass here. Best pile it in th' barn jest in case yer feed gets low. Can't let yer cow dry up fer lack o' feed."

A couple of daylight hours remained, so she ascended the hill again, this time with the scythe.

Swinging the heavy instrument went easier once she found her rhythm. Two days later, except for a wide swatch along the creek left for Hope and Della to graze, the whole claim looked as shorn as sheep in spring.

Though her muscles complained, gratitude filled her for the work. *Give us this day our daily bread,* Mama taught them. *We give thanks for strength to complete our work.*

Although Garrit's passing still weighed on her, these ordinary tasks provided a sense of purpose.

In five years, this claim would belong to them—to her. She had no idea how the rest of his dream would develop, but Mama also had taught her how to wait.

Idle hands are the devil's playthings, children… One waited by finding meaningful work to do. With the harder outdoor jobs finished, she took along her sewing when she visited the grave. The east slope sheltered her from the wind, and a doe frequented the area. Sitting quite still, Meta chatted with her in a quiet voice, and the doe stepped almost close enough to touch. At times, Meta spoke to her more than to Garrit.

"Perhaps you are the one Garrit intended to shoot, but you need not fear me. You are alone, too—we can be friends."

Though her fingers numbed, she completed a shirt for Franklin. If he crashed through the brush this very day, she could hand him an extra pair of warm socks, too. The thought of his face crinkling into a half-smile brought pleasure. Though basting and knitting had never enticed her, this task made them palatable. Mama would be proud of her careful work.

Now to start on a scarf.

Evening, like Iowa in November—a moist tinge in the air, earthy yet clean. Back home, this undeniable whiff of winter carried an air of excitement, for snow would soon be here. The first snowfall brought magic, covering the world in white. As a child, Meta foresaw sleigh rides and snowmen.

But tonight, she faced the same likelihood with a cavernous breath and fortified herself with a statement she repeated over and over. "Franklin will be coming soon. Surely he will."

Before settling the animals, she checked for anything amiss. Chimney smoke rose like morning haze, and Franklin's firewood had hardly diminished at all.

Leaning into the night to sniff accentuated her earlier sense of an impending storm. Yes, Winter—her very first in this country. Somewhere out there in the darkness, her doe friend reckoned with this same certainty and made her own preparations. In the barn, the animals knew, too—her hens frittered in their nests. Della and Hope eyed her and tossed their heads.

With the door barred and day-old cornbread sizzling in the frying pan, Meta fed the fire. The plowshare, such an unwieldly instrument, worked well inside, too. A triple set of wire strands held it next to her pot so she could bake three or four biscuits at a time. Ah, and Garrit had accepted her ingenuity, though he came to it in his own time. They had just been learning to work together. If only…

At an odd sound outdoors, she put her ear to the rough door. Some large animal was climbing the bank, perhaps a bear. She listened longer, and then came a human shout.

"Franklin!"

She unbolted the door as her new ally materialized out of the dusk. Urging Ethel toward the cabin, he wrestled with a pair of long-tipped snowshoes.

"Most there, gal. C'mon now."

"Oh, Franklin, you've come."

With a snort, he accepted her greeting, his frosted whiskers scraping her skin. He shook free and fastened his eyes on her.

"Howdy do?"

"Good, but better now that you're here."

"Lots more snow down south. How'd you miss it?" Unloading provisions stirred her heart—he had brought so much! She stumbled over the threshold with his saddlebag and jumped up to set a fresh pot of coffee over the fire.

"Oh, I so hoped you would come before the storm."

Franklin dropped onto a seat.

"Y' alright?"

"Much better. You gave me good instructions."

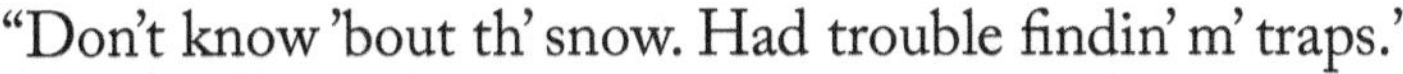

"Don't know 'bout th' snow. Had trouble findin' m' traps."

"Are you hungry?"

"Like a wild boar."

With a hefty portion of hot porridge before him, Franklin reached into his pack. His eyes twinkled up at her. "It's Christmas, child."

Child? Well, he could call her anything he wished. But what did he mean about Christmas?

Between huge spoonsful, he held out a packet four inches high and ten inches wide. Wrapped in brown paper, tied with string—what could this be?

"Them's letters fer ya."

Fire burned inside her eyes.

"Go on. Have yerself a look."

Her fingers fumbled to undo the knot. What if Mama had written? Or Betsy and Margita?

The contents spilled out and familiar names called to her like kindly apparitions. Hulda Tolzmann, Lissa Tolzmann, Margita Tolzmann. The fourth made her mouth go dry: Betsy Bishop, The Dalles, Oregon Territory. Franklin's grin spread into his beard.

"Got m' porridge. Jest go on n' read."

Mama's letter, she read aloud, and he leaned in as if he had met Hulda Tolzmann long ago.

"To see Mama's hand on this paper… And to think, her letter found its way to Herman and Anna's…"

He wiped his beard. "Sech a long way."

Betsy's letter carried the faint scent of lavender. "This woman I met on the trail has five children, but seems so young. In a Nebraska storm, her baby, little Michael, was thrown from the wagon. He died before his daddy even saw him."

The shimmer in Franklin's eyes spoke far more than words. Perhaps some day she would learn more about his past.

"'Most fergot. They's 'nuther somethin' in thet bag. Go on ahead."

A packet with a book of Emerson's essays, postmarked Nebraska Territory, and letters from Alma and Greta. They had remembered her, too.

When she finished reading two of the letters, Franklin got to his feet with a fair share of groans. "Ol' knees is cracklin' like ches'nuts. Best be makin' camp."

"Outside? Oh no!"

"Where ya think I been sleepin'?"

"At least make a bed in the barn."

He pursed his lips as she hurried to the trunk. "Take this extra quilt."

"If ya say so. But m' buffalo robe'll do me jest fine, gal."

Meta fought the impulse to hug him. "You have done so much for me, Franklin. Please, will you call me Meta?"

No reply. But a few minutes later at the door, he murmured, "'Night lil' Meta."

Tonight, she latched the door with a calmer touch. Before sleep utterly beguiled her, her whisper floated through the cabin.

"God has answered your prayers, Mama. He sent me Franklin."

Morning brought stored-up questions. "I hear water in the distance, but how can that be when everything is frozen? Where does it come from?"

"A warm spring 'bout a mile west, bubblin' clear as ya please."

Franklin pulled something from his pack. "Know th' date?"

"It must be November?"

"See fer yerself." He held out a small piece of paperboard. "Cheyenne General Store" stood out in black print against its yellow background. Published by the Army's Signal Corps, this one-page guide to the months until the turn of the century required calculation, but she would not complain. This would sharpen her brain.

November seventeenth. Almost Martin's birthday—she must write him in care of Mama.

"I think I told you about Martin, my brother in the Union army. He's two years older than me."

"Inf'try?"

"Yes, the Iowa Fifth."

"Bet he's got one o' these here logbooks. Hope he's in better weather then this. All 'round, they's snowdrifts. Cain't figger why yer claim stayed so clean." Franklin scratched his mustache. "Mebbe ya got a angel watchin' ya."

Until now, the incessant wind had seemed an enemy. But had those gales blown away the storms? "Maybe. But the only angel I see is you, Franklin."

"Hain't no kind o' angel no how." He sniffed and shuffled his feet.

"Do you suppose Garrit can see one here, watching out for us? I keep wondering that. Martin always said Papa was looking after us, even though he'd been gone so many years."

"Don't know nothin'bout them there things—nothin' a-tall."

Coffee and pancakes, sometimes with bacon thrown into the batter, became Clay's favorite breakfast. Afterward, he checked to see what critters trespassed during the night. So far, only jackrabbit, coyote, antelope and wild turkey, and of course, field mice. Once, wolf tracks edged the corral.

Pax welcomed him to the barn with a whinny.

"Well, boy, we've got a lot of riding ahead of us today. Can you smell snow coming? Hope it's no more than we got last time."

A cloudbank told him the storm would sweep in from the northwest. Foreboding thunderheads meant the same here as in Texas, but only a light breeze blew—plenty of time to ride to the far western end and back.

No sense taking chances—some of the cattle drive stories about winter heightened Clay's caution. But he could tell Pax relished the gallop, and sure enough, a campfire tale came to mind.

Most stories contained both fact and fiction, but the blizzard narratives stuck like honey on biscuits. Old Jerel, the trail cook, told one Clay could never forget.

"In Fifty-three, a storm blew in on my first drive. lost forty-seven head o' beef. 'Most died m'self, thinkin' to round 'em up, but the cook set a big fire to guide us. Boss like t' cried real tears when the wind finally went down with some men still missin'. Found two of 'em the next day."

Jerel kicked the toe of his boot against a rock. "They was young like me, thought they could ride out anythin'. One of 'em froze on the east side of a big rock, starin' off fearful like."

Clay left the campfire before Jerel described how they found the other fellow. Sometimes, knowing fewer details worked best.

Now he sniffed the air, determined to complete his watch in full daylight.

An hour later, a curl of smoke rose northward, but that old trapper's cabin ought to lie farther to the West. Riding closer, Clay brought Pax to a halt. Someone was on the claim, walking around outdoors. He urged Pax into a stand of cottonwood for a better look.

At first he detected only dark hair, but when he shaded his eyes, he could see the figure wore a skirt. A lone woman led a cow and a horse up an incline beyond the cabin. Pax stamped his feet in the cold.

"There, boy." The woman stood at the top of the hill, her hair flying loose from her scarf. With the horse and cow grazing, she began wending a scythe back and forth, back and forth, and even this far away, a faint dusty scent emanated. Sage and tall grass, same as an hour south of here, the gift of Wyoming Country.

The wind howled—Clay pulled up his collar, and as he did, words from Wordsworth surfaced. Mrs. Evendsberg read poetry in the evenings, and though he hadn't appreciated it at the time, some of the verses stuck with him.

> *Whate'er the theme, the Maiden sang*
> *As if her song could have no ending;*

I saw her singing at her work,
*   And o'er the sickle bending;—*
I listened, motionless and still;
*   And, as I mounted up the hill,*
The music in my heart I bore,
*   Long after it was heard no more.*

Spellbound, Clay urged Pax a little closer. When the settler gathered a load of her bounty and started down the hill, her animals followed like pets.

As she disappeared behind the cabin, an itch started in Clay's throat. If anyone ought to be working outside on such a day, it should be the man of the house.

Turning over in his mind how she would fare during the storm, he lingered longer than prudence allowed. But when the first wave of sleety snow slashed down, he pulled his hat low and headed for home.

Chapter Twelve

*The holiest of holidays are those kept by ourselves in silence
and apart: the secret anniversaries of the heart.*
~Henry W. Longfellow. 1807–1882

The wind slapped Meta's legs as she descended the hill. Such a comfort to have the animals nearby when she sat with Garrit. But today she stood before the grave only a short time.

Then it seemed only right to glean a few more sheaves she must have missed. Better now than in three feet of snow.

"Still goin' up there ever' day?" The day before Franklin left, his question made her wonder—did he fret about her state of mind?

"Yes, but I won't if a big snowstorm hits."

Her answer lowered his eyebrows. "Coulda worked in yer cousin's kitchen these cold months. Them young'uns was askin' after ya."

The thought of little Gustav and Helga running into her arms took her breath away. How she missed the chubby fingers and cherub eyes of Betsy's little ones! She might even have been able to teach at the school.

Back in Iowa, the school board recruited her when Miss Brunner took sick in the middle of the year.

Resolved that she could carry on in her teacher's stead for a time, they thrust her behind the oaken desk. And she relished the role—when Miss Brunner recovered and Meta returned home, the youngest students remained with her in heart.

"But I am here, and a portion of winter has already passed.

Mama stayed put after Papa died—of course, she had nine living children to consider."

Still, she would hate to leave Garrit here alone. Only his body lay buried on the ridge, and his spirit lived on, yet she could not think to abandon him. Franklin would come back, even though he disagreed with her decision.

If only she could speak with Mama right now. She would write a letter tonight, and another to Martin.

Before Franklin returned, she would finish his knitting. The last time he stopped, his ears were chafed and sore. A set of muffs knitted over a piece of leftover poultry wire shaped to traverse his head—surely she could manage this. Another scarf for good measure—why not?

On December third, a quiver came to rest under Meta's shoulder blade. Light snow fell overnight, so she searched for signs, but none appeared. Nonetheless, someone watched her—she knew for certain. A woodpecker drummed into the cabin's back wall. The first time one came, she thought someone had knocked. Such stalwart creatures—one had even tried to bore into the stone chimney the other day—what a racket! How did their beaks survive?

The uneasy sensation continued as she stalled on the stoop. A black-eyed junco flitted from the roof to a juniper branch. Still, she waited.

Sparkling snow brightened this brown and grey world. Della lowed, expecting to be milked, so Meta set one foot on the frosty ground.

A sound like oxen's hooves vibrated. What could be happening? Hope thrashed against the inside of the barn and the chickens clucked in a flurry.

Without warning, brown-haired heads, eight or nine of them, appeared above the creek bank. Elk—some at least seven feet tall, dashed over the crest. Never had she viewed animals so majestic.

Tan and dark brown hair shielded them from the cold, with black outlining their tails, eyes, nostrils, and mouths.

Antlers of various sizes rose like banners, and three calves, probably yearlings, edged from the group, curious about her, too. The adults stood like statues, alert for danger. *Deer venison's good, but elk meat's best.* She clasped her hands as Franklin's comment popped into her thoughts. Yes, she had shot squirrels and rabbits with Martin, but mostly to learn how to use the gun. Today, she knew she would never shoot an elk, however low her supplies sank.

How fortunate to live in what one of the wagon train settlers called a *riparian corridor* of this huge territory instead of a salty area with only desert shrubs like fourwing or shadscale saltbush and winterfat. Those places, often white with salt, Mr. Fortune had pointed out in the distance.

But they could not sustain the cottonwood, willow, and alder growing here. Near Franklin's cabin, she had even spied a boxelder tree. Thanks to Spring Creek, even larger animals like these elk lived here.

A male elk flicked his tail, and his obedient entourage snaked toward the grove. These silent visitors slipped in amongst the trees like shadows, leaving behind only their tracks and scat. Seeing them had brightened her morning, and she breathed, "Oh, please do come back."

Feathery, new-fallen snow and sunlight. Waking to this scene sent relief through Clay.

"Peculiar weather out here!" Less than twenty-four hours ago, he could have sworn morning would bring deep drifts.

"Must be a Chinook, like Mr. Dunbar said. *A warming wind in the middle of winter, so almost as soon as snow falls, the Chinook chases it all away. The Indian word means 'snow eater,' and that's exactly what the Chinook does.*"

Father Bernard used to call rare Texas snows, *heaven's chestnut cream.* His description of the filling for the croissants from his French boyhood made Clay's mouth water.

He used to play a game when strangers passed the mission. From their horses, he picked a herd for his imaginary ranch. He also volunteered to help the stable hand and took peculiar pleasure in brushing bays.

The structure's dim interior provided any number of hiding places that welcomed him after humiliations from the Sisters. Wailing his woes to the horses brought a measure of comfort until Father Bernard introduced him to human solace. Maybe because of that, or perhaps because he matured enough to stop annoying the Sisters, the humiliations lessened. Always, an assignment from Father Bernard kept Clay reading, off in another world.

A few years later, when heartsickness for his mentor still bore down on him, Pax came into his life. Their adventures soothed something irreconcilable, a yearning he could not quench. "There, fella. Enjoy the sun on your back." Clay tied Pax outside and attacked his stall with a pitchfork. Nothing like mucking to work up an appetite for the stew on the stove's back burner.

On December 20th, a few of Meta's childhood favorites looked up at her from the trunk. *Aesop's Fables, Robinson Crusoe,* and *The Leatherstocking Tales*—why not read these at night? And read through the Bible—Mama would be pleased. The second trunk produced *Tales of a Traveler* and *The Sketchbook of Geoffrey Crayon, Gent.* Mama's tenderness showed as she placed these childhood treasures from the Old Country into Meta's hands.

"The first Sketchbook reminds me of the folk tales my mother told, and so does Rip van Winkle. Do you know he and Ichabod Crane come straight from the old country?"

She touched the covers with care. "Imagine Papa's fore-sight—he wanted us to hear the old tales in English so we could learn the language. Somehow, he knew we would need more than

German some day. Greta took *A Tour of the Prairies* to Nebraska, and now these go with you, your inheritance."

The generations hovered near as the well-worn covers reappeared. Mama's books would see her through long winter hours, and one day her children—if she ever remarried—would hear these stories, too.

December 22, 1864

Cold winds sweep our claim clear of snow. I thought them a curse, but now realize they show favor. Elk and deer like our clearing, and antelope race up from the creek. Woodpeckers visit every day, their song more like a sneeze. The doe that used to come by must be nesting—I have not seen her for weeks.

Franklin will come for Christmas, I am certain.

For today, my thoughts run to Betsy. Christmas will be especially hard for her. And dear Martin—who would have thought the fighting would last this long?

I wonder where the Indians live in winter and speculate how they keep warm. Today I will begin to knit a scarf for Franklin. May God speed my stubborn fingers.

"And my stubborn heart," she added as the possibility of spending a solitary Christmas stole in. So many woes might befall even an experienced woodsman.

The next day, memories of last year's celebration sat like a weight as she lifted the trunk's lid. Exploring, shifting, and reorganizing—a perfect task for this long afternoon. Only a year ago she and Garrit chose their wedding date. The thought of Christmas alone spurred a pain high in her chest.

So much had happened since last December 24th. Now she wondered at her presumption. How could she have assumed she could manage this holiday alone? If only she had listened to Franklin, she would be helping Anna prepare for Christmas Eve right now.

Oh, to witness the delight on Gus and Anna's faces when they saw the lovely candlelit tree! And perhaps Franklin would have joined them—but no use to dwell on this. She had made her choice.

In the darkness, she could barely distinguish yellow fabric from brown. Time to light the lantern. Only the thought that Franklin would still come dissuaded her tears. As the hours passed, her spirits spiraled downward. Her hopes depended on a fallible, imperfect human at the mercy of Wyoming weather. She opened her Bible and read a Psalm:

"While I live I will praise the Lord: I will sing praises unto my God while I have any being. Put not your trust in princes, in whom there is no help. His breath goeth forth, he returneth to his earth. In that very day his thoughts perish. Happy is he that hath the God of Jacob for his help, whose hope is in the Lord his God..."

Trust in the Almighty, yes. Yet a human being must trek rough, snowy trails to get here. She meant to keep praying, but every time she tried, her voice became a reedy whisper, and salt washed her throat.

The next day, as she continued to re-fold fabrics and linens packed last February and March, Della mooed. An hour of daylight remained, but maybe she ought to move the stakes farther west.

The sun glided in and out of clouds, and the wind dispersed a light snow. If only Franklin would suddenly top the rise as the elk did every few days!

How could she bear being here by herself for Christmas? Her prayers for Franklin to come echoed hollow—what was it Mama said about the Holy Spirit praying for us? "Please do pray for me—and for Franklin."

Inside again, a shudder swept her—her thoughts for the future drooped like a threadbare frayed dress. How could a lone woman create a horse ranch? Starter herds never simply wandered onto a claim. Mama's God could be trusted, that she knew. But if only she could see how things would work out! "Oh, Meta Tolzmann Rausch—that would be the opposite of faith."

Restless and agitated with her lack of trust, she opened the door for sunshine, though the fresh air taunted the fire.

She tapped her fingers on the table, the shelf, her pots.

"Keep believing," she whispered to the murky, troubled countenance in her mirror. "Remember the eggs." Then she knelt to refill the trunk.

Donning her coat to fetch Hope and Della, she dithered. But finally, with them safely inside, she scanned the mound of wood chunks.

Words from Emmanuel Church floated like an early morning mist over the creek. *In common everyday objects we see God's love poured out...* Everyday objects. Bread and wine. The barn and the woodpile. The eggs and windswept countryside when she had expected snow drifts.

Through these, our Heavenly Father shows his care. And through an old trapper.

Freezing air stung her nose. This Christmas, the Almighty and Franklin came tied up in the same package.

To the south, the cottonwoods raised their arms against a darkening night. Latching the door, Meta made a fresh pot of coffee and knelt beside her bed, arms folded on the quilt.

"December twenty-fourth. Franklin tarries, but still, I believe. I do." She moved between dozing and wakefulness.

A sound—something right at the door. Then a toothy whistle. She flew up, unbarred the door and rushed into massive arms. Her face buried in cold rawhide, the heaviness flooding her released in a maelstrom. The visitor eased her to the hearth, where warm air sharpened his rasp.

"Oh, Franklin."

His beard scratched the top of her head, and the smell of stale coffee reminded her to pour him a fresh cup.

When she did, his eyes sparkled.

"Right glad I am t'be here, gal." His round nose, chapped with frost, attested to his day's walk. "Jest a minute." He disappeared into the night but soon shuffled over the makeshift step with a long, awkward object swathed in his buffalo robe. He set his load near the door and shook his head. "Snowin' agin. But ya still got way less than a little ways north." His forehead bunched. "Jest don't understand."

Her heart too full to speak, Meta prepared supper.

Franklin rubbed his hands by the fire. His swarthy face resembled Father Christmas from her childhood.

"I have missed you. I may talk your leg off tonight!"

Christmas Eve always focused on the candlelight service, but Mama mentioned the visits of *Weihnachtsmann,* or Christmas man. Sometimes she gathered all six younger children on her bed and told an Old Country story.

In America, we call him Father Christmas, children.

"Y' been all right?"

"Yes. I never open the door after dark."

"Be diff'rent come spring when th' days git longer. Animals gets busy with their young, but now, the woods b'longs t''em."

Meta baked biscuits and fried ham and eggs, while Franklin saw to the animals. When he came in, he perched at the table as she fetched the biscuits from the fire.

"Hain't had fried eggs since I stopped here last, n' thet was..."

"Three and a half weeks ago. My calendar tells me so, thanks to you."

They ate as if an Iowa Christmas dinner covered the table and finished with vanilla pudding. Even through December's cold, the hens kept laying—one of her best gifts. When he finished, Franklin held his middle. "Right fine meal. Thank ya kindly. Think I'll set me in thet rocker."

Meta scrubbed the iron skillet with sand from a bucket under the shelf, and shaved a little soap into the dishpan from one of Mama's bars The swish of her rag made music with the fire. She arranged the clean plates, took her Bible from her bedside, and set Franklin's presents near him. As she hung her apron, a gentle snore issued. Franklin's lips cracked in several places, evidence of wind and cold.

Did he travel longer than usual to make it back tonight?

So little she knew about him, yet he was all she had.

Chapter Thirteen

*I see a time of seven generations when all the colors of
mankind will gather under the Sacred Tree of Life and the
whole Earth will become one circle again.*

~Crazy Horse

In Papa's stead, Freidrich would read this ancient story on
Christmas Eve every year. Tonight would be no different, with
Mama, Henry, Lissa and her husband, and Margita's family gathered around.

Seeing Meta engrossed in the tale, Franklin asked, "How
'bout readin' thet out loud?"

She had been hoping he would ask and started over at the
beginning.

*"And it came to pass in those days, that there went out
a decree from Caesar Augustus, that all the world should be
taxed. (And this taxing was first made when Cyrenius was
governor of Syria.) And all went to be taxed, every one into
his own city. And Joseph also went up from Galilee, out of the
city of Nazareth, into Judaea, unto the city of David, which
is called Bethlehem; (because he was of the house and lineage
of David:) To be taxed with Mary his espoused wife, being
great with Child."*

She paused for a breath.

"'Least Wyomin's got nobody houndin' ya fer taxes. But
they's talk 'bout makin' th' Terr'tory 'ficial. Then we'd have t' pay th'
gov'ment fer sure."

Unable to recall having the Christmas story interrupted, she nodded. Franklin settled back as she began again.

"And so it was, that, while they were there, the days were accomplished that she should be delivered. And she brought forth her firstborn Son, and wrapped Him in swaddling clothes, and laid Him in a manger; because there was no room for them in the inn.

"And there were in the same country shepherds abiding in the field, keeping watch over their flock by night.

"And, lo, the angel of the Lord came upon them, and the glory of the Lord shone round about them: and they were sore afraid. And the angel said unto them, Fear not: for, behold, I bring you good tidings of great joy, which shall be to all people. For unto you is born this day in the city of David a Saviour, which is Christ the Lord.

"And this shall be a sign unto you; Ye shall find the Babe wrapped in swaddling clothes, lying in a manger. And suddenly there was with the angel a multitude of the heavenly host praising God, and saying, Glory to God in the highest, and on earth peace, good will toward men.

"And it came to pass, as the angels were gone away from them into Heaven, the shepherds said one to another, Let us now go even unto Bethlehem, and see this thing which is come to pass, which the Lord hath made known unto us. And they came with haste, and found Mary, and Joseph, and the Babe lying in a manger. And when they had seen it, they made known abroad the saying which was told them concerning this Child.

"And all they that heard it wondered at those things which were told them by the shepherds. But Mary kept all these things, and pondered them in her heart. And the shepherds returned, glorifying and praising God for all the things that they had heard and seen, as it was told unto them."

Franklin released a long breath.

"M' Christmas gift, hearin' thet."

"And mine. Every year my brother Freidrich reads to us all on Christmas Eve. I used to imagine Mary and Joseph wandering into our farmyard. I would answer the door and let them in. Mama would help Mary with the birthing. Baby Jesus would be born in our downstairs bedroom."

"Yer house had two floors?"

"Most Iowa houses have an upstairs because families have so many children."

"How many in your'n?"

"Ten."

Franklin snorted. "Thet's a passel."

"I am second-to-last. My sister Lissa is the youngest. Most of the older ones were grown up with children of their own when I was born. And a sister I never knew died as a little girl."

The fire crackled. Firelight danced on the wall. Questions rose about Franklin's family, but something told her to hold her tongue. "'s been a long time since I heerd thet there story. Mebbe twenty-five years. Winter o' Thirty-nine, I reckon. No, mebbe Forty, when m'..." He rubbed his thumb along his forefinger.

Outside, a coyote barked, and from another direction, its mate answered. Franklin squirmed in the rocker. "We was way out in Kansas Terr'try. Went there from Missouri th' year b'fore.

M' wife, she pulled out her Bible n' commenced t' readin'. Our little one, mebbe two months old, was sleepin' in th' cradle. Snow outside. Cold. She said, 'It's Christmas Eve. This here's th' night th' Christ child come t' th' world.' Somethin' 'bout thet riled me. 'Y' got religion?' I ast 'er, none too friendly-like. She jest said, 'I love th' Christmas story.'"

Franklin rocked back and forth a few times.

"I snarled like a cornered cat—put no stock n' books. In them days my pappy wern't keen on readin' nor 'ligion. But m' wife went ahead anyhow. Story seemed strange, like somebody made it up. I didn't pay 'er no mind a'tall, and she cried later thet night."

Snaps and pops from the fire filled the void, and Meta added another log. Franklin let out his breath in parcels.

"Thet spring I got th' urge t' go West. We headed thisaway with nothin' but our mule. One night th' wife got sickly. So did th' little feller. "Next mornin', neither of 'em woke up." Franklin stared at his big hand. "A'ready cold, both of 'em. Slept right through their dyin'." He ran his palm over his face. "Never forgive m'self fer thet."

The rocker's tread marked time. "Put th' babe in his Mama's arms. When I done it, them words '*on earth, peace,*' come to me, so I said 'em over th grave."

"Oh, Franklin, how sad."

His eyes filled. "Don't know why yer husband had t' die neither."

He looked into the fire for some time before the rocker began to creak again.

"Somethin' 'bout that story stays with a feller. Seems like yesterday she was readin' it back in Kansas."

"Did you ever marry again?"

Franklin countenance formed a wrinkled mosaic. "Come out here n' commenced trappin'." He shifted his weight. "Now, I kin hardly b'lieve I got me sech a good neighbor."

"I feel the same way. You have been so good to me." She handed him the earmuffs. "I made a little present to keep your ears warm."

Franklin turned the odd shapes over in his gnarled hands.

"Put them on like this." She slipped them in place over his wiry hair.

"Well, I'll be. These'll come in right handy. Ol' ears's had their share o' freezin'. Thank ya kindly." He groaned as he came to a stand and crossed the room to the awkward package he carried in earlier.

"These is fer you. Set yourself down."

Meta unwrapped the buffalo robe. "Snowshoes!"

His teeth, ragged and brown, appeared behind his mustache.

"Figgered they might come in handy th' next few months."

"You made them? Oh, thank you so much!" Meta grabbed him in a bear hug. "Will you teach me to use them tomorrow?"

"Sure's shootin'." Franklin drew back, but his whole countenance lighted. He really did resemble Father Christmas.

Before dawn, Clay opened his prayer book. The roll of the words brought back Father Bernard reading aloud each evening.

Worn into the shape of the bag, the leather-bound volume accompanied Clay everywhere. But this morning he took time to read. Lofty words about eternity enveloped him like the old priest's smile, and for the thousandth time, he wished Father Bernard could have lived longer.

When the priest took him in, he finally belonged somewhere. The next morning, Father Bernard declared that Clay must stay for good, that he needed him. That evening, the first of many spent listening, filled Clay with the same kind of warmth he felt here.

For months after the orphanage fire, night brought fear. Finally, he asked Father Bernard the question that haunted him.

"Those men who set the fire, will they burn in hell?"

"That is not for us to say. Only God judges the thoughts and intents of our hearts."

"Do you think they regret what they did?"

"Again, I do not know."

"But what do you *think?*"

"If they still have a conscience, they know regret. But people can snuff out the voice of scruples—we must take the utmost care."

Father Bernard gave Clay the job of burning the stable refuse, and as he tended the fire earlier that day, smoke curled into the sky like small clouds. Many times his own conscience rolled like that smoke, reminding him of his failures, what he had done as well as left undone, as the priest would say.

If only he could quiet its voice and the curiosity about those evil men that still haunted him. But those questions kept coming.

And Father Bernard never stopped listening.

"Do you think God can forgive them?"

"Our God is mercy itself—because of His desire to forgive us, He sent His Son to die for us."

That night Clay asked no more, but watched stars float above the church roof and pondered. Of course, God could forgive those men. The real question lay deeper: *would* he?

In the years that followed, Father Bernard began to speak of desolation and consolation. After he died and during the worst moments at the Crady ranch, Clay wished he had known Saint John. Father Bernard said this French priest taught Sixteenth Century people how to communicate with the Divine.

Even while locked in a dungeon, John still experienced consolation. "Do you wish to communicate with God, son?" The priest asked this and similar questions many times. "He dwells as near as your next breath, as real as your heartbeat."

Setting the prayer book aside, Clay saddled and bridled Pax and took off to check the range. He wanted to believe but lacked Father Bernard's faith. Under a cloudy winter morning sky, he lifted his desire to heaven.

"Show me what you want me to do. Teach me to love people like Father Bernard did."

Greater love hath no man than this, that a man lay down his life for his friends…

On this vast range, how did one locate a friend? Thus far he might choose from a grizzled trapper he had not yet met and a settler woman who most likely despised cowhands.

After breakfast. Meta put on Garrit's wool trousers and her wool coat and gloves and sat to strap on her new snowshoes. Her heart raced—she could leave the cabin in a new way now!

"Lemme help." Franklin threaded the straps in and out and gave her a hand up. With a gesture for her to follow, he took off.

Before long, Meta's steps almost matched his, and the beauty of black trees against fresh snow captivated her.

"Y' all right?"

"Yes, can we go farther?" He moved ahead. Trees began to appear much shorter than their actual height, and she understood Franklin's puzzlement at her lack of snow. He made a wide circle and stopped beside her.

"You'll be sore tomorra." He pointed southwest. "If'n y' folla thet hill n' veer left, y'll see m' place."

"Oh, could we go there?"

Franklin sniffed the air. "T'morra, dependin' on the weather."

When they reached her cabin, he unbound her shoes.

She slipped out of the trousers and pulled down her last bag of onions. She would add a small one to the ham for supper—no, a large one, and a carrot. Yes, for Christmas.

Franklin was taking Hope and Della the long way around to the creek She hurried to join him while the animals foraged. "Grave's sunk over th' winter."

Franklin added more rocks and shuffled away, but Meta lingered. "It's Christmas Day, Garrit. Remember Mama's yellow rose bush in the burlap bag? I covered it with straw before the first freeze—next summer I'll bring you a rose."

Her tears turned to crystals. "At least we had last Christmas together."

Back in the fire's warmth, her biscuits rose higher than yesterday's. No use trying to figure out why, as useless as speculating about the past. But the results in biscuits were far easier to accept. After dinner, Franklin's eyes sparkled when she produced a handmade checkerboard and fished the wooden checkers out of their burlap sack.

"My brother Henry made this for us, but we never got to use it. Will you try it out with me?"

"Not sure I rec'lect how." But he did. Meta had all she could do to win one or two games.

The exercise sweetened her sleep, and she woke to Franklin moving in from the barn. As he settled at the table, his brow scrunched. "Ethel's kickin' at her innards. Needs some tonic." Franklin combed his beard with his fingers. "I'll jest grab th' tonic, and we'll high-tail it home quick-like."

"But shouldn't someone stay here with her?"

"Cain't do nothin' no how, 'thout thet tonic."

Meta scrambled into her snowshoeing outfit. Franklin met her as she stepped outside. "Wisht I could git 'er t' walk." A wild look inundated the mule's eyes, her abdomen so tight she could barely stand.

Franklin roared off, but Meta set her own pace, pondering Franklin's fortitude. He had lived out here so many years.

At his cabin, he walked out of his snowshoes and unstrapped hers before she had a chance. Odd, she had no recollection of what his cabin looked like from the day she and Garrit had eaten with him.

"C'mon in." Her eyes adjusted to the darkness while Franklin reached for a large brown bottle.

He cracked the ice in his water bucket and handed her a cup. He drank a cupful too, crammed the tonic into his pack, and strapped her shoes once more. This time, she memorized his lacing motions. How could such gnarled fingers be so deft?

"I do hope Ethel will be all right."

"By t'night th' tonic'll work."

His woebegone cabin paraded before her on the way home. A single handmade chair, the outline of a bare bunk in a back corner. The quilt she had begun belonged in that sparse room. Tomorrow she would get to work on it.

When they reached the point closest to the creek, Franklin lopped off a thin reed protruding from the bank, stuck it in his belt and angled off again.

For a few minutes the trail belonged to Meta. A solitary speck in a world of white, she paused to take in the wintry beauty.

Bushes and trees iced in white, stark rocks softened by snow, mist still hanging in the trees—a small chickadee eyed her from a scraggly bush, his black cap accentuating the white around his eyes.

The stillness invited her to stay. Bare branches leaned with a message—some day her sorrow would disappear. But right now, Franklin might need help, so she sped home and cast her snowshoes aside as he threw his arm around Ethel's neck and grasped her by the halter.

In his other hand the tonic bottle showed the reed inserted. He gradually elevated Ethel's head by pulling up under her chin so the liquid flowed into her mouth.She wheezed and coughed, but Franklin kept her head elevated until she swallowed. Then he let go, taking care to protect the precious medication. Perspiration stood out on his forehead.

"How long does the medicine take to work?"

"Mebbe a couple hours t' start. I'll stay with 'er." He claimed a stump near the breathless mule, and Meta brought him a cup of coffee for his vigil.

What a day, snowshoeing to his cabin and back—now, she knew the way to somewhere. She swung her arms wide and climbed the hill to tell Garrit.

Chapter Fourteen

"You have tasted of death now," said the old man. "Is it good?"

"It is good," said Mossy. "It is better than life.

"No," said the old man: "it is only more life."

~George MacDonald

A brown elongated lump bulged from the earth, and Clay half-expected sudden movement. As Alan Crady taught him, he set each boot in place like a piece of fine china.

"We're stalkin' prey. Not a sound. My Pa's half Injun', ya know."

A strong human smell brought Clay back to the Dunbar ranch. A few feet closer, identical moccasins became visible, and oily black hair partially released from a braid. Bile washed Clay's throat as he took aim. Then he recalled Owen's statement.

"Only Shoshoni or Arapahoe live around here now, but they avoid the burial ground north of the Ross cabin, near Spring Creek. In the past few years, they've moved even further north."

Shoshoni or Arapahoe. An Indian was an Indian, but why should one come here? Then another scent wafted. Sickness.

Care for God's children.

Clay groaned. Father Bernard would have to show up now. This savage most likely came to steal. Despite the frosty air, Clay broke out in sweat. He could end this fellow's suffering right now with one easy shot—or try to help.

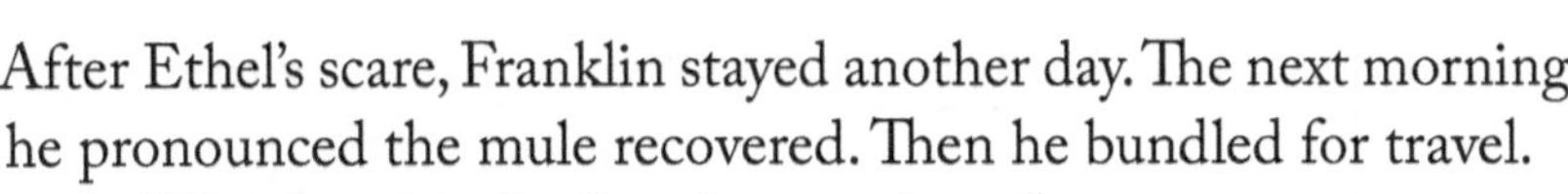

After Ethel's scare, Franklin stayed another day. The next morning he pronounced the mule recovered. Then he bundled for travel.

"Thank ya kindly. Best be on m' way."

Meta gave him her biggest hug, and he responded by calculating. "Be back this way agin come February." He gave his earmuffs a pat.

"Best gift I had me fer a long, long time. Be careful with them shoes. If ya got lost, I'd never fergive m'self."

"I won't go farther than the grave or down to the creek."

"Got 'nough t' feel guilty 'bout a'ready, ya hear?"

"Merry Christmas, dear Franklin." Meta's voice wafted lonelier than ever as she watched him out of sight.

Clouds hedged the sun, and the north wind compressed the bushes into a huddled mass.

The next days dragged. At work on a quilt for Franklin's cabin, Meta memorized the Christmas story. "Next year, I shall recite it by heart for Franklin."

Such a holiday it had been with him here—what a good friend he had become. The tonic had worked its wonders for Ethel, and now life moved on.

Franklin left other gifts for her—more sauerkraut, potatoes and parsnips from Anna, a warm knitted shawl, and stick-figure pictures the children had drawn. Not the least of what his pack offered, a selection of outdated newspapers now occupied a corner of her shelf.

The *Missouri Gazette* from June 1863, a copy of the *Rocky Mountain News* from later in the fall, and several of the *Daily Telegraph*, the first printed newspaper in Wyoming Country. Before Franklin left, Meta read hours and hours from these, but now, she searched them again for missed items.

Anna also sent her a pebble-and-string necklace from the children—she fingered it on January 4th as gray clouds basted the horizon like thick gravy. No doubt about it, a big snowstorm on the move.

In November, Franklin had told her to start milking Della just once a day, for such a time as this. Now the faithful cow would not suffer so much if the weather delayed her milking time.

As day waned, Meta filled the water trough and added extra dried grass to the manger.

"A storm's coming, girls. I will get here as soon as I can." Della and Hope blinked, and the chickens clucked a chorus. Five eggs today, a new record.

A barrage of flakes struck as she opened the barn door. "Watch out fer th' Wolf Moon," Franklin had warned before he left. "Ice'll run deep by then, drifts built up in th' woods, th' wind colder'n ever."

She took the shovel inside the cabin, made a bowl of porridge and settled down to read a *Daily Telegraph* dated late October. Franklin had exclaimed over one article that warranted another read, a story about President Lincoln's proclamation on October 20th.

"The year that is drawing towards its close, has been filled with the blessings of fruitful fields and healthful skies. To these bounties, which are so constantly enjoyed that we are prone to forget the source from which they come, others have been added, which are of so extraordinary a nature, that they cannot fail to penetrate and soften even the heart which is habitually insensible to the ever watchful providence of Almighty God. In the midst of a civil war of unequalled magnitude and severity, which has sometimes seemed to foreign States to invite and to provoke their aggression, peace has been preserved with all nations, order has been maintained, the laws have been respected and obeyed, and harmony has prevailed everywhere except in the theatre of military conflict; while that theatre has been greatly contracted by the advancing armies and navies of the Union."

Was this true? Had the theatre of fighting been greatly contracted by the movements of the army and navy? Such a hopeful note. There was no one to ask about its meaning—if only she might speak with Martin.

"Needful diversions of wealth and of strength from the fields of peaceful industry to the national defence, have not arrested the plough, the shuttle or the ship; the axe has enlarged the borders of our settlements, and the mines, as well of iron and coal as of the precious metals, have yielded even more abundantly than heretofore. Population has steadily increased, notwithstanding the waste that has been made in the camp, the siege and the battle-field; and the country, rejoicing in the consciousness of augmented strength and vigor, is permitted to expect continuance of years with large increase of freedom."

The plough…Meta had to smile, considering what service Garrit's plowshare provided every day in the hearth. *The axe*… ah, how it had enlarged this particular settlement. That is, until it took Garrit's life.

"No human counsel hath devised nor hath any mortal hand worked out these great things. They are the gracious gifts of the Most High God, who, while dealing with us in anger for our sins, hath nevertheless remembered mercy. It has seemed to me fit and proper that they should be solemnly, reverently and gratefully acknowledged as with one heart and one voice by the whole American People. I do therefore invite my fellow citizens in every part of the United States, and also those who are at sea and those who are sojourning in foreign lands, to set apart and observe the last Thursday of November next, as a day of Thanksgiving and Praise to our beneficent Father who dwelleth in the Heavens."

Surely Mama and *the boys* feasted on wild turkey that day—even if they were still working with the harvest. Most likely, Margita and her husband had brought her family to the farm, and the children played outdoors after the meal.

"And I recommend to them that while offering up the ascriptions justly due to Him for such singular deliverances and blessings, they do also, with humble penitence for our national perverseness and disobedience, commend to His tender care all those who have become widows, orphans, mourners or sufferers in the lamentable civil strife in which we are unavoidably engaged, and fervently implore the interposition of the Almighty Hand to heal the wounds of the nation and to restore it as soon as may be consistent with the Divine purposes to the full enjoyment of peace, harmony, tranquillity and Union."

Widows…how many thousands were there by now, whose husbands had fallen on both sides? One of the papers listed the fallen at Gettysburg alone as fifty thousand, but so many more battles had been fought since. Winter brought a respite, but camped outdoors somewhere with his unit, life could not be easy for dear Martin.

The wind grew even more violent. Whatever had kept this area free from snow, this time things might be different. How would she get out in the morning?

On into the night, she read, turning to Noah's story, Abraham traveling to the Promised Land, and Jacob meeting his wife at a well. Here, in her own Promised Land, the gale howled like a wounded animal and darkness persisted.

Black slits opened under feverish eyelids—if only this Indian would show fear or even anger. Paleness undergirded his leathery red skin, and his face burned to the touch.

Clay's touch. Disease had wiped out whole tribes—what if this man carried some dread sickness? But Father Bernard kept whispering, *Love thy neighbor.* The stained shirt barely rose and fell.

Clay slipped his gun back into its holster and hurried for a blanket, spread it on the frozen earth and seized the man under the arms. Rolling his dead weight took every effort. He shoved at the legs, like two heavy branches, tied the blanket ends together and pulled on the top. Finally he released the barn door and edged his load inside as Pax stamped his hooves. When the Indian lay against the far wall, Clay returned to the cabin for rags and hot water.

"It's all right, boy."

He wrung a cloth to smooth over the man's greasy face, dabbed again to swab his neck and chest. When he touched the cloth to cracked lips white with fever, the brave's eyelids fluttered. A soft groan and his eyes opened wide.

"Friend." Clay made the peace sign and touched his own chest. "Sleep."

The Indian's eyelids closed.

Clay retreated to Pax. "Glad you're here to help me, boy. I'll be spending the night with you and this poor fellow."

In Iowa, a heavy wet snow would block the door by morning, so Friedrich or Henry sometimes slept in the barn. Chores must be done no matter what. Could she pry open the door enough to scoop snow into her dishpan with her hands? Garrit had worked for hours fitting the door to the frame—perhaps he had matched them too well.

"Meta Tolzmann Rausch—so prone to presumption! You have no idea how things will look in the morning." In candlelight, she clucked at her image in the shadowy mirror.

Long into the night she read. At last, wrapped in Mama's quilt, she lay down.

When she woke, the wind sounded very different from the

mountain lion squalling through the night. Should she lift the bar? "Of course! How else will you ever know what lies beyond?"

When the door released with no struggle, she stepped back. A glistening world took her breath away. Snow had stuck high on the trees toward the creek, and as if etched by a giant white pencil, the cabin walls revealed where the windblown onslaught had reached.

But where had the snow gone?

Shimmering flakes everywhere, still at the wind's behest—she scooped up some of this dusty blanket that fell in a sphere around their cabin. Drier and almost powdery. Such a mystery, snow and wind drifting into deep intricate designs in the brush near the creek but mere rods away, leaving her a free path to care for the animals.

Somewhere, a chickadee twittered. Contrary to her anxious expectations, this glorious day, glossy and stunning, invited her out into the world.

Coal-colored eyes glimmered as Clay spooned the remaining porridge into his patient's mouth. Three days since he found the man, and except for brief range checks, he had played nursemaid.

The brave slowly raised his palms. A wild current buzzed in Clay's ears—he would live!

At the Crady Ranch, he had coaxed horses back to health, and cowhands called him, *Doc*. But he had never been party to a human recovery—still, this Indian had a long way to go.

Painful coughs resonated as he sought to clear his throat. Obsidian glints radiated from the shadows in the ensuing silence. Then two sparse English words emerged: "Thank…you."

Clay patted the Indian's shoulder and started to rise, but a muscular hand grasped his. Another word that took Clay's breath away.

"Friend."

Hours later, he returned Pax to the barn after riding the range. He crouched beside the pallet to check on his patient, but the blanket lay folded on the straw. The Indian had vanished. No way to tell which way he went. No way to know if they would ever meet again.

Inside, Clay blew on the fire's remains. After some moments, the kindling he added caught and burst into flame. Maybe his new friend lived somewhere near... by now, perhaps he slept in a warm tepee.

The fire made good company, but the warm coverlet failed to woo Clay to sleep. Such a brief time they had known each other, but the Indian's eyes kept passing before him. Never had he witnessed eyes the color of the darkest night—the eyes of a friend.

Finally, he bunched the covers and made for the fireplace, the closest thing to a campfire he could find.

By the time Franklin stopped again, snow had fallen several times. He stayed only two nights, and during daylight, checked his traps to the east.

The chickens provided six eggs over the past three days, so Meta fried them for supper. Franklin's eyes shone as he cleaned his plate.

"Saw your cousin. Got more letters fer ya. Them young'uns miss ya."

She missed them too. So many people to miss—Betsy, Lissa and Margita, her nieces and nephews, Henry, Mama—and of course, Martin. She even missed sober, somber Friedrich. Lately when she visited Garrit, a jumpy feeling plagued her. Maybe those five envelopes, two from Mama and one from Margita and Betsy, contained guidance. The last letter showed the name *Speigelhalter* in the upperleft corner—who could this be?

Mama's letter came first. Traveling back to Iowa, Meta forgot all about Franklin.

Dear Daughter,
We mourn Garrit's passing with you. He was so young.
We missed you terribly at Christmas. I am glad you can
be with Herman's family now, and pray for wisdom, my lieb-
chen, and peace.

The rest of the letter described sewing projects. Maybe it was better for Mama to believe she had gone to Cheyenne. A letter in Martin's fine handwriting, she set aside.

Mama's second letter, postmarked three weeks after the first, told of news from afar. Alma's oldest daughter carried her first child.

How I would like to see my first great-grandchild. But a
trip to Nebraska Territory, with my aches and pains—I cannot
consider such a thing.

After her signature, Mama added a short note.

You may receive a letter from our neighbor, Karl Speigel-
halter, three miles to the west. His wife died giving birth last
summer, and he asked for your address.

Setting the rest of her cache aside, Meta turned to Franklin. Just waking from his nap, he fidgeted.

"Everythin' a'right?"

"Yes. Thank you so much for bringing the letters."

"If ya have some ready, I kin leave 'em off at Fort Laramie. Goin' thetaway next."

He fell asleep again, and while he snored, Meta took up Karl's message, penned in German.

Dear Miss Meta,
I hope you will not consider me too forward. Your mother
told me the news of Garrit, and I send my sympathy.

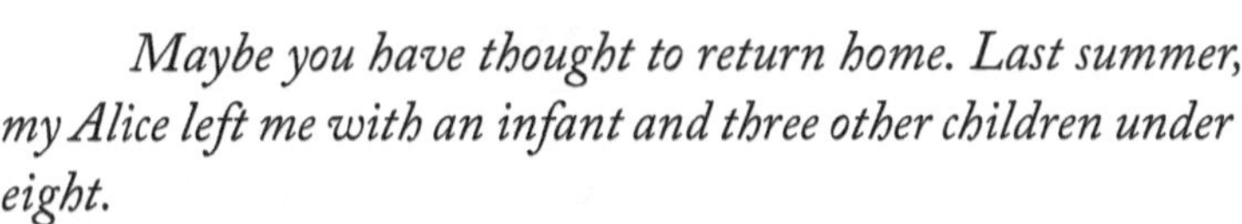

Maybe you have thought to return home. Last summer, my Alice left me with an infant and three other children under eight.

They need a mother and I a wife. I would be honored if you would consider me a suitor.

Yours truly,
Karl Speigelhalter

Friedrich had mentioned this farmer in connection with buying hogs, yet his face remained a mystery to Meta. But his letter made her think. What kind of future awaited a lone woman in her position? If she wanted to remarry—if ever her desire to be a mother were to be fulfilled—she must meet a man. But how would she meet someone out here?

Setting aside these impossible questions, she read Betsy's letter. Her description of their fertile land created a longing to visit Oregon. Towards the end of the last page, Meta slowed her pace.

Little Michael's memory burns in me, and my arms still feel empty. Sometimes I wonder if this will ever change, but find comfort in our busy life and the beauty here.

Still, every single day I must let him go again. Perhaps the same is true for you. You were God's gift in my loss. May He send someone to fill your emptiness.

Was this the reason for her restlessness, or did her answer lie in Iowa? She must be willing, but the thought of returning tensed her shoulders.

By bedtime the next night, a packet of letters sat on the table for Franklin to tote in his saddlebag.

"Must you go so soon?"

"Traps're waitin'. Cain't let some varmint get m' furs."

"When will you come back?"

"Don't rightly know. Sometime 'fore spring."

As soon as he disappeared, Meta moved some rocks at the grave, recalling their last conversation.

Over pancakes and ham, he had squirmed at her question.

"Franklin, how did you let go of your wife and baby?"

He took a long while to answer.

"Time jest moseyed on. Mae— thet was her name—Mae n' little Tad still go 'long with me, though."

A bitter wind whipped dark curls from Meta's scarf as she lifted her voice. "Help me understand what *letting go* means."

Another death in the herd with more hungry wolves preying at Mr. Dunbar's expense. Making the mark on the record reminded Clay that his boss expected such losses.

With no storm in the offing, perhaps he ought to check on that new settler's cabin. The night before, Bunyan's *Pilgrim's Progress* kept him company. Nearly a century after Saint John of the Cross, Pilgrim's slough of despond paralleled Saint John's desolation.Father Bernard agreed with their views—sometimes life became even harder when people believed.

So many cowhands lived worry-free without faith while other serious ones suffered no end.Where did consolation fit into all of this? If only he had someone to ask, but even if his Indian friend returned, they could never discuss such things. The recitations Father Bernard had him memorize—Copernicus, Galileo, Kepler... what use were they now?

By midmorning, Pax dipped his muzzle in Spring Creek. Such a bright, warm day—a translucent sky outlined willow saplings and young pines. Clay dismounted but froze in mid step at a vague, familiar sound—a woman singing. And he recognized the tune.

> *O God our help in ages past,*
> *our hope for years to come...*

*be Thou our Guide while life shall last,
and our eternal home.*

The breeze blew the rest of her words toward Fort Laramie. Years peeled away, transporting Clay back to Texas Hill Country as Mrs. Evendsberg instructed the orphans in a chorus. This song. He listened a while before taking another cautious step.

Several rods away stood the settler—the same one he had noticed before. Her dark hair escaped a yellow bonnet, but her earnest posture declared determination. Hands clasped, only her lips moved. Then she sank to the earth and rocked back and forth on her knees. The tremble of her shoulders twisted his insides. Longing to help her somehow, he could scarcely maintain his stance.

Who had died here?

He touched the warm muzzle behind him and Pax retreated soundlessly to the creek. Should he retrace his steps and ignore this woman—what would Father Bernard do right now? At last, he led Pax along the water's edge through barren brush and scattered willows. But the woman's face lingered. Fair-skinned, but hair darker than Pax's mane.

Sometimes bereaved mothers or wives visited Father Bernard's chapel. Clay never disobeyed his instructions not to disturb them, but he did listen from behind a pillar. Women and tears went together, this he knew—yet the Sisters never cried and snuffed out such displays from the children.

Surely his Mama must have wept. And like any child, so did he—but away from the Sisters' sharp eyes. Going to bed without supper taught him to shed his tears in lonely shadows. But Father Bernard had wept, and so did Mr. Evendsberg at the *Waisenhaus*.

How many times had he heard that kind man console a child in their household with never a raised voice, never a harsh command? So far from their moorings and having suffered so many losses in their small community, they trod a steady course, carrying on no matter what.

Little by little, the story of their early time in America came to light. One day Mrs. Evendsberg shared, "During the first year, cholera took three-hundred and forty-eight souls from our community. They all lie in the New Braunfels Cemetery. Living through that horror taught me never to withhold love."

A meadowlark's song emanated. A ground squirrel scurried across the ice. The day bore the season's clarity, but winter could not last forever. Warmth would soon alter everything, and Clay sensed change within, as well.

Twenty-some years ago, his life might have ended on the lonesome Texas prairie. He might have been killed by the fall from the wagon. A mountain lion might have come along, or a bear.

Why had he survived out there in the wilderness until the Texas rangers found him?

After Father Bernard's death. the Evendsbergs welcomed him, but when Texas seceded from the Union, urged him to avoid the Rebels. After a narrow escape from a Confederate band drove him north, he signed on at the Crady ranch. Then came the trail drive, which brought him here, farther north than he had ever imagined, to territory beyond both the Union and the Confederacy.

Today, as Pax made his way along the creek, his Texas past, through Father Bernard and the Evendsbergs, still mentored him. He must do something for this anguished settler, but what?

Betsy's words stayed with Meta. Four days earlier, on her birthday, she finished her usual chores and snowshoed along the creek. But that insistent tug continued, as though she must do something for Garrit.

A beautiful day to visit Franklin's cabin, but she had given him her word. Still, sitting inside like an old woman suited her ill.

Late that afternoon she trekked in wider and wider circles around the cabin before climbing the hill. There, a near-wail emerged, more a scream than a cry.

"Today I am nineteen. My life has not ended—no!" Afterward, with only the whistle of the wind, that sense came again. She must do something for Garrit.

Before darkness fell, she collapsed on her bed. In a dream, Mama swayed before her garbed in black crepe. "Let go, Meta. I had to, and you must also."

But how? Like the darkness, the meaning became impalpable. She made some porridge, but the image remained. "Let go... let go."

How had Mama coped after Papa's death?

Settled into her rocker with *The Deerslayer*, she gave herself to Cooper's vivid descriptions of life a century ago. The character of Natty Bumppo, a white man living in a native tribe, believed each living thing should follow its natural gifts. Though Indians had reared him, he still must follow his natural inclinations. For one thing, he should not scalp enemies. This he knew, but he sought more guidance.

In the final scene, his quest ended: "Truth was the Deerslayer's polar star. He ever kept it in view, and it was nearly impossible for him to avoid uttering it, even when prudence demanded silence."

Natty spoke his truth to Judith, a woman who wanted to marry him. She "read his answer in his countenance, and with a heart nearly broken... signed to him an adieu and buried herself in the woods."

The fire crackled and Meta pondered. Outside, a great prairie surrounded her, so different from the farm back home. How could she be true to herself here? Mr. Rausch's funeral flashed before her. Garrit's stepmother had worn black crepe, and not just any black— not even blue-black fit the guidelines. Mama and every other widow sewed crimped black silk over bonnets, dresses and coats.

When wet, the murky dye ran into other fabrics. On Papa's burial day it rained, so even though the crape ruined Mama's Sunday dress, she wore it for a year and a day after that.

"I have not done right by Garrit—he had no proper burial. I left our farewells to a stranger. No one prayed or sang for him."

Mama had taught her better than this. For the first time in several days she slept well and the next morning woke with purpose. The whole day, she considered what to say about Garrit.

An honest man, he died trying to save Della. He exemplified courage, believed in America's great promise, and left all to pursue his goal. What passage might she read aloud? Ah, Psalm 46 might do.

> *God is our refuge and strength, a very present help in trouble. Therefore will not we fear, though the earth be removed, and though the mountains be carried into the midst of the sea;*
> *Though the waters thereof roar and be troubled, though the mountains shake with the swelling thereof. Selah.*
> *God is in the midst of her; she shall not be moved:*
> *God shall help her, and that right early*
> *The Lord of hosts is with us; the God of Jacob is our refuge.*

The roll of these words took her home to the church of her childhood, where men and women sat on separate sides and decorum ruled. But tears fell when they bade loved ones farewell.

Here, salt licks edged sand dunes, cliffs rose from nothing, and lizards conquered all. In certain ravines, tall trees flourished, and with hard work, a garden might flourish. This land Garrit Rausch had chosen to claim, and here, he would now rest in peace.

Chapter Fifteen

The mind is its own place, and in itself can make a heaven of hell, a hell of heaven.

~John Milton—Paradise Lost

Oh God Our Help In Ages Past
 Our hope for years to come,
Our shelter from the stormy blast,
 And our eternal home.
Sufficient is Thine arm alone,
 And our defense is sure.
Before the hills in order stood,
 Or earth received her frame,
From everlasting Thou art God,
 To endless years the same.
A thousand ages in Thy sight
 Are like an evening gone;
Short as the watch that ends the night
 Before the rising sun.
Time, like an ever-rolling stream,
 Bears all its sons away;
They fly, forgotten, as a dream
 Dies at the opening day.

On February 12th, their first anniversary, Meta sang this hymn beside Garrit's grave.

She imagined their families present to honor him. At the

final word, her sigh lingered as a fresh sort of tears fell. Kneeling on the frozen earth, she willed his spirit to God. These sobs let him go.

Rising from the grave, her step felt light. Nothing had changed, yet everything had. Perhaps she would trek down to the creek. Could she try to ice fish?

Martin would be proud if she did, for fishing had been a highlight of many a summer's day. In the letter Mama sent along, he wrote,

> *Tell Meta we fish whenever we can, to add to the awful grub.*

The air had warmed. With her face raised to the heavens, in sight of the cabin, she twirled a full circle.

"I never imagined *The Deerslayer* would show me what to do!"

Just then her ankle rolled on a stray rock, and pain shot up her leg as she fell. She attempted to get up and tumbled again. What now? Call to Hope and Della, who watched with interest from where they were staked?

Then something crunched behind her. A tight band compressed her heart…indisputable boot steps. Who could this be? An outlaw running from the law, a trapper, or worst of all—a cowhand?

The all-too-human gait produced a shadow, tall with a wide-brimmed hat. As if to shrink herself, she hunched close to the cold, rocky earth.

"Ma'am?" A deep male voice harbored a tremor.

Meta turned to look up, but grabbed at her ankle. The fellow took another step and doffed his hat, revealing violet-blue eyes.

"I was—I slipped."

"Could I…" He leaned toward her, appearing faceless in the bright midday sun. "Would you let me help you?"

Hand to her throat, she stalled. But what choice did she have? Nothing to do but reach for his hand. "If I could hang onto your arm, perhaps…"

He pulled her up and the world spun. Regaining her senses, she took a step, but her leg folded. "Oh dear. Do forgive me, Mr...."

"Burns." He glanced around as a chipmunk skittered onto a rock. "Do you believe you could get on my horse? He won't move a muscle."

"Whatever you think..."

He whistled to a beautiful bay and turned to her. "Might make more sense to carry you, Ma'am."

She nodded, so he gathered her into his arms. Easing back, she tried to move her foot. "Owww!" Her cheeks flamed even hotter.

"Hold that ankle still now. Is that your cabin straight ahead?"

"Yes."

His horse followed like a pet, while Della turned her head to watch their progress. On the stoop, Meta strained to push the door open and stifled a groan as he maneuvered her onto the bed.

"Oh, thank you. What would I have done without—"

"You're welcome, Ma'am." He backed away. "Let me fetch some ice for that ankle."

He left before she could reply. A recollection churned within—where had she seen eyes that unique shade?

"Burns..."

She attempted to slide up on the bed, but a knife slashed at her ankle, and she slumped. How could this possibly have happened today?

When the man returned, he stopped just inside the door.

"Ma'am, do you have some cloth I could use?"

"Over there." She pointed, and he neared her shelf, found a towel, and wrapped the ice.

Nearing the bed, he hesitated. "Ma'am, could you... would you be able to take off your shoe?"

She stretched her arm, flattening her cheek against Mama's quilt. But another piercing pain made her shriek.

"Ah..."

He drew closer, tawny eyebrows pressed into a line. "I have some experience with horses. Mind if I take a closer look?"

"Go ahead."

His cheeks flamed. Her heart went out to him as her small leather buttons complicated his task. Finally, the last clasp came free. He placed the ice bag under her foot and stood to his full height, as tall as Garrit. No, even taller.

"Thank you."

She turned her head as he eased his fingertips over the joint.

"Tell me if I hurt you." He manipulated a bit more, and a moan escaped her lips. "Not a break. A bad sprain, though." He scanned her shelves. "Got any ginger root?"

She shook her head.

"Hmm. Keep your foot elevated. Good thing there's ice close by." He surveyed the cabin again as if the spice might appear. "I have some ginger root at the..." He angled his head. "I can get back before dark, Ma'am. Do you have anyone here to—"

"No one." A warning crawled her spine, but a peculiar sense of calm prevailed. "Please call me Meta. Meta Rausch."

He brought her a cup of water. "Are you hungry?"

"No... well, maybe you could bring me a biscuit and that honey pot."

He set cold biscuits, honey, and a knife near her. "Try not to move that ankle. You won't get up, will you?"

"No."

"I'll be back as soon as I can."

"Thank you, Mr. Burns." In the dim interior, his eyes still showed their distinctive hue. He added more logs to the fire and closed the door behind him. Soon the sound of hooves echoed.

The feather pillow caught Meta's tears, the ice soothed her ankle, and her thoughts meandered. Why had he come here today? Those eyes, like spring bluebells with extra violet—in the grove back home, a profusion sprouted every May along with Sweet Williams, Grandma Tolzmann's favorites. Then came the lilacs and honeysuckle, lending sweetness to the air even weeks after blooming—like the relief she still felt in spite of everything.

This temporary pain would pass, and all would be well. She had honored Garrit in the best way she knew. Natty Bumppo would be impressed.

Now, about this cowhand—could his first name be Johann? Aldrich? Fritz? No, she had never heard of a German with a name as simple as Burns.

"Oh, Mama, you were right to call me impetuous. I gave no thought to all I was leaving behind, and now—" Outside, a bird chirped, interrupting her train of thought.

But it was easy to find that thread again. Like Franklin, another stranger had found her.

That settler's cabin walls had almost closed in on him, but at the same time, Clay hated to leave. This young woman, about the age of the Evendsberg's eldest daughter, possessed such a quiet demeanor.

How did she come to live alone out here? The first time he saw her, she had stood on the hilltop like a sentinel. And this morning she stood there again.

Must've lost her husband. He resolved to check the inscription on the cross. Mayta ... one of the children at the *Waisenhaus* bore the same name. When he first lifted her, a faint whiff of some flower emanated. Like the incense at St. Augustine's, the fragrance stayed with him.

The fright in her eyes, he had witnessed often. A downed steer or wounded horse exhibited the same self-protective gaze.

"You're going to have to trust me. I mean you no harm." He would have crooned this to a hurt animal, but how could this girl believe him? Still, the wary light in her eyes had shifted.

Pax sped across the prairie. The rigid place between Clay's shoulders slackened—somehow, confidence had replaced the girl's suspicion. Surely she hesitated to tell him she lived alone, yet she had. Once again, a person rather than steers held his attention. He would do his best to help her. As Father Bernard would say, *As you wish that others would do to you, do so also to them.*

Not long ago, he had cared for that sick Indian—now this opportunity had appeared. Could loving others come down to something this simple?

With a tentative step into the settler's cabin, Clay's knock produced no response. As his eyes adjusted, he realized Meta lay silent. In her cooking pot, he covered several chunks of dried ginger root with steaming water and fed the fire.

Outdoors, her big mare and milk cow eyed him, so he introduced them to Pax and filled their water trough. Soon, their nickering and nose-rubbing with Pax created an agreeable background. Licking the rich foam from milking brought back learning to milk at the Evendsberg's. The hens clucked at all the activity, their wire cages catching fading light. Clay fumbled with the hooks and found four eggs, but the close air made his nose twitch. Then he recalled the ginger.

Boiling water had softened the roots, so he ladled the mushy mass onto a towel and folded it into a square before saturating it with the dirt-colored water. Wrapping the soggy mound in a second towel, he turned.

Dark eyes glinted at him from the bed. He stopped in his tracks.
"Mr. Burns?"
"Yes, Ma'am."
"You came back."
"This will ease your pain some."
He stepped closer. "Are you ready? It'll feel hot."
He removed the ice pack and placed the compress around her foot. Her lips curled ever so slightly, but tension drained from her countenance at the warm, spicy vapors. Perhaps ginger worked as well for people as animals.

"You..." Her voice, low yet distinct, quaked.

"I'll do the chores—don't you fret. Rest now." She sank into the quilt like one more shadow in this small cabin.

"*Don't you fret.*" When had he heard that phrase? He brushed Meta's horse and tried to recall.

Father Bernard, of course. The priest's French accent made a melody out of English as the r's rolled way back in his throat.

Don't you fret, son. I'll read a while longer, but you go to sleep.

When the luster on the mare's coat vied with Pax's, Clay bedded the animals and made a fire. Someone else had done the same at this campsite not long ago. Going back inside again set his heart prattling, yet he must replace the ginger pack with ice.

Moonlight glistened on the creek. Freezing in the morning, warm like spring this afternoon, iced over now. Hadn't Owen said something about women changing like the weather?

As he switched the compresses, Meta still slept, but her lashes fluttered open.

"Thank you."

"Ma'am... Ah... Meta, I'm camped outside if you need anything." She hoisted herself up against the wall. "You must be hungry. I have eggs and milk. Would you..." She waved toward the hearth. "I am sorry to ask, but—"

His stomach growled loud enough for her to hear. Her laughter waltzed over him like a song, and he chuckled too.

"I can make pancakes..."

"The flour... that red can, and..."

In ten minutes he created thick pancakes lush with honey and butter.

"These look so good, Mr. Burns."

"Call me Clay."

Until the last cake disappeared, the rich taste kept him busy. Finally, he realized she was watching.

"You must have been starving."

"Haven't had eggs or milk for... a long, long time. Nothing

ever tasted better. You were smart to bring that cow and chickens out here."

Her look darkened—had he said something wrong?

"And fresh churned butter. Nothing better—do you need more?"

"No thanks. The hens were my idea, but the cow... the credit for Della belongs to my husband." A branch scratched the cabin. "Garrit died some months ago."

"Awful sorry to hear. Grieving takes mighty hard work."

"Yes. I had no idea. My Mama lost Papa when I was very young and she had a child, too. Now I see what she had to do to go on."

He thought to ask after her family, but she continued. "I was born second-to-last of ten children."

What would it be like to sit around a table with your true brothers and sisters? Once again, she anticipated his question.

"Mama kept a strict household and everyone did their share. The older ones sacrificed most, especially when Papa died and my oldest brother became the man of the house."

"Such a big family." Something niggled at the base of Clay's neck, so he scraped back his chair.

"Ought to check my fire. Then I'll wash these plates, and—"

"Clay." Her voice sounded urgent, her eyes shone black as coal. Ham grease from the skillet wafted, mingling with his own fear. "Thank you for your kindness."

His voice cracked. "We are neighbors."

Outside in the night air, her gaze still warmed him.

The fire claimed every branch he could break, and he slipped into his bedroll. That pleasant sensation washed over him, the same as when he returned to his cabin.

Chapter Sixteen

Ubi caritas et amor; Deus ibi est.
Where there is charity and love, God is there.

Moonlight entered a crevice in the ceiling corner, outlining the dark rafters—even more mudding lay ahead. Then Meta remembered Clay Burns. Where did he live? Close enough to fetch the ginger. Not without hurting, she slid the chamber pot between the trunks, asking for the 20th time how she could have hurt herself. Now, she must depend on a complete stranger, but the chamber pot—surely she could manage.

A steady throb in her foot and leg reminded her of her foolishness yesterday. Yet at just the right time, Clay had come. Something about him attested to his honesty. What exactly was it? His hesitation showed he assumed nothing. His Mama must have taught him well. But those eyes—why did they seem so familiar?

He reminded her of Martin, timid as a fawn, but willing to help. Yesterday held such a muddle of emotions—relief, a different sort of pain, and now, propitious comfort. Perhaps she and Clay could become friends. The thought brought such a yearning. But at least for now, someone strong and kind slept within her call. The thought wooed her back to sleep.

Before she knew it, a pail clinked in the barn. She lifted her foot and groaned. Clay Burns must be doing her chores. Surely, though, she could make some breakfast. She shifted her feet to the floor, putting gentle weight on the tender side.

A tap came at the door.

"Come in."

Dizziness overtook her, and Clay strode within a few feet, leaving the door open for light.

"Careful now, a sprain needs time."

"I thought for sure—" She touched her hair, in wild disarray.

"A bad sprain takes two or three days to heal. You need more ice."

"I hate to be a bother."

"When do I get to eat fresh eggs and milk two meals in a row?"

His grin caught her off guard—he seemed at ease now after being so reticent yesterday. While he went to the creek, she replaced her hairpins.

After switching her ice packs, he blew on the coals and cracked eggs into the skillet. Soon the grease sputtered and spattered.

"Did you sleep well?"

"A perfect night out under the stars."

Clay wet a clean cloth and set it within her reach. As he flipped the pancakes, his profile showed against the hearth. No German nose—straight as an Englishman's.

Oh, the glory in a warm, wet cloth! By the time he finished cooking, words from Mama had settled her.

Be still, daughter. Trust.

When Clay brought her plate, she gave him a smile.

"Last night I talked only of myself. Now I want to know about you. Do you come from a large family?"

"Just two children, at least that's what Father Bernard told me."

"Father Bernard?"

"A priest I lived with." He sat down at the table.

"You are Catholic?"

"No, but the priest was." The hint of a smile graced his lips, but would he tell her more? "He took me in after a fire at our mission." He took another helping of pancakes.

"You lost your parents?"

"Mmm. Comanches." Might as well answer her unspoken inquiries. "In Texas long ago." He downed the rest of his coffee and carried dishes to the dishpan.

"Please leave them. I can do them later." Her dark eyes held him. "I'm so sorry about your parents."

Like a warning scent, that old closed-in feeling threatened. Clay offered, "I can come back tonight. If you stay off your ankle today—"

"I... Della..."

"I staked her and your mare nearby but with long tethers. I'll bring in the milk and fetch more water—I can see you do everything around here, but one more day's rest will stand you in good stead."

"All right. I—how can I ever—"

"See you later this afternoon."

Clay tipped his hat and was gone.

Until noon, Meta kept her ankle propped up, but reading and dozing could only last so long. If she could maneuver the three-legged stool Garrit made, she might open the door, glimpse the animals and enjoy the afternoon sunshine.

Using her good foot as an anchor, she proceeded with care. Soon, fresh air filled the cabin. A red shafted Northern Flicker slammed his beak into solid oak as sunlight found her. She rolled up her sleeves—such wonderful warmth! Six months ago right here in this spot, she had waited for Garrit during the storm.

The thought no longer crushed her.

That night seemed almost from another time, long ago and far away, like scenes from Iowa. Time had a way of playing with reality, it seemed.

But she could not sit here forever. Surely she might make something for supper, at least? And the chamber pot smelled. Balancing the enamel vessel to the doorway, she aimed the contents as far as possible. Thankfully, the wind cooperated. Two eggs lay on the counter—perfect for a batch of cornbread, and the task claimed her energy. After she slid the stool back to her bed, weariness struck, and she slept until a whinny sounded. When Clay peeked in, his eyebrows rose. "You have been walking?"

"Our stool works almost as well as a horse. I mixed up cornbread for you to bake."

The solemn lines around his mouth smoothed as he did her bidding. "Better give the animals some exercise."

When he came back, the cornbread smelled almost ready, so Meta manned her stool near the stove. Clay fried some meat and poured milk.In a companionable hush, he kept his eyes closed for an extra moment when she said grace. Then he tackled the bread.

"This tastes mighty good. You plan to stay out here the whole winter?"

"This has become my home. Garrit dreamed of building a horse ranch, to sell mounts to the Cavalry."

"A horse ranch—right here?"

"This may sound foolish, but I—" She halted, observing his reaction. "I hate to let his dream die."

"Foolish? Why?" When she stayed quiet, Clay left it at that. "I need to get an early start tomorrow after I milk Della and fill the water trough. You shouldn't have to go to the creek for another day."

Oh, to clasp his hand and beg, *Please don't go*. But Meta held her peace.

He washed the dishes amidst talk of the weather and his travels across Mr. Dunlap's ranch. But when he put on his hat, heaviness bore down.

"Clay." Her voice nearly strangled in her throat.

"Do you need something?"

"I—could I ask you one more favor?"

He leaned forward.

"I do get so lonesome here. Would you... could you please come back some day?"

"I will. I promise." At his whisper, the raw stab in her chest eased.

All afternoon, sunshine, hope's emissary, lighted even the cabin's dark corners. With the door open, Meta swept and dusted, organized and rearranged. Buds would soon transform with pale green growth, the earth would waken, its clean scent conquering all.

From a branch, her featherbed flapped in the breeze. She scrubbed shelves, table, chairs, the floor. Oh, for a way to let fresh air in at night! In spite of its beauty, the day moved like a wagon train. Work usually brought a song to her lips, but she caught herself staring south, as if to see beyond the cottonwood grove, and talked more with the animals.

"Della, if only you could tell me what you're thinking."

Della rolled her coffee eyes. With her ankle back to normal, Meta worked with a fervor and took three walks to the creek and back. Thoughts of Clay kept popping up until finally she chided herself.

"Face the truth: no amount of watching will beckon him back." She forced herself to stitch on Franklin's quilt. Any day now, he should appear, but Clay—counting on a cowhand's promise would surely be unwise.

Late February proved winter had no intention of dashing off, although mild weather teased the countryside with springtime temperatures. The dryness cracked Meta's lips and fingers—thank goodness for Mama's comfrey ointment. Evening by evening, her reading pile gradually shrank. By the end of the month, she completed the Old Testament, along with Cooper's stories.

One restless morning, the second trunk caught her eye. Toward the end of their packing, Mama added extra items—some surprises might await.

Soon, the hard back of a volume of poetry met her fingertips. Ah…from Miss Brunner, and she had asked for letters about this new country.

One entry leaped out.

Address To A Child During A Boisterous Winter Evening
~by my sister, Dorothy Wordsworth

What way does the wind come? What way does he go?
  He rides over the water, and over the snow,
Through wood, and through vale; and, o'er rocky height
  Which the goat cannot climb, takes his sounding flight;
He tosses about in every bare tree,
  As, if you look up, you plainly may see;
But how he will come, and whither he goes,
  There's never a scholar in England knows…
Books have we to read,—but that half-stifled knell,
  Alas! 'tis the sound of the eight o'clock bell.
—Come now we'll to bed, and when we are there
  He may work his own will, and what shall we care?
He may knock at the door, we'll not let him in;
  May drive at the windows, we'll laugh at his din;
Let him seek his own home wherever it be;
  Here's a 'cozie' warm house for Edward and me.

Interesting that she called the wind *he.* England must have wild gales, too. What was it Mama always said?

Like the wind, we cannot see the Almighty, yet His actions show He is real. Like Franklin and Clay—mysterious, both of them, but so tangible. If Clay ever did return, she must ask how he happened by when she fell.

Next, she found *Uncle Tom's Cabin.* No doubt, reading this influenced Martin to join the Fifth Infantry.

Hadn't Mr. Lincoln said when he met Mrs. Stowe, *So this*

is the little lady who made this big war! From the day Martin left to meet the troop train, they watched for word. His first letters depicted his unit moving south toward Mississippi, deep in Confederate Territory. In his last letter to Mama, he described a boil under a soldier's arm. Comrades tied the poor fellow's elbow around his head.

We applied hot cloths—oh, how the wretched soul screamed! But at last, the sore broke open and relieved his pain.

Once he wrote,

I looked into a slave child's eyes and know we fight for the right. In this, we take heart.

Dear Martin, battling hand-to-hand, marching where *heavy moss hangs from tree branches so thick it blots out the afternoon sun.* The humidity, he wrote, worsened every trial, along with mosquitoes and illness.

With *Uncle Tom's Cabin* on the keep-out stack, Meta added one more small book—Robert Browning. It opened to: "But what if I fail of my purpose here?"

It is but to keep the nerves at strain,
To dry one's eyes and laugh at a fall,
And baffled, get up and begin again,
So the chase takes up one's life, that's all.

"Let me not fail of my purpose here."

As she piled the books beside her rocker, her mind turned to Clay—so many questions she might ask him! Thankfully, Father Bernard had cared about his schooling, but how had he become a cowhand?

No answers, of course, so she turned to one of her perennial inquiries, *Why do birds sing?* A truly satisfactory solution never materialized, but this question often diverted other trains of thought.

The days plodded on until late one afternoon the next week, the hens cackled as Meta milked Della. "It's all right, girls. Soon it will be dark and you can have sweet dreams. Tomorrow I'll let you out again."

Then a shout came from the creek. She started up, nearly tipping over her stool and the pail. A few minutes later, Franklin pulled Ethel into the open and made his way up the bank.

Such an indescribable sensation—like a caged hen set free. Once more, Father Christmas had come.

Pax whinnied, so unlike him in the evening. Clay grabbed his coat and, at the last moment, his gun.

The plain shone clear as day. Pax whinnied again, so Clay traced around the fence. A strong south wind gave him no clues.

In the barn, Pax nosed him in the neck. "What is it, fella?"

Another nuzzle.

Clay set to work with the brush.

"Not like you to get lonely, but I'll sing you a song. 'Oh, the yellow rose of Texas'..."

After a while, Pax quieted.

"Won't be long till morning, boy."

As Clay neared the cabin, Pax whinnied again.

Clay halted, easing out his gun.

Then he spied something—was that an animal lurking in the shadows? Yes, and no small one. The beast lunged as Clay pulled the trigger. Pulled it again. A great bear still lumbered forward.

On his third shot, the giant swayed like a felled tree, hanging in midair for a long minute. A strangled cry penetrated the quiet as the bear crashed to earth a few feet away.

Clay finally released his breath and took in the overwhelming smell—heavy, musky, and penetrating. Owen said bears hibernated all winter, even with temperature swings, so what had wakened this one?

Half afraid the animal would rise up, he circled with caution before kicking at a back foot. A sparkling maroon channel drained from the massive chest.

Time to work—three thick blocks wedged under the giant's lower abdomen and legs increased the flow.

Back in the barn, Clay hugged Pax. "Thanks boy. You saved my life. Now, we've got work on our hands. Mustn't throw away good meat, and the smell will draw more predators—we have a lot of cleaning up to do."

He had never field-dressed anything this big, but used what he had learned butchering cattle at the Evendsbergs. After skinning the bear, he tugged the innards onto a tarp tied behind Pax, who dragged the smelly mass onto the range. Glad for the moonlit night and biting cold, Clay cut and hauled the quarters up a ladder on the barn's north side. Strung onto hooks under the overhang, they swung like pendulums.

Dumping two buckets of water at a time, he cleared the area, rinsed his shirt in the creek and set it to soak. Finally he splashed his hands and face. In the cabin he washed again and wrapped in a blanket—sweating one minute, freezing the next.

Four warmed-over biscuits and a can of beans later, a shaft of moonlight entered from the lone window. No doubt about it, Pax had saved him. Another living being made all the difference. This had proven true with the Texas Ranger who found him, with Father Bernard, and with the Evendsbergs.

Father Bernard might have breathed his last anywhere, but fever took him as they traveled near New Braunfels on one of their excursions to teach Clay more about Texas. Camping east of the Pedernales River, Father Bernard's natural friendliness must have brought contact with the disease.

When he became so ill he could not rise from his bedroll,

someone told Clay that just a few miles north lived Pastor Evendsberg, who would help them. And he did. He and two other men came to fetch the priest, and Mrs. Evendsberg nursed him.

German Lutheran through-and-through, they spent themselves on his behalf. The *frauen* in the household sought advice from Mexicans and Native Americans and used medicines they suggested. Whispered conversations about what to do next floated around Clay as he kept watch.

But Father Bernard's breathing worsened until he passed from this world. Stunned, Clay felt completely lost. When the Evendsbergs invited him to stay on, he accepted. As German *Freidenkers,* or Freethinkers, they opened not only their home and hearts to him, but their library—so many classics that he hardly knew where to begin.

Due to Father Bernard's instruction in Latin, he studied with the oldest orphans. Outdoors with the men, he learned animal husbandry and how to coax rocky Hill Country land to productivity.

The Evendsbergs kept a rigid work schedule, yet always made time for discussions. If not for the war, Clay might have stayed forever. But after two years, Texas turned Confederate, and the Nueces Massacre of German Union sympathizers shocked the community.

Dismayed by these events, Pastor Evendsberg encouraged his charges of conscription age to ride north and fight for the Union. Alternatively, they might flee South to Mexico, as the men in the massacre had chosen.

Two years into the war, Clay ended up in North Texas at the Crady Ranch. Something about the area seemed familiar to him—perhaps his parents had passed through here. When he met one of the Crady's drovers in town and realized the ranch needed workers, he took a chance.

Learning to drove took time, but the prospects were good— both the Union and Confederate Armies needed meat, and a Wyoming Country rancher sent his foreman to drive cattle back north. Better to work on the trail to Wyoming Country than shooting fellow Americans.

With these thoughts, the image of a soft-eyed settler, freckles framed by unruly dark curls, drifted before Clay—a good German girl like Mrs. Evendsberg's daughters, devoted to *kinder, heim, und kirche*—children, home and church. But Meta had been left all alone in this world.

Now that he had found a home in these plains, perhaps she might become a friend.

Chapter Seventeen

The meadowlark is a singer of a higher order, deserving to rank with the best. Its song has length, variety, power and rich melody; and there is sometimes a cadence of wild sadness, inexpressibly touching.

~Theodore Roosevelt

Franklin strained with Ethel, whose resistance proclaimed the weight of the bulky object on her back. "Extree oats fer ya t'night, ol' gal."

"Franklin! What on earth do you have?"

"Somethin' yer husband musta ordered."

Sturdy iron legs protruded from canvas wrap. It took Meta a few moments, but then she cried, "A stove!"

Franklin patted Ethel. "Best git this thing off."

"Here, let me help you." She steadied one side as Franklin bore the weight.

"Go on now. Give Ethel a good drink."

When Meta returned, Franklin grunted and heaved as he positioned the stove under the shelves. Finally he stood back, panting.

"How did you—? I thought you were checking your traps up north?"

He nearly fell into her rocker. "Yep. This here contraption was waitin' at m' cabin." He eyed the stove.

"Livery man musta had winter fever somethin' terr'ble t' make this haul."

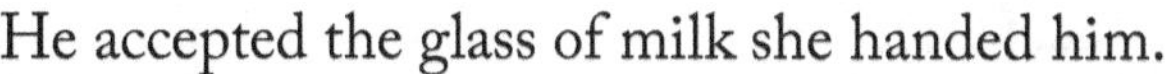

He accepted the glass of milk she handed him.

"I'll hurry with supper."

While he dozed, she acquainted herself with every knob and gadget. This would be her last baking on the plowshare—one more connection with Garrit gone.

Franklin jostled awake and joined her at the table. Before they began to eat, Meta took his knobby hand.

"Father in heaven, thank you for this food and for Franklin and Ethel, who carried my stove today. Amen."

Franklin grunted and took up his fork.

"Tell me about your travels."

"Same ol' trail."

"Did you see any Indians?"

"Sure 'nuff."

"Where?"

"In their camp." He studied his plate. "Injun young'uns help with m' traps. Sometimes, I bring 'em things from Cheyenne."

"What do you take them?"

"Mebbe a knife or cookin' pot—sometimes a sweet."

He ate a few more bites, so she started her story.

"One day I twisted my ankle. I was trying to figure out what to do when a man happened by."

Franklin narrowed his eyes.

"He works for the Oak Bar, and said Mr. Dunbar mentioned you."

"Cowhand?"

"Yes. But he helped me to the cabin and rode all the way home for some ginger root. The compress he made helped so much."

Humph.

"He took care of Hope and Della, gathered eggs and cooked pancakes."

Franklin pursed his lips. "From Texas?"

"Yes. Indians killed his parents when he was just a boy, so a priest took him in. Maybe you can meet him some day."

"Them cowhands…" He shuffled his feet. "But mebbe this feller ain't like th' rest."

"He took care of things here until I could walk again."

Soon Franklin began to yawn. "Time fer me t' turn in." He stood, and Meta hugged him.

"Thank ya fer supper." He pulled something from his coat pocket.

"Done fergot yer letters. Yer cousin musta sent 'em along with th' stove."

After the night's heavy work, Clay's arms ached. "Wish you could eat bear meat, boy. What will we do with all of this?" As he saddled Pax, an idea occurred. What if he took half of the meat to Meta, so she could share it with that trapper? And why not make the delivery today? He wrapped the quarters in a canvas and added two lengths of intestine for sausage casings. No scent from the gutting in the air. Buzzards would make short work of the carcass, and Clay made sure no trail led to the cabin before heading out.

For a time last night, he had felt so—what was the sensation? Perhaps it was being alone. Hadn't Father Bernard read him some story about this? After a few minutes, he recalled the details. More than two centuries ago the Bubonic Plague struck England—ah, this story centered on Sir Isaac Newton.

"Sir Isaac's life teaches us that solitude can be used for good, Clay." Little by little, the story surfaced. "In 1665, students at Cambridge University were sent home to avoid the disease. Instead of seeing this as a punishment, Sir Isaac set up his study and performed experiments that laid the foundation for his later work. He found consolation in what others perceived as desolation."

Hadn't his solitary life at the Crady ranch led to him coming here? As Clay rode, the thought of Garrit's dream returned. Surely he could drive some wild Texas horses here—his earnings from the drive might buy six or eight mares. But Meta would need a Fort Laramie connection. Would this prove difficult for a woman?

As he passed near a ravine about halfway between Oak Bar land and Meta's cabin, a splash of unusual color showed in the draw. Something blue. When he reached the spot, a U.S. Cavalry haversack rested near a scrub brush. Inside lay an Army-issue knife, an empty cartridge box, a fork, and a tin plate. A muslin sack held a few coffee beans, and what soldiers called *the housewife*—a rolled-up sewing kit that contained thread and needle.

Why would a soldier leave his haversack here?

The smell of salt pork laced the fabric, and with a good shaking, only a razor and some hardtack crumbs fell out. The bag fit under Clay's blanket, to deal with later.

At Meta's, he peeked into the barn and called her name. Straw rustled and she stood before him, freckles even more vibrant than he recalled.

"Clay Burns! You came back."

"Brought you quite a gift, too." He led the way to Pax. "A bear paid me a visit last night. Here's half of what's left of him."

She pushed curls out of her eyes. "

"Thank you—our ham is almost gone."

"Where shall we hang it? Needs to be salted down or made into sausage in the next few days."

"How about there?" She pointed to a log sticking out under the barn roof, so Clay maneuvered the bags over each side. "This'll do just fine, out of the sun." Meta wiped her hands on some snow. "I must be a sorry sight. I was cleaning out the chicken cages. I have forgotten my manners. Are you hungry?"

"Always, and toting raw meat is hard work."

"What if I make some eggs and ham?"

"Sounds good. I haven't had eggs since my last visit, and Pax is mighty thirsty. I'll take him down to say hello to Hope and Della."

He staked Pax and washed his hands and face. Might as well stretch his legs up the hill to Garrit's grave.

Garrit Kreiner Rausch
1835–1864

Twenty-nine years. So many graves like this in Texas and along the trail to Wyoming. But now the war had produced tens of thousands more. *We only have this moment. We must make the most of each day.* Something from a book at the Evendsbergs, or perhaps one of Father Bernard's sayings.

Back at the cabin, he noticed the stove right away. Meta happily explained.

"I had forgotten Garrit ordered it, but someone delivered it to Franklin's cabin. Now we can eat real bread instead of biscuits."

Over ham and eggs, her eyes glistened as she described Ethel's struggle. "Franklin has done so much for me."

"I hope to meet him one of these times."

"He disapproves of cowhands." Her dimple showed. "You would have to win him over." The quiet highlighted the cabin's creaks and groans. "How did you come by the meat?"

"Not with ease. Pax warned me, but I didn't notice anything until the bear lunged."

"Weren't you terrified?"

"I'll say, but everything happened so fast. Afterward, I got to considering how things might have gone without Pax. Amazing how animals see with their noses." Clay paused for a bite. "One more in a long list of deliverances. Makes me thankful for every breath."

"You think God was watching over you?"

"Father Bernard would say so, and I have no better explanation. But I do wonder why some folks live and others die. Your husband had a dream, but I don't."

"The ranch, yes. It has been on my mind, but sometimes I think I must be daft. What can I do to fulfill Garrit's dream?"

"They say dreams take time." Clay slid back his chair. "But I need to earn my keep. Thank you kindly for the eggs."

A long curl slipped from its pins, and with a frown, Meta tucked it back. "I have a stock of eggs—would you like some?"

With a nod, Clay went out, and after a few minutes she joined him to stroke Pax.

"Thank you for the meat."

"I've heard a little soda in boiling water takes out the wild taste." Clay tipped his hat and packed the eggs she handed him.

"You will come again?"

"Sure will."

The wind picked up, bringing the ever-present scent of sage, in spite of the season. Father Bernard said the ancient Romans used this herb for stomach and breathing ailments—such a healing essence over this land. Hopefully it would waft to Meta over the next few days and renew her strength.

Pax picked up the pace as if he sensed the urgency, and realization struck Clay. He had made this settler girl another promise.

Martin's letter kept Meta thinking. He referred to a relative who fought in the Revolution, a cousin on Papa's side—a Frenchman who joined the Patriots and eventually settled in Indiana. This time, Martin wrote more about that long-ago war than the present one.

> *A comrade from New York reminded me how things can change during war. In the summer of 1776, General Howe staged his force of more than 400 ships and 32,000 troops around Staten Island in New York Harbor. George Washington sent about 8,000 American troops to Brooklyn Heights—the western edge of Long Island.*
>
> *But the British landed 15,000 troops behind American lines—such heavy losses for the Patriots, their backs to the East River. But strong winds, an ebbing tide, and pouring rain prevented further British attacks and kept the regulars from moving warships into the East River to cut off an escape.*

General Washington ordered a nighttime evacuation. At about eleven, the wind died down, and a thick fog blew in. The next morning, the British discovered that the Americans had fled—but where? The fog shrouded the evacuation and many, including Washington, attributed their successful retreat to an act of God.

Some called the weather a heavenly messenger—without its aid, the the whole Army of the Potomac would have been killed or taken prisoner. Some term this deliverance, 'Miracle in the Mist,' since it allowed the Revolution to continue.

I recall hearing this story at school but had forgotten. So when you pray for our victory, please keep the weather in mind.

In full sun, Clay lined salted bear meat on a burlap bag. The rest, chopped fine and seasoned, he stuffed into casings before riding the range in the afternoons.

Now, his supply would seemingly last forever.

One afternoon, he pondered the mystery haversack he had found. Why not deliver it to Fort Laramie tomorrow?

Before dawn, he packed his saddlebag and headed toward the Chugwater River bend. From there, the Fort lay due northeast.

Over windblown snow on low-lying hills, Clay pulled up his scarf—Meta had used it to wrap the eggs she gave him, along with a message.

Thank you for being a good neighbor. Meta.

The brown knitted wrap still carried the same flowery fragrance as her hair. As evening descended, a slender half-canyon welcomed his campfire, and he bit into a piece of hardtack. The fire warmed him against a wind from the West, but how he would enjoy warm bread, Iowa honey, fried eggs, ham, and someone to share this meal.

The stars shone extra bright, igniting all sorts of thoughts. What role did the heavenly bodies play in this world? Father Bernard, of course, had ideas.

No one can count the stars, but we must ponder Copernicus and Galileo—the heavens fascinated them. And Sir Isaac Newton, though he called Nature simple, performed experiments to decipher planetary secrets. For now, remember this: the stars have long guided men on their journeys, including the Wise Men in their search for the King.

Father Bernard read aloud Newton's *Optics* and *The Principia*—how did using mirrors and spectacles affect light? What role did friction play in the universe? How did the moon draw the tides?

So many inquiries... Sir Isaac respected those who paved the way, like Descartes, but also explained where he believed they had erred. He did this by comparing his findings with their writings.

He wanted to know about the energy he labelled electricity—a vapor, a fluid, or an ether? Which, particles or waves, make up the light's essence and what forms rainbows? And how does putrefaction work to recreate life?

The earth is the offspring of silence and meditation. Sir Isaac believed time a moving thing, with velocity a function of time. Father Bernard paused a moment before asking, *What do you think he meant?*

The quote still danced in Clay's head without a satisfactory answer. But as time passed, he realized that no one concept meant everything. Above all, Father Bernard wanted to teach him to *think*. And think he did—out on these plains, Sir Isaac's inquiries still reverberated. A pleasant diversion at time, but these quandaries plied like thorns when he ought to be sleeping.

Despite the canyon wall, the wind reached his campsite. Finally falling asleep, Clay woke when his nose tingled. But Meta's gift had warmed his neck.

A few hours later from a hilltop, the convergence of the North Platte and Laramie Rivers near Fort Laramie proclaimed the Army survey team's expertise. Guards could view miles on every side. Compared to Fort Clark in Southern Texas, the outlay resembled a town.

Wagons awaited approval for entrance under a high-flying Stars and Stripes——too busy a place to dawdle.

The flag flapped, alerting Pax. Clay crooned in his ear as a sentry finally gestured their way.

"Your name?"

"Clay Burns."

"Business?"

"Thought someone here might want this haversack I found."

"Sure you just found it?"

He returned the soldier's stare.

Finally, the fellow retreated into the guardroom with the pack and returned few minutes later with a private.

"Follow me." The private swung onto his horse. Several two-story officers' homes lined one side of the parade ground and a line of enlisted men's barracks the other. The whole place buzzed with activity—any amount of time here would be more than enough. At the largest building, the guide motioned Clay down a hallway. Inside a small office, he addressed an officer behind a desk.

"Man says he found this, sir."

"Thank you, Private. Dismissed." The sentry retreated as the officer sized him up.

"Tell me where you found this, Mr.—"

"Burns. I spied the pack in a ravine."

The officer rifled through the contents and held out his hand. "I'm Captain Reynolds. Anything else in here when you found it?"

"No."

"A photograph of a woman?"

"Nope. I put everything back. Found it a few days ago."

The captain shuffled through the haversack again.

"A deserter might have swung down that way."

A sick sensation rose—how might a deserter treat a solitary young settler woman?

"I'll keep an eye out, sir."

Captain Reynolds thanked him as he turned to go, and then

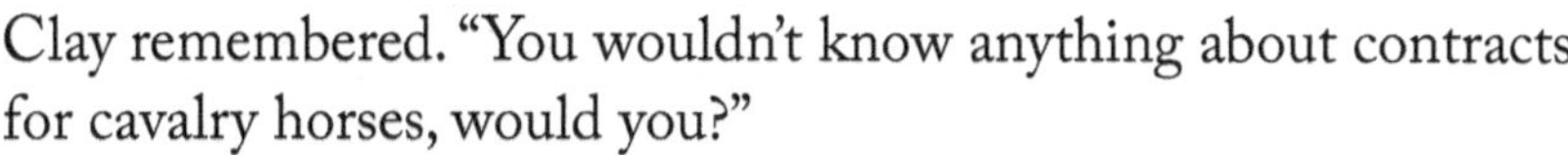

Clay remembered. "You wouldn't know anything about contracts for cavalry horses, would you?"

"Some. You're interested?"

"Maybe."

"If you move ahead, contact me or Major Miles."

Near the parade ground, eight soldiers in blues stood at attention with rubber ponchos over their left shoulders and tied under their right arms like fat black snakes. Everyone carried a canteen, a rifle, and ammunition in homemade cartridge belts. Prepared for a march, they had tied their socks around their pant legs.

This life held no appeal—too much like his years with the Sisters. No one to be found if you needed help, yet when you made one wrong move, someone always appeared.

Across the parade grounds, a native interpreter stood out. His leggings and wide hat seemed more practical than the uniforms. His prominent nose and brow brought recollections of the sick Indian he had cared for.

What had become of his friend?

Chapter Eighteen

*Late at night we were awaked by the sergeant on guard
to see the beautiful phenomenon called the northern light: along
the northern sky was a large space occupied by a light of a
pale but brilliant white colour: which rising from the horizon,
extended itself to nearly twenty degrees above it. After glittering for some time its colours would be overcast, and almost
obscured, but again it would burst out with renewed beauty;
the uniform colour was pale light, but its shapes were various
and fantastic: at times the sky was lined with light coloured
streaks rising perpendicularly from the horizon, and gradually
expanding into a body of light in which we could trace the
floating columns sometimes advancing, sometimes retreating
and shaping into infinite forms, the space in which they moved.
It all faded away before the morning.*

~Nicholas Biddle,
expanding on Lewis and Clark journals, 1814

All too soon Franklin had to leave, but until then, he spent
evenings listening to Meta's letters. He seemed never to tire of
hearing the same old news, and neither did Meta.

Betsy's perfect handwriting contained news of someone
Meta thought she would never hear of again.

*Hildegard and Rudolph's children have been taken in
by others, since the cholera took her almost overnight. I carried
food to them, and Hildegard had shrunken to half her size. Such*

a strong woman at the beginning of our trek—I still find it difficult to believe she has passed.

Rudolph, I think, realized he could not carry on with the children, and began to parcel them out soon after Hildegard's burial. So tragic, but I hope they have found good homes. Two of them have, for certain, for Elsbeth and Adolph took them in—what a comfort they will be in their old age.

What will become of Rudolph? Even my imagination fails me—he has little strength to work, and even less heart. He gave their wagon to a family in need, and rides in the back all day like a child.

"Soun's like thet feller jest give up."

Talking with Franklin sufficed, but oh, to spend one single hour with Betsy, discussing all of this! Letters were the next best, so Franklin's saddlebag toted hours of Meta's writing when he left, including a letter to Miss Brunner, describing several native plants.

A few days later, she started more correspondence for the next trip, penning long missals to Greta and Alma as well as Mama, Lissa, and Betsy. Then one to Martin, to include in Mama's envelope. At the same time, she began sketching the plants she could recall for Miss Brunner. Karl Speigelhalter came to mind, but what to write? Finally, she began.

"Dear Mr. Speigelhalter, Thank you for thinking of me in your sad loss, but I plan to stay here until..." Until what? She scratched out *until* and placed a period behind *here*. Then she added "Sincerely," and signed her name.

"There."

Outdoors, she yearned for a long trek, but recalled her promise to Franklin. The animals scavenged near the creek, so she followed it north until the hilltop came into view. Even this short venture enlivened her—so much to explore. Winter would soon abate—bitter cold always softened into springtime.

Her ruminations halted, for ahead something stirred—a

coyote or a startled rabbit? Near some tall grass on the opposite bank, a peculiar gleam beckoned.

Against thin ice, the glinting object showed a handle—a tin cup—and nearby, a blue swatch. Muddy boot prints blurred where someone had crossed in a hurry. A frigid finger traced Meta's spine—she must get home. One more glance revealed an insignia on the blue fabric—an Army cap like Martin's. But why would a soldier come here all alone?

Panting, she passed Garrit's grave. Logic said this ought not frighten her so, but her heart drummed. The wayfarer had fled her approach—baffling and chilling all at once.

Before dark, she settled the animals, barred the door, and fixed hot coffee. In her rocker, "In Thee do I put my trust... God is our refuge and strength... He that keepeth Israel shall not slumber..." calmed her.

Oh, for Franklin's familiar, *howdy*. The long evening pulsed with sounds that normally would not have troubled her. Like ants on honey, her qualms multiplied. What if Della went missing in the morning, or Hope, or both?

Did she need to reconsider Karl Speigelhalter's offer—perhaps returning home would be best. Her prayers sifted back from the rafters, but she must talk with someone.

"My heart fails me. Help me to trust."

Long hours passed in fits and starts. When Della mooed, Meta crept to open the door. A light snow, but everything appeared as she left it. A sparrow twittered from the juniper.

Then one simple truth dissolved her tension. This snow dusting would reveal tracks if anyone had come close. Perhaps an Indian had found the cup and hat, but why would they have left them here?

Betsy's last letter mentioned a Lakota uprising near the Bighorns, and over his last breakfast here, Franklin's opinion sided with the Indians.

"Chief Red Cloud's war party kilt a whole Army patrol in December up toward Montana Territory. Thet off'cer Fetterman let Injuns lead 'is men too far from th' fort. Mostly Arapahoes here. Congrigate west o' Laramie,with th' Fort built up. Lakotas stay in Dakota Terr'try."

"But why did Red Cloud—"

"Cheyennes like th' Powder River country by th' Wolf Mountains. Shoshones and Arapahos stick pretty fer northwest. Lakotas been forced here by th' gov'ment—two-sided talkin'. Gold diggers struck gold in Bozeman, passin' through th' big huntin' grounds—thet's all Injuns got left fer huntin'."

He ate a few bites of ham.

"Gov'ment called a council. Red Cloud come, but th' gov'ment brought hunderds o' troops. Riled Red Cloud. Then Covington set a line Fetterman weren't t' cross. But he done it anyhow."

Quite a speech—Meta understood only parts but waited with her questions.

"I tol' th' Chiefs 'boutcha. Most of 'em owe me favors. 'Sides, Injuns shy away 'tween Spring Creek n' the burial grounds a mile off."

He drew two squiggly lines on the table and pointed far south. "Yer man picked a fine claim. If Injuns ever does come, jest say, *Ross*."

His certainty buoyed her.

She determined to follow the same short route. Seeing the hat and cup would mean the owner had moved on.

And the two abandoned objects still lay covered with snow. Sunshine caught a bare spot like a glory. "When we are faithless, our Creator remains faithful." Pastor Schultz said this over Papa's grave, Margita said.

Last night she had turned faithless, unreliable like the weather, sunshine and frost at once. Perhaps Bergita's death had changed Papa in the same way. A *thrum* vibrated as she turned. As if to mock her, her heart went wild once more.

A Mid-March wind provoked more pondering. Wildflowers would soon brighten this landscape—did blue bonnets grow here as in Texas? Pax's rhythm steadied Clay. A day had passed since meeting Captain Reynolds, leaving a troubling question. *What if the deserter became disoriented again?* Clay made up his mind and turned Pax toward Meta's cabin.

Less than an hour later, Meta burst from the cabin door before Clay could even dismount. The look in her eyes pitched his heart into his throat. Before he could take a step, she flung herself into his arms. He caught his breath and grasped her shoulders.

"What is it? Has someone . . ?"

"I have been so frightened." Her body trembled.

Heat and ice chased his spine—*if that deserter had been here*—every heartless cowpoke he ever met coursed through his mind.

"Has someone hurt you?"

"N-no." She wiped her cheeks. "But someone has been here."

"How long ago?"

"Yesterday afternoon north of the creek, I saw—" She cradled her throat with her fingers. "I heard something like a rabbit, and saw a tin cup, a blue cap, and boot prints." She pressed the sides of her dress with her hands.

"Show me where you saw the cup." He reached for her hand. "Take me there." With Pax close behind, they started toward the creek.

After a few minutes, she paused and pointed. "See where the water narrows into ice? The tracks went that way."

Clay gathered the deserter's belongings. "A Fort Laramie officer mentioned a recent deserter. Pax and I will follow him for a distance—then you can rest easy."

"Oh, thank you. I let my fears—"

"With good reason." He pulled Della and Hope's stakes and led them toward the barn.

"Let's put them inside early. Bar the door. I'll be back before dark."

Her freckles and wayward curls bespoke her youth. But the look in her eyes, so vulnerable, shrouded his heart. Responsibility slipped over his shoulders like a breeze, a reason to wake up in the morning.

Captain Reynolds was probably right—the confused soldier threatened only himself. Otherwise, why would he dash off at a woman's approach? Yet Meta's fear was as real as this rocky earth. Within half an hour, Clay realized the soldier had gotten hopelessly lost. Eventually his tracks crossed back over the creek and headed due east. Frozen to the bone, most likely.

Recalling the terror in Meta's eyes, he turned back toward the cabin. Having her run to him—holding her for those moments—had changed things. Like Father Bernard's riddles or the Evendsberg's evening readings, he puzzled over the meaning.

Sir Isaac's axioms offered no help now. What mortal might ascertain things of the heart?

Clay's findings quieted the storm inside Meta. Toting the milk pail, she kept watch as dusk stroked the sky reddish-orange. Three fresh eggs nestled in her apron when Pax whinnied from the creek.

The sunset profiled Clay's lanky form. All was well, of course. He must think her daft. He led Pax up the slope and paused at the campsite. Soon sparks flamed against twilight... so lovely juxta-posed. The hollows of his cheekbones reflected a steady blaze, and gratitude swelled in her like a song. A second time he had arrived just when she needed him.

She cooked dried corn with bear meat for stew. Soon they devoured everything with bread and honey.

"Our woebegone soldier finally ventured northeast. Circling North to be sure he stays on track won't take me long in the morning." Clay filled his plate again. "Good stew. Right now, I'm glad that old bear woke up."

She returned his grin. He helped her with the dishes and made to leave.

"Thank you for following that man."

"He left so many clues, any cowpoke could have tracked him."

"But it's you who did."

Full dark had descended. "There's quite a spectacle in the sky of late. Comes, let's look at the lights."

Grabbing her shawl, Meta stepped into a world of wonder, filled with a peculiar pale light. Unique varied shades of green and gray undulated above, sometimes with vertical streaks like pillars. But those pillars kept moving, forward and backward, nearer and farther away.

Leaning against the cabin with Clay nearby, she stood in awe. What could be happening in the heavens? But this was no time for words, and Clay seemed to sense the same.

This was a time to watch, to wait, and to ponder.

At breakfast, Meta's voice pared to a whisper. "I knew this would be difficult, but—" Her shoulders slumped. "Maybe I cannot see Garrit's plans through."

"Sometimes waiting qualifies as action. Like with those lights last night. We only watched."

What he had learned from Captain Reynolds sat on the tip of Clay's tongue. Against his better judgment, he found that the message would not wait. "You know that Army Captain at Fort Laramie I spoke of? I asked if he knew about horse contracts."

"You did?"

"Yes. And he does, and said to let him know if I am ever interested."

Like waterfall in a canyon, her laughter swept over Clay. Then she sobered.

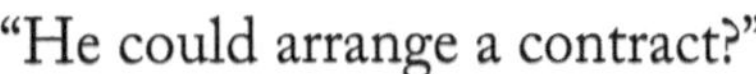

"He could arrange a contract?"

"He gave me a Major's name."

Color returned to her cheeks. Excitement engulfed him, too, coupled with niggling doubt. "There's no guarantee."

"How would we find the horses? How would we—"

"I have some ideas. Would you consider working together?"

"You mean you would—" Her eyes fixed on his. "Oh, Clay. This gives me hope. That's how we named our mare, the beginning of our herd. How did you name Pax?"

"From the sign over an archway a long time ago. I passed under that word often with Father Bernard."

The morning's warmth heightened as she digested his answer. Then she whispered, "Peace and hope. They go together well."

Chapter Nineteen

The pain passes but the beauty remains.
~Pierre-Auguste Renoir

Surely he must be nearing the deserter's trail—Pax had galloped several miles. Just then, something moved in the distance, and Clay watched for a long minute—a fuzzy rectangle bobbed this way. Soon he made out a fur cap and beard, knitted ear coverings, a rawhide coat.

The poor fellow stumbled in the snow, so Clay dismounted. Bushy eyebrows, white beard crusted with ice, Franklin Ross materialized before his eyes. He extended his hand.

"You must be Mr. Ross. Clay Burns, sir."

"Cowhand?"

"I work for Owen Dunbar of the Oak Bar."

Humph.

"An Army deserter scared Meta, so I tracked him up Spring Creek."

Humph. "He's headed outta th' Territ'ry."

"Good." Clay saw that Franklin's moccasins were frozen to his buckskin. "Are you headed to Meta's?"

"Mebbe."

"Would you—" Finally, Clay blurted, "Want to go together?"

"No use slowin' ya down. Feet bin givin' me fits."

"What if you ride my horse?"

"Don't know's I could make it up there."

"It's worth a try." Clay made a step with his hands.

Grunting and groaning, Franklin pulled himself up and turned midway. "Ethel, you corperate with this here fella now."

Clay picked up the reins, and Ethel followed Pax.

"Didja see thet greenhorn? Stockins' froze right t''is skin."

"You gave him your boots?"

"'Bout all I had t' offer."

An oft-quoted phrase from the past filled Clay's mind.:

Greater love hath no man...

Garrit's grave called, so Meta set the animals to graze and climbed the hill. From this point, vast grasslands extended east, interrupted by lonely clumps of twisted trees, markers of fierce winds and bitter winters, with quartz outcroppings here and there.

Time had worked its art, bending the trees and even altering the shape of rocks. And so it would with her. This truth crept along her bones…like Mama, she would shrink with age, and her bones turn brittle—but not her spirit.

"Garrit, remember in Nebraska before we spied Scott's Bluff? You said, It has to be over the next rise. This is how I feel about Spring." She rearranged some shifted rocks that had sunken. Once again, time at work.

Voices drifted then—*Clay's and Franklin's?*

She hurried toward the cabin for a better view. *Ah…Clay leading Ethel, and Franklin… astride Pax?* Alarm skittered her backbone. *Hurry…a fresh pot of coffee.* She sliced bread and set out the honey. By the time she went back outside, the two men neared.

"Howdy do!" Franklin perked up as Clay helped him down. Looking like a snowman, Franklin grabbed his knee and muttered. Clay bore his weight as Meta scurried to help. In the cabin, Franklin remained silent when she warmed his hands between her palms while Clay unlaced his moccasins.

"We need water at room temperature." He hoisted Franklin up with the quilt. "Can you sit?"

"Course!"

"All right, we'll pull your legs over the side."

During the process, Franklin fell asleep. Several toes looked white and waxy, the skin a mottled gray.

"They feel soft underneath—not the worst case." Clay's eyes darkened.

"Shall I—"

"Pa's drinkin' agin. Gotta get Ma outta…"

Over their patient's head, Clay caught Meta's eye.

"Franklin, would you like some coffee?"

He twisted and turned. Then, "Gotta get 'er outta here."

"Bring a cup. We'll see if he can drink."

A swallow did wonders, and Franklin lifted his hand when Meta poured a little more coffee into his mouth. After another sip, he sat up straighter.

"Got me a powerful hunger, gal."

The best words he could have said—Meta set to cooking. A powerful hunger and a strong memory of home, like the *hiraeth* Betsy spoke of—*a place to which you can never return, perhaps a place that never even was.* For Franklin, perhaps not so pleasant, a place you took leave of gladly.

Now Franklin seemed aware only of the present, so Meta asked, "How did you two meet?"

"This young feller jest come right up." The twinkle reinstated itself in Franklin's eyes, and Clay took up the tale.

"We had been tracking the same man." Clay turned his attention back to Franklin's feet. "And this fella gave his boots to an Army straggler."

Franklin bristled. "Feet's seen worse days. Been frostbit many a time."

"Can you move your toes?"

Water splashed as Franklin responded.

"Then I can leave you in good hands and be on my way. I do hope you rest here a while."

The two men shook hands. "Right glad ya come 'long with thet good horse." Franklin leaned back exhausted, and Meta followed Clay outside.

"Our deserter's likely across the border by now, nearing home in Franklin's boots and socks."

"He gave them—"

"To a total stranger. Meeting your trapper friend scared me at first, but what a good heart he has."

"You were afraid?"

"You said he scorns cowhands." Clay tipped his hat.

"You mentioned the ranch—"

"I need to think on this some more. I'll check on Franklin in a few days."

Clay mounted and Pax turned south as if he knew the way, and the vista soon swallowed them up.

Those old gnarled cottonwoods told a story. After these winter months, the tale had become part of Meta. She belonged in this Wyoming Country. Her declaration carried on the wind.

"Franklin and Clay—my only two friends in the whole of this huge land. Yet they somehow found each other."

"Dang blasted feet!" Franklin's wince hurt Meta too.

"Ain't fittin'—"

"But Franklin—"

"Be hornswaggled if I sleep in yer bed!"

His show of spirit brought a relieved sigh. Only a few hours ago, Clay brought Franklin home with frostbite.

"Just for one night—you can use the rocker or sleep by the hearth."

"Heered ya—jest one night."

Relishing this victory, she set to work on some biscuits as creaking floorboards announced Franklin using the bench and table to reach the rocker. A mighty heave announced success.

Such a faithful friend—his eyes had already closed. What would have become of her without him? She turned the fritters and poured the milk.

He awakened when she brought his supper plate, and accepted it with his usual zest.

"Biscuits n' Ioway honey. Ain't nothin' better."

"Tell me about that deserter, Franklin."

But he had a question first, his eyebrows forming a sincere line. "Do ya think the Lord'll git me fer swearin'?"

"We both can be hard on ourselves. I worry about my disobedience to Garrit, too."

"Nothin' t' do 'bout thet now."

"I know, but my feelings don't. I believe it's more likely God notes you helping a stranger rather than your language. Now give me the whole story."

"Ain't much t' tell—farm boy skeered n' sick. Soldierin' weren't right fer 'im, anybody could see thet."

"You gave him your socks and your boots?"

Franklin worked around the topic. "Hardtack n' beans was all I had fer 'im. Froze clear through. Early on, I wouldn'a give a plug nickel fer 'im."

"He slept by your fire?"

"Mmm. By mornin' he could stand. Said he oughta move on."

"Do you think the Army will find him?"

"Not if he keeps t' 'is course."

"How did you meet Clay?"

"Why, he come up n'—" Franklin wrinkled his nose. "Reckon th' good Lord sent 'im."

"That's how I felt when he came along to help me, too."

"I s'pect some folks has second sight. They jest know things."

"I imagine—what a special gift. Do you remember Garrit's dream?"

"'Bout them horses."

"Clay may want to raise horses too."

"Ya reckon?"

"At Fort Laramie, he asked an officer about a contract."

"Fort—say, I got ya some letters from there—lookee 'n m' saddlebag." Franklin knit his brow again and soon a loud snore issued from the rocker.

She found the packet—oh what treasure!

Spits and sputters from the fire marked the evening's passage, comfort in each spark. And the letters—Martin had traveled home during a lull in the fighting. Mama called this her best gift. Franklin snorted but stayed asleep. In every way but blood, this mountain man had become her Papa. Leaving the other letters for tomorrow, Meta took up her needles. Providence had led her here and was knitting something, too, beyond her knowing.

"Come'n, ya blamed orn'ry pole!"

On her way from washing clothes, Meta stopped by. "Franklin, whatever are you doing?"

"Riggin' a clothesline. Dad blame it!" He nursed a black-and-blue thumb.

"Thank you. This will make hanging clothes so much easier."

Did his beard hide a shy smile? Little-by-little, she'd begun to ascertain his mood despite that hairy outgrowth.

On this clear spring-like day, what else might she hang out here? The featherbed, Mama's quilt, all the clothing she had neglected during the cold months. For now, though, she contented herself with gulping great drafts of warmer air—just like back home, Spring did not disappoint.

Each breath signaled a renewed beginning. Garrit would be pleased with the clothesline—with Franklin's attention to the small things. And perhaps—just perhaps—Clay would come along one day soon, with news portending the future.

The dream entered Clay's consciousness intent on staying. Whether he rode the range or cooked or read, the ranch idea grew. This morning, a hint of green dusted the range, and sunshine on his back reminded him of Texas. That thought led to finding a starter herd. A fox whizzed by, rusty fur gleaming. Must have a nest somewhere around here, and perhaps small mouths to feed.

Across a wide meadow with tiny white and purple flowers, the partially frozen ground turned mushy. He urged Pax around, dismounted, and walked back. In a few seconds, the heels of his boots dampened. In another, they sank an inch. Water gurgled from somewhere, steady, reliable. Could this be one of those artesian wells Mr. Dunbar mentioned?

With such a well, one might pipe water to a trough—this land could become a homestead. The concept scuttled like a grass-hopper in August, and by the time he rode on, a new determination formed. Before round-up, he would claim this land. Some day, he might show Meta this well. But not until he could also tell her something else, an undeniable reality that nestled deep down within alongside the home feeling.

As Pax galloped the hill before her place, her skirt danced in a strong spring wind. Beside her, something snapped—a rope of some sort. Ah, a clothesline! Clay hurried to grab an end of the blanket she struggled to secure.

"Oh, thank you. These do get heavy."

The sun glinted on every curl, and her voice flowed like music.

"How'd you get yourself a clothesline with this hard ground?"

"Franklin—sheer determination."

Her eyes turned darker, if that were possible.

"He has me worried."

"His feet?"

"No, they're much better. He went down to his cabin this morning to stretch his pelts."

She hung some dishtowels. Clay overturned her empty basket and water drops flew into the breeze like children at play.

"One day, though, he said he feels useless now." She bit her lip. "I—Mama said that men sometimes have trouble with big changes—especially growing older."

She clipped the last clothespin and turned away. Clay had to lean in to catch her last words. "I should never have told you."

"Why not?"

Without looking his way, she sought a bucket in the barn and headed toward the creek. Clay tied Pax near Hope and went to say hello to Della.

Down the bank, Meta filled her bucket. Her concern about Franklin made sense, but the old trapper would find something to do, wouldn't he? When Clay turned, she had slipped right beside him. He had never seen her face so intent.

"Let me try again."

"Is this only about Franklin?"

"I told you Papa died an untimely death, but..." The sun dipped under a cloud as she hesitated.

"He—" She smoothed her collarbone. "He could never forgive himself for an accident that killed my little sister. He backed a wagon over Bergita in our yard. She passed in his arms, and one night, he..."

Those dusky eyes pooled. "He hung himself out in our hayloft." Sickness engulfed Clay, and struck him wordless.

"When Franklin talks like this, I get so afraid he might—"

"Oh, Meta."

She looked off into the distance.

"I don't even remember Bergita. Papa—I do recall him, but barely. But every time Franklin— Maybe he would never do such a thing, but he means so much to me."

"We can help him make a new life."

Her sigh split the air. "You think so?"

"I do." About halfway up the hill, Clay pulled her around.

"Remember a few months back when you said you were sorry my parents died? Now it's my turn. What a terrible end for your Papa, and such a misfortune for your family."

"I have never told anyone. Our whole community knew, of course, but Mama never allowed us to mention Papa."

"Mmm. Secrets from the past sure do weigh us down."

She started back to the cabin, and the moment ended. But she had trusted him with a long-held confidence. This truth warmed him through.

Chapter Twenty

"If I owned Texas and Hell, I would rent out Texas and live in Hell."

~General Philip Henry Sheridan

"Where'd you get those boots, Franklin?"

"From Meta—good uns, too."

Garrit's boots. Clay laid down his axe to shake hands.

"Fixin' t' light some big fire, son?"

"Another storm might still be lurking."

"Talkin' like a real Wyomin' man now." Franklin glanced northwest. "Wouldn't be s'prised, neither, so I stretched m' pelts quick-like."

"Your feet all right now?"

"Like new, but ol' buzzards like me gits rheumatiz. Ain't good fer nothin' no more. So show me how fast ya kin bust thet branch, cowhand!"

A few blows brought success, and they stacked wood until Meta called them to eat. Murmuring to Pax and Hope, Clay washed up.

"If horses can pray, you two, I need help. The last thing Meta needs is to get her hopes up only to be disappointed."

Their nickers followed him up the incline, where Franklin met him at the door.

The warm aroma of egg noodles cooked in bear broth would have enticed a king. Franklin rubbed his belly. "Mmm—nobody but Germans make noodles like this."

"Where did your people hail from, Franklin?"

"Don't rightly know. Mebbe some was Scots. "Member my Da' sayin' somethin' 'bout hurkle-durklin'."

"What does that mean?" Meta fetched seconds.

"Don't rightly know, but I think it was the Scottish in 'im."

"That wood pile grew a lot this morning."

"Good work for cowpokes."

Clay cleared his throat. "I told you I would think about the horses..."

Her eyes shone so bright, he had to collect his thoughts. "I have tried and tried, but..."

Her chin rose a smidgeon.

"I can find no fault with the idea." He turned to Franklin.

"What do you think of raising horses for the Army?"

"Gotta git 'em somewheres. Why not here?"

"I know where we could find a starter herd." Clay swabbed his broth with his bread. "You know much about horses?"

"What I rec'lect from Missouri—after thet, it was all mules fer me. But I ain't skeered a horseflesh, neither."

"We would need a shelter, harness and tack, a few mares and a stallion."

"We brought some tack from Iowa, and I have seventy dollars left. How many horses would that buy?" The glimmer in Meta's eyes increased.

"Mebbe two."

"My pay from this winter could buy a few more."

At Clay's admission, Franklin kneaded the fringe of his buckskin with his calloused fingers.

"Got me some gold stashed. I got hides I kin build fer harness n' tack. You two want 'nuther pardner?"

Meta threw her arms around his neck. He luxuriated for a second but shook himself loose with a sputter.

"So, whaddya say?"

"You would make the best partner we could ever imagine."

Meta's smile ignited two dimples as she took her seat again and poured more coffee.

Clay leaned his chair back. "Such wild country between here and Texas—storms, Indians, bandits—"

What he saw in their eyes stopped him short. They believed in the dream. And they believed in him. Now, he would have to believe in himself.

Two rabbits, still warm, lay on the stoop when Meta opened the door this morning. Had Franklin gone hunting so early? When she checked, his thick buffalo robe still showed trapper-sized lumps.

Rabbit stew... such a treat! She would surprise him with dumplings. Fetching her dishpan and knife, she headed for the creek, all the while pondering who had brought the game.

Halfway there, she sensed someone watching. Knowing Franklin slept near at hand calmed her, but her curiosity rose. Peering into the foliage revealed nothing, and soon summer's leaves would obscure even more.

Spring brought out the worst in the wolves, and the stench of carcasses. But riding range provided a perfect chance to recollect.

Franklin now talked of building a new cabin on the northernmost end of his claim, adjoining Meta's. This would double their grazing land.

Clay analyzed their plan once again, searching for flaws. But why not expect good things? Nearly ten years ago, Father Bernard left him with a blessing: *Good will come to you, Clay. The Almighty will take care of you.* With his last breath, he repeated his blessing. *God... will take... care of... you.*

Mrs. Evendsberg held Clay close. "What a good man you have known."

Such a powerful gift, this memory. And now the future

beckoned brighter than ever before. Yet he must not act on impulse. Father Bernard emphasized careful preparation in every undertaking, so he must consult Owen Dunbar.

Then the trip to Texas would come soon enough. Either way, one decision had been made. He would stake his claim. The dream would mean both sacrifice and consolation. As with those dancing lights he had witnessed in the sky with Meta, so many questions remained. Did Sir Isaac, way across the Atlantic, ever see this heavenly phenomenon? Oh, for a mind that worked like his!

But there was only one way to discover the answers—move ahead step by step. At the same time, two other people in this world needed him now—this understanding rode with him like a quiet, reliable benediction.

"Mebbe some Injun left them rabbits."

"But I thought they never came near here because of the burial ground."

"Naw." Franklin chewed a chunk of bread the size of his fist.

"Better find some bees 'roun here. 'bout t' finish off your Mama's honey."

He had yet to learn that bringing up a new topic did nothing to diminish Meta's concern.

"Mebbe Clay brung 'em?"

"You believe he would ride all this way without talking to us?"

Franklin rolled his eyes and changed the subject again. "Been thinkin' bout ol' Stonewell Jackson n' how he died, ridin' forward on the Plank road t' see the ground his men took that day. 'Twas dark. His own men, Carolinians all, fired a volley, thinkin' his party was Federal troops."

"Yes, I do remember hearing that. I think we heard it in Cheyenne, in late May. Someone brought a newspaper from out East before we left Herman and Anna's house."

"Three bullets in his arm. Got pneumonia. Everthin' woulda

been different fer General Lee last summer with Jackson still 'live. Now the South ain't got much hope."

Meta started washing dishes—no harm in letting Franklin explore this diversion. But she had to wonder—if he were thirty years younger and still in Missouri, would he be fighting for the Confederacy?

Empty speculation, like so much about the war. If only this year would see the end of the fighting!

But the gift on the doorstep still troubled her.

As Clay provisioned his saddlebag for the trip to Cheyenne, Owen Dunbar and three cowhands rode up.

Owen offered his hand. "How you holdin' out?"

"Got your list." Mr. Dunbar scanned the record.

"About what I'd expect. We got the itch and came a little early, but I'd rather not leave any steers isolated."

He singled out two hands.

"Cover the north and west boundaries with Clay. Joe and I will ride east." He turned back to Clay. "Has winter seemed long?"

"Not especially."

"Good. Nothing like a satisfied hand."

"But you saw the losses—"

"You did your job, and the range did its job. I hope you'll stay on."

Words wrangled in Clay's head until he finally blurted,

"Could we talk more tonight?"

"Right after our beans n' bacon, son."

By evening, the corral boasted a passel of steers. Time to tell round-up tales.

"We was at th' holdin' spot, fixin' to lay the brand on a calf. The roper calls out *Circle X. Crop the right.* My flanker grabbed the hind legs. 'Nother hand held the head and front leg, so I sizzled 'er down. First thing I knew, that flanker started jumpin' like a flea, smoke rollin' off his chap. That brand wore clean through the leather. Sent 'im t' th' cook fer some linament."

Guffaws led to another tale. Mr. Dunbar nudged Clay toward the cabin and across the table, nursed his pipe.

Clay searched for words.

"That old trapper, Franklin Ross—"

"Good fella."

"Yes. And a settler along Spring Creek stayed on after she lost her husband last summer in a flood. She's all set on fulfilling his dream."

Mr. Dunbar stroked a day's stubble.

"Mr. Ross is going in with her to sell horses to the army."

Not even a blink from Owen. "I—I'm thinking on going in with them."

"Hmm." Owen nodded and the rest came easily.

"We need to round up a stallion and some mares in Texas. And something else—that stretch of land north of the creek, between your boundary and Franklin's? I plan to claim it."

"So I keep my cowhand, but you would have a place of your own?"

"As soon as I can build a cabin."

"Tell me about the woman."

"From Iowa. German background."

"No children?"

"No. She survived this winter all alone."

"Impressive. So, you three would go in together. And the horses?"

"Wild herds roam the ranchland and hills where I used to work."

"You would still have time to ride my range next winter?"

"I think so. Training might take up some mornings, though. I would let you know if my plan was failing."

"If you can do both jobs, fine. A man has to make decisions or waste his life avoiding disappointment." Owen took a puff. "Just one thing, though. I always wanted to see Texas myself—never got to go on one of my father's trips down there."

He looked off into the distance. "Did you see those lights in the sky back in March? Purple and green and white, moving like snakes in a pit. The Indians think they're the spirits of their ancestors, or the game they've shot. Anyway, watching them made me think. Life is getting shorter. Whatever I'm going to do, I need to make a plan. So I'd like to ride along with you to Texas."

Stunned, Clay absorbed his words.

"If you'd have me, that is. Might have a couple of hands interested in going, too."

"Why…sure."

"When you figure on leaving?"

"The first week of May. Back by mid-July."

"Deal." Owen held out his hand, and they shook on it. Just like that, another solution.

Restive most of the night, Clay finally chided himself.

"Father Bernard said good things would happen to me. No use trying to figure this out." The next thing he knew, the men stirred outdoors. Before they rode out, Mr. Dunbar handed him an envelope.

"Your pay. And check in Cheyenne. For range property, building a cabin might not be necessary. See you in a few weeks."

They rode off, so Clay gathered some provisions, saddled Pax, and locked up the buildings. This would be a big step toward his future, and if life had taught him one thing, it was to expect change.

On a stained map, the solicitor explained his situation. "We hope to have an official land office soon, but for now, I keep careful records of claims here in my office. Do you plan to graze cattle on your claim?"

"Horses."

"Hmm. All right. Sign here, and the land becomes yours in five years. Stop back in an hour for your copy."

No mention of a cabin, so why bring it up? Time to mark this occasion with a sarsaparilla. The saloon's cool dark interior welcomed Clay like a comrade, but after a few sips of his drink, a woman in a shiny red dress and high-heeled shoes swayed down the stairs. The mirror reflected her glance toward the portly, balding barkeeper.

The closer she came, the more Clay's neck heated. In spite of the sarsaparilla, his throat dried out.

"Hey there, cowboy." She eased onto the stool next to him, her heavy perfume hovering like evening fog. Clay's shirt tugged at his neck. "Whatcha drinkin', hon?"

"Sarsaparilla, Ma'am."

Her throaty laugh hailed the barkeeper.

"Hear that, Hank? This boy called me Ma'am."

"Best not call 'im *boy*. Men younger'n him'r layin' down their lives for the Union right now."

"What's the latest war news?" Clay figured engaging the bartender might stall off the woman.

"Still reelin' from Gettysburg n' Chicamauga. Too many men died from both sides. Got a grandson in th' cavalry, m'self. They pulled his men aside to help build th' National Cemetery. Got to hear the President's address at Gettysburg. They been in winter quarters since, but now Grant's launchin' th' Wilderness Campaign—attackin' over n' over till the South's all done-in."

With all this talk, Clay moved a couple of stools over. Clearly, he had asked the right question.

"Mighty glad California went Union—the gold out there woulda made a big difference to the Rebs. Good thing all them compromises fell through in Washington, too, 'cause we're fighting 'bout the West. Most o' the men that freed Texas hailed from the South and wanted slavery in th' new territories. "Ol' Jeff Davis was a Mexican War hero and Secretary of War from '53 to '57—he made

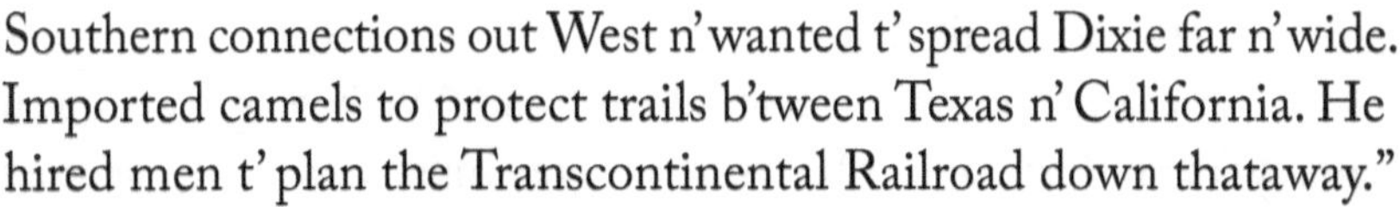

Southern connections out West n' wanted t' spread Dixie far n' wide. Imported camels to protect trails b'tween Texas n' California. He hired men t' plan the Transcontinental Railroad down thataway."

So far, so good. The woman seemed immersed in this information.

"He had plans, for sure, but Senator Douglas from Illinois proposed pop'lar sovereignty. Ya heard of such?"

"No—what does it mean?"

"Each territory decides 'bout slavery themself. That's what led to "Bleedin' Kansas," a long shoot-out 'tween border ruffians n' anti-slavery free soilers."

Most likely this bartender was first to read the newspapers when they came. You never knew what you might learn in these places.

"That slaughter led to this war we're fightin', n' then 'publicans introduced the Homestead Act, favorin' small farms 'stead o' plantations. Finally passed, but only 'cause the Southern states seceded n' took their senators with 'em. Same with th' railroad n' land-grant colleges."

About to ask a question, Clay felt something touch his shoulder. That woman moved her hand down his back. Then her whisper brushed his ear.

"Wanna come upstairs for some fun?"

"Nope. Got business to attend to." He set down the right change and headed for the door.

But she persisted. "Ever have a girl?"

"Got me a girl."

Her laugh trailed him to the door. "Don't believe ya, hon."

Outside, he re-uttered the statement.

"I've got me a girl." Sounded right. Sounded true.

At the general store, three men shared a wooden bench. One tipped his hat as Clay passed.

"Fine day." He wore a wool vest over a silk shirt, and such a hat—black, narrow brimmed—useless against this alkali dust.

"I await the Overland Stage. Do you ever take it?"

Clay shook his head.

"I'm with the Union Pacific Railroad. We have government surveyors on that stage." His trimmed grey mustache fairly gleamed as he looped his forefinger through a gold watch chain.

"You live around here?"

"Not close."

"My family back in Boston would be pleased to see a real cowboy." The Easterner caught Clay's sleeve.

"Suffer me, sir. Hear that hammering out north of town?"

No one could miss the racket, so Clay simply nodded. "Those men are building the Union Pacific Depot, you know. Won't be long and folks from far and wide'll be coming this—"

A dust cloud rose at the far end of Main Street. But the fellow seemed in no hurry.

"That must be the stage coming. You'll soon see a depot here, and a fine fort between the two creeks. There's even talk of founding a new city some distance to the north."

Pulling away, Clay retreated inside. At the entrance, rows of coats hung on either side. Along the other three walls, merchandise spread in orderly fashion, upwards on shelves, outward in well-tended bins. The establishment smelled of sardines and pickles, tobacco and leather and dyed yard goods.

Hadn't Meta said a pickle a day made a person hale? He set a pound on the counter and added a pound of dark coated creams.

Then an object on the wall caught his eye—a window glass framed between solid boards—perfect for her cabin. Studying it, he judged it just the right size—he could install it before he left. While the owner double-wrapped the package, the commotion outside died down. A hand led weary horses away to the stable as two wizened men stationed themselves like sentries beside the door

"In '57, that James Haslem fellow carried the letter. Don't believe me, go ask Mandel, what brought the hay fer th' team."

"All right, I b'lieve ya."

Dust had settled like tiny seeds on the storyteller's whiskers,

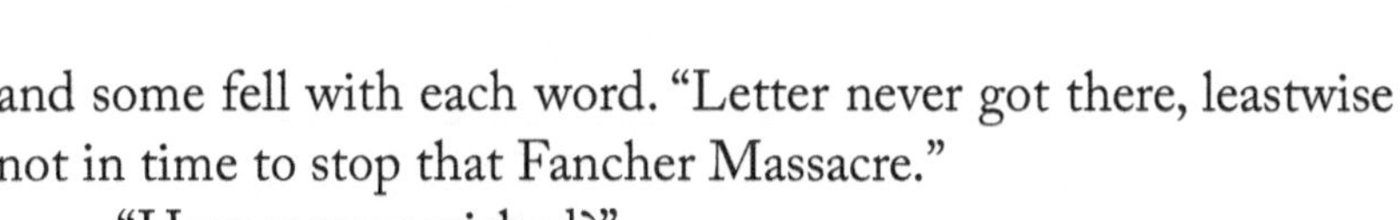

and some fell with each word. "Letter never got there, leastwise not in time to stop that Fancher Massacre."

"How many perished?"

"A hunderd n' thirty. Whole party—Iron Mountain Mormons out for Gentile blood."

"Now I rec'lect—some Arkansaw prophet got kilt n' them Fanchers hailed from there. Kilt folks out here for revenge. Anyways, thet Haslem rode almos' five-hunderd miles from Mountain Meadows t' Salt Lake City n' back in a hundred hours."

"Naw."

"Had a fresh horse for 'im ever so often. Kept jumpin' off n' on."

A story new to Clay, but it stirred questions. If this Haslem fellow rode an average of five miles an hour, could their party make the trip to the Crady ranch in a week? Returning would present more challenges, but with a bell mare as herd boss and a stud to halter and lead, things would go faster.

Just then Meta's hankering for tea came to mind. Clay returned to buy some, loaded his purchases, and led Pax to the livery stable.

The liveryman, a friendly sort, brushed a massive steed. "How many horses? Twelve, ya say? And three or four hands? Done that route. Keep close watch fer bandits—don't want t' lose your herd." *Swish... swish.*

"A chuck wagon'd slow ya down. Mebbe get a pack mule or two. String th' mules, n' one hand leads the stallion. The other three hands'd still have their work cut out, peers t' me."

After thanking him, Clay retrieved his copy of the deed and headed out. So much to take in from all across this great land. From Washington to Salt Lake City and California, history unfolded all the time. New forts, new cities—and a giant railroad snaking through the miles to connect them.

The trip to Texas, one small undertaking in this ever-changing world, but like alkali dust, the details overwhelmed him—so many dimensions to consider.

Still, Mr. Dunbar would be riding with him.

Chapter Twenty-one

Therefore am I still a lover of the meadows and the woods,
and mountains; and of all that we behold from this green earth.
~William Wordsworth

Garrit's wool trousers, clotted from past labors, still worked for mudding. Franklin had started building the shed, and Meta knew mudding as well as any man.

The work lightened her heart—with Franklin so near, she would never have another winter alone. That knowledge slipped through her consciousness throughout each day, reason to smile.

Spring had come—the future summoned like a dear companion. Soon her precious seed packets would reveal their treasures. Carrot and turnip rows on the right; onions, potatoes, and horseradish toward the back; and peas shaded by the potato plants. Mama had taught her well. In afternoon warmth, her yellow rose was beginning to show signs of life. One day, it would sprout leaves—later, blossoms would come, just like those on Mama's bush beside the back porch. In late August, she would set a yellow rose under Garrit's cross.

Just last summer, he filed this claim, and with such rocky soil, her garden had had to wait. But this year, its time had arrived.

Franklin vowed to find her some seed potatoes—why hadn't she thought to ask Anna? How her hands itched to pull sprouting potatoes from Mama's gunnysack! Still clothed in last summer's soil, they symbolized hope—that huge Iowa patch produced hundreds of pounds each season, and so it went, year after year.

And cabbage—she must find some to plant. Maybe from Anna, the next time Franklin visited Cheyenne. Anna had replenished their supply of sauerkraut when Garrit filed this claim, but it had run out weeks ago. How could a good German girl face a long winter without a goodly store?

This morning Meta searched out the kerchief of forget-me-nots Betsy had pressed into her hand. Soon they would prosper here, reminding her of her friend's gentle eyes.

Laying out the garden in her mind brought satisfaction, but a sudden tingle trilled her backbone. Someone must be watching her again—she turned a slow circle and midway, her breath caught in her throat. Tall and wide-shouldered, a solitary feather in his hair and bare legs braced, an Indian stared at her from between her cabin and Franklin's new one. Erect and still, he might have been a sturdy cottonwood sapling. His buckskin shirt extended to mid-thigh, and a colorful sash adorned his waist.

He held up his right hand. *Peace.* She forced her breathing to slow and returned the signal. Black eyes locked on hers, he advanced. Her legs turned to stone as the high ridgeline of his nose and intricate beading on his sash came into view. His skin matched the soil, and around his neck hung a rough rawhide box on a leather cord. Then he spoke, one simple word.

"Ross."

As though connected to some pulley system in the sky, her arm pointed south, so the brave altered his course and she sank on the stoop.

She had failed to follow Franklin's instructions.

"So he said *Ross* for me."

Her tension drained, but her mind still spun. It was one thing to hear her Mama tell of Indians from years past, peering in through the window of her childhood cabin; quite another to encounter one.

Now the Indian towered over Franklin and they spoke as if they had known each other forever.

Twenty minutes later, they had vanished. A single set of boot tracks led away from the new cabin toward Franklin's old one.

Perspiration soaked her back, but Meta grabbed a rake—time to check the garden plot. Two hours later, she had made some progress smoothing stubborn clay clumps, so different from Mitchell County's lush black earth.

Thankfully, Garrit hadn't planned on farming. A garden would prove challenge enough.

Suddenly, the silence felt too close. She folded the morning's washing into her basket and set out. Perhaps Franklin's visitor would share their noon meal. But the worksite lay empty as a beetle's shell at the end of summer. A few hours later, meadowlarks sang from the bushes along the creek. Still no sign of Franklin and the Indian.

On a day like this, she wanted to stay out in the sunshine. How long had it been since she had read a book outdoors? She buttered some cornbread, donned her bonnet, and flipped a blanket over her arm. Freidrich and Henry would be plowing, Mama and Lissa cooking meals, baking pies and bread—so many loaves, so many pies! They would have no time for reading, but no other task tugged at her.

With a view of Della and Hope, both cabins, and the path to Franklin's old place, she spread the blanket. After sinking into Crusoe's adventures, she munched the cornbread. Then a *thud* came from the scrub pines.

Was that some movement? Staring produced no further sound, so she returned to her reading.

A few minutes passed before another peculiar sound emanated. *Probably just an animal*, but her skin prickled when she surveyed her clothesbasket.

Like Franklin's worksite, the basket lay bare. Someone had taken his shirt, her camisole, a pair of stockings, and a tablecloth.

They must have sneaked up while she read, but why leave the basket? Perhaps Indians who knew the brave visiting Franklin?

Only her trapper friend could solve this puzzle. Meta staked Hope close to the cabin, fed the hens and milked Della. Surely he would return soon, ready for a good meal.

Daylight changed into evening as Clay reached home. Hungry and tired, Pax nuzzled his arm. "There boy. Let's get you brushed down."

Leaving the door open for light, he soon smelled something neither animal nor human and investigated.

Near the back wall, a bulky object drew him along with the milky scent of cooked corn and meat.Later, lantern light revealed several items wrapped in dark wide leaves. Inside, he discovered soft dough and pinched some to taste. While the coffee boiled, he devoured more of the pastry-like food.

Four dough and meat packs altogether, and a faint rosy pudding. On his final evening check, Clay studied the place where he found the pouch—right where the Indian had recovered from his sickness.

Pax nickered as if he understood.

"Guess we've got us more than one friend now, boy."

Drawing up a contract should take only a short time—having his claim secured somehow made this decision easier. On the way to Fort Laramie, Clay could check on Franklin and Meta. After loading up Meta's gifts, he set out—a man on a mission.

Sure enough, at the artesian well, clear water bubbled forth as if powered by some new-fangled machine. The soil in his palm reminded him of incense in Father Bernard's hand—incense to bring a sweet smell into the chapel.

For all practical purposes, this land would belong to him— such a solemn thought. He had become a landowner like Owen Dunbar!

He wanted to break the news to Meta, but hesitated. Not

even a year had passed since she lost Garrit. All the way to Franklin's worksite, his thoughts bounced back and forth. He felt sure about her—sure that their future wound together. But they both must share the same desire. Strangely, a silent worksite awaited him.

Why had Franklin stopped building on such a perfect day? A fresh question to consider. Clay staked Pax near the other animals and set Meta's gifts beside the barn.

A *thump, thump thump* came from the cabin's other side. Out of sight, Clay watched Meta attack a stubborn clump with her hoe. When he cleared his throat, the hoe flew heavenward, sending patches of earth and grass everywhere. Her eyes twice their normal size, she clutched her chest.

"Clay!"

"Didn't mean to scare you. Are you fixing to farm this land?"

His humor fell short, and he noted dark shadows rimming her eyes. Even her freckles seemed to sag.

"Where has Franklin gone?"

"I don't know. Yesterday he left with an Indian and still hasn't come home."

"Another sleepless night?"

"I don't know how long that Indian watched me before I saw him. It tries me to think this might happen again."

She smoothed a spot below her collar.

"And clothes disappeared from my basket. Another thing— one morning, two fresh rabbits lay on the stoop when I woke up."

"Looks like you're taking out your worry on this stubborn clay."

This brought a rueful grin.

"I'm about to starve. How about I tackle these lumps while you make some food?"

Like a candle flame, the light returned to her eyes. She let out a sigh as big as Wyoming Country and set out for the cabin. Afoot, Clay headed south—best do some scouting.

Some ninebark and an occasional boxelder edged an alder thicket where Ethel's prints led south. Yes, but no sign of any Indian.

He might have explored more, but he must not disappear, too. Meta needed him.

Bear meat sandwiches lined a basket beside thick slices of cake Meta made while waiting for Franklin. Her very first Wyoming cake, using the last Iowa honey—she started it late yesterday afternoon, when the evening ahead seemed so long, and took it from the oven in full dark.By the time she carried her basket to the plot, Clay had finished hoeing a good-sized area. He glanced up at her approach and wiped his forehead.

"You must have some farmer in you."

"Possibly. Most likely, I will never know."

He helped her spread the blanket and bowed his head.

"We give thanks for this food. And please bring Franklin back safely. Amen." He reached for a sandwich at the same time as she did.

"Don't you love to be outdoors after the winter?"

His mouth too full to answer, Clay nodded. He chewed a while, then gestured to a gopher racing across the meadow toward the cottonwoods."Sure would be nice if you had a window. My cabin has one—helps on dark days."

"Maybe Franklin can find one." She glanced toward the building site. "What do you think happened?"

"For some reason, he must have had to go with the Indian."

"But what could be so pressing?"

"Father Bernard helped me with things like this. He used to say, *We can usually ponder circumstances to a logical end.*"

"Mmm. Maybe the Indian's horse was sick, and he needed Franklin's tonic."

"Good. But he could have taken a minute to tell you. What about this—the brave wielded a gun and forced him to go along?"

"He had no gun. Besides, Franklin says the Indians owe him favors."

"Maybe this tribe has a politeness custom. If someone asks you to do something, you show dishonor by taking even the slightest detour."

"So Franklin might have made his choice for my sake?"

"Possibly. But then time slipped away—"

"And you would offend the people if you left. I like this game."

"Except you can take it too far." Clay took a bite of cake.

"How?"

"Giving someone too much leeway. Making a bandit into an angel."

"Mmm, I see what you mean."

"This cake tastes so good."

"My first here—I should call it *upset cake.*"

"What shall we celebrate?"

"I wish it could be the end of the war. The other day some soldiers came by with mail for me. It sounds like the North and South are going to keep slaughtering each other until someone holds up a white flag—Martin wrote about some terrible things he has seen." She shuddered and shook her head as if to shoe away a fly.

"But we can celebrate Hope. And dreams."

She handed Clay a second piece of cake.

"Wait." He ran to the barn and called, "Close your eyes." Then he set something beside her. "Now you can look."

Two packages wrapped in brown paper sat at her feet.

"Both for me?"

"For you."

She opened the smallest first. "Tea! *Nothing like tea to soothe our troubles,* Mama always said." She untied another string.

"Chocolates and pickles! Where did you get these?"

"It's a secret. And now, Madame, final package, so close your eyes again."

He settled the window beside her.

Her hand trembled unwrapping the paper.

"Oh, my!"

"Shall we put this in now?"

"I can use some of our savings—"

Clay toted the window inside. "Decide where you want this while I finish off your garden."

From the doorway, she watched him hurry out back. Her vision blurred—once again, this Texas cowhand came to her rescue. Having him here would have been enough, but now, this cabin would have light!

"Right here?" Clay held the axe against the wall. Right above her rocking chair—afternoon sunshine would warm her shoulders. "A little closer to the stove?"

"Right there."

"You're sure?"

"Yes."

"Certain?"

"Yes!" Her giggle escaped like a melody.

"Absolutely?"

This jesting reminded her of Margita's bubbly little Johann, whose antics always cheered her.

Time to sew curtains. The softness of extra nighties and petticoats hidden away in Meta's trunk took her back to Mama's parlor, where she stitched these items in the weeks of filling the wagon. With only Lissa and her husband, Friedrich, and Henry there, Mama wrote that she used one of the bedrooms for her sewing now.

Suddenly, clear sky beckoned through the open square. And sunshine! Stowing all but a gingham checked piece back in the trunk, Meta hurried to the opening. "You did it! This whole cabin thanks you."

Clay hefted the glass outdoors. Soon the frame slid into place. His hat askew, sandy hair on end, Clay raised his eyebrows through the glass, igniting another chuckle.

"What a wonder to see daylight!"

Clay disappeared, and the barn door squeaked open—he was going for mud. Time to mix up some biscuits for supper.

Scratch…dab…scratch. The sounds of mudding—this window must be secured against storms, and this time, someone else went about the task. In her basket lay enough eggs to make a pudding, and where had she put those dried chokecherries? Finding them, Meta carried her wooden bowl and pestle to the stoop.

Clay hailed her as he returned to the creek for another bucket, his face smeared like a playful child's.

"Almost done."

Breadcrumbs blended easily with cream, butter, and three eggs, to heat and thicken over the stove. Without constant stirring, the pudding would stick to the pan—and worse would follow. After burning one of her first puddings, she never left the stove again during this process.

Swish… squeak. Now Clay washed the glass. Why, she could see clear to the south grove! Even in winter, she could claim the morning sun—the whole world was opening up. She poured a dab of vinegar into some water to rub the inside of the glass.

A young meadowlark perched on the ledge to peck at the strange new sight. He pecked at the glass and angled his head in puzzlement. Next winter, a feathered friend like this one would shorten long, cold days. Only a window, but what a difference!

Soon, Clay sat with her to eat. "How did you make the pudding?"

"With chokecherries from down by the creek."

"Remember the Indian I told you about? Now I can identify the taste in the pudding he brought."

"You're sure he brought it?"

"As sure as I am about most mysteries out here."

"Ah. I must get used to them. Franklin's secrecy about the Indians, the rabbits, the absent clothes—"

"I'll close up the barn and build my fire." Clay's eyes darkened.

"You look so tired—wait to do the dishes."

As evening descended, Meta gathered her shawl as the first star blinked. His fire aflame, Clay started toward the cabin but halted when he saw her.

"Want to sit by the fire?"

"Yes—but I might fall asleep."

She sank onto a log as the sun rolled under the horizon. So lovely, this splash of persimmon, gold, and purple to end the day. "Thank you for the window and all of your work."

"My pleasure. And thank you for the good food. Feeling better?"

"Fretting about Franklin surely does weary me. But I've begun to wonder if he might be hurt."

Clay added several logs, and heat enveloped them. "My thoughts, too. In the morning, I'll launch a search."

It seemed natural and right to lean on Clay's shoulder. Later, he draped his blanket around her. Long after darkness fell, they rested. The same stars shone over her sisters in Nebraska, over Franklin, his Indian visitor, and Martin.

But someone shared this fire with her—someone kind and caring. The thought eased her like the scent of wild plum drifting from the creek.

Chapter Twenty-two

"No man has a good enough memory to be a successful liar."
~Abraham Lincoln

Flames sketched figures on nearby trees as Meta fell asleep. Clay pillowed her head in the crook of his arm. Her eyelashes, the arch of her brows, her spattering of freckles entranced him. Her curls caught the light like miniature dancing campfires.

Often, he had warmed an orphan calf, but now, something like the home feeling encased him. A fresh realization occurred—maybe in caring for him, Father Bernard had found consolation. Meta's eyes fluttered open, and she breathed his name. Then she pulled him closer. Their lips grazed, and he drew back, but again, she whispered, "Clay."

In the silence, he awaited a word. At last, one settled upon him like a blessing from Father Bernard.

Pax.

Ethel's bray disturbed the quiet of an early morning. Between her bellows, muttering wafted to Clay's campsite. After he carried Meta inside last night, he lay awake considering what he must do if Franklin failed to return. An Indian near a burial ground; the vanished clothing—even a Texas cowboy recognized these as bad signs.

Hopefully Meta still slept—she had been so worn out. After milking Della, he led the animals toward—

"Franklin?"

The old trapper looked up from kindling the campfire.

"Meta has been fretful about your whereabouts."

Bright blue eyes clouded as Franklin looked away.

"Cain't tell her ever'thin'. Mebbe you kin help me figger how."

How to be sly—or deceitful? Clay kept his thoughts to himself. When the coffee heated, they both poured a cup, and Franklin released a harsh sigh.

"Have you been awake all night?" Clay asked.

"I'll say. Got somethin' t' puzzle out. A fire helps a feller think."

Clay sat on a log and sipped his coffee, waiting for the older man to collect his thoughts.

"Twenty some years ago a chief—friend o' mine—give me one of 'is daughters to wife. We married th' Injun way. Had us a boy, but 'is mama died in th' birthin'." He sucked in a profound breath, and somewhere nearby, a jay squawked at a chipmunk.

"Th' tribe raised m' Injun son—he's more theirs then mine. 'Nuther mistake I made." He fell silent as the sun peeked over at the earth. "Thet Injun yesterdee said a council's decidin' 'bout settlers." He drained his cup. "They's talkin' raids n' scalps, so I jest took off."

"Meta said you had to go all of a sudden."

"Waal, I know no Injun'll hurt her. Know fer sure. But she don't."

Clay poured another cup. "You could tell her you're sorry."

Franklin rubbed his forehead.

"She sees you like her father. That's why this troubles her so much."

"She's like m' daughter too. Thet squaw—we warn't married Christian-like, so I'm afeard—"

"Meta loves you no matter what. And she needs you."

"Th' dang-blasted meetin' lasted till mornin'—even Dakotas chiefs was there talkin' blood. But Tall Elk held 'is groun'."

"Did you speak?"

"Sure did. Tol' 'em a few whites is bad jest like Injuns. But whites don't kill th' bad 'uns till they prove they's bad."

Those bandits from Clay's childhood appeared in his mind's eye, yelling and whooping and burning down the orphanage. They deserved to die—maybe he had part Indian blood.

"Trouble is, they's set on raidin'."

"Here?" Clay choked out the word.

"No. Dakota, down Cheyenne way, n' Colorady." Franklin paled as Meta's door opened and she started toward them. "What'll I tell 'er?"

"I can't decide for you, but you need to make up your mind quick-like."

"Franklin, you've come home!"

"Course. I—"

"But... That Indian..."

"Set yerself down. Want some coffee?"

Clay pulled up a stump for her.

Franklin scratched his head. "Right sorry fer leavin' like thet."

"You had to go so fast?"

"Not so fer, but—ya riled?"

Her silence produced a squirm.

"Could ya—fergive me?"

"Surely. But that Indian startled me so."

"Shoulda knowed you'd be afeared. I'm so used to 'em..."

A long minute passed. Black-capped chickadees twittered morning greetings while the breeze still held evening coolness.

Forgive me.

Hadn't the Oregon Trail taught her this?

Clay waited as Meta continued.

"I tried to say *Ross*, but my voice failed. Then the Indian said it, so I knew he was a friend."

"Yep. If'n I kin help it, won't never let this happen agin."

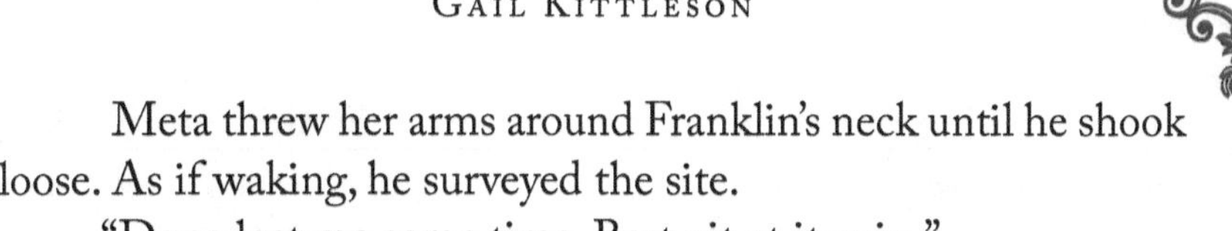

Meta threw her arms around Franklin's neck until he shook loose. As if waking, he surveyed the site.

"Done lost me some time. Best git at it agin."

Clay got to his feet.

"And I'm headed to Fort Laramie—got a contract to sign."

"You both need some breakfast first."

Meta started off and Clay followed her. Then, like a hawk returning to its nest, an idea circled. Why not ask her to go? They could stay at a stage stop halfway, and some time alone might be good for Franklin.

Only one way to discover Meta's response. After another minute pondering, Clay knocked on the door.

"Pour yourself a cup of coffee."

She cracked eggs into a bowl.

"You came here last summer?"

"The second week of June."

She poured batter into a pan and set it in the oven.

"Would you like to get away for a little while?"

She turned. Her fingers fluttered at her collarbone.

"What do you mean?"

"How would you like to sign this contract?"

"You would bring it all the way back?"

"No. You would ride to Fort Laramie with me."

Her eyes darted to the window.

"You know how to ride, and you like to?"

"I love to—it has been so very long, but…"

"Always comes back…kind of like breathing. Franklin could watch out for the animals. You would only need a few things—"

"You would take me?"

"That, Madam, would be my pleasure."

"Do you really think—"

As if signaling a momentous occasion, the eggs sizzled.

"We can bunk at the stage stop tonight, finish our business tomorrow, stay over again, and be back on Wednesday. Take your time thinking about it. I'll fetch more water and tell Franklin breakfast is ready."

When he returned, Franklin in tow, a neat row on the bed provided Meta's answer. A small stack of clothing, some bear jerky, a canteen, and a bag of biscuits—traveling fare. Over breakfast, she and Franklin discussed the disappearance of the clothes while Clay imagined patterns from one of her freckle to the next.

"Doncha think thet's what happened?"

Franklin's question startled him. "Wha—"

"Injun young'uns took 'em. Fer them, stealin's different then fer us."

"How is that?"

"Injuns say everthin' b'longs to ever'body. They see clothes n' think they're fer th' takin'."

"Makes as much sense as anything.

Franklin turned to Meta. "So yer goin'?"

"With you here to take care of things—"

"I'll be feastin' on eggs n' milk. Leave them dishes. I kin wash 'em."

Hitching up her skirt to slip on a pair of trousers took some doing while outside, Clay latched the saddlebags, and Franklin held Hope's reins. When Meta put her foot in the stirrup, Clay took note.

"Ready?"

"Anything can happen, I know. But if I break something, you make great ginger compresses."

His laugh eased her tension. Hope pranced a bit but obeyed, and Franklin waved them off. Once she found her rhythm, Hope took to running and before long, the joy of riding overtook Meta. The wind in her face felt better than anything. The kerchief around her neck—Garrit's—would come in handy with her wayward curls. His things had become hers, like his dream.

Near some trees a runoff gurgled over rocks. Clay slowed Pax and offered his hand. He leaned in to calm Hope as Meta dismounted and stayed with the horses while she searched out a private spot.

No wildflowers showed their heads yet, but the countryside burst with promise. So many birds at work on their nests, and all around, other creatures preparing for new families, too.

When she returned, Clay pointed north. "Through this break in the hills, we ought to reach the Chugwater long before dark." He buried his face in Hope's muzzle when she mounted—so thoughtful.

"Thank you, Clay, for asking me to come."

He tipped his hat, revealing those purple flecks in his eyes.

An hour later, a log structure showed in the distance—two stories, like home. Meta stayed with the horses while Clay asked about spending the night.

Burdened stage wheels had carved deep ruts in this yard. In a long, low shed, horses stamped, awaiting their turn to pull the coach. Soon a familiar-looking woman emerged with Clay. Her voice jogged Meta's memory—she had stayed with them after Fort Laramie. The woman held her at arm's length.

"You do remember me?"

"Yes—Matilda. Matilda Hanson. You have had your baby."

"I did, and now—" She gave her midsection a knowing pat. "You can sleep with me—Tom often camps out with the travelers."

Clay took Hope's reins and set out for the stable. Not knowing whether to laugh or cry, Meta fell in pace with Matilda. "I am so glad you have come, but what of your husband?"

"Garrit died last fall. He had an accident on our claim during a dreadful rainstorm."

"Oh my. How have you—where did you spend the winter?"

"In our cabin."

"All alone?" The tears in Matilda's eyes brought back the long winter.

"Yes, but I did have a neighbor. Maybe you have met Franklin Ross, who traps all over these parts? He brought me supplies when he passed through."

"Ross…maybe Tom knows him. Ah, well nowSpring has come at last. Come on in. Almost time to cook supper. All winter alone." Matilda shook her head. "Oh my."

In a kitchen not much larger than Meta's, Matilda cooked for stage drivers and passengers. She waved away Meta's offer to help.

"Oh, no. You deserve a home-cooked meal after all you've been through."

Glad to stand after the day of riding, Meta scanned pails, rags, and shelves brimming with foodstuffs. The stove, as large as Mama's, took her back to Iowa. When Matilda wrapped her hand with a dishtowel to lift a huge pot of potatoes, Meta ran over and grasped the handle too. "This is awfully heavy."

"Thank you. I get so used to doing these things myself—"

"But you carry a child. Mustn't you be careful?"

"I am expecting more often than not. Work never waits an opportune time."

"I thought you and your husband planned to settle a claim?"

Matilda wiped her forehead.

"Yes, but Tom's family told us the stationmaster had a severe injury, and the company needed a replacement. We came to investigate and found a cabin, a good water supply, and regular customers—we moved in the next day."

"You have blossomed here."

"Tom and I love having people around, and he can talk faster than anyone I know. He gets to do that every day."

The door flew open. "Mattie? Looks like three for supper this time."

Matilda's older daughters appeared, and she turned to Meta. "You can help me fix breakfast in the morning, all right?"

The stage brought several travelers, along with the driver and his helper. Children ran in and out, Tom spoke with one man, then another, and Matilda scurried about to feed the whole crew.

At the end of the table, Clay gestured Meta to a seat. After a succulent stew, berry pie, and more Wild West stories than she could recall, she leaned back against the wall. "So, young man, I have seated myself beside a real cowboy?"

Clay replied to the passenger across from Meta. The buzz of conversation continued, but she could hardly stay awake. Then Clay slid back his chair.

"Thank you kindly, Mrs. Hanson. We'll be leaving early in the morning." He picked up their dishes and turned Meta's way.

"Good night, Mrs. Rausch. Let's start out right after breakfast."

"Girls, at the dishes, now." The Hanson's daughters spun into action, and Matilda led Meta to her bed off the back of the cabin.

"What a gentleman your Clay is!"

True—but no need to reply.

And no fretting this night—sleep tucked Meta in like Mama's quilt.

At Fort Laramie, the gatekeeper and sentries treated Clay like an officer.

"State your business."

He gestured to Meta, who leaned toward the soldier.

"We wish to see Captain Reynolds, sir."

Perhaps mentioning a specific officer's name made the difference—the soldier cleared the way, and they rode in together.

"Did you and Garrit visit the trading post when the wagon train stopped here?"

"No, Mr. Fortune warned us about the high prices. But the blacksmith did pull Garrit's tooth—I had tried oil of cloves and wild geranium root tea, but nothing helped."

A soldier walked by and tipped his hat.

From then on, she greeted even the most rumpled private crossing their path, and Clay relaxed.

I've got me a girl. In Cheyenne, he had believed these words,

but today, that girl's presence made all the difference in the world.

"Do come in. Clay, wasn't it? And?" The captain stood as he saw them coming.

"I've brought Meta Rausch, Captain. If you recall, I asked you about horse contracts."

The Captain made a slight bow. "Sit down, folks. You are ready to move ahead then?"

Clay deferred to Meta, and she responded. "Yes, sir. I—*we* intend to have a number for sale by Spring, at least eight or ten."

"Wait here. Major Miles keeps contracts on hand."

Meta's eyes sparkled.

"I can scarcely believe we are here—an actual contract!" Her dimple showed, and his heart did a turn.

Captain Reynolds re-entered with a sheaf of papers.

"Take time to read through this." He handed them to Meta, and she scanned the top one before passing it to Clay.

They would deliver the horses at sixty dollars a head. Clay's surprise must have shown, because the officer explained.

"We pay ten dollars more a head with delivery. You can imagine how much effort that saves. Any questions?" Meta spoke up. "I have never been party to a business agreement, especially with the U.S. Army. Would you continue to be our contact?"

"Possibly, although one never knows when reassignment to another post will come. But Major Miles would treat you fairly." He held out a pen. "We shall need your signatures. You work as partners, correct?"

Meta and Clay exchanged quick glances and nodded. "Well then, here's pen and ink."

Just like that the deed was done. This meant he was Texas-bound for sure. They all shook hands, and Captain Reynolds rounded his desk. "You have my permission to visit the cook for provisions. And you might find something at the trading post."

They stopped by the water trough to check on Hope and Pax before entering the post. At the door, Meta asked, "How much time can we spend?"

"Look around as much as you like."

While she crossed the central aisle, Clay looked at the tools. After a few minutes, she spoke with the clerk before hurrying to him with an excited glint in her eyes.

"The clerk told me the gardener gets his seed potatoes from the cook. Could we go to the kitchen?"

Clay guided her there, and the cook, up to his elbows washing pots and pans, filled a gunnysack half full of sprouting potatoes. "The United States Army delights to share, Ma'am. I threw in a bag of parsnip seeds, too—plant them two or three weeks before the last frost." Meta grinned like a child with unexpected candy. He sounded so much like Mama, and this sack held such a simple treasure.

"Thank you so much! I never expected to find these here."

She held the burlap bag open, and the rich earthy scent took Clay back to the Evendsbergs' large garden. The whole family nurtured an array of vegetables to see them through the winter, and hours of hoeing and weeding taught their own lessons.

As he hoisted the sack to his shoulder, the cook called them back. "Plenty of beef left over—want to take some along?"

Another bag in hand, they headed for the horses. "Sure you don't need anything from the store?"

"Only sugar, but honey works fine. My money is set aside for a horse."

"All right. We'll be on our way."

Clay's saddle horn bulged with burlap as they took leave of the fort. In an hour, the sun cast cloud shadows on the Laramie Mountains, welcoming them back to the high plains. Some men described women as chatterers, but Meta had no such tendency. For her, riding must be thinking time, too.

Chapter Twenty-three

In the North, where success was certain, they could afford to have bitter division. On the beaten side the departure of hope left only the resolve to perish arms in hand. Better the complete destruction of the whole generation and the devastation of their enormous land, better that every farm should be burned, every city bombarded, every fighting man killed, than that history should record that they had yielded.

~Winston S. Churchill
The American Civil War

At the Chugwater River, hills and rock formations took precedence. A grassy place provided their table, and that beef—so tender and filling. "Every time I look at those cliffs, I see something new. First a lamb, now a coyote—see its snout?" Meta's eyes danced, inviting Clay to join in.

"I do. Last night Mr. Hanson said the Chugwater got its name from a Mandan Indian chief hurt during a buffalo hunt. His son took over and ran the buffalo over one of these cliffs. When the animals landed, their bodies sounded like *Chug!* Chugwater means *water at the place the buffalo chug.*"

"Tricking them seems so sad."

"Yes, but their poor eyesight has a lot to do with this way of hunting. If hunters can startle a few of the female leaders by hitting them hard in the rumps with their gun butts, they'll head in the other direction, and others will follow. For the tribes, what an easy way to get meat and hides for winter."

"I guess so." Meta stood and stretched. "We have officially become partners now. Because of you, Garrit's dream will come true after all."

Her energy beckoned him to walk with her, but Clay clung to caution. Maybe he had done nothing but steal a dream.

"Clay, is something wrong?" She whirled around. "When I signed that paper, the dream became real. What is a dream besides an idea? Maybe one person receives an inkling, but someone else can make it work." A juniper shadow darkened her freckles, and a curly waterfall escaped her calico bonnet.

"With Franklin's help, we can accomplish what would be wasted otherwise. When he perked up at the thought, things started to fall into place. Do you understand?"

He kicked at some loose stones.

"I would never want to pilfer..." The seriousness in her eyes arrested him.

"In death, Garrit, gave up earthly things. Don't you think Providence has given us this opportunity to see his dream into being?"

Birdsong surrounded them as they turned back toward the horses. Then Meta burst out again.

"Garrit believed folks could do anything here. He worked so hard—for ten years—to prepare for this. And now we can prove his conviction."

Her dark eyes bade Clay to let go of his doubts. His misgivings fled, and he swung her arm like youngster. Then, under the outline of the cliffs, he lifted her onto Hope.

After the evening meal, full of news from parts East including ever-present war reports, Matilda invited Meta for a walk, so they followed the stage track, where meadowlarks welcomed twilight. In another corner, three redheaded woodpeckers sneezed at each other in a squabble.

"I have two cousins still in the fighting. How about you?"

"My brother Martin. Do you think what that traveler said is true, that the South will only give in after much more fighting?"

"My daddy came from Tennessee and used to say there's nobody stubborner than men born in those hills, so I expect he know of what he speaks. But how tragic."

"What will they be like when they return? How can they ever be the same after all this?"

"I cannot imagine. But for now, how did you meet Mr. Burns?"

"I had finally given Garrit a proper good-bye—that had been bothering me. My birthday reminded me I had my whole life yet to live, and giving him a funeral service helped me move ahead. But then, just when I started feeling so hopeful, I twisted my ankle, and Clay rescued me."

"Mmm. He lives nearby?"

"Not really, but that day he had ridden farther north than usual."

"Sounds like guidance from above. I lost my first husband, too. My Joseph went out to shoot wild turkey, and two men toted his body back that evening. They said his gun misfired." Matilda waved to warn Meta of a deep rut. "We had two little ones and a third on the way. I learned no one can tell you how to grieve. When Tom came along, even though only three months had passed, I could hardly afford to wait much longer.

"Some folks judged me rash, but Tom took a liking to the young'uns right away. That meant everything to me, and I knew I would love him as I loved Joseph, to the end."

As they followed the curve back to the station, daylight shifted into dusk. "In the beginning, God gave us each other. My Tom..." Matilda's laugh spread into the darkness like firelight. "We lived way out in the hills, and one day, Tom came by with Joseph's horse. She'd startled at the gunshot and run herself out."

"And you invited him in?"

"Yes. Before he left, he played horsey with the little ones on

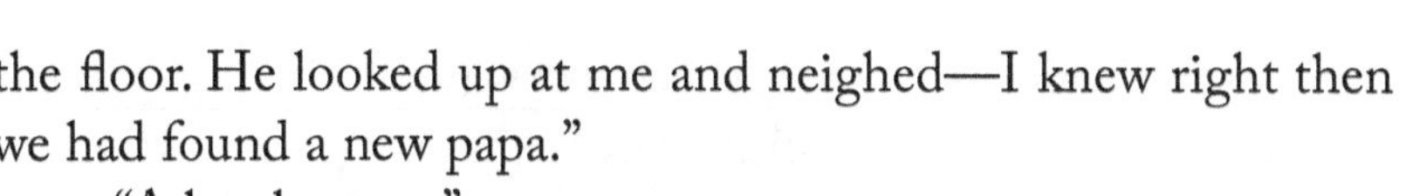

the floor. He looked up at me and neighed—I knew right then we had found a new papa."

"A lovely story."

"Do tell me more about Clay."

"He worked that trail drive that joined our train—remember how Mr. Fortune warned us to stay away from the drovers? He has been so kind to me. I—" Suddenly she recalled the cowhand who found her petticoat. Had that been Clay? Yes, surely…his eyes told her so. So they *had* met way back then—how could she not have remembered this before?

In the light of Tom's evening campfire, Matilda patted her arm. "Keep in mind what Betsy went through with her baby. Life goes far faster out here—we never know what might happen by the end of a day. I'd say a whole winter alone surely counts as a full mourning year. And remember, the idea of courting came from above."

Only the fire's crackle dotted the evening stillness. The men had gathered, and Meta searched for Clay's hat as Matilda went on.

"Trust your heart. You will know."

The men's voices created a resonant undertone as the flames put on a show. A few phrases filtered through.

"…with all of the North's victories and General Grant in place, surely the fighting will end…"

"Virginians will be hard-pressed to surrender…matter of honor…"

Surely not…surely Martin will soon be relieved of duty.

"…out in New York state back in '60, the sky filled with supernatural light that rushed above us. Nothing like this before or since. Now no one can say 'twas not a portent…just consider how many have perished…"

"Oh, how I tire of that war talk!" Matilda's voice lowered. "But, Meta, be certain that Clay cares for you. The way he follows you with his eyes proclaims it, though he takes pains to protect your honor."

"You think so? Now that we have signed this contract, perhaps things will will come clearer, but—"

"Believe me, his eyes declare the truth."

The sun peered over the horizon as the women bade each other farewell, and Clay helped Meta onto Hope. He turned so quiet this morning—had all of yestesrday's dream talk offended him? By midmorning, clouds covered the sun as they watered the horses. As she returned from her walk, bright rays broke through. A light rain fell as Clay led the way into an intoxicating stand of pines.

"Franklin calls this a spittin' shower, sun and rain at the same time. He says the sun spits rain."

Clay kicked pine needles with the toe of his boot. "This place reminds me of hunting for strays in Texas high country. The piney air made sleeping grand."

Shadowed by the branches, his eyes became bright specks. Then, as it had started, the shower ended. Each blade of grass glittered as they mounted, and at the stretch leading to Spring Creek, Clay reined in and waited.

"Ready to get home?" Dark splashes sullied his eyes like rain clouds.

"Yes and no."

He succumbed to silence. Like faithful friends, Mama's words filtered with the sunlight.

Patience, daughter. Men must take time to know their hearts.

No rain here, for a whorl of dust and debris rose from the plains. *Ah, dust to dust.* So fragile, this earthly vale of tears, yet the Creator cared for all.

Still silent, his hands tight on the reins, Clay finally turned. Words—more than usual—bubbled out.

"Such a gorgeous expanse. I have not felt so—" Errant curls bade Meta shake them back. "I want this journey to go on, like April. But May will soon be here."

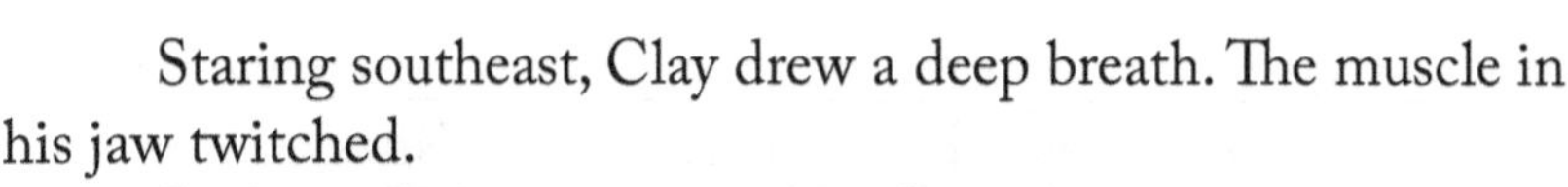

Staring southeast, Clay drew a deep breath. The muscle in his jaw twitched.

Such a telltale movement, like Garrit's when she displeased him. Only later, she recognized his love wrestling with fear.

A jackrabbit tore through the grass and Clay squared his shoulders. "Come with me?"

"How far from here?"

"Twenty minutes' ride."

Trust in God. The back of her neck tingled. A whole lifetime had passed since Mama's voice, strong and sweet, encouraged her. Today, the lessons reverberated to the rhythm of the hooves.

Trust in God. Trust. Trust. Trust.

Green with promise, the land smelled of rain and earth, sage and expectation. Early grass waved like hundreds of tiny green flags.

Wyoming Country had so much to offer. Her garden was growing, she had visited Fort Laramie now, and Matilda Hanson lived a only pleasant ride away.

Trust, trust, trust. A different meaning surfaced—to trust meant to act—to plunge forward. This, Mama had done after Papa's calamitous passing.

Her whisper escaped into the wind. *Whatever lies ahead, I place my life in your hands.*

Wait, trust, give him time.

Ahead, water sparkled under the grass but then disappeared. Lush growth flourished here like the backdrop of a dream.

Now Clay was helping her down. "Mr. Dunbar calls this an artesian well—water trapped by the earth. Pressure down below keeps it bubbling up."

An artesian well? Would this be like having a creek cross your land?

How could anything be so lovely? This dark-eyed beauty—not

painted like that saloon madam, but pure and true—here on his claim—*his claim*. Had Clay wandered into a fantasy?

Something inside him guarded words as if, once spoken, they might explode like the black powder paving the way for a transcontinental railroad. *Dyna*... what was that word... created by a man named Nobel?

So much change these days. A railroad crossing the entire country, East to West, and now the telegraph bringing news to citizens far, far from Eastern cities. All of this deepened his hunger.

Mr. Dunbar allowed that a man must make decisions or spend his life avoiding disappointment. Now Meta and the ranch went together—this partnership formed a cornerstone, for how could they remain separate?

That kiss beside the fire the other night told its own story, but could even such a tender touch be trusted? Did she truly care for him, or was she simply lonely for Garrit?

A rainbow shimmered as she splashed water and leaned back into the sun. Her sigh tore at his heart.

"How did you come upon this place?" She made a wide circle around the well, and Clay fell in step. But his voice became a Johnny Reb.

"Clay? I asked you something."

"On the way to... the day I brought you the bear meat."

"Mmm. All this green reminds me of Iowa—feels like our back pasture—like home."

The word startled him, and his tone issued low, raw. "Meta..."

She looked so stricken, he grasped her hand. His voice cracked. "Please don't be afraid."

Her eyebrows formed one fretful dark stroke. A drop of water balanced on the tip of her nose.

"I... I want this land to be *our* home."

She covered her mouth with her hand.

"I know not even a year has passed—" He cursed his slowness of tongue, but her eyes begged him to proceed.

"The other day I went into Cheyenne and claimed this tract. I want you…" His words faltered. "I will wait as long as you need."

Tears bathed her eyes.

He had done this all wrong. A scratchy whisper was all he could muster. "Forgive me. I mustn't take what…" Near their feet, the spring gushed forth. "But my caring for you keeps growing."

Flames sparked her eyes. She stepped closer, and he gathered her in as all of his yearning years shrank into nothingness.

After a while, he drew back. "One day soon, this will be our land. We can build a cabin here."

The plains spread before them forever, winter's long hold releasing sage and brittle bush into new life. Meta nestled against him.

"Shall we call this the H and P Ranch? H for hope, P for peace?"

No need to reply. This cowhand had himself a girl—smile, dimples, freckles, trust, love—right here in his trembling arms.

"Git up, ya durn mule." Franklin batted his soaking forehead with his gnarly hand, leaving yet another muddy streak.

A shadow laced the log pile as though a cloud hid the sun. Intense in his struggle with Ethel, Franklin failed to hear anyone approach, but that shadow…

His heart leaped—always the same when a certain brave neared. He grasped the tall Indian's hand.

"Father." Black eyes unfathomable, the visitor surveyed him without emotion. "You come."

"Agin?"

"*Hiibeh' ithoowotonin.*" Arapahoe, part English. The brave slapped his chest for emphasis.

Franklin shook his head, unsure of the meaning. Tall Elk said something about the chief doubting him?

"Awright." Years ago he got himself into this, and now, when he wanted to live a simple life, he could not say no.

Earlier, he had milked Della, gathered the eggs, and fed the other animals. As long as he came back by nightfall, he could keep his word to Meta and Clay to watch over things here.

"Go n' git yerself hitched. Don't worry 'bout nothin' here. I ain't leavin'." He had made a promise.

But Tall Elk rarely asked for anything—how could he deny the urgency in these somber eyes? Usually silent as stone, Tall Elk spoke again, using the Arapahoe word meaning *now* with the word for *destroy*.

So Franklin followed the young warrior westward from Spring Creek. The normal meeting place had changed—an extra hour of walking, so Tall Elk must not witness the weakness in his legs.

"Ethel, I know ya got yer own rheumatiz, but…" Ethel snorted as his weight landed on her, but fell into rhythm soon enough.

One day Tall Elk would become chief, since all other blood relatives had fallen in battle or to disease. One brave, then another, until only he remained.

Around a bend, the encampment appeared, exposed and vulnerable, warriors from several tribes seated in mysterious hierarchy. When his native grandfather motioned him to speak, Tall Elk nodded to Franklin.

"Our trapper friend stands with his Indian brothers always. I have brought him with the Chief's approval."

"Ross." The aged chief nodded to Franklin as a boy folded a blanket for their guest.

After all these years, revenge had become the main impetus for Indian raids, but the bonds between this chief and Franklin held fast. The White Man would never stop claiming native land— everyone knew this.

At the same time, the Cavalry sought Franklin's advice. Such a riddle!

Tall Elk stood near the chief. The towering brave's high

forehead and pronounced nose proclaimed him Arapahoe, yet two bloods mingled in his powerful person. Oh that both worlds would reason together for the good of all.

"Our children hunger, yet each day brings more settlers. We must protect our hunting grounds."

One-by-one, Franklin interpreted the chief's expressions, as he did for the Army.

"Speak, Ross." All eyes focused on Franklin as he gripped the smoking pipe Tall Elk passed. An unwelcome awareness enveloped him: the chief and Tall Elk would weigh his words, but some of the others here would always see him as White.

Chapter Twenty-four

Mother, I have news to tell you which I hope you won't blame me for. I was married last month on 26th to the one I have spoke to you so often about but then I did not think of marrying until this was was over but we both changed our minds and married while Billy was with us. The ceremony was read by W.C. Harris, an old friend from home and now a stationed Preacher at this place or near here. Ma the only thing that worries me is that you did not see us married.

Joanna Painter Fox
a Confederate Civil War nurse
concerning her marriage
to a druggist she met during the Civil War

"**B**efore God and this witness, we gather to wed this man and this woman."

Hand-hewn planks, horsehair and leather, the smells of working men, riding men—no Sweet Williams and lilacs inundating the aisle of Emmanuel Church with sweetness. But scents and conversation from the cook's gardens told Meta someone out there labored in the soil as the Army Chaplain's voice riveted her attention.

Against the background of Fort Laramie's make-do chapel, sun speckled Clay's brow. His moist eyes held hers as the Chaplain continued.

"Marriage is not to be entered into lightly. If anyone hath reason that these two should not be joined in holy matrimony, let him speak now or forever hold his peace."

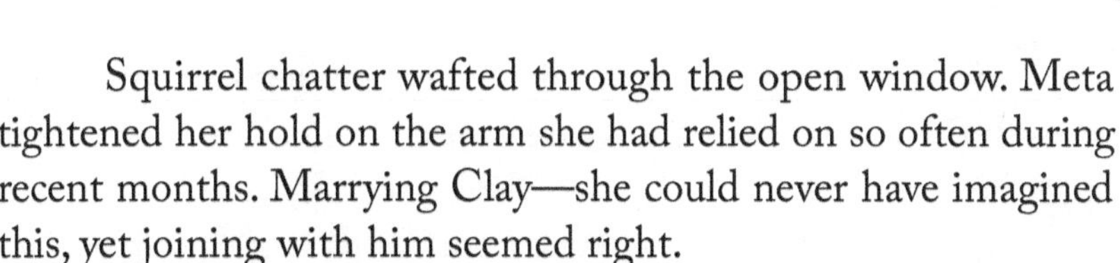

Squirrel chatter wafted through the open window. Meta tightened her hold on the arm she had relied on so often during recent months. Marrying Clay—she could never have imagined this, yet joining with him seemed right.

The chaplain turned to Clay. "Do you take this woman to be your lawful wedded wife, to have and to hold, for better, for worse, in sickness and in health, till death do you part, according to God's holy ordinance?"

"I do." Clay's broken whisper heated Meta's eyes. Such a trustworthy soul, he felt things so deeply.

"Meta Rausch, do you take this man to be your lawful wedded husband..."

"I do."

So much had changed since the last time she uttered these words in the presence of her family—shadows and sunshine alike. But Mama's guidance had sustained her, and through it all, Providence remained faithful.

As the chaplain pronounced them man and wife, Meta twined her fingers through Clay's. Death might part, true, yet love remained. And a different, fresh love could rise like a morning breeze.

"Mrs. Burns?" Clay leaned down to look into her eyes. "You have made me happier than I ever could have hoped."

His fingers tightened around hers. "I love you, Clay. Always and forever."

The Chaplain handed her a steel-tipped pen and opened a bottle of strong acidic ink. The stiff paper crackled at her touch, and after Clay added his signature, the chaplain signed and handed the pen to Captain Reynolds.

The Captain grinned as he clapped Clay on the shoulder and shook Meta's hand. "Hearty congratulations. About time I attended a marriage rather than a funeral."

The Chaplain waited for the ink to dry. Then he rolled the license into a scroll and handed it to Clay.

"Ma'am, Mr. Burns. May Divine protection guard you during these Indian wars. Take good care of each other." He stepped out into the sunshine.

Captain Reynolds held the door for them. "Thank you for this privilege, folks. We will stay in touch."

Meta reached to Hope's saddle horn, where she had tied her best bonnet. Freckles already ruled her nose, but Mama would say, *Keep trying*.

"Do visit us, sir."

"Ma'am, I expect I will, although most of my travels call me northwest. In that country, Red Cloud continues to threaten."

A shadow crossed Clay's face. "Have you made some progress?"

Captain Reynolds pushed his cap back. "Such cantankerous tribes. We never know where the next attack will come."

Clay slipped his arm around Meta's waist. "Why don't you find something in the trading post to remember our wedding day? I'll be along soon."

"Thank you again, Captain Reynolds." Meta turned toward the store, aware that Clay would voice to the Captain his concern about leaving her.

He discussed this with Franklin yesterday, to make sure their trapper friend thought it safe to ride to Fort Laramie. The Indian threat had monopolized the dinner conversation at the Hanson's stage station, too, where they stopped for the night.

Two privates who looked too young to be fighting Indians, but definitely not too dirty, made their way toward her and she gave them her best smile. What a lonely life, far from their families.

Ah, Martin—such a dear brother. After Appomattox, he had joined the cavalry in Arizona Territory with his captain from the war. What adventures they must be having! If only he would write again.

"So, what shall it be? Some chocolates and tea?" Clay caught her waist in the post store and turned her toward him.

"You're a poet."

A packet of each in hand, they left, and Clay helped her into the saddle. Heading southwest toward the stagecoach station, it seemed they were alone out here. Perhaps no lilacs or Sweet Williams graced the breeze, but the pervasive, almost sweet smell of everyday sage wafted around them.

Faithful sage, an aroma for an everyday girl. What Matilda called *all you've been through* faded with each of Hope's strides. The winter had indeed passed—no time to waste reconsidering that time.

About an hour from the Fort, the horizon showed filmy dust spires. Dusty blue uniforms came into view, and at the station, Tom and Matilda Hanson gave them a cheerful welcome. The night before, Matilda shared her bed with Meta while Clay slept by the campfire. But for their first night as husband and wife, Matilda insisted on a small cabin for Clay and Meta.

"The overnight travelers already have their bunks, and the stage driver always sleeps in the lean-to. Why bother setting up camp outdoors?"

They accepted, and after supper Clay Meta her down the moonlit lane. From the campfire came the chatter of stage travelers discussing the latest news.

"Do you want to hear what they have to say?"

Clay shook his head. "Only your words, Mrs. Burns."

Hours later, dawn altered the cabin's darkness to misty grey. Meta memorized the sound of Clay's heartbeat, strong and sure. He stirred, and she burrowed into his muscles like a rabbit in the cold.

Stagecoach wheels scrunched against hard-packed soil, metal clashed with metal as a hand hitched the horses. On any other visit, she would be helping Matilda in the kitchen, but this morning belonged to her and Clay.

The ride back took only three or four hours. Why not stretch these moments as long as possible?

Life is fragile—every second matters. During their marriage, she would strive to live in the moment and pause more often to enjoy whatever came their way. Neither past nor future would pilfer present blessings.

She washed up at Matilda's house while Clay joined the men outside. Invigorated by cold water and lye soap, she rounded the building, and the men's voices reached her.

"That Loving fella owns a thousand acres of Texas. Met him in '60, drivin' a herd up Denver way. He'd still be there but for Kit Carson, who convinced th' Army t' let him git back home."

Clay's back faced her, but she could imagine his intensity. What a boon, to find men familiar with the trail to Texas.

"After that, he supplied the Rebel Army with beef, but never collected much money. Heard last year, he drove a herd up to Fort Sumner in New Mexico Territory. Rounded up cattle with a Texas Ranger name of Goodnight."

"He sold them to the Army in Fort Sumner?" The speaker looked as though he had seen a few trail drives, his skin as bronze as an Indian's and riven with deep lines.

"Roundabout. Gov'ment's holed up eight thousand Apache and Navaho there, tryin' to civilize 'em, make 'em into farmers. Had t' feed 'em somethin' and Loving knowed it. Went through all sorts o' troubles, Injuns stampedin' his cattle, cattle divin' off cliffs over the Pecos." The man spat far and wide.

"But, he come out good n' made a profit. Like as not, you'll meet him."

"Do Indians still haunt the panhandle? They gave us no trouble a year ago." Clay lowered his voice.

"H'ain't gonna stop raidin' till they's all in reservations. But you're bringin' back horses. It's cattle they want."

Clay slipped beside Meta like a shadow, and they sat down inside. She itched to help Matilda and her daughters serve the food, but Matilda forbade it.

"Next time I'll put you to work like always."

A traveler launched Clay a question before he took his first bite.

"Leavin' soon?"

"In about a week."

"Got 'nough men ridin' along?"

"Five. One older man and three seasoned cowhands."

"That oughta do. Jest don't all sleep at once. Never know when them thievin' Injuns might come outta nowhere, but white bandits're as bad. With the Palo Duro Canyon stretchin' so far—"

He filled his mouth, and Tom surveyed Clay and Meta. "Ain't no worse than here. A week ago, some bandit robbed a stage in Dakota." All eyes turned to the driver, too busy chewing to answer, so Tom continued.

"We live in perilous times. If we took note of every danger, nobody would accomplish a thing. We keep a watchful eye and do the best we can."

Matilda gave Tom a smile, one hand across her growing middle. "Our grandfolks would have said the same. The journey from New York City to Wisconsin took some lives, but they kept going." She eyed their children. "Maybe by the time all of you are grown, things'll settle down here, too."

Clay's knee pressed against Meta's. The violet-blue of his eyes showed darker streaks this morning. Was he saying, *Everything will be all right*, or *Perhaps we ought to re-consider this trip?*

Chapter Twenty-five

Once you make a decision, the universe conspires to make it happen.

~Ralph Waldo Emerson

Franklin bent to pick up the shards from a log he split a few minutes earlier. He and Clay heaped more cut wood on the growing pile that would transform into a corral fence during Clay's absence. The space between Franklin's cabin and theirs would soon hold ten to twelve horses.

After he completed the holding pen, Franklin would build a shed to shelter horses during winter. He swore they could produce a finished barn but agreed with Clay on a three-sided shed. Now, buildings fled Clay's mind as vexation plagued him at leaving Meta here.

"This claim's th' safest in th' whole Ter'tory, son, but th' tribes has lost patience. Bound t' be bloodshed up north. I'll do ever'thin' t' pr'tect her."

"Sure wish I didn't have to go."

In three days, he would leave for the Oak Bar and parts South. How could he possibly bear the thought of his new bride here in Indian Country?

"Ten years ago, I'd go fer ya, son. But—" Franklin turned back to the chopping block.

"Glad you're able to stay here."

"I'd b' worried, too, if I was you. Took m' wife 'long with me n' lost her. M' firstborn, too. But back then, nothin' coulda stopped me."

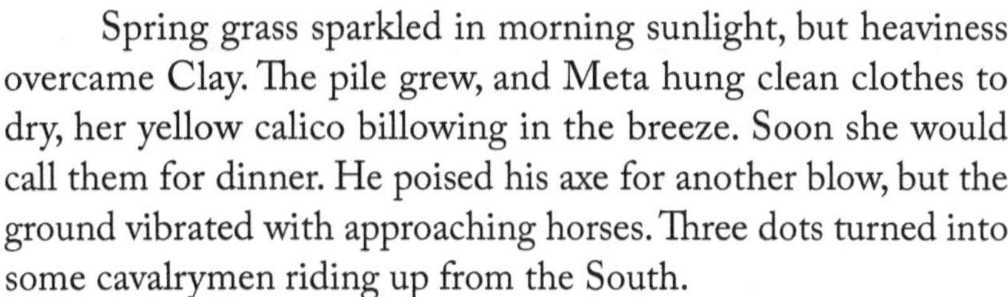

Spring grass sparkled in morning sunlight, but heaviness overcame Clay. The pile grew, and Meta hung clean clothes to dry, her yellow calico billowing in the breeze. Soon she would call them for dinner. He poised his axe for another blow, but the ground vibrated with approaching horses. Three dots turned into some cavalrymen riding up from the South.

"Good day, Captain. What can I do for you?"

"We're checking on this area—heard your axes. Everything all right?"

"So far. What news do you have?"

The officer blinked in the bright sun. "So far, the raids are all north of here in the Bighorns. Still, we reconnoiter everything east of the mountains."

"Do you have time to stop in? My wife's a good cook."

"Ah, no, but thank you. We'll water our horses at the creek."

"I'll be heading to Texas in a few days. Any trouble down there?"

"What route will you take?"

"From Cheyenne through Fort Morgan, across the South Platte northeast of Denver, then east of Pueblo. North of Fort Sumner, we veer off the Goodnight-Loving Trail to the diagonal across North Texas, along the Red River to the Red River Station, then south to Dallas."

"You know the Army's closing Fort Morgan?" Before Clay could nod, he went on. "Take care for the Overland Stage. One fellow got away with his life but lost his horses and buckboard on one of the wooden bridges—the Stage always has the right-of-way. Those Easterners headed to the *diggings* in the Rockies won't appreciate you slowin' 'em down."

"I... I hate to leave my wife here."

"We'll stop in when we pass this way. Godspeed."

That evening, long after Franklin retired, the coyotes howled. Silent as the slice of moon in the east, Meta snuggled against Clay.

Suddenly, fumes stung his lungs. His limbs turned to wet sand as he struggled to sit up. Through a sea of orange and gold, he made out men on horseback waving their shotguns, flares in their hands, laughter pouring from their mouths.

Then a torch sailed his way. A child screamed and scuffling broke out. A wall gave way, and a boy added his cries as Clay choked on dust and smoke.

"Help! Get us out—" reverberated from his own throat.

Finally, smooth fingers pressed against his forehead, and a voice so mellow it dried his tears. Ah... Clay shook hair from his eyes. Meta. One of his bad dreams had paid a visit. He sank against the feather tick.

"You dreamed about the fire?"

Words forsook his parched throat. She ran her fingers over his forehead again, through his hair, over his cheekbones.

"I can't imagine what that must have been like." Her silky curls touched his neck. "Maybe in Texas you will find some peace about the fire."

Her even breathing calmed his own. *Peace?* He had no desire to re-enter the scene of so much pain. He must be crazed to think of leaving.

All winter long, Meta had needed him. Now, she slipped back into sleep, but this dawn highlighted his need for her. At last, light showed under the cabin's door and Clay pleaded for strength to do what a man must do.

Still he lay motionless, allowing her to rest. Then she stirred and reached for the prayer books beside their bed.

"What if you take my prayer book and I keep yours from Father Bernard? If we both read a little every day, we shall know each other better by the time you return."

She opened Clay's treasure and commenced. With each word, sunlight filtered into his soul.

God is our refuge and strength, a very present help in trouble. Therefore will not we fear, though the earth be removed and the mountains be cast into the sea... Heavenly Father, we

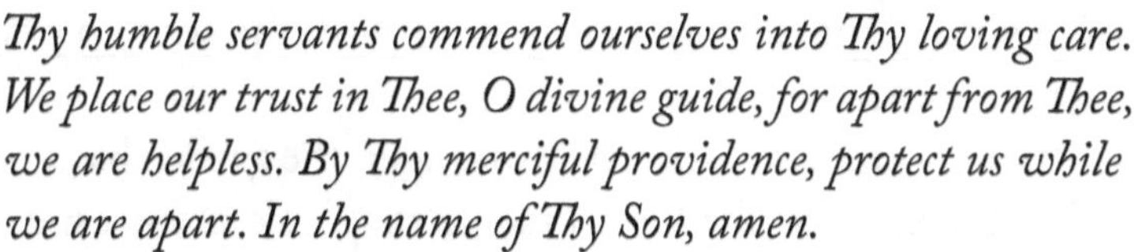

*Thy humble servants commend ourselves into Thy loving care.
We place our trust in Thee, O divine guide, for apart from Thee,
we are helpless. By Thy merciful providence, protect us while
we are apart. In the name of Thy Son, amen.*

"The reading for today?"

"Yes. God goes before you and will bring you back. On this,
I stake my hope." Light burned in Meta's gaze.

"I would give anything—"

"I know."

"How does a dream get such a hold on us, we become willing
to sacrifice so much?"

She shook her head.

"You have given up so much already. And yet—"

"And yet." She kissed him, then drew back. "One of us must
get up first."

Their feet hit the floor at the same time. Meta cooked
breakfast while Clay did the chores and called Franklin, whose
last-minute advice rolled between bites.

"If ya find a courier at Fort Morgan, ya can send us a letter.
Got everthin' ya need? Got yer contract, jest in case?" He set his
plate aside and stood.

Clay followed him outside with Meta close behind. Franklin
stamped like Ethel in the brisk air. "Got yer money?"

Clay patted a bulge in his saddlebag.

"P'visions?"

"Mmm."

Clay clung to Meta, rested his chin on her head before
pulling back. At that moment, he would gladly have given up the
dream. But a pained pledge rasped from his lips.

"I'll be back, I promise."

Meadowlarks and wild canaries, busy feeding their babies, chorused as Meta wrung out clothes. With every twist, she sent up prayers for Clay's safety.

Right now, Lissa would be working in the garden back home. How hard it must be for her to tackle that task alone, especially since she always liked indoor work better.

Henry Jr. and Freidrich would be steadying the plow down a furrow in the west forty this morning. Mama always called her two eldest sons *the boys*, even after they turned forty. Friedrich must be forty-four by now, and Henry forty-two, both unmarried.

They would make good husbands and fathers—like Franklin. But neither of them would marry, for duty called them to tend the farm.

Last night, she asked Franklin the year of his birth.

"Don't rightly know." He studied her as if she might guess and gave no further reply.

Dreaming of the future, she secured the clothes with wooden pins her brother Henry carved. Imperfect but made with love, and workable—like life.

The breeze grasped her sigh—oh, how she missed Clay! But three days had passed, and so would all the rest.

Franklin loaded rough-hewn logs into his cart to join a growing pile where he and Clay had drawn the shed's foundation. Of a sudden, her thoughts stopped altogether, for an Indian stood ramrod straight a few yards from Franklin.

She hurried into the cabin and grabbed a plate of leftover cornbread. Franklin glanced up as she approached, then turned rapt attention back to the brave. When she stopped a couple of feet away, they quieted.

"Will your visitor eat some food?" She gave the Indian her best smile. "For you, if you wish. Please tell him, Franklin."

As bronze as Mama's wedding pitcher from the Old Country with eyes like rich Iowa soil, the brave glanced from Franklin to her, then back again. Birds twittered in the brush, but otherwise, the afternoon turned silent, so she returned to her garden.

Later, Franklin came over. "Lookee them clouds. I'll bring th' animals up in case th' storm comes sooner'n I think."

Not a word about his visitor. Her questions all returned, but he plunged down the creek side. She yanked the clothes off the line, and just in time since the wind changed direction before she reached the cabin. From the northwest, thunder rumbled. In the barn, the hens' eyes glittered from their roosts, and Della settled in next to Hope.

Just as she reached the door, rain's cooling promise swathed her. Franklin joined her to stand watch, a sturdy pillar planted under the canvas tarp—an ideal opportunity for him to tell her about that Indian, but nary an utterance from his lips.

Soon the sound on the roof turned into pounding: hailstones, white and sharp, glanced the earth and rattled against the cabin wall. Finally, Franklin volunteered something.

"Hit's a flower moon—bound t' be rain."

If only he would tell her about his visitor, but experience had taught her to quiet her questions. When he wanted to impart information, he would, but not until.

Owen Dunbar's warm handshake welcomed Clay to the Oak Bar, and a cowhand took Pax to the barn. Within a few minutes, the dinner bell clanged, so Owen led Clay to the bunkhouse.

"Roy here's our trail cook. He's been practicing." Owen gestured to a mustached hand. "Boys, meet Clay Burns. Clay, Reece on your left and Buck behind him."

They all shook hands as Roy dished up steak with biscuits and gravy. Slim conversation peppered the meal, and Clay filled his plate a second time.

"Good grub, Roy." Owen tipped his chair back. "So, this is our crew—what do you think?"

"You all look like better men than me."

"Let's get an early start so we can make good time by tomorrow night."

Owen's estimate worked, and by the third day, they entered Laramie County where Colorado's rolling hills tinged with green. Owen rode beside Clay a distance behind the others.

"Things have changed since I came through here. Back then they called the Fort, Camp Tyler, and after that, Camp Wardell. Prime location on those bluffs." A little farther on, the South Platte River bisected the fertile area.

"In the days of Camp Tyler, whole bands of Arapahoe and South Cheyenne crossed here toward upland buffalo grounds. Lakota and Pawnee, too. Not many settlers had moved in, so we had little to fear."

On a homestead, a settler had dug a ditch to his claim from the Cache de la Poudre River. Several small children played near his cabin, and his wife worked in her garden.

"If I were twenty years younger, I might settle here. Gold miners passed right over this country—once belonged to Nebraska Territory. Colorado got lucky when some Washington bureaucrat decided to re-divide the land."

They gave the horses a rest where sharp outgrowths signaled the beginning of the Arapahoe Range. Being on the trail reminded Clay he would never have met Meta if not for his first trail drive. Every splashing clear-water stream reminded him how she had changed his life.

"Indians! To the left on that ridge. Just keep moving." Owen rode on to alert the others, and ten minutes later, circled back. "We ought to reach Fort Morgan late tomorrow—won't mind having somebody else keep watch."

Cool mountain air descended from the front range. A hundred miles in three days. If they could keep up this pace— Owen's calm matched the fading of daylight as the cowhands made camp.

"Trips like this make me think of the Pony Express. After they telegraphed President Lincoln's inaugural address to St. Joseph, riders delivered it to Sacramento in seven days and seventeen hours."

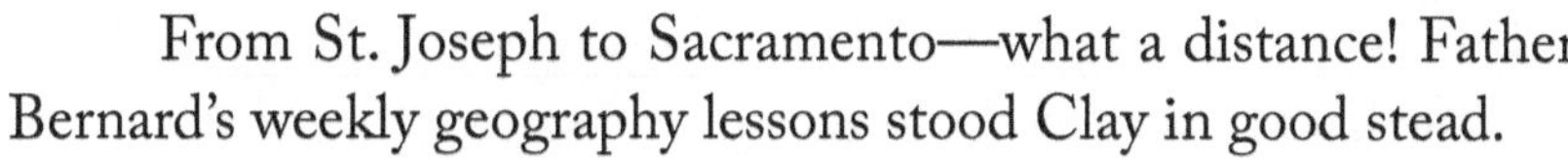

From St. Joseph to Sacramento—what a distance! Father Bernard's weekly geography lessons stood Clay in good stead.

"Why such a hurry?"

"Any day, California was scheduled to vote North or South. A lot depended on the new President's speech—money counts in war, and they had gold to offer either side."

"Do you think it made much difference?"

"Hard to tell. Hate to think how much the South would have gained if the vote went for them."

Owen stared into the fire after they devoured beans and bacon. "My first cattle drive about thirty years ago, my wife cried herself sick when I left."

The ranch had shown no sign of a woman's presence. Clay squelched his curiosity—none of his business.

By midafternoon the next day, Fort Morgan came into sight.

A guard stood watch at the gate.

"How far'd you folks come?"

"A few hours southwest of Fort Laramie."

"See any Indians?"

"Just once, two days north. Mind if we spend the night?"

The guard pointed to an adobe building. "Plenty of empty beds, and we've still got a smithy. Next bugle call will be mess."

Later, the cook ladled them beefsteak and potatoes. Even before they sat down, Owen initiated a conversation with a major.

"How long have you been out here?"

"Fourteen months. From Indiana."

"Got your stripes in the war?"

When the officer nodded, a scar on his neck shone in the lamplight. "Never thought t' command *galvanized* Yankees, but they sent me here when the conflict ended. Most of the men had been Confederate prisoners of war."

The talk turned to the Indians. When Roy got up to leave, Clay went with him to check on Pax.

"Good boy. Rest now, we'll hit it hard again in the morning."

Clay climbed to a corner watchtower with cannons positioned over the fort and approached the guard.

"Mind if I take a look?"

The guard stepped aside to reveal a plateau about half a mile from the South Platte. No wonder people called this *the Fort Morgan Cut-off*. The Overland Trail left the river here, veering across the plains toward Denver City.

"How many men do you have?"

"Don't rightly know. Durin' Injun troubles, three companies—four hundred men each."

As Clay climbed down to circle the fort's circumference, snitches of conversation wafted from a group of wagons parked near the entrance.

"I say we leave in the morning. The twenty of us can surely ward off bandits in the Arapahoe Range."

"Not just outlaws, the Colonel says. Indians, too. I don't mind waiting for more able-bodied men."

Dusk colored the distant range purple—the natives' homeland. But outlaws like the ones who burned the mission—what stirred their fighting? The answer came with the evening's coolness. Hatred—sheer hatred.

Years ago, his father had ventured out into danger with only a wife and young children. Had his dream clouded all common sense? A slipshod wagon and a man with a dream—no wonder the Comanches found them such an obvious target.

Chapter Twenty-six

For four long years the civilized world was engaged in killing men. Christian against Christian, barbarians uniting... anything to kill. It was taught in every school, aye in the Sunday schools. The little children played at war. The toddling children on the street. Do you suppose this world has ever been the same since? How long, your Honor, will it take for the world to get back the humane emotions that were slowly growing before the war? How long will it take the calloused hearts of men before the scars of hatred and cruelty shall be removed?

~Charles Darrow

No more Indian bands through southern Colorado, into New Mexico Territory and across the Canadian River. Except for small irritations, the men got along. Buck whistled through his teeth, but no one mentioned it until New Mexico Territory. Clay had already settled in his bedroll when Owen broke rank.

"Buck, you mind giving us some quiet?"

"Sure." Buck took off beyond the campfire, and Owen went on. "I've been thinking of those galvanized Yankees who agreed to join the Union Army if they wouldn't have to fight former comrades-in-arms."

"Was that the deal? So the command sent them out here to build forts and provide security?"

"Yes. Must've been tough for them to forsake the South, and they'd never faced the Indians out here. But I can imagine, after they'd fought for so long and been held prisoner, that anything would have looked good."

"Hmm."

"But don't you think they had trouble sleeping out here?"

No doubt they had, but Clay stifled a yawn. He longed for sleep himself—perhaps if he withheld comment, Owen would drift off, too.

Weariness badgered Meta as she dipped her spoon into the honey jar after caring for the animals and sweeping the barn. Her legs moved like posts as she returned to the cabin. Once inside, she sat for a minute in her rocker.

An early summer haze, heady and warm, accompanied the *plunk* of logs not far away. Mellow sunshine reached the back of her head, neck, and shoulders. A horsefly buzzed near the window.

At a sharp knock, she jumped to her feet and opened the door to a cavalry officer.

"Ma'am?" The soldier stepped back when she came into the sunlight.

"Yes?"

"I seek a Mrs. Clay Burns and a Mrs. Garrit Rausch."

"I am Mrs. Burns, and I know Mrs. Rausch."

"A letter for you from Clay Burns, Fort Morgan, Colorado Territory. And some others for Mrs. Rausch."

"Oh, thank you. Would you take the noon meal with us? You can fetch Franklin Ross out back. Dinner will be ready by the time you water your horses."

The captain tipped his cap and reached into his pack. "Your letters, Ma'am."

Her fingers trembled as she pulled out her flour can. Enough time to make fresh biscuits and some ham.

After Franklin and the captain found seats, the door opened

again and Captain Blaine gestured in another soldier. "Mrs. Burns, Lieutenant Anders."

Franklin took charge. "Have yerself a seat."

Meta transferred golden biscuits to a basket and speared thick ham chunks onto a platter while Franklin engaged the soldiers.

"Saw Clay Burns, didja?"

"His party stayed the night at Fort Morgan about a week ago."

"They meet any Injuns?"

"Only one small band with no pursuit."

"How's things b'tween Denver n' Cheyenne?"

"Raiders make life miserable for settlements distant from Denver, and ranchers reject Lieutenant General Sherman's advice to gather at stage stations but blame the Army when they lose stock and horses. General Sherman and Governor Hunt keep a sharp eye.

"Sherman would have flushed out warriors down the Platte and Smoky Rivers sooner, but Washington stymied him with just five hundred men, only three hundred carbines, and no money for equipment. Governor Hunt faces the same situation."

"Afore '50, some numbskull agent separated th' Cheyenne, North and South.

"Before the Homestead Act?"

"Yep. Settlers piled in, so Injuns lost more land. Treaties shoulda set things right, but nobody carried 'em out."

"I wish the agents would ask your advice." The Lieutenant exchanged a look with Captain Blaine. "Tell us more, Mr. Ross."

"They sent the Cheyenne t' Oklahomy Territ'ry, but Chief Dull Knife got captured n' sent t' Dakota. Broke out n' got captured agin. Ended up in Montana, but th' tribe lost ceremonial trinkets n' sech. Injuns takes 'em right serious."

"Like the objects in their burial grounds?" The young Lieutenant seemed earnest.

"Yep."

"Did you know Dull Knife?"

The question stopped Franklin's forkful in midair.

"Met 'im a time 'r two."

"Can you tell us more about him?"

"A honest Injun. Cared 'bout his own."

"Governor Hunt can do so little without Washington's support. This Indian war covers an area a thousand by two thousand miles. General Sherman has only six companies at Julesburgh, and even with Custer coming down from the Smoky Hill..."

Lieutenant Anders continued to eat, but the captain patted his stomach. "The stage customers rely on regular schedules, but if the companies would vary the times and carry passengers willing to fight, they could avoid raids."

"Zac'ly. This Sherman sounds like a smart feller."

"True, although the Confederates would tell you different. Lieutenant, it's time we move on." The captain turned to Meta. "Such a hearty meal. Sorry for all the talk of Indians, Ma'am but—"

"Oh, I would rather know."

"I anticipate more troops advancing north. We have our share of troubles from Chief Red Cloud—the Lieutenant and I will have to deal with them."

Franklin extended his hand. "Things h'ain't gittin' better."

Meta watched from the doorway as the men mounted and headed north. Franklin peeked in a few minutes later as she washed the dishes.

"Jest 'member, Owen Dunbar's lived out here all his days."

"You're sure this canyon's too dangerous? Looks a lot closer to where we're goin'." Of the three cowhands, adventure ran strongest in Reese. From a sudden drop-off, a lush valley, rough but stunning, led to a creek winding through the base. There, rock outcroppings rose in various formations.

"Absolutely. Red said Palo Duro's beauty deceives men. That

pillar over there looks like an hour's ride but might take a full day. That's one thing that attracts outlaws."

"How far does it go?" As usual, Owen sought geographical details.

"A hundred and twenty miles. Red said he crossed through once, called it the prettiest place he ever saw but was glad to get out still breathing. Last summer, he had us cross beyond the south entrance, to Fort Sumner and then north."

Owen interjected, "Red doesn't have much to say. When he does speak, I tend to believe him."

May 29, 1867
Dearest Meta,
Five days gone by and we spent the night at Fort Morgan. Ate hearty, but I miss your cooking.
All is on schedule. The hands are good men and Owen has so much to offer.
The stars remind me of you, the creeks and the sunshine, the breeze… everything.
Beautiful country, beautiful Meta.
Take good care of yourself. With continued good fortune, I hope to see you in July.
Your loving husband,
Clay

She pressed the thin paper close. The rocker's sway lulled her, but she went to check the hens. By now the men might have arrived at the Crady Ranch and even rounded up some horses. She unwound the latches on two cages and set warm eggs in her basket.

From the downy underside of the last laying hen, three eggs appeared. Twelve today, a new record. But her mind went back to a conversation before Clay left.

Do you look forward to seeing the Cradys?

I only worked there.

Did you have any friends?

Cowhands came and went. Mr. Crady ignored me until he gave me Pax. But Hank, the foreman, seemed to understand my puzzlement.

The Cradys will welcome you, won't they?

Clay had taken her hand. *I'm going there for our starter herd— it's the only place I know. I don't plan on any welcome.*

Clay showed no emotion about his childhood, so opposite from her memories. Only his descriptions of the horses roaming North Texas excited him.

Near the Crady Ranch, herds run wild. In spring and early summer, you can hear them miles away. After clearing the hills of grass, they retreat to cool shallow canyons with creeks. Mustangs, sorrels, and paints blend in a hundred variations. A man only needs desire and a lasso to capture them.

The tall stranger's thick-heeled, square-cut leather boots reached just below his knees and extended to brass tips on pointed toes. His silver spurs clipped with an air of authority as he held out an over-sized brown hand.

"Name's Moberly." His eyes glinted as sunset created an aura around his head. Owen shook his hand.

"Owen Dunbar, Wyoming Territory. Join us for supper?"

"Always say yes to an invitation like that."

"We're down here for a starter herd."

"Selling to the Cavalry?"

Owen nodded.

"Makes sense—a stable market." Moberly replaced his sombrero.

"You wouldn't happen to be a Texas Ranger?"

"How did you know?"

"Just a wild guess."

Clay poured their guest fresh coffee. He handed a mug to Owen, who tilted his head toward the Ranger.

"Clay Burns, sir."

"Burns. That an English name?"

"I'm not altogether sure."

Owen swallowed a whiff of his steaming coffee, with one hand on a long-handled spoon stuck into the skillet. Tonight, he had taken over the cooking.

"Moberly's English, isn't it?"

"My nose declares my folks sailed from there about a hundred years back. Names and faces intrigue me."

"Dunbar's Scottish, a town near Edinburgh on the southeast coast."

What would it be like to know your origins—Clay lapsed into conjecture. Father Bernard knew his French ancestral line, and Meta's German heritage filled her childhood.

"You Rangers have quite the reputation, even up in Wyoming Country. I imagine some's true, some's legend. Maybe you can straighten me out."

"Depends what you heard."

Owen flipped biscuits one by one. "Unmarried. Some drinkers, but mostly sober men who risk their lives doing their duty."

"My wife died years ago, but my work made her life anything but easy. I try to follow the law. Had my days of drinkin', but that don't set well with trackin' outlaws. Better to keep my wits and surprise them without theirs. Not much glory, but a whole lot of riding till you're stiff in the saddle."

"I can imagine. This trip reminds me how sore a body can get."

"Mmm. Trouble is, a man can't stop. Always one more scoundrel that haunts you at night."

Clay leaned back against a sapling. The sky had dimmed to gray, and a breezy whisper lazed through the campsite. The faint beat of hooves told him the hands were scouting the area before bedding down.

"Who you hunting right now?"

Moberly's jaw clenched. "Depraved fellows from the town of Jefferson. Killed a Negro, Rough Alexander, for sport. The instigator, Hugh Freeman, has been known to beat Negros in broad daylight, and did so to Alexander a week before the murder—a revolver to the head. Forced an argument with him and that night, got another Negro to call him outside."

Moberly swigged some coffee. "Man named John Shepherd pulled the trigger, point-blank. Alexander fell into his wife's arms while a young man, Tomlin, stood guard with Freeman. I'll find 'em, even in the Canyon."

Night sounds hushed as evening fell. A little later, a hearty belch echoed from the river.

"A bird?" Owen addressed his question to Clay.

"No, little brown frogs you can hardly see. But they make that big noise."

The Ranger leaned in. "You lived here before?"

"Most of my life."

Buck and Reese shuffled into the circle, looking hungry. Owen handed the first plate to Buck, who headed toward Roy, standing watch.

After a second helping, Clay's eyes grew heavy. He gathered the plates, swished them in hot water and set them out to dry.

The tale of Rough Alexander's death hung just below his breastbone. His killers had a lot in common with the desperadoes that torched the mission.

When he returned from dumping the dishwater and checking Pax, Reese had gone for an evening stroll, and Buck, next to stand watch, took to his bedroll. Owen fed the fire as Clay settled in, his hat over his face, but Owen had another question for Moberly.

"Got a story that's stayed with you through the years?"

"Sure do. Must've been the fall of forty-four, maybe forty-five. Comanches attacked an immigrant wagon, and by the time I got there, everything had burned. Sagebrush caught some of their papers, written in another tongue. Buried the man, his wife, and a child."

A pair of quail twittered from a lone tree. "You recall even a name?"

Shoving his hat aside, Clay surveyed Moberly's profile from the shadows.

"*Dusek.* Must've been a steamer ticket, I figured. Found out years later that means *soul* in some Slavian tongue."

"Anyway, that day I saw somethin' like sheep's wool rolled under a sagebush." He fell silent for a spell. The mellow twang of pipe tobacco reached Clay, Owen's evening indulgence.

"Then the bundle started movin' up and down. And down in there nestled a ruddy-cheeked boy lookin' up as though he expected me."

A knot formed in Clay's stomach. Twenty-three or four years—No way would he ask his burning question. At the same time, he willed the Ranger to continue.

Chapter Twenty-seven

I can't say as ever I was lost, but I was bewildered once for three days.

~Daniel Boone

Franklin maneuvered fence posts all morning as Meta cleaned the chicken roosts and hoed her garden plot. Potatoes, carrots, and beans sprouted—along with determined weeds.

A long narrow cloud passed through the heavens, slim but double-barreled, like a shotgun. The billowy column rolled from horizon to horizon.

The steady *whack, whack, whack* of Franklin's mallet set a backdrop as she thinned the carrots. Having his new cabin near, she could do her work, cook for him, and fall asleep in peace. Still time before the noon meal—perhaps she might visit her neglected journal.

June seventh. Prayers for Clay and Martin, both in Indian Territory.

With sunny days and showers, the pea crop has begun. Mama's bountiful rows put my scraggly turnips and potato vines to shame.

Tomorrow will be Martin's birthday. And Clay... how peculiar not to know his birth date. I might have to create one for him. Yes—one day I shall surprise him with a cake.

A low stirring of earth and air—the rhythm increased into a rumble. A heavy wagon approached from the north. She leaped to her feet—Franklin must not have heard yet. At the screech of a brake and voices from the creek, she hurried faster.

Down the bank, a man with blacksmith's arms lifted three young children from a wagon.

"Can we wade in the creek, Papa?"

A slight red-haired woman answered from the buckboard and the young'uns splashed with glee. Nearly down the incline, Meta hailed them, and the couple started her way.

Company... a woman! Attending to ruts and tree roots, Meta advanced. By the time she reached the creek, Franklin called from above.

"Ho there. Who ya be?"

"Butler. Passing through to Cheyenne."

The woman's clear hazel eyes shone bright. Meta held out her arms. "I am Meta Burns. Welcome to Spring Creek."

"Stalwart Butler and my husband Bryant."

"Oh, I am so glad to see you. When did you start out?"

"Yesterday. We're mighty glad to see someone besides Indians."

"You have seen some?"

Her husband answered. "A few, but none with painted faces."

"Will you take the noonday meal with us?" Meta tossed her head in Franklin's direction. "Franklin Ross knows more about the Indians than anyone."

"We hope to make Cheyenne by sundown, so we ought to keep on."

"That's a hard day, even without small children."

"You have made the trip?"

"Twice. But you can eat and still get a few hours in before nightfall, so tomorrow will see you there in daylight."

Stalwart placed her hand on Bryant's sleeve. They looked as though they could use a hot meal.

"We got eggs." Franklin could not have issued a more enticing invitation.

Bryant called, "All right, sir. Thank you kindly."

The children's chatter echoed as Stalwart joined Meta, describing their journey from Bighorn country and stopping at the Hanson's overnight.

Scenes from the stage stop came alive—always enough food there. She would fry eggs, slice up some salted bear meat, and serve dried corn fritters with butter and honey.

"Lookin' for someone?"

Clay started back. "Why no. I couldn't sleep."

"Ah. You'd think when others are keeping watch, we could sleep."

"Thinking about that Alexander fellow?"

"Yep. But you're at the start of a grand adventure. Have a wife?"

"I do, sir. We married at Fort Laramie about three weeks ago."

The Ranger sighed. "Must've been hard to leave her so soon."

A longing for Meta swept through Clay as Moberly continued. "Leaving mine was the worst. Once you get your herd going, you can stay put?"

"I plan to."

"Good." Moberly squinted at Clay for a long moment, but Clay found no words to ask about the Ranger's story.

Moonlight played tricks with Pax's coat, midnight blue, black, then dark brown. Perhaps a similar thing happened in life, since destiny played a hand, as that fellow—what was his name—said in the saloon on last year's drive.

Our main duty lies in trusting. Father Bernard, always somewhere near.

"We'll see you in the morning."

Stalwart Butler reminded Meta of Betsy. Washing the children's faces and hands, she taught them about plants.

"Notice how Mrs. Burns separates and replants her carrots?

See where she stopped? She will do the same with the rest to multiply her crop. Each plant needs its own space, like people. Ellie, keep your hands clean now."

The other two urchins, two boys a year or two older, circled the garden patch like frolicking lambs. Meanwhile, Franklin spoke with Mr. Butler about Indians.

"Franklin, would you please bring in a couple of stumps for extra chairs?"

Both men headed for the log pile as Meta fried every single egg while her corn fritters browned. Nothing like having guests!

At just the right time, Stalwart entered. "I left Bryant in charge. How can I help?"

"You could pour everyone some milk."

"Milk, butter, and honey. How wonderful! We had to leave our stock behind." Stalwart's voice wobbled. "Our cow, the chickens—all pets, but—" She stared out the window. "When we started out six years ago, *stalwart* described me. Papa said when we left Indiana, "You're as strong as any son.'" She poured the last of the milk. "But after three babies, and losing two others, I am with child again, and every day another homestead gets burned. So frightening, but at the same time, we wanted to stay.

"You must think me very weak. Once, I believed faith would see you through."

"Of course you did, and so did I. We still do, but maybe our faith has gone deeper, like—like transplanted carrot roots." Meta hugged away Stalwart's tears.

"Protecting your family shows no weakness. What if Providence put the desire to move in your hearts?"

Voices sounded outside, and the scuffling of little feet. "But why build our homestead only to leave?"

"I think the same way. Why should my husband's dream lead to his death?"

Stalwart took in a long breath. "Yes. Out here, I guess the question is always, *why.*"

Ellie toddled toward her. "Children, Mrs. Burns has prepared a special meal. She's an angel to cheer us on our way."

"You kept Ranger Moberly company during the night?" Owen plied Clay with coffee as the sun made a feeble attempt to rise.

Scorching his throat with the black liquid never failed to clear Clay's mind. With Meta beside him, he had slept more in the past three weeks than he could recall. Should have known the trail would revive his old habits.

Boots scrunched on rock and Ranger Moberly accepted Owen's steamy offering. Owen turned his attention to the pancakes.

"How far you fellas going?"

"The other side of Dallas."

"Should get there by nightfall, I'd say."

"You know the Crady ranch?"

Moberly narrowed his eyes. "No trouble there for a long time."

What did that mean? Instead of asking, Clay headed to Pax. Halfway there, Moberly fell in step.

"Son, look at me."

The Ranger's scrutiny shot lightning down Clay's spine.

"Seen lot of faces in my time but eyes like yours only once." Moberly's cheek muscle worked back and forth like a calf scratching an itch. Time stopped as he spoke again.

"Where'd you get your name?"

"I think the Sisters gave it to me."

"At a mission?"

Clay needed air, but his lips clamped together.

"The orphanage out east of Dallas in the grand prairie? You have no recollection of your mother and father?"

Somehow Clay shook his head.

"Could be wrong, son, but I think you're the one. All these years, I've looked and looked for eyes like yours. That fire at the mission. Wish I'd have been closer…"

"Father Bernard took me in."

A wide grin softened Moberly's expression. "And you have a wife." He drove his fist into his hand. "Sometimes a man wonders if what he does makes any difference. My wife died without having children, but you're starting a family of your own."

No reply came—for all this time, this Ranger had pondered over him. Such a wonder, and now it was true. He would start a family. His parents' seed would live on in this great land.

The Crady ranch had to be near. Always questioning, Owen caught up with Clay. "Reminds me of a section of the Rockies."

"You lived in Colorado?"

"Sojourned is more like it."

"Did we come close on our way?"

"No." They rode a while before Owen continued. "What happened with Moberly?"

"He believes I'm that baby he found under the bush."

"He's sure?" Clearly, the question had churned in Owen's head "Bet your eyes gave it away."

"You ought to be a detective. But how did you know Moberly was a Texas Ranger? The sombrero?"

"No, his holster. Most marshalls adjust them low on the thigh, but rangers wear them high on their hips—easier to shoot from horseback. So your real name is *Dusek*?"

"Seems so."

"Going to change it, then?"

"Meta will have a fright if I leave as *Burns* and come back as *Dusek*."

"If I could, I'd change mine to Beauregard, for my mother's side." They rode farther, and the lay of the land became familiar.

"Tell me about the Cradys."

Clay pointed east. "What little I know, you'll figure out soon enough."

The winter before Clay left, Mr. Crady had suffered a severe illness. If he were still alive, would he do business with a novice horse rancher? And all those years ago, why had he hired him in the first place?

Father Bernard had made sure Clay could ride and fire a gun, but he had so much to learn when he first arrived. So many questions churning, churning.

Hopefully Mr. Crady's son would not be here, but even his malice drove Clay to manhood. Allan Crady taught him to ignore sharp tongues. Clay developed a *flat face*, diminishing Allan's pleasure in torturing him.

A crude wooden sign greeted them at the turn-off. Owen reached out to the middle log with two slats forming a T.

"Why do they call this place the Triple T?"

"Never thought about it."

In the yard, Mr. Crady occupied a chair on the ranch house porch. Even in afternoon heat, a blanket circled his shoulders.

He raised a thin arm. "Still got that horse, I see."

"I do, sir. Right now he needs a good rest."

"What brings you here?"

Clay glanced toward Owen, who dismounted. "Owen Dunbar, sir, of the Oak Bar Ranch, Wyoming Territory. Clay, here, has done fine work for me. Now we hope to buy some halter broke stock."

Clay looped Pax's reins to the hitching post as Mr. Crady broke into a violent cough. "Thought this lad might come back to live in Texas."

Owen jumped back in. "Wyoming Country stole him away. He's claimed some land, even found himself a wife."

Another fit struck the rancher. As soon as he quieted, Owen guided the conversation.

"We need breeding horses. Be mighty grateful to do business

with you, sir."

"Take care of your horses." Mr. Crady struggled to sit up "Plenty of room in the bunk house with most hands at roundup. Come back in about an hour for supper."

Clay would much rather eat in the bunkhouse but accepted his fate as he rubbed Pax with an old blanket. "You rest now, boy."

"Tell Anna at the restaurant that Meta sent you." Meta handed over a letter filled with news of her marriage, Clay's trip, and Franklin's work.

"She has far too much to do, and Herman might welcome Bryant's help, too. Cheyenne bustled with new businesses last spring when we stopped there."

As she and Stalwart said farewell, birds chirruped afternoon messages. Bryant hoisted two tired boys into the wagon bed and turned to wave to Franklin on the bank.

Ellie came running, smeared with mud, and Stalwart wiped her face and hands. "Time for a nap." She grasped Meta's hand. "We will deliver your letters, and..." Her hazel eyes glinted. "Thank you for your kindness. Will you come visit us?"

"Maybe some day. In the meantime, we can write. Keep a letter ready—Franklin stops in when he checks his traps, and cavalry men often carry mail, too. Godspeed, my friend."

Ellie nestled against her Mama, like baby Michael with Betsy. Had Betsy's faith grown deeper through her trials, too?

Chapter Thirty-one

*Look not mournfully into the past, it comes not back
again. Wisely improve the present, it is thine. Go forth to meet
the shadowy future without fear and with a manly heart.*
~Henry Wadsworth Longfellow

Wainscoting bordered a ceiling decorated with plaster, and
ornate wood formed rows around the room. The table's ponder-
ous legs and thick top must weigh five hundred pounds, but Clay
focused on his thick steak, grateful for Owen's gift of chatter.

Mrs. Crady's black collar backed her neck like a flag. Her
head erect, she presided over dinner.

"Tell us about your plans, Clay."

He had scrubbed in the creek, put on the extra shirt from
his saddlebag, and run his fingers through his hair before coming.
But they wanted to hear his voice.

"Like Mr. Dunbar said, Ma'am, we aim to supply horses for
the Cavalry."

"When you first came here, what were you, sixteen? One
thing hasn't changed, your unique eyes."

To avoid her gaze, Clay took another bite.

"Tell us about your wife, won't you?"

Oh, for Owen's ability to speak with ease! Clay's focus kept
slipping to Mrs. Crady's silver-rimmed widow's peak.

"Meta... my wife. Ah... she comes from Iowa. Her eyes..." he
sought for words. "Why, they're as dark as this floor, and her hair
too. She grew up in a big farm family."

Through this little speech, Mr. Crady's stare agitated Clay. Mrs. Crady touched her stiff collar. They all ate in silence until she addressed him again.

"We wish you the best. Family constitutes a special gift." She squeezed her husband's quivering hand. Bones stood out in his sunken yellow cheeks, like windblown cattle skulls. Maybe Mrs. Crady referred to his lonely childhood.

Clay looked to Owen, whose drawn brow could have meant, *Say something!* or *This old rancher looks too sick to be at this table.*

Their hostess touched her lips with her napkin. "And your family, Mr. Dunbar?"

"My wife passed on a few years back, Ma'am." Mrs. Crady murmured in sympathy as Owen returned her question.

"Do you have sons and daughters?"

She lit into her description as a visible shudder took Mr. Crady.

"Three sons and a daughter. Gold fever wooed our sons to California, and our daughter married a railroad man from Ohio."

Mr. Crady suffered another spasm, so his wife handed him some water. When he recovered, the rancher made his announcement brief.

"We have four halter-broke mares, twenty dollars a head." He took another drink. "You can round up more—use this as your base camp."

Owen half-rose to shake hands with him and thank his wife for the meal. Clay followed suit, breathing easier as they departed. In the kitchen, an older Spanish woman busied herself at the table.

When his feet hit the ground outside, Clay turned to Owen. "Glad that's over."

"They think highly of you."

An evening breeze meandered to them.

"I never even met Mrs. Crady before."

"She seemed awfully concerned for your welfare." Owen's eyebrow shot up, his eyes on the sunset. "Get an early start tomorrow?"

Clay nodded, and Owen gave a gentle snort.

"Sure hope I remember how to use a rope."

He disappeared into the bunkhouse, and Clay checked on Pax. In fact, he slept in the next stall.

Chapter Twenty-eight

Friendship is a sheltering tree. Advice is like snow—the softer it falls, the longer it dwells upon, and the deeper it sinks into the mind. The happiness of life is made up of minute fractions—the little, soon forgotten charities of a kiss or a smile, a kind look or heartfelt compliment.

~Samuel Taylor Coleridge

The letters Captain Blaine delivered cheered Meta. The last time Franklin brought news from Iowa, Friedrich's stilted hand bore word of Mama's death. Reading this, something had entered her soul, a stillness, perhaps, impossible to define.

All things changed. Nothing remained the same.

Now, an address made her gasp—Mama's fine writing. She rocked for a while, the familiar squeak oddly comforting.

The Lord is my shepherd. Freidrich had written this concerning Mama's funeral service. *As the Shepherd guided her in life, so it was in death.*

As she prepared to open the last letter Mama wrote her, more came to mind. *He leadeth me beside the still waters. He restoreth my soul.*

In those long winter months, was that what had happened? Memories swarmed as she hesitated a bit longer. Mama's careful strokes would give one last glimpse into her earthly life, one last blessing.

Everyday occurrences filled the letter—Freidrich and Henry's newborn calves and getting the plow stuck on the first planting day. A visit from Margita with her four youngest children, who tracked so much mud into the back porch that Lissa slipped and hurt her wrist.

A fetching bird perched on the windowsill, much like the blue jays in Iowa, but a darker shade of blue. Perhaps Mr. Audubon would call them cousins.

Margita, the third oldest, would have laid blame on the little ones for Lissa's accident. But Mama had a way of acknowledging error without causing shame—what a lovely legacy.

The night of that visit, she slipped away during her sleep after a day of meaningful work, engaged with her loved ones right up to the end. A fitting closure to a comely life.

This letter must have gotten waylaid at some post for several weeks, for Mama said Lissa would have her first baby in June. Now to put into practice the generosity Mama instilled.

The blue bird's breast swelled before each verse of his song— he was at work, too, guarding his nest. Just like Mama, always diligent.

"But here I sit, dawdling in the middle of the day. Better put my mind to Lissa's gift. What might I sew? Maybe the pale blue stripe in the trunk would make a sleeping gown."

The next thing Meta knew, Della mooed down by the creek. The sun had already slid into its late afternoon position—she had fallen asleep once again. She bustled up, glancing through the door.

Franklin must not realize how she had loitered. She cut ham to fry. While the food cooked, she scraped under the noodle dough and turned it over to dry the other side.

By the time Franklin came, dinner awaited him. Meta wiped her hands on her apron. "How is the work going?"

"Hit my thumb with the blamed hammer." He held up a swollen hand.

"But you kept working."

"Course. What else would a feller do?"

She fetched some linament. "Let me put this on."

What else would a feller do? Or a woman. With an ounce of self-pride, any woman would keep working. Garrit would disapprove of her lazy spirit, and heartily. What would Clay think?

Franklin labored so hard while she took naps like a lazy cat. And she had not even opened Matilda's letter.

Franklin interrupted her remorseful thoughts, "Ya' feelin' a'right, gal?"

His first spring here, Clay rode along to Hollow Canyon with cowhands he barely knew. Skinny and scared, he had offered little help, but did learn some things. Today at the Canyon's mouth, Owen waited for instructions like the other men, so Clay devised some.

"The herd used to graze at the far end, and we split into two parties, one to rile up the horses and rope the lead mare and stallion. It's about a half-mile—one of you ride with me and the rest of you stay ready for when the horses start running."

Roy joined him, and after covering about half the distance, Clay dismounted to look for tracks. Nothing.

"Haven't left yet. That's a good sign." Alert, they slackened their pace as the canyon wall curved. When he spied a flash of white, he signaled Roy with two fingers. Roy glimpsed the horse too and eased closer.

So far, fortune seemed on their side. Clay spread his fingers —slow and quiet. Then he tapped the reins and Pax proceeded another few rods.

On the far side of a creek, he and Roy counted twenty-five horses.

Clay picked up a little speed, aiming ten yards behind the last visible animal. A loud whinny split the air as the herd's leader reared in a magnificent pose, bright sun bedazzling her mane.

Hooves hit the earth in a display of thunder. Manes and tails flashed like thousands of insect wings. Vaguely aware of Roy twelve feet to his right, Clay sensed their oneness of purpose.

In what seemed like no time at all, the top of a cowhand's hat appeared in the distance. They both drew back as the lead horses approached the canyon's mouth. Just when it appeared the herd might escape, a lasso winged like a bird.

Another lasso found its mark. In less than two minutes, only two wild horses remained in the canyon. Finally, those two exhausted their fury. Owen's wild hurrah might be worth the ride to Texas.

"Got two of 'em!"

The exquisite mares, one mostly white with a little brown, the other as dark as Meta's hair, brought satisfaction.

In midday sun, the future pawed the earth. Three other mares joined the belle mare, though they might have chosen freedom. Five horses plus four at the ranch—nine healthy animals.

Mr. Dunbar exulted, "Everyone did their job, and you have five fine horses." Everyone whooped and hollered.

"Now what?" Holding his hat high, Owen looked ten years younger.

"They say stallions are the most difficult to capture. The herd might head to another canyon I know. Shall we follow them or get these mares back to the ranch?"

Roy spoke up. "I'd as soon see these beauties in the corral first.'

"Besides, I'm getting mighty hungry," Reese chimed in, and they started off, bantering back and forth.

Franklin's new cabin door hung open, and in fading light, he snored with his chin on his chest. He woke when Meta placed her basket on the table. "Such a long day. Here is your supper. I'll take care of the animals."

"Be sleepin' b'fore m'boots is off. But what did them letters say?"

While he ate, she shared Clay's news. "I waited to read Matilda's letter, but one Mama wrote before she died must have taken the long route here."

Franklin's thick eyebrows shot up, so she shared Mama's descriptions of spring on the farm.

"'Minds me o' Missouri as a young'un with a passel o' brothers and sisters." He half-stood when she started to leave. "No fire t'night, my git-go plumb run out."

"It's all right." She turned to leave.

"Now, don't fergit t' lock th' door."

As darkness fell, she hung her apron on the hook and considered lighting the lantern. In a moment, she changed her mind. Why waste oil?

She accomplished little today but could make up for it tomorrow. As she undressed, she pictured Stalwart tucking her children into bed at Anna and Herman's. What laughter and delight they must be enjoying—but the image only highlighted her isolation.

Only Mama's quilt would do for this evening, for weariness had become her master.

"This morning took me back to when we started up ranching. But we only went as far as Colorado Territory for horses." Owen stretched his legs. "Something to remember the rest of my life. One more adventure before I'm as old as Mr. Crady."

Sparks shot toward the stars, and the few cowhands on the ranch joined them. A man who worked in the stable told them how he acquired his bad leg.

"A few years back, them Confed'rates run wild here. Roped myself a stallion, n' was about t' bring 'im in when a passle o' dirt soldiers rode up. Stallion got tangled in the rope. Pulled me right out o' m' saddle."

He rubbed the side of his thigh. The grey in his hair shimmered in the firelight.

"A quick-thinkin' Reb off'cer kep' me alive—spurred 'is horse n' cut the rope. Stallion took off in a cloud o' dust."

"Did you break your leg?"

"Here n' here n' here." He pointed to three spots from his hip to his knee. "Warn't fer Miz Crady, I mighta died, but she watched me like gold nuggets. Dressed m' wounds n' fed me like a baby till I healed."

"Mr. Crady kept you on?"

The cowhand squinted at Owen. "'Spect that was th' Missus' doin'. If they's angels here, she'd be one.

"Some folks don't take t' sharin' their freedom with black men. Durin' th' war, a leg'slator started th' Loyal Texan unit down in Mexico. Now he's fightin' fer ed'cation fer e'vry chil' born here. Some whites is up in arms, Miz Crady calls 'em carpetbagger pol'ticians. She's all fer edju'catin' folks, says it's th' hope o' this here state." He spat and replaced his chew.

"Say—a Ranger come by, tellin' 'bout a outlaw clan what kilt some Cav'ry of'cers up by th' border. Says t' keep an eye out. Mean bunch, four 'r five of 'em, outa Colorady, mebbe."

Owen's chin rose. "Ranger Moberly?"

"Thet's the one. Them outlaws don't stand no chance." He limped away, and Owen turned to Clay. "Thanks again for letting me come along."

"I'm the one to thank all of you."

Laughter and good-natured talk floated around the fire longer than usual. Buck even pulled out a mouth organ he had kept secret. He played until Owen reminded the cowhands of tomorrow's plan.

"Let's get another early start, all right?" No one argued, but as usual, Clay lay awake beside the fire after Roy collapsed in his bedroll. Thinking of Owen, Clay took a walk around the ranch, ending beside Pax.

"Hey boy, here I am again. If I ever see that Edgar fellow again, I'll tell him you're part of my destiny." He bunched some hay and soon fell asleep.

With the roosts cleaned, Meta brought in wood and chopped some ham into the stew pot with beans. Homemade biscuits would taste good. She set to work, and after dinner Franklin's sawing resumed, so she opened the trunk to choose fabric for Lissa's gifts.

In the process, she came across some seeds packaged in brown paper and tied with string—sweet peas and white daisies—better get these planted. The yellow rose slips beside the cabin door already sprouted leaves. Sometimes she stooped to speak to this reminder of home. "You will brighten our doorstep, just as your cousins do in Iowa."

Plenty of goods for a warm baby sleeper and a winter nightgown for Lissa—by the time this package arrived, fall would be in the air. When her fingers tired from cutting and stitching, Meta took Matilda's letter between the cabin and the creek where Della and Hope grazed.

Against scratchy wild plum bark she lifted her face to the sky. Blue above, green all around. If only Clay worked across the meadow with Franklin, life would be perfect.

A child's greasy fingerprints marched along the envelope, one of Matilda's wild brood hovering near when she sealed the letter.

> *Dear Meta,*
>
> *We are right happy you and Clay have married. Now you will not be alone again. We hope you will stop by next time you come this way.*
>
> *We keep so busy I wonder if I will ever leave here. Soon the garden will need weeding, and Tom says why don't I bake bread to sell to travelers when they take their leave for their claims? A good idea, but when will I find the time?*
>
> *The men have built half of the schoolhouse. Our baby grows every day, and I am in the family way again. Maybe this July birth will be our last.*
>
> *Some settlers have come to sojourn until the Indian troubles pass, and the children enjoy having new friends. The*

cavalry may set up their own way-station here. I hope the situation does not come to that, since so far, the raids stay in the north.

I hope to hear from you.
Your friend,
Matilda Hanson

*Y*our *friend.* Betsy, Matilda, and now Stalwart. No matter how desolate the miles between them all, the word *friend* described these women. Sunshine filled the cabin like a blessing as Meta wrestled between dreams and wakefulness.

Matilda had such a way with words…the images of her busy life crept in and out of this morning's snooze. She must get up, but— Ah, she would rest her eyes only a few minutes more.

For the third time in two days, she woke with a start long after Franklin began his work, and hurried inside to start the meal and set the table. Then she walked out to the new shed, where Franklin wiped his brow with his sleeve. "Only th' middle o' June, and hot as blazes a'ready!"

"You could slow down a little, you know."

He shook his bulky head. "How would I face yer man?"

"Can I help with anything?"

He frowned as if she had offered to carry him to his cabin. She braced herself, hands on her hips.

"Remember how I survived the winter? I have worked out-doors my whole life. I can carry logs, I can—"

The old trapper picked up a specimen, about seventy pounds. "Yer doin' th' chores, cookin' n' cleanin'."

No use arguing, but a perfect time to visit Garrit's grave. So much had happened since last fall—surely years instead of months had passed.

Smoothing the rocks into a row, she sank to the ground. A yellow and black butterfly dipped and flitted away toward the north.

"I have married again, Garrit. Clay and I will carry out your

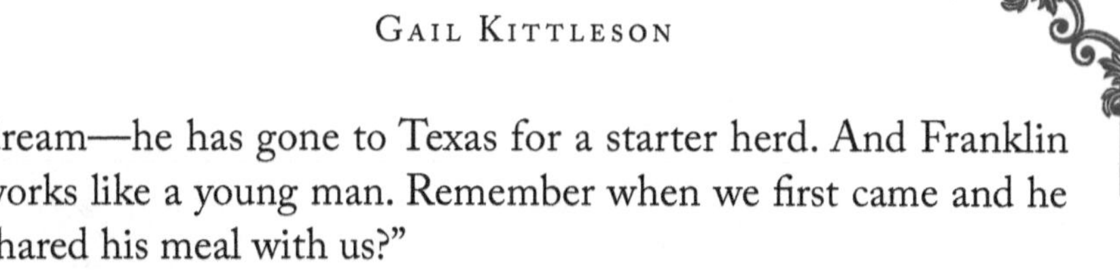

dream—he has gone to Texas for a starter herd. And Franklin works like a young man. Remember when we first came and he shared his meal with us?"

She pulled some dry weeds. "We had some company one day, settlers coming South because of the Indian troubles. I met a new friend, Stalwart. I sent them to Herman and Anna, in hopes that her husband can find work."

A new patch of wildflowers had taken root, delicate white petals around yellow buttons. Meta picked one for the grave.

"And Mama passed quietly, in her sleep. May you both rest in peace."

Pierce Crady's cough proclaimed his dying. His harsh breathing filled the room where his wife, Antonia, kept watch.

Thirty-two years with Pierce had taught her not to pray out loud, but he had mellowed in measured degrees. During the past six months his mean streak rarely revealed itself

She quieted herself by focusing on something beautiful, one of her gardenias, a newborn colt, or the painting on the opposite wall. Half an hour ago, she propped his pillows just so, but her restless thoughts waylaid rest.

This waking-sleeping ritual occurred often. The hallway clock chimed three as she paced the room, recalling how she had made her choices.

At the very first, when Pierce's outbursts began, she might have begged for reinstatement in her family. But she could not, and now, she faced this death alone.

Who else would help Pierce? Glimpsing the bunkhouse across the yard, her answer arrived. Perhaps Providence had sent Clay back for more than horses.

Chapter Twenty-nine

Visions of flames and black veils jolted Clay awake—oh for Meta beside him, but the slow in-and-out of Pax breathing would have to do. Tomorrow, capturing the stallion would complete their mission.

Finally, he gave up on sleep, and a moonlit sky quieted his jumbled thoughts. A lantern flickered in one room of the ranch house while lace curtains puffed at a window like miniature clouds.

After some time, a human form passed—surely Mrs. Crady. Had she lived here when he bunked in the bunkhouse? The cook had watched out for him, and his only troubles came from Allen Crady.

He spent evenings reading Father Bernard's books. But one morning, a new set of clothing lay folded beside his bunk. And several times, he discovered a new book perched beside the rest.

Had Mrs. Crady reached out like this? And if so, why had she never spoken with him?

Meta could help him unravel this riddle. He lay down again and stared up at the stars—she said the same stars would shine down on them both. When he woke, Pax snorted a few feet away. Clay turned over and beheld Owen, arms crossed over the divider, studying him.

Clay started up and almost banged his head.

"You all right?"

"I... yes."

"I told the others you had business to attend to, and that we'd be right along."

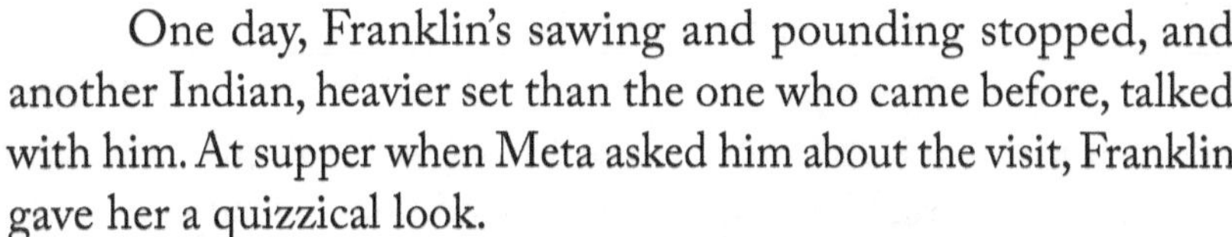

One day, Franklin's sawing and pounding stopped, and another Indian, heavier set than the one who came before, talked with him. At supper when Meta asked him about the visit, Franklin gave her a quizzical look.

"Thet's an old friend o' mine."

"Did he bring news?"

He took another helping, so she tried again.

"Can you tell me why he came?"

Shadows flitted over Franklin's countenance.

"Not knowing things frightens me, Franklin. Please tell me anything you can."

He drummed his fingers. "Yer right. If anythin' happened t'me..."

"What if something happened to you?"

"They's blood b'tween me n' th' Arapahoe; th' Shoshone, too."

"Are you related to one of the chiefs?"

"Somethin' like thet." Color rose under his rough skin, and he worked his mouth. "I tol' 'em yer fam'ly." He set down his fork. "Done 'em favors years back." He took another bite.

"What kind of favors?"

"Talked t' th' Army fer 'em. Saved some bloodshed, mebbe."

"Why did that man come today?"

"Some gov'ment agent's makin' things powerful tense. Lots o' talk o' raids."

"Where?"

"Up in Powder River Country."

Later, she realized he had never explained the specific reason for the Indian's visit. But she must trust him.

Later, her reward came.

"Of all th' Injuns, Arapahoe might be th' trickiest."

Meta sat on a tree stump finishing Franklin's shirt. This morning, some cavalrymen had stopped by and brought mail, including a packet. After they left, Franklin hurried over with that *Christmas* twinkle in his eyes.

"Got somethin' fer ya…a s'prise some soldiers brung."

Something from Martin, postmarked Virginia. Her fingers could not move fast enough, and this thoughtful gift could not have meant more. His simple note piqued her curiosity.

Another soldier introduced me to Charles Dickens, an author from England. I hope you like his story as much as I do. Soon, my Captain and I will leave for Arizona Territory—mail might be even more unreliable there, so I want you to know I am thinking of you.

Your loving brother,
Martin

A copy of *For These Times*—the volume felt like silk against her fingers. How difficult had it been for him to mail this? He gave no explanation, but Margita or Lissa must have sent him her address. Once that excitement had passed, she had a hard time settling back into her work, so she joined Franklin for a while.

To her surprise, he offered more insights about the Indians. Peculiar, since she had not even asked about the soldiers' visit.

"Raids in Colorady got settlers fightin' mad. Th' Arapahoe want horses, so they been stealin' 'em."

"So Clay's trip home will be even more dangerous?"

"Arapahoes're all tied up with Cheyenne and Ute nowadays. Soldiers keep 'em under control down thetaway. Else, the gov'ment would never a' closed Fort Morgan."

Images of fierce Arapahoe warriors circled through Meta's mind. At any time she might see a solemn red-skinned brave staring at her, but what if a whole band rode up?

"Franklin, will you teach me some Arapahoe words?"

"S'pect so. Can't hurt none."

Antonia Crady trolled the soil around her rose bushes, her shawl skimming the ground. She raised her head and reached out when Clay neared.

"Pierce drifted off, so I came out for some fresh air. Working the soil calms me."

Clay paused, uncertain what to say.

"Have you succeeded in your mission?"

"Yes, Ma'am. Roy roped a white stallion today, and two more mares followed him. That makes twelve, everything I had hoped for. Is Mr. Crady—I would like to pay him."

"He hovers near death." She wrenched her hands. "And calls your name."

"My name?"

"Yes, and two other words, *fire* and *father*. The priest came yesterday but that visit left him with no peace." Clay's heart hammered as she paused. "I have something to tell you, not an easy thing. I— Perhaps you came here for two reasons.

"Pierce's father, a man of no honor, left his children homeless. Pierce chose the wrong companions, but I believed his promise to change. My father owned land far to the south, and Pierce worked for him. Father had high hopes his children—he hired English tutors and would have educated me in Europe.

"But Pierce appeared like a knight, with such bravado. I disregarded my father's blessing, and my family turned away when we married. I never saw them again." Thin lines tightened around her mouth. "I believed I could transform Pierce. But then one terrible night, he and his comrades carried out a despicable act."

Her face swam before Clay, and he sank beside her.

"They burned a building—the mission where you lived."

"Mr… Mr. Crady?"

"Yes. When he heard some orphans had died in the fire, I thought he might end his life, and begged our Merciful Father to help him."

Clay's throat turned raw.

"He has repented, yet faces eternity— In his mind, perhaps you and the priest at the mission have become one."

"Father Bernard?"

"Yes. I—I went to see him after the fire. He spoke of God's forgiveness. When I asked what we might do, he pointed to you out in the courtyard."

The clothes ... the books ...

"So Mr. Crady hired me, and you made the clothing?"

A bleak smile broke through Mrs. Crady's tears. "I wanted you to be our son, but seeing you revived the worst in Pierce. You became his redemption yet his curse at the same time."

A sob escaped her lips. "He forbade me contact with you, but I prayed every day." Her trembling hand warmed Clay's shoulder.

"Ma'am, I—"

A violent cough sounded from the house.

"Perhaps I ask too much, but could you possibly—"

Those haunted eyes and tear-stained cheeks... how could he say no? Clay rose and she took his hand like a child.

"Shall I come now?"

"Please."

"Give me a few minutes."

In a few weeks Clay would return, but the time loomed like years. Lissa's blanket and nightgown lay wrapped in brown paper, ready to send. Franklin wore his new shirt, and Meta's garden kept her busy.

She gave thanks for all the work, but constantly calculated. Surely, Clay had left the ranch. By now they must have crossed from Texas into Colorado.

If only he could watch their garden progress and see flowers sprouting between the cabin and the creek where she created a small patch. If only he could note the fence taking shape under Franklin's hand. Sharing the moments of life—wasn't that the essence of marriage?

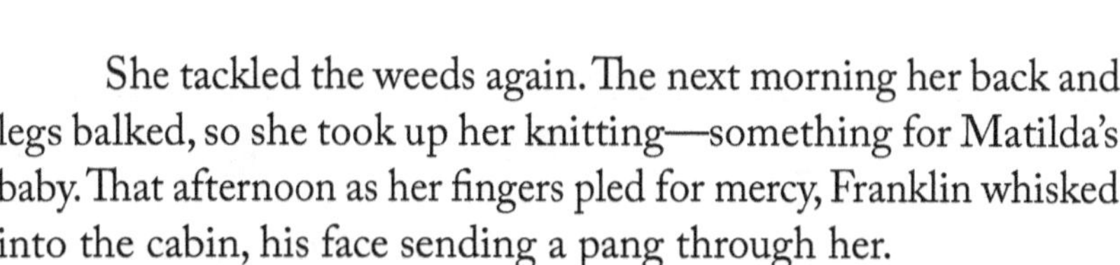

She tackled the weeds again. The next morning her back and legs balked, so she took up her knitting—something for Matilda's baby. That afternoon as her fingers pled for mercy, Franklin whisked into the cabin, his face sending a pang through her.

"Rider's comin'."

She stood behind him in the doorway. Two cavalrymen dismounted. One watered the horses, and the other approached the cabin. Meta followed Franklin outside as the soldier removed his cap.

"Franklin Ross, Cap'n."

The soldier extended his hand. *Captain Reynolds!*

"Mrs. Burns? So good to see you."

"Captain."

"I'm afraid I bring bad news. An Indian council has met, war parties have formed, and already attacks have occurred in Powder River country."

Franklin stood steady. "Th' meetin' a coupla months back? Over west?" As if he knew Meta's thoughts, he turned toward her. "Injuns allays comes up with a meetin'. Got 'ny coffee?"

The men came in, and she hurried to make a pot and put together some ham sandwiches as Captain Reynolds answered Franklin's questions.

"Tall Elk have anythin' t' do with this?"

"I don't know. What difference does that make?"

Franklin sputtered. "Long's ya have Tall Elk's ear, yer way ahead with Red Cloud."

"The Bighorn tribes have gone on the warpath. That means—" Captain Reynolds hesitated. "Has Mr. Burns already gone to Texas?"

Franklin's nod animated the captain. "The time has come for all women and children to seek protection. If you wish, we will escort you."

"Where would we go?"

"Some families are staying at Fort Laramie. Others have

gathered at the stagecoach stop north of here. Part of a unit will station there."

"Thank ya, Cap'n."

"We must notify another settler some miles across Spring Creek but will pass through here again tomorrow."

"Please do stop—we will discuss this." Meta handed Captain Reynolds his coffee, which he downed in an instant. He accepted the packet of sandwiches she offered and took his leave.

Franklin followed him and started out for the worksite. But she ran after him, touched his sleeve.

"Franklin, please. Will you tell me who Tall Elk is now?"

Without a sound, Clay closed the porch door behind him. Mrs. Crady's urgent plea overrode his preparations for the trip, even his preoccupation with Meta. Upon entering the kitchen, he steeled himself.

Wrought iron defined the space centered on a large iron cookstove. An intricately carved wooden cross on the wall brought Father Bernard to mind. An arched doorway led to the dining room where he and Owen ate the first night. An embossed door opened to a wide hallway where a scrolled rug stretched upward, step-by-step, over a hand-carved stairway.

His footfall echoed like hammer blows. Surely Mrs. Crady must hear him coming.

Suddenly Edgar's countenance appeared in the dim light. Could this be part of his destiny? A drunken fellow may have posed the question, but what twist of fate placed the name *Clay Burns* on Mr. Crady's lips?

In the upper hallway, Clay hesitated. Then from the second door on the right, Mrs. Crady beckoned him. Inside, she leaned close to her husband, her hair slipping to shroud his face. Her whisper echoed against dark papered walls.

"Pierce, Clay has come to see you."

A long minute passed. Clay lifted his foot to leave but stopped when the sick man's eyelids shuttered.

The quiver in Mrs. Crady's voice twisted his heart. "Please speak to him."

"Mr. Crady?" The rancher's right forefinger stirred. "I came to say good-bye. Thank you for your kindness, sir. We leave in the morning."

A single word scratched. "Fa... ther."

"Father Bernard. He—he forgave you, sir."

The eyes opened a squinch more. "Fi... fire."

"Do you mean at the mission?"

A single tear escaped.

"Our God forgives all sin."

"Fa... ther..."

"Father Bernard forgave you—I heard him say this."

Utter stillness, and then one final rasping breath. A small cry issued from Mrs. Crady, and she held a mirror near her husband's mouth.

A minute passed. She leaned to kiss that tortured forehead, then fell into Clay's arms. "*Mijo. Mijo.*"

Her son? Astounded, he blurted, "Shall I let Hank know?"

"*Gracias.*"

Moonlight reached Mr. Crady's still form, and a barely perceptible breeze carried the scent of sage into the upstairs. Sage for healing, Meta said. Perhaps this tormented man, beset for so long by his choices, rested in peace at last.

Like a ghost, Clay started down the stairs. A whitish haze filled his thoughts. Had the scene he just witnessed truly taken place? Gulping fresh air on the back porch, he wrapped his arm around a corner post.

"Want to talk?"

He startled at Owen's voice. He had settled on the bottom steps, and Clay sank near him.

"Look up there. When has Sirius shown so bright? The dog

star, in the midst of summer's heat—the Hunter's Hound. No wonder they call this time the "dog days."

"Mmm."

"You went to Mr. Crady's bedside?"

Clay could only nod.

"You're doing some mighty hard work, son. Need something to eat?"

"Mmm…wouldn't mind."

"I know my way around the bunkhouse kitchen. Come on."

"I need to tell—"

"Hank. Done—I noticed when Mrs. Crady drew the shades over the windows." Owen led the way to leftover steak and biscuits, and somehow, what words could not say passed between the two of them.

"Thanks. I think I can make it to my stall now."

"We've put off leaving one more day. This way, we can tame the horses a mite more and help with the burying."

"Thanks for seeing to it."

"In the morning, I'll see what else we can do for Mrs. Crady. Try to take your rest now, Son."

No wincing this time. Now, even Mrs. Crady had called him her son. Clay simply nodded and headed toward Pax.

Such a night of pondering over Franklin—why did he believe she would be safe here despite the Indian uprisings? Only a man of honor would have searched for Garrit after that terrible storm, and gone to the effort of burying him. And then he had watched out for her over the winter—without doubt, he amended his normal route to check on her.

With every reason to trust his good heart, she fought against doubts that struck like arrows in the darkness. But at the dawning, the sensation that he was hiding something still hovered.

Determined to comprehend his way of thinking, she took

his coffee and waited for him at the worksite. Who could imagine, in this peaceful early morning, with prairie scents—earth, wild-flowers, and always the banner of sage over all, that danger might lurk so near?

When Franklin approached, he seemed nonplussed to see her here. The skin around his eyes puffed with lack of sleep, and he spoke softer than normal, so that she had to lean in to hear.

"Mebbe y'd be better off at th' stage stop. Mebbe I been trustin' them Injuns too much." His shoulders slumped. "Ya think it's a sign thet the Cap'n come by?"

"I don't know. I will do whatever you say."

"No use takin' foolish chances. What'd I ever tell yer husband if'n somethin' were t'…"

"I would rather stay—you know that."

"Mmm, but t'won't be fer long. It's fer th' best." Franklin bent to his work, and she went home to consider her preparations. At sunset, after their evening meal, she joined him beside his fire. "You mentioned Blackrobe to Captain Reynolds. Who is he?"

"Father DeSmet. Named a whole Bighorn lake after 'im. From Missouri, but he traveled all over the Northwest t' start missions, but then th' gov'ment asked 'im here in fifty-one, with a passel o' injuns fer a big council. Them Injuns trusted 'im."

"This doesn't turn out well for them?"

The flash in his eyes warned her. "'Bout thirty traveled from Dakota Territory where th' Missouri meets th' Yellowstone—Fort Union. Astor built it fer 'is comp'ny. Thousands o' tribes lived there till th' pox wiped 'em out in th' thirties. 'Most all th' Mandans died, n' the Hidatsu.

"But them chiefs trusted Blackrobe n' rode t' Fort Laramie. Then th' council got moved west—called it th' Big Smoke."

"You were there?"

"'Most six-mile long, thet lake. Ten thousand Injuns with a hunderd traders throwed in. But nary a mile o' beaten track 'tween Fort Laramie and them Red Buttes."

He threw another log on the fire, creating a mighty blaze, blue and green and orange at once. "Comiss'ner Mitchell done th' talkin'. Bout th' future, more settlers comin'. Said th' Great White Father wanted good fer his red childr'n. But at the same time Blackrobe was baptizin' babies n' tellin' 'nuther message."

Franklin shifted his weight. "Makes me rec'lect m' little one—never thought t' 'tize 'im a'tall." He let a long minute pass.

"Injuns promised t' keep peace amongst 'emselves, but th' gov'ment'd lied 'bout punishin' bad whites. Injuns kep' their part, and Mitchell promised each tribe a'nu'ties that never come." He studied the stars for a moment. "Wonder how thet DeSmet feels 'bout things now, if he's still breathin'. He come back but never stayed."

The fire popped like Meta's unspoken questions, but Franklin's yawn could be heard over the whole claim.

"Done played out a'ready, gal."

Chapter Thirty

Love is the root of all joy and sorrow.
~Meister Eckhart

Under a heavy lace veil, Antonia Crady led the small procession with Hank by her side. Sultry heat bore down, but she held herself erect as the men lowered her husband's body into a rocky grave.

The priest who visited Pierce raised his voice. "*En el nombre del padre, de Hijo, e de espiritu santo...*"

Only portions of the homily made sense, but they rang with Father Bernard's chief lesson: *The Creator values all souls.*

The old cowhand who mentioned Mrs. Crady's care for him during his recovery straggled over with two pieces of wood for a cross and shoved the pointed end into place.

Pierce Crady
November 1860–July 1867

Afterward, Mrs. Crady pulled Clay aside. "Come to the house tonight. I have something for you."

Meta gathered a few clothes and searched out a gift for Matilda, some soft fabric with thread, a needle, and yarn. She wrapped one of her best dishtowels around a jug of honey, too.

"Riders comin'." Franklin's gruff warning—only a few minutes left.

"I don't want to leave you—"

His beard scratched her forehead. "Hits fer the best. Be back 'fore ya know it."

Captain Reynolds approached. "Mrs. Burns, let's get you up here behind me."

Franklin handed him her saddlebag, and they spoke while she mounted. Then once again, the stagecoach stop became her destination. Such a difference from the last time she and Clay, fresh from their wedding vows, had spent the night.

This time, the landscape revealed a route she recalled—why, one day, if needful, she might ride to see Matilda all by herself. But the Indian troubles cast a shadow over the journey. Captain Reynolds, always the gentleman, spoke of other things when they stopped to refresh themselves, and asked after Clay.

But aside from the letter she had received weeks ago, how might she reply?

Sensing her discomfort, he turned to another subject, Matilda and Tom's sprawling family. "I expect one day your claim will have little ones running about."

Yes, perhaps. Her longing for a child had not been fulfilled, though, with Garrit. No need to borrow trouble—who could know the ways of Providence?

Northern Texas produced a lavish display—wild sorrel, Indian paintbrush mixed with tiny wildflowers and common daisies. Clay took a mental picture of the scene, the horses they had caught— their own horses—against such a splendid backdrop.

If only Meta could see this wild array of flowers, too. Every seed she planted meant so much to her—hopefully Betsy's for-get-me-nots and the yellow rose would bloom. Though they had to endure this separation, at least he would return with consolation.

She understood Father Bernard's teaching right away.

"Mama never used those exact words but taught us that life blends sorrows and joys."

Last night, Mrs. Crady echoed this. "I found something of yours, Clay—it must have fallen from your bookshelf."

One of Father Bernard's volumes. She also pressed into his palm Mr. Crady's payment.

"We have no need for this, *mijo*."

The gold Meta and Garrit had saved for the dream now occupied Clay's pocket—she would be so surprised. Ah, *consolation*, penetrating like this summer sun.

With good weather, the journey would take almost a month—with *good* weather. They had become one already, but then their new life would truly begin. This drive connected the past with what lay ahead, the future. And the future beckoned, as tangible as the reins in Clay's hands.

After supper, he unrolled his blanket and pulled out Meta's prayer book and another of Father Bernard's. On the inside cover he had written, *John Vianney: brought common people back to faith at great sacrifice.* In the back he inscribed: *God is more apt to forgive than a mother to snatch her own child from the fire.*

John Vianney's prayer highlighted the volume. *My only desire is to love you... and I would rather die loving you than live without loving you.*

Father Bernard sacrificed enjoying a wife and family, home and hearth. He never showed a sense of loss, but met each day with great energy, even after the fire.

A horse whinnied in the distance. Reece snored in his bedroll, and Mr. Dunbar groaned. Clay covered his face with his hat. Loving God wound together with loving Meta, this much he knew for certain.

Meta helped Matilda carry a pot of stew to the serving table. Her lower back ached this afternoon. Some settlers cooked over their camp fires, but others fled their homes without time to pack. Everyone chipped in, gathering wood, chopping logs, and kneading dough on makeshift breadboards. The Army supply wagon had become Matilda's general store.

This bustle resembled a church picnic. Women pinned laundry on lines strung between trees. Dark blues, bright reds, yellows, and greens, checks and calicos and whites formed a huge counterpane swaying in the breeze.

Although danger lurked, voices and laughter filled the air. The children had a heyday with a set of marbles and a ball. Cavalry horses rested in the sun, and pots clanked from the cook's tent.

Mothers with faces worn by constant care greeted her. Soldiers stood guard all around the station. What a relief to share family responsibilities with so many others—these little ones would not be snatched away by Indian warriors.

"Have you ever cooked a frosting?" Matilda wiped her brow.

"Mama thickened a cup of milk with a third cup of flour. When that cooled, she added a cup of butter and whipped it all with a cup of sugar."

"Would you mind making a double batch? The cakes should be ready in about ten minutes, in case I get waylaid. I'll show you where we keep the butter and milk. Since we're so near the creek, Tom thought of a way to cool things out there." Matilda whisked out the door.

When she returned, the cakes cooled near the window, and Meta had dispersed a big bowl of frosting over them. Now, it glistened in the afternoon light as Annalee, Matilda's eldest, checked the roast.

"Glad the cakes turned out. The other day, the tops caved in." Matilda dabbed her finger in the frosting. "Tastes perfect, too."

The rest of the afternoon passed from one task to another until Matilda's brood arrived, worn out from playing under their sister Sarah's supervision. She shooed them to the water tank.

Annalee volunteered, "The table is set, Mama. I'll go help Sarah get them washed up."

Matilda handed Meta three tin serving spoons from her utensil drawer.

"You remember Annalee from your last visit? She has found her first beau now—I can scarcely believe she has come of age." Matilda started toward her bedroom. "Let's get you settled—I am so glad you've come."

"But where will Tom sleep?"

"Outside. He often does. But tonight, with the Injuns riled and all these menfolk around, sleep will be the last thing on his mind."

Sleep came in an instant, and when Meta woke, Matilda had already gone to the kitchen. Her stomach rolled when she rose, but she paid no attention. Soon, though, she had no choice. During the next hour, she found herself out back retching three times.

The third time, Matilda followed with a cool wet cloth to dab her neck and wrists.

"Must have been the traveling yesterday."

"Are you sure? Do you feel feverish?"

"No." Meta took a long breath, spying a beautiful dark blue jay on the clothesline pole. "Let me walk a bit." Matilda returned to her work as Meta started out.

"Hello, Mr. Bluecoat. Did you come to cheer me?" The white line above the bird's eye looked ever so much like an eyebrow. He studied her back but took his leave at a cacophony of chirps from a scrub oak.

With every step, she felt better. Such a strange stomach upset, just when Matilda needed her so much. After a few minutes, she went back inside.

By midmorning, piles of clean dishes dripped from the wooden drying stand Tom fashioned for Matilda, and half of dinner preparations were complete. Meta's stomach growled, so she tried a piece of bread and met with success.

Another low rumble, so she wolfed down two more slices with a cup of tea. Just before Matilda clanged the bell, hunger pangs struck again, so Matilda offered her mashed potatoes with butter and salt.

"Doing all right?"

"Yes. Maybe I was just hungry." Then the pungent aroma of baking venison wafted, with onions, turnips, carrots, potatoes, and summer squash in thickened broth, and the bilious sensation returned. Once again Meta rushed behind the cabin.

The sky darkened as she recovered. Checking the front of her dress and tucking stray curls into place, she readied herself once more. Dinner guests would come in ten minutes.

After the meal, her stomach cried for food and more bread contented it. So much cleaning to be done after a meal—dishes, pots and pans, tables, floor. After the children climbed to the loft, Matilda found her.

"How long have you felt sick?"

"For about two weeks. Morning used to be the best part of the day, but now I wake up like this."

"Have you had your regular this month?"

"Not since Clay left."

"And you married about… let me see… two months ago? You may be extra glad you came—you may have someone else's safety to consider."

Every evening Clay spent time with the horses. He couldn't count them often enough—a stallion, four bays, two grays, two paints, and three sorrels. He fed them sweet meadow grass, his very own horses! Their flesh-and-blood reality proved the dream was real. He spoke to them in soothing tones and took heart when one stepped closer.

The next morning, they crossed big Sandy Creek a little before noon. Owen refilled his canteen. "Do you have any sense about this place?"

"What do you mean?"

"We're being watched. I'll feel better within range of Fort Morgan." Owen's voice deepened. "What do you say we take turns at watch? I won't be able to sleep anyhow. I'll take the first."

"Sure. Wake me?"

Owen clapped him on the shoulder. "As if you ever sleep."

On Saturday night, the settlers formed a circle. All day long, older children planned the evening. Annalee asked if her friends might bathe in the creek, so Tom kept watch.

After the meal, the girls took over the dining room, twining purple hare bells into their hair. Meta and Matilda tucked stray hairs and cheered their efforts.

"Surely you have these flowers at home? They seem to grow everywhere."

"I think so, down by the creek. And another purple one with stems that shoot out from the center—I think I've seen it here, too, with little puffs for flowers?"

"Mmm—sounds like purple prairie clover. So many varieties grow close at hand. I hope to start a garden out front—when I find time." Matilda patted her middle and chuckled.

Soon lanterns swung from tree branches or wagon hooks. Energetic fiddle music floated into the kitchen as Matilda and Meta dried the last of the pots.

"Always wished my Tom liked to dance, but tonight I'm thankful to sit and watch." Matilda's movements had become so awkward that two settler women helped with meals now.

A light wind sprayed the land tawny orange. Meta tapped out "Little Brown Jug" against her thigh when she and Matilda found a bench to share. Annalee and her new beau, his hair slicked down, joined other couples in a square dance. Next, an accordion player launched "Beautiful Dreamer," and three married couples waltzed. Some of the younger girls danced together while the boys clustered around the edge. Even a few soldiers joined in the festivities.

Anna Stelling sighed. "Don't seem that long ago since Harold and me courted, yet we have four children."

"Yes, I know." Matilda's laugh floated toward the dancers.

"How long have you been married?"

"We came to Dakota with Annalee, Gabe, and Lucas. Annalee was eight, so we married in '48. Will you ever forget your wedding date, Meta?"

"It seems entirely possible. But at least both anniversaries are just one year apart, in February and May."

One woman told the story of her trek from Ohio, but Meta daydreamed about Clay. Where did he camp tonight? How many horses would he bring? How would he react to her being with child?

Anticipation found a home in her heart. What better way to learn about childbirth than observing Matilda's, with experienced women nearby to help?

A baby! She must write Betsy and Lissa soon, but not before she told Clay. They had talked about many things, but not children—or dancing. Maybe one evening, she would teach him simple steps from barn dances back home.

"You ladies can stay up till all hours, but my time has come." Matilda braced her hands on the bench and arched her back.

"Your time?" Meta leaped up, too, but Matilda chuckled.

"To go to bed. Stay and enjoy the music a while longer."

As Anna tapped her toe, it occurred to Meta that she might live near the Butler's homestead. When she described Stalwart and Bryant, Anna recalled passing a deserted claim near their home.

"They could live over one of the foothills and we would never know. It's even more isolated between here and the Bighorn."

When Owen shook his shoulder, Clay woke with a start.

"Everything's quiet, no trouble yet."

After a cup of coffee, Clay circled the horses in mellow night air. Then he heard something at the far end of the line, muffled by the fire's crackle. Touching his weapon, he checked the bedrolls before gliding through low trees in a wider circle. He paused every few feet to listen.

Up a steep ravine behind the camp, he stopped short. Gradually side-stepping over a granite outcropping through low sage, he waited again. Silence, so he checked the ropes.

The last knot had one less loop—the animal could break free. He pulled the knot tight—only insects and small animals broke the silence, but sure as sunshine, someone had been here.

If anyone watched their progress, they would have sought one of the lead animals, not the bay. The obvious answer—Indians—seemed unlikely. The question troubled him until the first faint light of dawn.

Early morning stillness offered no clues as he made one last round before boiling coffee and waking everyone. With each step he took, Owen's sense of impending danger wriggled down into Clay's heart.

After sweeping the floor, Meta fell into bed. The children's evening prayers brought Mama to mind—a woman had so much responsibility. Next winter, she would be a mama herself.

Did Clay sleep or star-watch from his bedroll? Had the men met Indians on the return trip? If only he might send word.

A few hours later she woke to a wet sensation and Matilda's moans.

She lit the lamp. "Shall I fetch Tom?"

"Stay with me... Boil water... clean towels."

After feeding the fire, Meta moved a kettle onto the large burner. Back in the bedroom, she pulled off soggy bedclothes and helped Matilda into a clean nightgown. Perspiration lined Matilda's forehead, and a cool cloth did wonders.

Her calm gray eyes expressed gratitude.

"So glad... you are here..."

"Shall I fetch Tom?"

Struck by another contraction, Matilda shook her head.

"Noth... nothing he can do. Better to... let him sleep."

After more than an hour like this, it seemed the baby might need help. Should she fetch someone who had given birth? She started to pull away, but Matilda's "No" halted her. Panting, she tried to sit up, and Meta reached for another pillow.

"Just a little longer."

Soon, Matilda leaned forward and grasped her knees.

"Tell... when... you see... head." Then she cried out, and a shiny wet mass of dark hair appeared.

"Oh my. Right now!"

In seconds, the baby's face emerged. A tiny slippery miracle, this boy entered the world with a squall and doubled fists.

Covered from scalp to toes with a wet, chalky substance, his tiny perfection defied the imagination. Meta wrapped him in a blanket and transferred him into Matilda's arms.

They wept and laughed at the same time, and Matilda explained how to cut the cord. That completed, Matilda exclaimed over the tiny fellow, "Isn't he beautiful?"

Speechless, Meta nodded.

"And he's so big compared to the others. In a little while, he will suck. He needs to get used to this new place but stopped crying because he hears my heartbeat."

Meta piled towels and bedding outside the back door and made the bed with fresh linens. At full light, Tom burst into the room, disheveled.

"Thought I heard something." He approached Matilda and their new son.

"Oh, Mattie, he's perfect."

"In the top drawer—" Matilda gestured to Meta. "You dress him for the first time. You will be his godmother."

Flawless arms and legs, toenails and fingernails already

needing a trim. What helpless wrath as she worked a soft garment over his shoulders! Swaddled in a warm blanket, he finally quieted in his Daddy's arms.

Matilda's eyes closed, and Meta slipped into the kitchen to start the porridge. Matilda would be mighty hungry when she wakened, along with a whole crowd of people. The brightness of the rising sun, the first birdcall, an early breeze unfolding the curtains.

And for the first time in days, she had no urge to run out back. This morning, the whole earth whispered, "Holy."

Perseverance is more prevailing than violence; and many things which cannot be overcome when they are together, yield themselves up when taken little by little.

~Plutarch

Midday sun tempted Clay to rest, but he shook himself—Owen got even less sleep. With that loosened knot on their minds, they determined to double their watch.

A full twenty miles yesterday. By noon tomorrow they should reach Fort Morgan. Clay breathed easier when a band of soldiers crossed the trail.

Mountaintops, stark gray and black above the tree line, outlined startling blue sky. Hawks and eagles swooped on airways higher than man could know. Franklin had told him the highest peak here stood over 14,000 feet.

The scene's beauty flooded Clay's senses. Had his ability to take in earth's beauty been asleep a year ago? Had dwelling on the past stunted his appreciation?

A shout interrupted his reverie. The sun had slid a few degrees since he last noticed. The horses drank, and upstream, everyone filled canteens. A dark streak filled Owen's eyes.

"Someone marks our every step."

"How do you know?"

"A puff of dust rises from time to time."

"What if we light a fire as if we plan to spend the night, but move out after dark? Daylight should bring us to the Fort."

"Worth a try."

Darkness fell over the plain, and the Front Range loomed even larger.

Then, a few feet away, Owen whispered. "To our right—two-o'clock."

A campfire. Unmistakable. As he slipped away, Clay's earnest prayer rose like candle smoke.

Tiny Benjamin Thomas Hanson spent nights in Matilda's arms, and Meta wakened for every feeding. After a few days, she no longer heard them.

With Annalee's head in the clouds over her beau, Matilda remarked, "I'd much rather have you watch him—in her state, she might forget."

"People seem so worked up today."

"Two families have decided to leave despite the warnings."

"Where will they go?"

"Back to their homesteads in Powder River country."

"Right where the Indians—

"Anna had a vision."

"A premonition?"

"Mmm. So vivid it froze my insides, but the men are determined. In the morning, we will wish them Godspeed."

The door creaked and Gabe peeked in.

"Ready for the bell, Ma?" Matilda nodded, and after six clangs, he joined the other children at the water tank.

"Right on time. But did you see those muddy hands?"

"A fine farmer in the making."

"Those families... Tom will try to change their minds."

Anna's husband, a spindly fellow with an arched nose, hurried about. Anna chatted with the children but left with her brood soon after supper.

In the morning Matilda tried to talk Anna into staying, but

her husband would not hear of this. So Meta and Matilda hugged her and the other woman, who spoke only Polish. Matilda grumbled, "Mule-headed men."

An unnatural hush quelled the men's normal chatter. Baby Benjamin's warmth reminded Meta of Anna's young'uns. How could she possibly go along with such a decision?

In darkness they passed the overland stage turnoff. Not much later, a sharp command arrested them.

"Halt!" When the dust calmed, a soldier followed Owen toward Clay. Owen's eyes relayed an unreadable message. The soldier shouted, "You the boss here?"

"Guess so. What do you want?"

"We accompany all crews to the fort." The soldier's hair grew low on his forehead and he wore a wrinkled uniform. But what could anyone expect at a closing outpost?

"How far to Fort Morgan?"

"Jest a little ways. Here's where we cut off the normal trail. Gotta keep them Injuns guessin'."

Clay stalled a bit more. "Have you spotted some?"

"Come with us—now. You're dealin' with th' United States Cavalry." He pointed his gun. "Shut up and git movin!"

Owen and Clay turned their mounts.

"No talkin', hear?"

The rancher stared straight ahead. What sort of misfortune had come upon them?

A few hours later, Clay struggled to sit with hands throttled behind his back. Owen sprawled in a corner of this makeshift building. Something warm and wet trickled down Clay's temple. His memory produced foggy details—two other men in cavalry jackets had joined the first soldier.

How could this have happened? They had fallen for the oldest trick in the book: pilfered uniforms. Sunlight filtered through a wide crack. After several falls, he reached the middle of the building, but still Owen remained motionless.

"Owen! Owen! Can you hear me?"

Silence mocked him—Owen might be dead. Then something Father Bernard had him memorize sifted through. Specific words failed him, but the meaning came down to, *Keep your head. Do what you can.*

Morning sickness became a thing of the past as summer's heat burned the high plains. Matilda taught her to chew some bread before getting up.

One day after dinner when Matilda took a rare afternoon nap, a whimper came from Ben's crib. Meta sat on an outdoor bench with him. Men circled under a willow tree, and a woman with a young child dabbed her eyes. An odd chill hovered even on such a hot day—and a peculiar silence.

Benjamin's trusting brown eyes surveyed Meta through thick black lashes, and the glimmer of a smile played at his lips. Perhaps one of the mothers busied all of the older children in a quiet after-dinner game, and they could watch.

But the Hanson children, along with several others, sat cross-legged under a tree. A woman and two men spoke with them as Meta drew near.

"You have heard some bad news about Evie, Lilly, and their brothers. Remember, we don't know anything for sure."

Tom joined a gathering of men, so Meta meandered over.

"So tragic, especially the children..." Seeing her, Tom's shoulders slumped.

"Let's sit down for a minute." He took little Ben and gazed at his cherubic countenance.

"A messenger came through. Indians raided a settlement and... I'm afraid the Stellings..."

Meta caught her breath.

"The Indians slaughtered them all and burned everything to the ground."

Anna Stelling, mother to four small children—she had asked the women to pray for them. Meta visualized a smoldering chimney, stones scattered, and an eery silence.

Tom's dark eyes moistened when he slipped Benjamin back into her arms. Wooden, she laid him in his crib. Matilda still had not returned to the kitchen, so Meta pulled out the cutting board and filled the biggest pot with water.

Tonight, they would serve ham and beans with cornbread, so she walked out back to the larder, where large hams hung from ceiling hooks. Trees and bushes protected the space from the sun, so its stone shelves held milk, meat, and butter from the cooler in the creek. But as she stepped in, a sob caught her ear.

All alone on the cool floor sat Matilda. Time stopped as they held each other. At last, Matilda wiped her face with her apron. Her green calico appeared as gray as her eyes.

"Mama's older sister left Pennsylvania for Iowa in the early fifties, and the Sioux killed her in a massacre." She sniffled. "This news hit me so hard—I stack up my griefs, and then when something horrible happens, I cry over everything at once."

A mourning dove cooed outside, and Matilda's words took Meta back, too. Her sixth-grade class studied the Spirit Lake Massacre in western Iowa, when Chief Inkpaduta and his band killed several families.

"I once wrote a report about the Spirit Lake massacre. For a month, I became Abbie Gardner. My sister brought it up when we were leaving, but things have changed so much in Iowa, I thought—" Meta paused, and all of the details flooded back.

"Inkpeduta's other name was Scarlet Point. Rowland Gardner, his wife and four children and their son-in-law Harvey Luce with his two children invited the Sioux into their cabin in the northwest, near the Minnesota border. The Indians came from a Wahpetuke band of Santee Sioux who suffered a food shortage during a severe winter."

The larder's coolness enveloped them. Years had passed since Meta thought about the Massacre, but today, it became more real than ever.

"When the settlers shared their food and trusted the Indians, they thought they were forging strong ties. But the fourteen Indians turned violent, and I have always wondered if they deliberately deceived the settlers."

A mourning dove cooed its song from an aspen.

"Who found the Stellings?"

"We don't know. Captain Reynolds said a survivor straggled through on his way to Fort Laramie—stopped only long enough to water his horse. Maybe we'll know more soon."

"I was fourteen at the time of the massacre, like Abbie Gardner. Miss Brunner said Abbie watched her whole family die and witnessed the raiders' wild war dance around their campfire that night. She saw her family's scalps hung on long poles. Can you imagine?"

Matilda buried her head in her hands.

"The next day, the warriors killed thirty-five or forty settlers, all except three women. Only Abbie and three other women lived.

"By then, a contingent of Fort Ridgely soldiers tracked them and one of the women, Mrs. Thatcher, became ill. The Sioux threw her into the Big Sioux River, clubbed and shot her to death when she tried to crawl out."

"My aunt was one that perished." Matilda's voice broke. "How did Abbie ever escape?"

"A native sent by an Indian agent found the group and bought one of the women, Mrs. Marble, for a keg of powder, a gun, some trinkets, and some blankets. When only Abbie and a Mrs. Noble remained, the older woman refused to obey Inkpaduta's son, so he killed her.

"That summer, the agent finally sent friendly Indians to buy Abbie. They paid two horses, twelve blankets, two kegs of powder, twenty pounds of tobacco, thirty-two yards of blue cloth, some calico, ribbon, and other items."

"You recollect the exact list." Matilda let out a long sigh.

"Yes, Miss Brunner was a stickler for memory work. We grew up without fearing the Indians, but then—"

"I heard. Last year over one hundred Minnesota settlers died in an uprising. Some stage passengers told us. And now—"

Matilda's groan sent a shudder through Meta.

"After Tom told me, I sat with little Benjamin, so steady, so unaware of this world's evil. I heard soldiers telling the settlers their retaliation would lead to more safety. But that will only mean more deaths."

Matilda held out her hand to pull Meta up.

"Two families' love and labor, hopes and dreams, all gone. And we must go on." She reached up for a ham, and Meta carried milk and a butter slab.

Back inside the kitchen, Meta recalled the day the Stellings left. If they had traveled south, she might have asked to ride along.

She wiped her eyes and watched Ben's soundless sleep. Little Ellie Butler's bright eyes shone before her—so wonderful the Butlers had decided to leave their homestead for Cheyenne.

Why, oh why hadn't Anna refused to go back home? But a woman must obey her husband.

Matilda had the right attitude—even with so many unanswered questions, they must go on. True. If only Clay were here. Talking this over with him would help.

If he returned before she did, he would come for her. In the meantime, she would care for Matilda's precious child and waste no time fretting about getting back home.

The next day, the men gathered around two officers. Captain Reynolds removed his cap as a Major Hess dismounted and addressed the crowd.

"The latest casualties include Ambrozy Zieliski, his wife, his children, three in all, and an unidentified woman in the same party. The family has been properly buried, and scouts are now hunting down the warriors."

Heavy dark circles under Captain Reynolds' eyes testified to his weariness. A coarse murmur ran through the circle.

"To the south, the area remains safe. We spotted no Indians to the end of Horse Creek, due to a burial ground between there and Spring Creek. Still, we advise you to remain here another week.

"Better to err on the safe side. Those of you who live between here and Montana, we expect things to simmer down before mid-summer."

A low groan came from the onlookers. One man spoke up, "Somebody's gotta teach them savages a lesson."

The captain nodded. "We track and punish the bands responsible, sir, but the Indians have been pressed further than many thought wise. Now, we deal with the consequences."

As if to remind Meta of its presence, her unborn babe kicked. What a marvel, new life about to unfold even in the midst of such tragedy.

The outlaws left Clay's canteen, but he must free his hands. He called to Owen every few minutes with no response, then knelt beside him, nudged his shoulder with his own and listened.

Owen's breathing regulated little by little. Clay's raw wrists testified of progress, but the binding still held strong. He could think only of water.

Moonlight still filtered through wide cracks in the wall. He rested his hands for a while and must have dozed off until Owen stirred. Between working with the rope and nodding off again, he jerked awake.

"Howdy." Growing light revealed a jagged gash across Owen's left eyebrow and dried blood matted in his hair.

"Ready?" Owen drew a screeching breath. "Ready... to go... get 'em?"

"Sure." Clay wormed his way around so Owen could reach his wrists.

After what seemed forever, the rope gave way, and Clay faced the rancher. Bruises and cuts spread across his forehead and cheeks. His normally dark tan shone sallow and clammy.

Water—he must find some.

His arms rebelled as he moved them, but at last he could stretch them out. Although every inch tingled, nothing seemed broken. It took only a minute to loosen the other knot.

His hands shook, but at long last, he reached for the canteen, painfully twisted the mouth open, and gave Owen a sip. Brightness returned to the rancher's eyes. Clay took a sip, and grateful for no broken ribs, pushed against the door. If only he could pry a loose plank away from the others…

Owen drew short sharp breaths as he worked himself up against the wall.

"Not so smart… to leave us alive." Owen had not lost his humor.

Clay braced himself to pull on the plank until it gave way, then banged it against a corner. On his fifth whack, the wood cracked. On the next, a board splintered. He tackled another and another.

Owen closed his eyes as daylight entered. No one guarded them. Clay paused a moment to acknowledge this hard-won victory.

Chapter Thirty-two

*Our chief want in life, is, someone who shall make us
do what we can. This is the service of a friend. With him we
are easily great.*

~Ralph Waldo Emerson

Benjamin wrapped his stubby fingers around Meta's as she
indulged him by tugging back and mouthing a wide O that produced a giggle. Tomorrow would be his one-month birthday, and
his christening, since Captain Reynolds fetched the chaplain on
his last trip to the fort.

Time raced since little Ben's birth—Clay left almost two
months ago. Her days hastened by as she helped Matilda and
watched Ben change by the minute. He smiled now, real smiles,
and her heart flipped over when he cooed.

Matilda gladly shared her *last baby.*

Bathing his heat rash in an old dishpan, she commented,
"After he outgrows that dishpan, I'm planting flowers in it. They
all took their baths in there."

She handed him to Meta to dress, and in the process Meta
ran her fingers along Ben's silky eyebrows and button nose. With
him ready for bed, they rested outside while the children played
a while longer.

"Oh, how can I ever thank you? I expected to battle worry
all these weeks but your family has given me so much joy."

Her energy flooded back as she felt better, but she still could
not imagine how Matilda fed her family and a passel of strangers.

Now, only two families remained, since the cavalry announced all settlements safe except the far northern ones.

On this night before Meta joined the last family headed south, Matilda gave her a hug. Then she drew back and studied her up and down.

"Are you sure you must go? The stage ride would be so much easier, and you could choose your day. Do stay longer—you make my life so much easier."

Meta dreaded the trip in the wagon with a family of six. Franklin had told her the stage passed only a mile or two west of Spring Creek, so Matilda's suggestion made sense. "Do you mean it?"

Matilda smoothed Benjamin's head. "You've become the sister I left behind in Dakota."

"And you mine. If only I had known last winter how close you lived!"

From out of the past rose Mama's simple statement, *Always listen to your heart above your mind.*

"I think I will stay then. It seems so selfish, but—"

"On my part, maybe, but you must think what's best for you and that little one you carry."

After the children slumbered, Meta pulled out a chair in the dining room to write a note to a man who could read nary a word.

> *Dear Franklin,*
> *I will be coming home soon on the stage. Matilda has a new baby and I am helping her. I have news for you. I am with child, too—soon you will be Grandpa Franklin.*
> *Thank you for taking care of Della, Hope and the hens. I miss you.*
> *Love,*
> *Meta*

In the morning, she searched out Captain Reynolds, who prepared for the trip south.

"I'll make sure Mr. Ross gets this." He slipped the envelope into his breast pocket.

"Please read it aloud for him, Captain. And tell him I send my love. Godspeed."

Her hands on the growing mound that once marked her waist, she knew she had made the right decision. For once, no plaguing herself with speculations.

Another task would occupy her next week, one not to relish. Her dress could no longer contain her burgeoning body, and Matilda had offered her a wide cut of yard goods from her fabric stash.

Owen Dunbar had encouraged Clay this whole trip. Now the tables turned. More than ever, Clay knew that Owen signing up for this trip had been no accident.

With every step, his confidence rose—he no longer believed in coincidence. Though their plans had been waylaid, he must continue on—they must live to tell this tale. Owen would be healed, and the horses—surely the Almighty knew what they meant to him and Meta.

The closing from Father Bernard's prayers ran through his mind as if the priest prayed with him.

Thy will be done. Amen.

Back inside the shed, Owen stood on his own, staggering toward the gaping hole. Clay gulped at his painful stance, shoulders hunched and one hand cradling his ribs.

Although barely able to walk, Owen faced the brilliant sun as rocky outcroppings and the steep ridge of the Front Range soared two thousand feet above. Clay explored the rocks on the left while Owen searched out the outlaws' trail. Like Moberly, they focused on signs.

Clay advanced upward a few steps at a time and widened his circle. There must be water nearby—variegated green splotches colored the landscape as far as the eye could see. How far had they ridden yesterday? His memory stopped when an outlaw pointed a gun barrel his way.

These thieves determined he and Owen threatened their operation, so they had knocked them out near the shed. He must have gone down without a fight, but Owen's shredded shirt and abdominal cuts revealed resistance. A sharp rock most likely administered the gash above his eye.

Horse flies landed on Clay's sticky skin, and a little to his right, a doe and her fawn lowered their heads. When he investigated, they bounded off in the opposite direction.

A faint gurgle urged him left, to mountain water sparkling in a fast-flowing stream. He let the cold immerse his smarting wrists, then refilled his canteen and hurried back to Owen, who stood near the shed as if sniffing out a trail. When the rancher grasped the canteen, his fingers trembled almost as much as Mr. Crady's.

He drank his fill and handed the canteen back. "How far away did you find the water?"

"About a furlong."

Owen motioned just ahead, to two sets of horse tracks. Then a simple plea burst forth. "Show us which way to go."

The same lightness enveloped Clay as when Father Bernard prayed about some problem years ago on the Grand Prairie.

"Should we follow the water or the tracks? Which will it be?"

This time, Owen's urgency required a reply, so Clay did his best. "I could walk to Fort Morgan for help, since we have no food, weapons, or shelter. That one officer would remember us and start a search."

Owen stood for a long time, arms slack. Then he whispered, "Show us, Lord."

He asked with such confidence. Against all tangible odds, Clay expected a revelation, but kept moving.

He took his time climbing a few yards higher. About halfway

back, some loose stones caused a stumble, but he caught himself on a branch and landed near a dark object.

Closer, he kicked at a black leather bag as if rattlesnakes might slide out. On the top, a narrow leather flap fitted into a buckle—why not try to open it?

The lid landed behind the bag with a thud. The contents sent chills down Clay's spine—so much gold he could never guess its worth, nuggets stuffed in a velvet pouch like beans in tomato sauce.

Why hadn't someone buried this treasure? He glanced up to see Owen limping toward him. The rancher's jagged breathing prickled Clay's skin. Owen leaned his hands on his knees a couple of yards from the trunk.

"Full of gold nuggets." Clay hoisted the velvet pouch so Owen would not have to stoop.

Owen's eyes darkened. "Turn that bag over."

Leather scrunched against rock. A lumpy area revealed an outside pocket with a yellowed paper. Folded in fourths, the piece crackled as Clay opened its folds.

A weathered receipt with a G or a J penned in longhand, and a D. Surely his eyes deceived him—he squinted at Owen's blanched countenance and handed over the paper. Owen read for a moment and shuddered. Then he sank onto a rock and held his chest.

No mistaking the name. *J. Dunbar.*

Even more color drained from the rancher's face, if that were possible. He moved a hand to his forehead and breathed, "J. Dunbar. N Route, 7/62."

Feeling even more helpless than when Owen lay unconscious, Clay recalled how this man had supported him at the Triple T. Nothing to do but lift Owen's private suffering on high.

Shadows floated over the sweltering slope. Small animals scuttled through the brush, accenting forest green against indigo clouds.

For Clay the heat came as welcome balm. He extended his arms and rolled his shoulders as warmth soaked through his shirt to his cramped muscles. No good came of wishing he were back in Wyoming Country, but in order to get there, they must make some decisions.

Owen looked up into the mountains. "I've been here years ago, maybe twenty. Back then, we scoured the canyons west of here for wild horses."

"I used to bring James along on our drives to make him strong." He whistled through his teeth as he let out his breath.

"Rain's gathering. Better draw up a plan." He stopped again, and Clay winced at his effort to breathe.

"We've got maybe three, four hours before dark. To Fort Morgan, I'm guessing it's a four-hour walk, but to the first canyon, probably two. The boulders have cutouts to make a fire without being spotted."

A long night with no blankets. But if these canyons could hold horses, it only made sense to head toward them.

"What shall we do with the bag? Probably weighs more than fifty pounds. Still, the gold might come in handy as bribe money."

"No. Leave it."

With a rock, Clay pawed a hollow in the soil and squeezed the trunk into it.

"Just a minute." Owen opened the lid and took out several gold pieces.

"Stick some of these in your pockets. Maybe they fell into our lap for a purpose."

Clay did Owen's bidding and heaved a rock over the trunk. A good shower would completely conceal the hiding place.

Owen sniffed the air. "We need to follow the water. If I remember right, this ridge rises steep on the east but slopes down into a canyon. The far south end's a perfect place to hold a herd. At the top, we'll be able to see down there and figure out a plan."

"You can walk that far before dark?"

Owen wiped his mouth with his sleeve. The dark places in his eyes shaded even more in his silence. Clay scrambled to fill the canteen again before they tackled the task.

"Unparalleled opportunity," the speaker insisted. His voice fanned out over the hot crowd. "In this free land, a man can set out with confidence and expect to see his dreams come true. America holds promise unlike any other nation, my friends."

"Some of you missed our nation's birthday celebration." The speaker pulled on his collar, surely soaked by now.

"Mr. Hanson informs me that the Indian wars have taken their toll here. However, since our coach is delayed, it seems fitting to present the speech I gave on July fourth in Cincinnati, Ohio."

The Hanson children formed the first row, and he took advantage of their interest.

"You youngsters mark my words, soon you will live in the state of Wyoming. Your thriving cattle industry will lead to a sterling future, and you will one day gather on July fourth with no fear of Indian attacks."

A feeble hurrah rose from one of the stage passengers. But this speech produced mostly murmurs from stragglers still at the station.

He spoke the truth, but ought to take into account the complications of distance, danger, and disaster. Meta could give her own speech on this topic, complete with an introduction, a closing, and three cohesive points. Miss Brunner, who insisted each upper level student give speeches every two weeks, complete with outline and note cards, would be proud.

The speaker continued, and Meta's thoughts wandered to Clay. At dinner last night, this fellow regaled them with tales from his life, and in one, recalled a sermon describing people motivated to pray for someone during a certain time. Later, they discovered that the person experienced a dire need precisely then.

When Garrit disappeared, she endured a long night of trying to control the uncontrollable. Even afterwards, though she lost her bearings for a while, winter finally came to an end and despair made way for hope. Now her womb held the most amazing expression of a new love. Clay had no idea but would know the moment he saw her.

Nearly finished with her waiting dress, she brought the calico out under the big cottonwood to stitch while she listened. Nearby, Matilda's knee swayed back and forth to keep Ben asleep. Soon they would all eat sandwiches made earlier.

"The great railroad will extend this far one day. Count on it, ladies and gentlemen, and your cities will grow and prosper. Hundreds of miles lie completed, while hoards of men labor to cross the mountains and plains."

Why not speak of Martin's unit stumbling through harsh terrain so recently, or the tenacity of General Grant's troops through disease and storm, with the nation waiting to hear the outcome of their prolonged siege? The Confederacy had split because the Union succeeded at Vicksburg—why not talk about that?

This orator ought to tell how that victory came on the same day as the hard-fought win at Gettysburg, and how many men died before soldiers raised the flag on July fourth. But he referred to none of these.

In the same way, the colonists fighting the British secured freedom a hundred years ago but paid a dear price. Such an undertaking required more than aspirations.

Fat baby fingers curled around Matilda's, and Ben's cry brought Meta back to the moment. Matilda nuzzled his neck, and his coos touched Meta's heart.

People applauded. Matilda stood up, and Meta rose with her.

"What did you think of the speech?"

"I fixed his outline as he spoke."

Matilda grinned. "If only Jacob and the older girls could have a teacher like you." She shifted Benjamin to her other arm as Meta opened the kitchen door. "I am so glad you decided to stay with us longer."

Perspiration and blood caked Owen's head. An hour's climb put them above a sharp ravine bordering a creek four feet wide. Rock pillars spired into peaks against the heavens.

At times they walked north to south, then the opposite, but always westward and upward. Coon and coyote droppings, full of ravaged mesquite beans, draped the path. Once, they smelled bear, but, Clay saw no tracks.

As the mountain's shadow deepened, bright green bracken ferns decorated small ledges cut into the rock by wind and rains. Heavy moss, rusty from water seepage, covered much of the rock face. Calcified formations crumbled in the hand while others shattered on the path.

A massive cottonwood towered over them, roots so entangled in the caliche and rock conglomeration it was impossible to tell where the tree began and ended. Smaller roots poked from the rose, blue, and gray pattern of tiny embedded stones and pebbles. A calcified root the width of Clay's finger had succumbed to the action of water heavy with lime. Without its crust, the actual root boasted half its size. Another knobby piece showed a thick tuber's inner pathways.

In the shade, Owen's breath became less labored.

"A little farther on, this wall will weave, with indentations big enough for a house. We'll find one and make a fire."

Owen pulled a black stone from his pocket. "Got my flint—never travel anywhere without this."

After another half hour, an old trail worn into the earth by animals and Indians revealed some unfamiliar droppings.

"Mountain lion. Looks like a mama and her cub."

Owen never asked to stop but drank when Clay did. Here, pines grew so close they hid the trail. Grey and tan patterns formed on dense needles underfoot.

At a sudden wide space, aspen and pine encased an oval mountain lake. A meadow led to the water's edge, and a mother eagle, stark white against blue sky, led four dark brown, furry-feathered chicks on one of their first flights.

Tiny yellow flowers on fragile vines and purple larkspur colored the meadow. Owen grunted as he rotated a slim stem in his fingers.

"Bullhead flowers. Hard to imagine but these little beauties will soon turn into stickers. Who would ever think such a pretty flower could produce something as vicious as bullhead thistles?

"Waning moon tonight, so we can expect denser darkness up here. How about making our camp just beyond the lake?" Owen pointed ahead. "Won't take much longer to make it."

"You think the canyon's just over the top?"

Owen glanced toward Fort Morgan and let out a moan at the movement. No turning back now, but Clay wished he could offer something besides water.

"Looks as if our stream ends at the lake, but I expect we'll find some water on the other side. We can follow a new stream over the top in the morning." They crossed the meadow and started toward the wall.

"The canyon lies due west about three miles." He made a slow circle, his eyes intent. "On the downside of the ridge."

They could not have found a better hideaway. An open-ended entrance led to plenty of space for a fire. Hidden by rocky extensions on both sides, the shelter even exposed a roof about six feet high and ten feet deep.

Owen painfully gathered dry needles and short twigs, knelt in a central location about eight feet from the wall and pulled out his flint. Clay scrambled for dry brush and larger chunks for the night. When he returned, flames burst forth.

Sorrow, pain, and exhaustion—seeing Owen head-on in the reflected light ignited fury. A makeshift cushion could never heal the rancher, but sleep might lessen his pain. Such an abundance of soft needles—Clay raked in a big pile and shaped beds for them both.

Owen fed the fire until it crackled, and then dropped onto a mound of pine needles and boughs. He covered his face with his hat, and Clay tiptoed back to the creek.

To the rhythm of Ben's regular breathing, Meta wrote to Lissa, now a married woman with an infant. What would it be like to make Mama's house her own, even though Freidrich and Henry still lived there?

Probably she and her husband, Alfred, would care for the brothers into their last days, although some men got the urge to go west in their thirties or forties. By the time this letter arrived, Clay would be back and working on the shed with Franklin.

Dear sister,

My friend Matilda's baby, whom we call Little Ben, sleeps in his cradle a foot away. Your first baby does the same, in the cradle Mama used for us. I picture you as a happy mother and wife. How I wish I could have been there to help with your birthing, as I did with little Ben's.

And if we were together, you could help with mine. Yes, Clay and I will have a baby too, closer to Christmas. Please tell Margita and the others. I vowed to tell him before spreading the news, but am making an exception for my baby Sis.

Now, I await his return from Texas territory, where he has gone for our starter herd. I wait, too, for my own return home, since I have come to Matilda's for safety during Indian troubles. She and her husband run the stage stop, and there has been plenty of activity here.

You would be pleased with my stitchery progress, sister. I sewed a waiting dress for myself from some of Matilda's yard goods. Though it makes me look like a big yellowed leaf, my growing body fits inside.

I hope you received my package by now. I await word of your new little one.

Your loving sister,
Meta

Little Benjamin stirred as she addressed the envelope and sealed it with candle wax.

"Benjamin Hanson, have you wakened from your nap? Come here to Aunt Meta. I'll sing you a song before we bother your Mama, all right?"

"Bye-oh, baby-oh. Daddy's gone a-hunting, oh.
Down to old north Texas way,
but he'll be back on one fine day.
Bye-oh, baby-oh.
Bye-oh, baby-oh."

From across the room, Matilda's smile warmed her. They shared another bond now, as well as the work and little Ben's care. Something about that time in the larder, when weeping was all they could do, strengthened her.

Aware of goodness enveloping her, Meta leaned back. The goodness of these kind people, the goodness of this innocent child, the goodness of a Creator who watched over her and her unborn baby. Sorrow had played a part in her journey, but so did goodness, sustaining her through everything. As she rocked and sang, she lifted herself up, along with all her concerns. Clay, Franklin, and the dream they shared, the Indian problems, her family and friends spread from Iowa to Texas, Nebraska to Wyoming, Arizona to Oregon.

Stalwart Butler's family with Anna and Herman in Cheyenne, Betsy in Oregon Territory, and Lissa with her new baby. Her mind flitted to her older sisters and their families in Nebraska, and as always, to dear Martin.

For some reason, Mr. Dunbar came to mind. She had never met the owner of the Oak Bar, but prayed for him, whatever his present needs.

Running water—once again, Owen's instincts served them well. Sure enough, a stream crossed the rise. After filling the canteen,

Clay squatted in deepening shadows, nightfall's first quiet. Would Meta's star shine tonight?

He dipped his forearms into the cold flow and watched the day's dust disappear. A slender moon reflected the water as an evening breeze whispered. Then he froze.

Close by, something was flapping. *Slap, slap, slap…* a bear lapping water? No, he would smell that.

He shifted a few feet and searched along the streambed. Finally, a shallow pool revealed the source—a large trout caught in the rocks—must have worn itself out.

Owen needed food, and their fire could roast this tender fellow. He threw his shirt over the fish, a dripping foot-long package. With the sleeves around the still-writhing body, he started back toward the campsite. Had he been lost, Owen's snore would have led him there.

Clay whittled the ends of two sticks into sharp points, gutted and skewered the fish and hung the flanks above the fire. As the trout roasted, scenes from evenings with Father Bernard came to mind—manna in the wilderness, oil in Elijah's empty flask, flour for one more batch of dough.

The stories Father Bernard read him about Moses and the burning bush, the starving widow and her son, and Jesus feeding five thousand people with a few fish took on new life. This night, he and Owen shared a divine gift. When the skin had browned, Clay waited a while longer.

The wind made music in the pines. Warmth emanated in their campsite, far beyond what the fire produced. Owen turned onto his back and moaned. His eyes opened a twinge, and Clay left the fish.

"Owen!" The rancher gaped back at him. Clay pointed toward the wonder as Owen's eyes widened.

"Hungry?" Clay carefully removed the skewer from its holders and split the meat into four chunks on a flat rock.

With a square of pine bark in his hands, complete with two large pieces of meat, Owen managed to speak. "Where did…"

"The stream. Saved for our supper."

Though his stomach had complained for hours, Clay took a small first bite, and imagined Owen did the same. The elaborate meal at the Crady's table could not compare to the wild yet mellow taste of this particular fish.

No more words passed between them that night—their mission would succeed. When Owen's snore filled the cavern, Clay fed the fire and lay down, breathing easy.

Chapter Thirty-three

*Friendship is a sheltering tree. The happiness of life is
made up of minute fractions—the little, soon forgotten charities
of a kiss or a smile, a kind look, or heartfelt compliment.*
~William Wordsworth

Something cold and wet nudged Clay's forehead. He opened his eyes to sun shining through the opening and reached for his gun. Then he looked into a doe's grey-brown muzzle and black eyes. She twitched her head and took a step backward.

Owen still slept, forming an S shape in his needle bed. Clay crept past the fire and toward the enclosure's mouth. A hot meal and a night's sleep had done wonders.

Every solitary pine needle dripped shimmering evidence of rain during the night. Stiffness plagued Clay's back, arms, and legs as he sidestepped down the short slope to refill the canteen. Shafts of light shone through heavy, wet branches, and the pine smell worked its way—each breath seemed wider and deeper here.

If they could top the ridge today, they could spot the outlaws' set-up before dark and attack under cover of darkness. As far as they knew, they were up against four outlaws, but the number mattered little. Success depended on making the right moves at the right time.

With any luck they would find the other cowhands in their party tied-up, hungry, furious, and itching to fight as soon as they could. But the outlaws would likely have a lookout, so they must disarm and disable him without being discovered. Then everything else would fall into place.

Sunlight splayed through pine branches as Clay doused his face and shook off the water's shocking cold. Patches of blue sky peeked through—Meta would love this place, like the cliffs below the stagecoach stop.

He had never been much for gunplay, but Father Bernard insisted he learn to shoot and enlisted one of the best marksmen in north Texas to teach him. Clay got the idea that his instructor had transformed from a scoundrel to an upright-citizen.

So every Saturday afternoon for several hours, they met for practice out in an open field. The man's tall wiry frame and bald head intrigued Clay, along with a definite English accent.

The best lesson he learned was how to aim without balking at the back talk. This had to do with preparing for the noise. Once learned, though, he had never again startled when firing.

Father Bernard refused to be satisfied with minimal skill. The first night, after an unsuccessful afternoon, they ate their evening porridge in silence. Clay's arm ached from holding the gun, and he had no great desire to try again.

But his mentor knew exactly how to comfort him. "If an expert like Alexander Bloomfield learned how to shoot with his handicap, there is no question you can do it."

The logic stymied every possible self-doubt.

"Nine out of ten bull's eyes, son—make this your goal, and nothing less." Father Bernard stayed beside him through grueling practices. "You must be able to defend yourself and your family. We live in dangerous times."

Finally hitting nine out of ten, Clay felt as though he had gained manhood, even without hair on his chest. Now, he breathed another thank you for Father Bernard's foresight.

To save Owen's life, would he shoot an outlaw? No question—the rancher had become family. Only one problem: the outlaws had taken his gun.

Though Owen declared himself healed, reaching the ridgetop took longer than they speculated. Clay could hardly wait to look

into the canyon and refused to consider what to do if they saw no horses or men.

When the stage disbursed its passengers on the twenty-third of July, a small older woman gripped the sidebar until Tom steadied her. She clung to him, but her eyes shone bright. Meta wiped her hands on her apron and held the door for her.

The woman extended her hand as Tom released her. "Mrs. Beckley. Kate Millicent Beckley."

"Meta Rausch Burns."

"Does your father run this station, child?" Mrs. Beckley must not have noticed her condition.

"No Ma'am, but let me help you with your things." The woman handed her a parasol and a brown paper parcel.

"Could I get you a cold lemonade?"

"Oh, that would be lovely, dear."

Meta hung the parasol on a hook and placed the parcel on the bench below. Mrs. Beckley took a seat, and when she received her lemonade, she rubbed her hip. "So, what does your father do here?"

"My father... ah, he died long ago." Meta had been cutting homemade noodles for what seemed like hours, and her feet thanked her when she sank into a chair. "I have a husband, and we own a ranch to the south, Ma'am, a horse ranch."

"A horse ranch. Oh my, how exciting!" Mrs. Beckley's left eyebrow arched, and she drew a shaking hankie over her forehead's fragile skin.

"I guess you could say so."

"How did you meet?" Mrs. Beckley sipped her drink, and her pallor took on some color. "This sooths my parched throat. Thank you so much."

"He happened by my claim one day. He, ah... helped me out with something."

"Oh my. You must be as brave as my niece Sarah, who lives far off in Oregon Territory."

"And you, Ma'am? What brings you here all alone?"

"Oh, a dear family friend, Mr. Lawson, who will be in shortly, accompanies me."

"And where will your journey end, in Oregon?"

"The Dalles, with my niece and her family. I..." She pulled another delicate crocheted hankie from her satchel to wipe her mouth.

"My husband passed during the winter. I—we—had no children, so Sarah invited me westward."

"Sarah. What a lovely name. You will be seeing your family soon."

"Yes." Mrs. Beckley pulled at her black bonnet strings. "Although I must say this stage travel wearies one dreadfully."

"Ma'am, I will talk to the owner's wife. Perhaps she could arrange a hot bath after dinner tonight?"

Mrs. Beckley's chin quivered. "Why, dear, you have no idea how much that would mean."

Oh, but Meta did, and so did Matilda.

The new stream maintained its size, and as they stopped for their second drink, sharp stickers grabbed at Clay's clothing when he refilled the canteen. He and Owen devoured bunches of dried black raspberries hanging low on the bushes, staining their fingers and mouths dark blue. Nearer the ridge top, they found red raspberries.

"If we can't outwit those outlaws, we can at least scare them to death with our dyed skin. But where there's berries, there's bears."

The berries fortified their spirits, but they wasted no time. At last, the ridgetop lay beneath their feet, and a sheltering boulder beckoned.

Owen exhaled as he studied the mountain's huge fold.

"I'd say they took your horses clear down toward the south end." At first they saw no movement. Then something white flashed.

"To the left of that pine leaning north—see them?"

Clay's stomach lurched into his chest. *His* horses. This was why men risked everything for land and possessions.

He could make out the herd, but not individual animals. Together, they looked like a swaying wheat field, tails flicking at flies in the noonday sun.

"When the sun casts shadows on this side, we'll sneak down for a better look."

For the time being, they needed to rest. Healed or not, Owen's raspiness reappeared toward the end of their climb. With no quarrel, he rested while Clay kept watch.

Now to find a rock for a weapon. One hard blow from a sharp piece of iron ore would knock the guard senseless, and his gun would become Clay's.

Over and over he rehearsed the scene. Finally, the perfect rock came to his attention, eight inches long and narrow at one end.

Owen had said nothing more about James. What if they discovered his son had some connection with these rustlers?

While Mrs. Becklly bathed, Meta penned a letter to Betsy. Earlier, Matilda had grabbed Meta's shoulders. "What a wonderful idea. Consider yourself in charge of making this lady happy."

A half-cup of soda, a pinch of lavender from a sachet, and steaming water. Towel and cloth hanging over a chair back, Meta fetched Mrs. Beckley from the dining room as twilight fell.

"How kind of you, dear." Mrs. Beckley paused at the kitchen entrance. "Oh, lavender? That always puts me right."

"I'll be right outside if you need me. And Ma'am, might I ask you a favor?"

"Surely."

"I have a friend, Betsy Bishop, in The Dalles. We met on

the wagon train, and I would be obliged if you would deliver a letter to her."

"Why, of course. Sarah mentioned other families just across the meadow. I wouldn't doubt she knows your Betsy. I have a little extra room in my bag, if you want to send anything else."

So Meta poured out all the news of the last weeks. July would end next week—she shared her worries and fears with Betsy too.

> *You will like Mrs. Beckley. She asked no special favors, but Tom arranged for her to sleep in one of the guest cabins. She regaled us with stories of her youth over dinner, but her eyes show such weariness.*
>
> *It pains me to think of all the jolts and bumps she endures day after day. A wagon would be worse, but at her age... what a positive attitude!*
>
> *In the packet you will find something small to remember me by, like my forget-me-not seeds. I planted them near our cabin and asked Franklin to water them.*
>
> *A similar flower grows wild here, so I made you a remembrance. I hope your new life in Oregon overflows with joys, dear Betsy.*
>
> *Your wagon train friend,*
> *Meta*

Beside her on the table lay a drawstring bag—leftover calico from her waiting dress. One of the settlers' wives taught the children to press small blue wild flowers into flat rocks and seal the outlines with a heated flatiron, so Meta made several.

"Dear, could you please come now?"

Wary of slipping, Mrs. Beckley took Meta's hand. "I will never, never forget your kindness. You have made me feel at home."

When Owen woke, Clay went to get more water. The canteen

would have to last them through the attack. Owen half slid down the slope a few yards ahead. Halfway down, he discovered a niche in a granite outcropping to observe the camp's action. They could see the layout, with the herd far back in the canyon. A creek flowed a few yards from the bandits' fire.

"They sleep between the creek and the fire, so the running water will hide our movements. The guard will be between them and the horses."

"I'm going to slip above the horses to see where they've got Roy and the others." Owen took off without further explanation.

Above the horses—he must mean on the steep canyon wall itself.

Clay focused on learning as much as he could about the enemy, moving like dots far below as the sun reflected on something—a tin roof? Perhaps Roy and the cowhands were locked in that small shed.

One day soon, sweet Benjamin would roll over. Meta spent every possible moment with him, but an insistent tugging began to pull her home. That evening, the stagecoach driver took off his hat and joined them at the table.

"Slow mover's comin' through on Thursday. Won't make near the time as the night coach, but there'll be two seats for passengers headin' South."

After the meal, Meta pulled Tom aside. "I'd like to be one of those riders on Thursday."

"All right, we can arrange for your passage."

As soon as they put the kitchen in order, Matilda made it clear she would be sending gifts. From an old steamer trunk she piled yard goods on the table, put her hands on her hips, and grinned.

"Let's see how much we can sew for that baby of yours in two days."

They cut and sewed that night until Meta's eyes hurt. The next morning Matilda assigned the kitchen and little Ben to Annalee and Sarah. She stormed to the table, a woman on a mission. To the slim pile of baby wraps produced the night before, they added two blankets and three buntings before midafternoon.

She packed loaves of bread, too, and jam from the berries they picked near the creek. Thursday when Meta stood beside the stage door, her fingers on sleeping Benjamin's cheek, Matilda's arm caressed her shoulder.

"I know Clay is due any time, and the officer declared your area safe. But…"

"That burial ground lies close to our cabin. So far, every Indian I have seen has been a friend of Franklin's, and he's certain they won't hurt us."

Matilda pulled her close again. Her eyes said it all, *thank you,* and *come to see us again,* and *Godspeed.*

Less than two rods away from the creek and north of the campsite, Clay and Owen froze at their new watching post. The moon appeared and insects started their incessant whirring. Just before nightfall after a showy sunset, a big brown frog emerged near Clay's boot. The animal stared through slanted eyes below two slender black lines. Finally, it spread its toes and hopped into some brush.

Earlier, Owen had returned with valuable information. They had guessed right on several accounts.

"Roy's tied to a pole about ten feet south of the fire." Owen made an X in the earth. "We can cross the creek here. Somebody pulled a tree trunk across the water."

From below, men's voices floated upward.

"One of us diverts the guard, and the other comes at him from behind with a knock-out blow."

Owen's eyes flashed when Clay pulled out his ore.

"Been getting used to my weapon. Just the thing for bashing somebody in the head."

"Takes stealth and determination. You've got both."

"I'll get the guard to the creek." Owen frowned. "But be careful—might be another guard."

"This weapon can be used more than once. I'll double-bind their hands, like they did ours."

"Good. A man can look like he's out cold one minute and…"

"The outlaws will sleep with their guns. How can we secure them all without someone getting shot by a man startled awake?"

"These scoundrels were thoughtless enough to leave your canteen on you. We can outsmart them." Owen shook Clay's shoulder. "That's the part we'll live to tell in campfire stories."

Some low whinnies wafted up the incline, a door squeaked open and shut, and the quiet resumed as the guard strode toward the fire. The next time Clay looked, four bedrolls lay like sleeping sheep near the fire. Five against five.

A rock landed near the creek with a thud. Owen's diversion jerked the guard's head east. The tall, muscular man hunched his shoulders as he stared toward the sound. Not a stir among the bedrolls.

Clay glided behind the shed and heard Reese's snore. A board creaked as someone turned over, but he resisted the temptation to untie these two.

No, the guard might hear them. Owen made another artful splash, and Clay slunk ahead in a wide circle, his weapon a part of his body. The guard took a step toward the water when another splash came from the opposite side, like someone thrashing through dry brush. He clutched his rifle, moving forward.

Within a yard, Clay made his thrust. The crunch of rock on bone set his teeth on edge as the guard collapsed with a dull crash, like the bear that visited last winter.

Easy to slip his gun belt from his body. Clay raced to Roy and tugged on the rope binding his wrists.

"Where did they hide the guns?"

Roy gestured toward a wagon. His forehead bore a long wound that needed tending.

"I'll tie this one. You get the guns and go for the others in the shed."

First Clay pulled off the guard's boots. No human could go far barefoot over bullhead thistles. Overturning the man, he gasped at the mustached outline of a younger Owen Dunbar.

Distinct cracks from two strong kicks to the lout's ribs with the sharp toe of his boot provided a peculiar satisfaction. James ought to hurt like his father.

Then Father Bernard's face came to mind—despite this outlaw's betrayal of his own father, he still had value. Clay shook himself.

By the time he arrived at the shed, Roy had retrieved three gun belts and untied Reese. Buck slept through it all, so Roy jostled him awake with a warning shush and untied his hands. After both cowhands buckled on their gun belts, Clay led the way out and almost ran into Owen, who wheeled back into the moonlight. Clay followed him around the corner, the others not far behind.

"Ready your weapons. There's four more."

In the firelight, Roy gave a terse nod.

"Take one apiece. Knock them out first." Owen's muted command reflected certainty.

Without a fight, Clay brought the guard's gun down on the first man's skull. Around him, similar dull *cracks* splintered the night air.

Owen handed ropes around like a woman serving Johnny cake, and they all set to work. Owen pilfered jackets from two of the men, put one on and handed the other to Roy, shivering from lying on the ground.

Pulling off boots, Owen moved from man to man. Then he headed toward the creek with Reese. Reese launched the boots far and wide. *Smack! Slap!*

"Shall we put 'em in the shed?"

Clay threw a chunk of wood on the fire. The need for stealth had passed—might as well create some light.

"Tie three of them in there, one to a corner. Take this one and the guard over there by the wagon." Owen took charge—had he recognized James?

Reece dragged a his man to the wagon wheel. Clay saw to James Dunbar, positioning him like Owen, doubled over, face in the dirt.

As he shoved the dead weight into place, he thought to search inside the box, where he discovered his own warm jacket and two more coats. He took out all the harness and tack for morning.

Using an extra-long rope, he tied James' feet and hands again, then looped the ends through the latch and secured them with hog-ties. Back at the fire, Buck piled their bedrolls a short distance away, and Roy put on the coffee pot and heated ham and beans.

The men went at the food like wolves.

"One thing—they took good care of the horses." Roy's eyes shone. Must be their reg'lar camp. They even have hay stockpiled."

Clay set his plate down and strode toward the animals. Pax nickered when he smelled him and receive the best brushing of his life. The night stirred with horse talk as Owen and the hands counted the stock. In the end, they had lost only time.

Consolation swelled—all of their work had not been in vain. The fire drew the men back, and Owen began the story.

"This young man saved my life. Got me over that ridge when I was hurting bad. Even brought me a fish to eat."

Clay shoved back into the shadows.

"Reminds me of when your pa saved my hide, Roy. We like to froze to death when that April blizzard blew in, but old Slim McGraw slipped away. When he came back, he dragged a buffalo robe to keep us through the night."

Roy returned Owen's grin. "To his dying day, Slim never told me where he found that robe. Did he ever tell you?"

"Not outright. But he gave us a hint. That night, we camped closer than anyone realized to a band of Sioux, and Grandpa was half Sioux..."

Mr. Dunbar's forehead folded into a terrain of wrinkles. "That's right, and your pa had a way with them. Slim disappeared for only half an hour. When he walked toward us, huddled around a meager fire, no one said a word.

"We thought he was a bear with that robe around his shoulders. Lucky we didn't shoot him before we thought twice."

Buck reached for the empty plates. "I'll wash these and stand watch. Been sleepin' all day." He nudged Reece. "Snorin', too, I 'spect." Reece thumped him in the arm and Buck's smile widened.

"Best way to sleep—couldn't hear a thing after they knocked me out." He strode toward the creek as Reece went for their bedrolls.

Clay found his bedroll and saddlebag, still holding Meta's prayer book. A tipped shell of moon shone down, along with her bright star. Sleep would be hard-won tonight.

"These shipment stages always have plenty of room. The cavalry can figure out how to transport everything to your cabin. Looks to me like you'll be traveling with gold." Tom gave Meta's shoulder a fatherly pat.

Matilda came forward with Annalee, Sarah, and the rest of the children. Meta bent to take in Benjamin's charm one more time. Tom gave her a hand onto the stage and handled the driver's scowl at her extra parcel.

"Only one bag on this run. Got a full load a'ready."

"The scheduler said you could take two."

The man's grip tightened on the whip laced at his side. "All right. Count the parcel as a passenger."

Tom pounded fourteen nails into the crate early this morning, after Matilda squeezed in a few more items. Matilda launched the driver a stern scowl. "Must be having a bad day."

"All right, then. Up you go." Tom hoisted Meta into the stage and shut the door. The accompanying soldiers mounted, and her heart squatted in her throat. Having Captain Reynolds nearby would have helped, but he was not among the four cavalrymen riding watch.

Soon, dust covered her, and she gave full rein to her distress at leaving the Hansons.

When her breathing returned to normal, she leaned back, balanced her left arm on the box, and listed its contents to calm herself. Matilda's huckleberry pie, baked before dawn and triple-wrapped in brown paper, lined the bottom.

On top rested two dishtowels, baby diapers—she lost track how many—three buntings, two little hats, several blankets, and even a christening dress Matilda said she no longer needed.

"My Mama made that dress, and it has seen my seven properly baptized. After your baby wears it, throw it away and make a new one. A dress can last only through so many births, dear."

Staring at the horses as they rested in the stillness of late evening brought Clay unique satisfaction. An occasional flick of a tail or a nicker rode the wind as a shooting star sailed across the heavens.

How could horses sleep standing up? Even Father Bernard's explanation failed to completely quell his curiosity.

Since horses fall prey to wolves and mountain lions, God made their legs able to hold them up even while sleeping. If they get startled, they can run away.

A bat flew by, then another, perhaps youngsters home late from their feeding. Footsteps approached from the camp, and the sharp outline of Roy's distinctive hat profiled against the night sky. Buck and Reece made fun of its high arc, but Roy claimed it cooled his head better than theirs.

"Got yer horses back."

"Mmm. And we all survived. But Owen looks a little worse for wear." Clay perched on a rock. "Two days ago I had my doubts about him, but he's not one to go down without a fight."

Roy chewed off a bit of twig and spat. "After that sick-lookin' one knocked you out, Owen went wild. Got in a durn good kick before the cook banged him over the head."

"That doesn't surprise me. You've known him a long time?"

"I was ten or so when Ma died and Pa heard th' west callin'. He knew ol' Mr. Dunbar—lived near 'im back in Minnesota. Dunbar wasn't one to stay put, even after he built the ranch. Once he mentioned this territory, Pa was doomed to go."

"Ever been back there?"

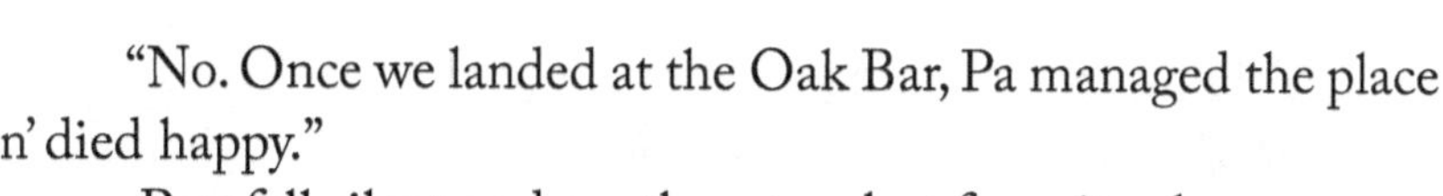

"No. Once we landed at the Oak Bar, Pa managed the place n' died happy."

Roy fell silent and another star shot from its place.

"You know Owen has a son?"

Clay nodded, and Roy chewed for a long time on his twig. "You know which one he is?"

"I…ah…I believe so."

Roy lowered his voice. "The last time we came here, Owen had to stay at the ranch so Pa and me made the trip with some hands. Mr. Dunbar's son offered me a share in his gang. Pa said he'd like to shoot 'im for Owen's sake. Woulda saved 'im heartache in the long run."

It would be a hard night for sleeping, after all. At dawn, the truth would be impossible to ignore.

The rhythm of cavalrymen riding outside the stage lulled Meta to sleep. When they stopped to water the horses, the door flew open and a soldier offered his arm.

Past some juniper pines and scraggly wild oaks, she found a private place and hurried back so the surly driver would find no fault. The guard, a friendly sort, chatted when he latched the door.

"We'll change horses at the next stop, since this load weighs far more than most. Then it's only an hour to the Spring Creek turn-off."

After another nap, no cavalrymen rode next to the stage. A whirring noise filled the air and the driver yelled at the team. The stage creaked and swayed like a tree in a storm, and Meta gripped the sidebar with both hands as her box shoved against her, then slid the opposite way.

Now the crate reversed direction, so braced her feet while smoothing her bulging stomach with her other hand. But what protection could she afford her baby?

"Oh God, do keep our baby safe."

A blunt *thud*. Gunfire whistled, but the driver kept slapping his whip. An Indian passed her window with long black hair flying and an unearthly yell. Black marks ran down the side of his face.

Gunfire issued from above, and the warrior crashed from his horse. His gun flew above his head, blood spattered the window. Meta's mind raced with images of the Sioux Massacre from her school days.

Roy and Owen led the way to Fort Morgan as Clay, Reese, and Buck kept the herd in line. The sky had never shone so blue.

Fresh biscuits cooked in an iron skillet with bacon in the batter constituted a celebration this morning. They all ate their fill, and Clay checked on the outlaws. Two in the shed had regained consciousness.

Owen rolled out of his blanket in far better shape than yesterday. In the middle of the night, Clay heard him get up. How could he mistake the form of his only son?

They followed the wagon road within easy reach of the gold stash. Clay fell back beside Owen. "Shall we fetch that trunk?"

"Let the Army find it or let it rot. Might well be blood money."

"Clay Burns... or is it Dusek?"

"I never thought we'd see each other again." Clay shook hands with Ranger Moberly.

"Nor I. But I'm tracking some scoundrels, part human, part jackal." Moberly dismounted and led his horse to the creek. "You run into any trouble so far?"

"A gang stole our horses and added a few more days to our ride."

"Same good-for-nothings attacked some couriers at the New Mexico border. Killed two cavalrymen, stripped their uniforms and left the bodies to parch."

"The ones you sought before?"

"No, I caught them a few days after we met. They're behind bars over in Jefferson. Probably hanged by now, if there's any justice."

"How many men're you looking for?"

"Four or five—good chance they also robbed a stage and killed a guard here, but I get first chance at 'em. What I want 'em for happened in Texas, where the authorities suspect them of some other mischief."

"Does one have deep-set eyes and a low forehead?"

"That's the fool of the bunch. Where did you leave them?"

"Into the wind about an hour, then up past an old shed. If you take the road, it's three hours. We left early this morning."

"Tied up?"

"And hungry. We'll report them at Fort Morgan."

The wind carried Moberly's spittle like rain. "Don't bother. They belong to Texas."

"There's gold, too. A small leather trunk uphill from the miner's shed, with a rock up against it. We found a bill of sale inside to J. Dunbar."

"Ah. Tell the army about the trunk." The small muscle in Moberly's cheek worked as he eyed the ground. "The way they left those soldiers—ought to pay with their lives."

The ranger spat. "How did things go at the Crady ranch?"

"Fine, sir." Clay gestured toward the horses with his free hand. "Mr. Crady died the night before we left."

The Ranger issued a grunt. Clay thought he might say something more, but Owen walked up. "Ranger Moberly, I'm surprised to see you've come this long way."

"That right?"

"Yes, sir." He glanced at Clay. "Ready to saddle up?" Quieter than usual, he headed back to his horse.

"Awful glad I found you out on that prairie back in '44, son."

"So am I. Hope you're still glad when you see what we left you."

"Waiting for their escort." A grim smile spread across the

Ranger's face. "Bringing their kind in—why, I can't put the satisfaction into words."

"If you ever happen to chase anybody to Wyoming Territory, we live northeast of Cheyenne."

They both mounted, and Clay rode toward Owen and the hands. Just before Moberly disappeared, he glanced back for a final glimpse of those granite shoulders.

Another warrior rode by. Two more, then six, then Meta closed her eyes. Dust sprayed her clothes, stung her face. More shots resounded, and a different kind of yell rose from the driver or the guard—a shriek.

With her trunk boxing her in, she could barely breathe. The coach lurched again and something like cat's feet sounded on the roof. Gradually, dust rose like ashes, the pounding of hooves slowed and just when she thought the coach would stop, her door flung open. Bronze fingers grasped the framework.

She shrank back as a muscular arm extended and obsidian eyes held hers. Partridge or quail feathers stuck from his leather headband. Those eyes seemed vaguely familiar as he drew her into a sweet, woody essence—hyssop.

Time stopped, though horses and stage kept jolting. Arms like iron lifted her onto a horse. A thick forearm drew her near.

Treetops flew by as a strange sense of safety enveloped her. Behind them, shouts and shots still splayed. The wind lifted her hair as she eased into this brave's embrace.

Such an odd feeling of falling yet not falling, hanging between reality and nightmare. The Indian held her helpless, yet this odd quietude prevailed.

Abbie Gardner's saga ran through her mind, but she focused on the life within her. As she did, her shoulders relaxed. Something she had sung to little Ben wafted. *Lullaby, and good night, go to sleep little baby...*

They rode for what seemed like hours before her captor reined his horse under a clump of elders. He lifted her as he dismounted and put his finger to his lips.

Near a creek bank, he patted the ground opposite him. Then he cupped water in his hands to wash his face and drink. He cupped more and held it to her lips. Ah, as sweet as Spring Creek.

She blinked dust from her eyes, and he reached his wet finger to wipe it away. Then he uttered, "Ross."

Her throat clogged.

He tapped his chest with his fingers. "Ross... fa—ther."

The great white father? He believed Franklin spoke for the government? She shook her head.

He licked his cracked lips, unblinking eyes as black as her stove. He tapped his chest again. "Ross... father."

"Your father... Ross?"

He thumped his fingers on his chest five times.

"*My* father."

Then she saw it—the curve of the eyebrows, the line of the nose, the thick neck, the bulk of arms and shoulders. This couldn't be true, and yet...

"Franklin Ross is—your father?" Breathless, she reached toward his chest.

His lips curved into a slight smile, and Franklin's twinkle lighted his eyes. How could she have missed the resemblance?

He patted his stomach, then motioned toward hers.

"Papoose?"

Her eyes burned—he read her fear. "I take care... you." He pointed toward her. "Take home... Ross..."

Meta leaned back against a sapling. Franklin's son had come for her. How had he known her peril? No answer but one—Providence had sent him. He stood and swooped her up.

"Home... Ross."

Clay could think only of time already wasted. Now, a Fort Morgan officer warned that Indian troubles might still loom ahead. When they set up camp the second night, no one spoke of an earlier departure in the morning. No one needed to. During their last water break, a contingent of soldiers on their way to the Bighorns described recent clashes.

"Wiped out more than one settlement. Red Cloud's on the march." Clay's stomach wrenched as Owen questioned the man.

"Where exactly did this happen?"

"Two families were killed a few hours west of Fort Laramie. Now, others have holed up at a stagecoach station south of there."

At least four hours away from . . .

That night as soon as Clay pulled his blanket over his shoulders, the half-moon, like the lantern Father Bernard often burned into the night, summoned him. He rolled over again, but finally gave up and wriggled out.

Reece had first watch, so Clay offered to take his place.

The lanky young man showed his sense of humor. "'Preciate the offer, but you got a wife waitin'. Better sleep while ya can."

Vegetation had thinned out, and brittle brown grass already broke with every step. The scents of juniper and sage reigned. Coyotes yapped in the distance, and a jackrabbit skittered across camp.

The Oak Bar could be no more than two days away. Then back to the cabin—to Meta.

Counting once again, Clay rounded the herd. He greeted each one and came to Pax.

"Hey boy. You asleep?"

Pax nudged his side. "You've worked hard. In a few days, we'll be back with your old friend Hope."

"Can't sleep?" Owen's voice startled him. "Me neither. Think horses ever have trouble sleeping?"

Clay chuckled. "I doubt it. Used to wish I was one."

Owen eased onto a rock a few feet away. "A lot's happened on this ride. You had quite the time with the Crady's."

"That's the truth."

"And in the Rockies.—" Owen twirled a dry branch in his fingers. "I expect you have some questions about my son."

Clay pondered what to say. Where was Father Bernard, or Saint John of the Cross when he needed them?

"Anybody would."

"I do wonder about James."

A coyote's howl pierced the night.

"A man can't keep things like this inside forever. James grew up with—" Cicadas took over the silence.

"Before the boy was two years old, my wife—" Owen passed his hat back and forth between his hands.

"I should have known better than to take a city girl so far from home. Met her in Minnesota. Never thought she would up and leave."

A tremble entered his voice. "When she left, she took James. Can't say I ever got over the shock. I rode into Cheyenne to see him from time to time. His mother started working at a saloon, so James grew up seeing the worst of things."

The air cooled as a breeze blew in from the Rockies.

"One time when he was about twelve, I brought him home for the summer, even though Lorraine fought me. Took some doing, but he learned to ride and rope. I thought he might want to stay, but he went back to town in the fall. Fetched him again the next year, and it took the first month to make up for what he had lost."

Owen put his hand to his forehead. "That second summer we built your cabin. I kept thinking maybe someday James would take care of the herd during the winter. But near the end of August, a buggy drove in. Lorraine and her new beau, all dressed to travel, with James along."

"I told him he could stay, but my wife said a boy belonged with his Mama. They could start a new life in Denver City. Sounded exciting to him, I suppose."

Glittering stars flooded the sky as Owen ran his knuckles along a stick.

"Thought my heart would give way when James left. I rode down there to find him the next year, sent the hands to drive the cattle back up to the ranch. Folks said she moved on to Utah or was in California. Said she left James behind, but nobody knew for sure.

"That's why I tell people she passed on." His sigh reached the Rockies. "I searched and searched, but never caught wind of James. Thought I would never see him again in this life."

"Can't help but wonder if he was already out in those mountains back then, if he had already hooked up with—" Owen's voice fractured.

"If only I—" In a hoarse whisper, he continued. "Guess I gave him up back then."

An itch began in the middle of Clay's back. No telling what hard times people had gone through.

"But more than ten years later, here he is, no mistaking. A grown man, mustache and all." Owen twisted away. "What I heard the two in the shed say, I vowed never to repeat, but I owe it to you. They bragged about killing those soldiers down in Texas. Laughed about leaving them to die. It's more than—" He choked on his words and Clay's stomach turned.

"You did your best for your son. You tried so many times. . ."

A shudder passed through Owen as if someone had struck him. He stumbled off toward the horses.

Like Ethel when Franklin wanted her to move faster, indigence prevailed over Meta's better instincts. She wanted to accomplish so much, but her willingness shrank as the temperature rose.

Horses and cows flicked flies with their tails hundreds, probably thousands, of times a day, but the movement fascinated her all over again as she observed Della and Hope. At the Hanson's she spent most of her time indoors and reveled to be outdoors again.

Hours with old Tobias, her pony, had filled her childhood. Most people would look at tails as an addendum to an animal's body. But when battling nagging insects, those tails proved essential. Why, she could write a three-point essay on the amazing feats of horses' tails.

Throughout the day, her thoughts went to Tall Elk. The whole vast high plain spread before her in a new way, now that she knew one native. It took Franklin until this morning to recover from hearing their story.

The day before, as she and Tall Elk rode up to the cabin, Franklin emerged, shotgun in hand. When he saw Meta, he paled.

Tall Elk whisked her off the horse and walked her to Franklin, who swallowed her in his arms. She leaned against him, her throat aching. Seeing him again brought back the long winter. When she held out her arm to Tall Elk, the brave retained his posture, hands at his side.

"Thank you for bringing me home to Ross." She touched her chest to signify gratitude. The brave's lips moved in silence, his eyes locked on Franklin's.

"Please tell him for me."

Franklin launched in, though she understood not a syllable.

"He saved my life, Franklin. And he told me he is your son."

The old trapper's mouth opened, then shut. Storm clouds rode his eyes, and a flash of something new. Stupified, he stared from Tall Elk to her.

"Why don't you invite him to eat with us? He must be starving, with only a drink of water since he rescued me. Please don't let him leave. I can never repay him for what he did."

Eyes still wide, Franklin stayed outside as she went in. He spoke to Tall Elk in short bursts, and Tall Elk responded with grunts. Four eggs lay on the table, so she mixed cornbread and poured milk, set the honey pot on the table, and cooked a bag of dried venison. By the time she cut the cornbread, Franklin walked in carrying the butter mold from the creek.

"How did you find time to churn butter?"

"That cool spot in the creek needed somethin' in it, n' I missed havin' butter."

"And I missed you. Did Tall Elk tell you how he found me?"

Franklin rubbed his beard. "Somehow he figgered you'd be on thet stage. He mixed up with th' warriors n' grabbed ya outta there."

"How could he have found out?"

"Injuns send messages we don't know 'bout. When he come here a few weeks back, I tol' 'im where you was."

"Even that far away, he watched out for me—so very brave and so loyal." Franklin shrugged, but Meta gave him her best smile. "And he looks like you."

The trapper's cheeks flooded red. "Didn't mean t' hide nothin', but..."

She looked up to see her rescuer standing in the doorway and waved him in. Franklin showed Tall Elk where to sit, and she served them.

At first the warrior looked askance at his plate, but when he had cleaned it, he crossed his arms. "Good—more."

During the meal she asked every question she could think of. Franklin interpreted until at one point, he blustered. "Lemme eat, will y'?"

Meta complied, but before the end of the meal, she had Franklin tell Tall Elk she wanted him to visit them often. "Ask him to stay here tonight, Franklin."

Franklin bit his lip.

Facing Tall Elk, she tapped the table and looked around the cabin. "You... here." Tall Elk's forehead creased, so she turned to Franklin.

"Tell him for me, please."

Tall Elk mounted and touched his stomach. "Nokuhehe."

"Little rabbit, he says. He means your baby. Take care of your little rabbit."

Meta touched Tall Elk's hand. In one smooth movement, the brave made a sign with his hand.

"He's sayin' *peace*, 'r, mebbe *good luck*."

Then Tall Elk spoke: "*Thootheenebi.*"

"What does that mean?"

"*'Member me*. He wants ya not t' firgit 'im."

Not the slightest chance. She put her hand on her heart and Tall Elk did the same. Before she or Franklin could say more, he turned his paint and disappeared into the brush along the creek.

All evening, Meta repeated the word as the babe within her stirred. She opened the trunk—a dark gray flannel might do for a wrapper during the cold season ahead. This little one ought to arrive around the first of the year, and by the end of her time, her green calico would not be warm enough.

The trunk reminded her of Martin and her sisters—so many gifts they bestowed for her dowry. Her books brought back the old days; sisters and brothers sitting around Mama for reading time.

And Father Bernard had read to Clay in the evenings. There in the quiet, a fresh revelation came—James Fennimore Cooper had written of Natty Bumppo, a white raised by Indians—now, a century later, Tall Elk roamed these western lands.

"I have my own Natty Bumppo!" Clay would marvel at the way Tall Elk had saved her and that Franklin had a son.

Only one way to face the days ahead, days of more waiting. As Mama said, *Even in the waiting God is at work, and so must we be, as well.*

Finding her needle, threading it for morning, Meta had to smile. Lissa would appreciate this—one more opportunity to tackle her least-favorite task.

If only Clay would come home soon.

Chapter Thirty-five

Prickles traversed Clay's spine when Owen sighted Indians crossing the trail and signaled a stop. But the party moved on without incident. Crossing into Wyoming Country a few hours later, the cowhands made for the Oak Bar.

They would leave the starter herd there to rest before bringing them to the north corral. That space would have to suffice until Clay and Franklin finished the new one between the two cabins.

Last year when he passed through Cheyenne on the way to the Oak Bar, the place held no meaning. Now, Clay spied a woman on the porch of the saloon and thought of Lorraine. And James. An arrow pointing to *The Café Rausch* piqued his curiosity—this must be Garrit's family.

Owen nodded when he said, "I need to stop and meet Meta's relations. Maybe they have mail for her. I'll catch up with you."

He rode past the establishment first, noting that Garrit's cousin had worked to make the place stand out. Three rows of rocks, placed by hand in a façade on both sides of the door, did exactly that in a thrown-together town built entirely of wood.

He tied Pax and opened the door that boasted a small hand-lettered sign hanging in the window: *OFFEN FUR GESCHAFTE*

A dark-eyed woman with flour up to her elbows acknowledged him. She started to wipe her hands, but Clay held up his palm.

"Mrs. Rausch? I am Meta's husband, Clay. You must be Anna?"

Anna's hands flew to her face, and she rushed toward him. "Yah. Husband for Meta. She write letter."

The cool interior invited him to sit, and so did Anna, who threw words his way as she ran out a side door. "Husband," was all Clay could comprehend.

In less than two minutes, the door burst open, and Anna returned with Herman in tow. He held out a massive dirty hand, and Clay stood to shake with him.

"Clay Burns? Welcome to our home." Herman's English exceeded his wife's, and he pulled out a chair.

"Can you stay? Anna has *rumskeller* for dinner." The smell alone would have convinced him, but Clay shook his head.

"Thank you, but my cowhands are already headed north with our starter herd. I need to catch up with them. I thought you might have letters—"

"Oh, yah!" Anna beamed and produced a stack. "Yah, Meta for happy."

Clay took the pile, but to leave so soon seemed awkward. "Thank you. I wish I could stay. Maybe some day I will bring Meta to visit."

"Yah. You bring her." Anna linked her arm through Herman's, and he extended his hand again.

"We are glad to know you."

Clay stepped out and unlatched his saddlebag. The letters safely inside, he had his boot in the stirrup when the door opened, and Herman handed him a burlap bag.

"For your supper." He tipped his hat.

Pax headed north through the streets of Cheyenne. Not much had changed here since late last summer, but on the inside, everything had. Along the boardwalk came a man and wife followed by their children.

He had never thought much about families, except to wonder. But something about meeting Herman and Anna initiated a new perspective. He and Meta had formed a family, and they would build a home. Maybe one day he would be a father and small children would call him Pa.

The idea nearly made him laugh. So outlandish, but hadn't Father Bernard always predicted good things for him?

Two days after her arrival, Meta had cut out her dress and began stitching the arms to the bodice. A rap sounded at the door, and Franklin stood there beaming like a young'un with a surprise. His eyes twinkled as they had when he arrived on Christmas Eve.

As he had then, he brought the perfect gift, handmade with care. In the winter, he bore snowshoes of wood and leather lacings bent into shape and stitched with his gnarled fingers. Now, he had foreseen another need.

"Got somethin' t' show ya."

She followed him around the cabin, where Ethel swayed under a high-backed wooden object. Franklin hurried to untie the leather straps.

"Franklin!" A simple wooden cradle, sanded to a sheen, rocked back and forth on the hard earth.

"Mebbe it's too big. Have ya got room?"

"Oh, yes! You thought of just what we need."

She touched his sleeve, and to her surprise, he pulled her close. For a few moments, she leaned into his smell: well-worn buckskin, wood shavings, the musky flannel of laboring in the sun. His beard scratched against her temple. Then they each stepped back with moist eyes.

He loved her. She might never understand everything about him, but this one thing his words and actions made clear.

Franklin lifted the awkward piece through the doorway and paused with a questioning look. "Where d'ya want me to put it? Close to the bed, not too near the stove?"

"What if—what if we move the trunk closer to the table and put the cradle between the bed and my rocker?"

Franklin surveyed the space. "Ya sure?"

She grabbed the trunk's leather latch and stooped to pull

it out, but he roared. "Ya ain't gonna be pullin' on nothin' heavy long's I'm around." He waved the backs of his hands at her like a woman shooing away chickens. "Git outside. Hunt fer some eggs 'r somethin'."

"I never thought I'd see the day you would order me out of my own house."

He grunted as he waved her out. A mourning dove called to its mate from a juniper, and the creek, low now, beckoned. On the right-sized sapling, she rubbed the small of her back, slid her feet out a few inches, and let her body slip down. Low-hanging leaves created a welcome bower as the baby moved inside her.

Then another kick came. She took a deep breath and let it out.

"Little one, I will bring you here often. I can almost hear your laughter as you play in the cool water."

Faint wisps of pearly clouds tinged the sky. Maybe Clay would come home today. Maybe she should pick wild berries and bake a pie to welcome him. Franklin had been faithful to water her garden, so they could eat new peas and potatoes with onions for dinner.

Soon they would have fresh carrots, beans, and parsnips, summer squash and later, winter squash and pumpkins. A cardinal's cheerful song gilded the gentle roll of water over rocks. Red-winged blackbirds, thrushes, and wrens darted from bushes to nests, teaching their young to fly.

Suddenly a strong hyssop essence lingered. Meta opened her eyes. Four feet away stood Tall Elk, a bronze statue.

When she struggled to get up, he held out his hand, motioned for her to follow him and turned up the bank. After a few steps, she panted. Halfway up, he twisted and slowed his steps.

As they approached the cabin, she realized the reason for his visit. Lying near the step lay her boxes from the stage. One looked battered, with scrapes and digs in the wood, but the nails had held. Franklin met them, hammer in hand, ready to pry open the slats. When he lifted the lid, the aroma of huckleberry pie oozed forth.

The package Matilda had so carefully placed in the bottom of the crate unwrapped with ease. A jumble of crust and fruit appeared, so Franklin went inside for spoons. As she lifted out baby clothing tinted a violet not that different from Clay's eyes, Franklin and Tall Elk consumed the pie like two happy children.

Sitting on the stoop to watch, she stilled a wild urge to embrace Tall Elk. Perhaps that was one custom of whites he might never claim. Small matter. If he had not watched out for her the day of the attack, where would she be?

Now, how far had he ridden to retrieve her belongings? No doubt Franklin would give her the details, but one fact solidified. This tall Indian with huckleberry all over his hands and face had become a fast friend. And today, even though he took her completely by surprise, she had not been shaken. From now on, she would watch and wait for him.

Clay wandered to the campfire where Owen kept watch with a cup of coffee. Clay poured some and sat down. This Wyoming night belonged to the nearly full moon and a million stars, the earthy aroma of sage, and ever-present insects.

"Almost home. Thanks for letting me come."

"I needed your help, and the hands deserve the money Mrs. Crady gave me."

Owen cut him off with a wave. "Do what you want, son. But they're getting paid plenty already. Money doesn't mean a thing." The image of a black leather bag filled with gold nuggets passed before Clay.

Looking off into the heavens, Owen took a drink. "I've had years to build up the ranch. What I lack is family."

He grew silent for a few long minutes. "That wife of yours, Meta. Tell me more about her. You said she's dark and pretty, grew up in Iowa?"

"Yes, she spent the whole winter alone near Spring Creek

though she could have gone into Cheyenne after her husband died. Her husband's cousin and his family live there. Meta's a spunky one, for sure."

"I'd like to meet her. A woman has to be strong to make it out here."

"Good German blood, she says. Her Mama prepared her for life's ups and downs, and she's already seen quite a few, but never lost her faith."

"I'd like you to bring her down here sometime. And one day if you have children, I'd like to… If I could get to know them—" Owen's voice came from far away.

"We've got no family near the claim except Franklin. I expect you to come up—someday maybe we'll have a son you can teach to lasso—my talent fails me there."

Moonlight glimmered in Owen's eyes. "That, I can do." A log sizzled in the breeze, wafting a whiff of autumn.

"I've a mind to move up north to the cabin. The ranch house rambles all over—built it for Lorraine." Owen settled back against a boulder. "What would you think about me living that close?"

"We'd be happy to have a new neighbor. And I expect you could teach me a few things about running a ranch."

The last time Clay rode this path, he had no intention of staking a claim or managing a herd, much less of taking a wife. Last year on that late September day, though, as Mr. Dunbar first showed him the lay of the land, the high plains had seeped into his soul. Now, nearly a year later, he rode toward a woman he loved.

A place to go and someone waiting for him—what more could he want? His own father, Mr. Dusek, had given him life. Some questions would never be answered—where had his parents intended to homestead? Where did they board a ship for America? What possessed them to face the wilderness alone?

But at least he knew their family name—his name. And he

knew who had discovered him after his parents died—what better deliverer than a Texas Ranger?

A whirl of sagebrush whisked into a frenzy and raced until it blew into nothing. That symbolized his life a year ago. Now, everything had turned around.

The plains rose little by little until the Lodgepole River sparkled ahead. Pax galloped as if he, too, sensed the homeward call. Clay let him graze and made camp as darkness covered the land. In the morning, they would cross the north range, the range that led to Meta.

August 14th dawned bright and clear, but by early afternoon, a gully washer looked imminent, with barrel-headed clouds riding the northwest. Sudden thunder sent Meta down to the creek after Della and Hope. Franklin buzzed around the side of the cabin with his tools just as she barred the barn door.

"Goin' fer Ethel. I'll drop th' window board on m' way back."

Thunder rolled and lightning burst across the sky. By the time he returned, Franklin was winded and plopped down at the table. Meta poured coffee left over from dinner and sat with him to wait out the storm.

Then the strangest thing happened. The heat, mild that day, suddenly turned intense. Even inside the cabin, Meta almost felt faint.

"Heat's hittin' like a blizzard, gal. Never seen one o' these, but I do recollect Lewis and Clark writin' 'bout it while they was out this way."

Sudden gales whipped the cabin like mad men out of Mama's tales from the old country.

"Hits like a summer snowstorm." A cold wind swept under the door, ruffling Meta's skirt. From warm to blazing, hot to cold— what could this be?

"Durin' a terr'ble ice storm once, a feller tol' me he met up with a man what traveled with Lewis n' Clark."

"What kind of storm did they record?"

"'Twas 1805 on th' Clearwater, Idaho Terr'tory now. Clouds piled atop each other like baby pups 'roun their mama. From a hole in th' heav'ns come a fierce hot wind."

A blast of thunder shook the cabin, and Franklin opened the door. His eyes snapped. "Durned if th' sky don't look jest like thet story."

Meta hurried to his side. She always loved storms, but being with child heightened her awareness. Lightning left jagged writing in the squall clouds below foreboding thunderheads that took her back to Iowa.

The storm displays our Creator's might, children. Mama taught them to stand in awe of the weather's power, but also to appreciate the unique beauty before them. In Spring, tornados sometimes devastated the countryside there, always preceded by oppressive humid heat and sometimes a green glow in the atmosphere.

Nothing to do but watch with Franklin until rain fell. Finally—relief from the pressure. The intense heat disappeared as if sucked away by a giant animal. Now, sheets of silvery water pummeled the cabin, as they had the night Garrit passed.

The garden needed moisture badly. Blessed rain.

As the storm died down, Franklin went back to work on the shed. So much progress—Clay would be pleased. Meta picked up her sewing. Only a few hours left on the huge dress that would soon wrap her like a blanket. Sunlight shone in a steady stream through the window, and she determined to finish by bedtime.

The next time she looked up, a rainbow filled the sky from horizon to horizon. This sign brought a surge of longing for Clay.

"We only get one chance." Clay whispered the words to his blurred image in the mirror. He peered closer and tried to make out the color of his eyes, which had such an effect on people. Meta remembered them from the first time they met, when he happened on her petticoat on the Oregon Trail.

Her embarrassment could not have exceeded his own—it had taken everything he had to approach her. Back then, he never would have guessed she would remember his eyes. But now he had begun to realize their distinctiveness—wasn't that how Ranger Moberly recalled him?

The mirror almost touched his nose now. But to him, the color looked about like Owen's eyes, or Franklin's.

Like *Pilgrim's Progress,* which still lay on the small bedside table, he had slogged through the slough of despond. Now, the gates of the city signaled him. He felt rather than saw them as he raced off to fetch Pax from the creek. Only a matter of minutes now.

Meta dropped the hem of her wrapper on the table—hating to sew as she did, any excuse amounted to enough for a rest. But steady hoofbeats from the south bade her peer out the door. Then Franklin summoned her with a shout, and they watched a rider approach.

Sparse patches of grass brightened considerably after yesterday's heavy shower, and her garden grew inches overnight. What a lush late summer this was becoming. As the rider neared, she clutched Franklin's sleeve.

"Oh, Franklin..."

A minute later Clay's hat became visible. Half a minute closer, she felt sure. Then Franklin pronounced the verdict.

"Why, hit's Clay Burns, gal. Fer sure n' certain!"

Meta's skirt swished against his buckskins as they both rushed forward. Sunlight outlined horse and rider as Pax glided toward them on a sagey Wyoming Country wind.

Everything seemed to happen in such an orderly fashion, as if she stood outside the scene watching. First, Clay's boots hit the ground. Franklin hurried forward to take the reins and shake his hand. Then Clay's scent filled her, and like a nestling chick, she hid in his arms, her tears a torrent. His incredible eyes took her in. He pulled her close again, and his kiss caught her tears. Then his gaze lowered. His brows reared like wild horses, his eyes full of unspeakable questions.

"Yes, a little one, our firstborn. In the new year—maybe February.

He chased away a tear. Then he kissed her again.

"A' right now, cowpoke. Yer mount's mighty tired. Git this here saddle off so's I kin take 'im down t' th' creek."

Clay shook himself as if waking and turned toward Franklin. "Yes, sir!"

Words have always been comfort food for Gail Kittleson. After instructing expository writing and English as a Second Language, she began writing seriously. Intrigued by the World War II era, Gail creates historical fiction from her northern Iowa home and also facilitates writing workshops/retreats.

She and her husband, a retired Army chaplain, enjoy grandchildren and in winter, Arizona's Mogollon Rim Country. You can count on Gail's protagonists to ask honest questions, act with integrity, grow in faith, and face hardships with spunk.

Visit Gail online at:
www.GailKittleson.com